LIVIDITY

CARITA NELSON

Cover Design by Liz Byrne
LIVIDITY
Nelson, Carita
ISBN-13: 978-0-6451254-0-5

This book was written on land rightfully belonging to the Turrbul and the Jagera peoples.

I pay my respects to the traditional custodians of this land and their Elders, past, present and emerging.

Always was, always will be.

I would like to thank my husband, Woody who bore the brunt of my frustrations during all stages of this endeavour from conception to publication and every painful point between. Thank you to my parents, Rhonda and Ian Nelson. I would be hard-pressed to find better parents in this world. A special thanks to Mum for reading my feeble drafts and being tactful in her honesty.

My sisters, Talia and Reanna, thank you for your support and being an endless source of inspiration, comfort and joy.

For Woody and Burger.

Lucia Hughes actually liked cutting onions. She liked how quickly and precisely she could slice and dice them. It made her feel as though she was actually good at something. She hardly ever shed a tear while she did it, something that Lucia had bragged about on more than one occasion. The truth was that Lucia was good at a lot of things. In the way of tangible skills, she had impeccable balance and a strong throwing arm, she was handy around the house and had a bit of a green thumb. The things her loved ones praised her for were less tangible, but skills nonetheless. She had an excellent memory, especially for things that people mentioned in passing, meaning she was also a great listener, not only for the words, but the meanings. She had good instincts, usually about people and all these combined meant she was an A grade gift giver. But it was while cutting onions that Lucia felt the most skilled.

The Autumn sun had set a while ago and a cool breeze wafted through the open kitchen window. Lucia had set her phone on top of the bench, her podcast rising above the sound of the street, but not quite loud enough to cover the sound of the occasional hooning car. The hosts of "Beg Your Parton" were nattering about their respective weeks and both of them had completely forgotten the word for "hollandaise."

Lucia set the onions into two piles, a quarter onion very thinly sliced into a plastic container for later and the rest more roughly cut and set to the side of the cutting board. She had gotten the taco Tuesday routine down pat. Next slicing a red capsicum and finally a tomato. She ordered the cutting in such a way that the messiest was last. Not that cutting capsicum in tomato juices would affect the dish at all, but this was the order she liked best.

Lucia turned up the volume on the phone in anticipation of the pork mince sizzling violently in the pan. "...The Courier Mail presents *Bite* an in-depth investigation into the mysterious deaths of seven…" The flare of meat hitting the pan drowned out the podcast advertisement.

Crumb had set himself up right behind Lucia's feet in an effort to cheat extra food, despite being already fed. He sprang up and made for the front door. A definite sign that Win, Lucia's husband was making his way down the street. Sure enough a couple minutes later his keys were jangling in the lock and the front door creaked open. Win made his way for the kitchen, Crumb meowing hopefully with every step.

Samuel Huyhn was what some would call "compact," not so tall, but taller than his wife and very lean. He had been a gymnast during high school and college, his nickname Win taken from a tournament chant. "Hew-Win for the win, Hew-Win for the win!" Even though he hadn't competed in years, Win retained both the nickname and an unmistakable elegance in his movement.

"He's been fed," Lucia advised just as Win was reaching for the cat food.

"Nearly tricked me you little guts" Win scooped up Crumb and hugged him close "family cuddle!"

Lucia hugged them, planting a kiss on both of them before turning to add onions and capsicum to the pan.

"You're limping," Lucia added in the kind of accusatory tone that comes when someone you care about is being reckless.

"I know, it's really not that bad" he replied, "I'll stay off it."

"Hmmm" Lucia sighed, unconvinced. "Dinner will be another ten."

"Cool, thanks. I've just got to check some things on the computer."

"Hmmm," Lucia rebutted again, this time less out of concern and more as a warning that Win better not get carried away.

❖

Even though she technically wasn't supposed to, Lucia found herself doing some cleaning in her down time. Lucia had three patients and usually ten-hour shifts. Some days she would be absolutely run off her feet, but not with Ruth. In Lucia's opinion, Ruth didn't even need a home care nurse. Ruth was very self-sufficient, a little wary on her feet sometimes but overall in good health. A fall about a year ago sent Ruth's children into a frenzy. She broke her hip and lay alone for hours until she was finally able to call an ambulance. In response Ruth's children got her two Pomeranians and a nurse.

Lucia tried very hard to not judge families. In the cases of her other patients the families were great. They only needed a nurse so that they could actually live their own lives a little. They were kind and thankful and spent a lot of time helping their loved ones. Ruth's family on the other hand threw money at the problem because that is what they thought she was. Only a few visits would show them that their Mother was still quite vital. Visiting her just after a broken hip did not accurately portray her ability, and the thought that came behind getting two small dogs for someone they thought was prone to falling was beyond Lucia's comprehension. Ruth loved those dogs though. Lucia was a cat person through and through, but she had to admit they were cute pups. Despite Ruth's protests and Lucia's advice, Ruth's family kept her on. They truly believed Ruth was an invalid and wouldn't hear otherwise.

Apart from checking her vitals and insisting on Ruth doing her physical therapy mandated exercises, Lucia had very little to do. She couldn't leave Ruth during her shift, so she usually just shadowed her. They took the dogs for walks, went to the post office and shops. The pair were happy to have chats, but mostly Ruth just wanted to be independent. Lucia babysitting her did not make for a loving relationship. Ruth didn't resent Lucia, just the idea of her. In turn Lucia liked Ruth just fine but wished she could be of more help. So that's why Lucia sometimes did some of the cleaning.

Ruth was outside, putting a second load of laundry on the line. The loads were dutifully divided into darks, lights and linens. Ruth was of an age where they still did that. Lucia watched through the kitchen window that looked out on the back yard, her hands wrist deep in scorching water. The palms of her hands were flushed and felt a little prickly, but she'd rather that than using lukewarm water. Daisy and Delilah, the Pomeranians, were dutifully watching Ruth as well. They lay on the grass beneath the Hills Hoist and every so often Ruth would stoop to pet them. With her basket full of white sheets, dress grazing her calves, olive skin and masses of grey curls that had all been jet black a couple of decades ago, Ruth looked like a vignette of some Italian Nona. Though she was neither.

At four o'clock both Lucia and Ruth were released from their duties. Lucia bid Ruth farewell and reminded her that she'd see her the next Monday.

❖

Wednesday nights were left over taco nights, so Lucia didn't need to make any stops on the way home. She changed into work out gear as soon as she walked through the door, intent on going for a walk before the sun went down. On the way out Lucia saw the garden looking a bit dry so made a detour to the hose. She watered each bed thoroughly, waving to passers-by. The same people could always be found walking around the neighbourhood. Elderly couples, thirty somethings with dogs, and kids, usually in a little gang and usually with bikes. There were others that were serious about their fitness. Proper running clothes, reflective patches, pedometers and headphones. They were usually too puffed or concentrating too hard to say hello, a weak smile here or there. The serious joggers were the most intimidating, Lucia liked to get out for a walk, there was a lot of beautiful bushland in easy walking distance, but she could be convinced by nearly anything to opt out. Today a dry garden bed was more than convincing enough to stop her from actually exercising.

❖

Win wasn't a huge help during cooking, or maybe he would be if Lucia would release more control of the kitchen. Lucia took a lot of pride in her cooking; she'd been doing it from a young age. She loved bold flavours and had an impressive collection of spices. Her favourites were, in order; sweet paprika, chilli flakes, thyme and cumin, but allspice, cinnamon, cloves, oregano and basil got a pretty good look in as well. Lucia had tried teaching Win to cook but eventually they kind of gave up. She liked cooking and he didn't so it worked out ok. Sometimes Lucia worried about when they were older. If she died first that he'd be unable to feed himself good or healthy foods, but that wouldn't really be her problem. Hopefully the nieces and nephews wouldn't let him starve.

Despite not being a good help Lucia liked to have him around when she cooked. She didn't mind cooking alone. Sometimes she whiled away the time, flitting around the kitchen, listening to podcasts and having several pots on the go. She imagined the bubbling broth to be like a cauldron and the final potion spread her love to whomever she served it to. Lucia preferred it when Win was there. Win's main job was to pass her things, which wasn't a big job. Lucia was so organised and prepared that she rarely needed him to even do that. She liked him there to chat, to cuddle in between stirring and to be sure he wouldn't be in the middle of an online game when she served up dinner.

Lucia had been proving the pizza dough all day. She bloomed the yeast first thing in the morning by using the leftover water from the kettle. She found that by the time she finished breakfast and enjoyed her morning cup of coffee the kettle had cooled just enough to be the perfect temperature for yeast to activate. Once the tangy bubbles were practically spilling over the lip of the jug, she would mix the dough and let it rise all day. She liked to make her own sauce, which is what she was doing now. Win stood out of the way, leaning casually against the kitchen bench. He had changed out of his work clothes and was wearing flannel pyjama bottoms and a fitted t-shirt. He was on the phone to Lucia's mother-in-law, Linh. Lucia didn't speak very much Vietnamese at all, which she always felt guilty about. She knew enough that she usually got the gist of what was being discussed. It was especially helpful that in the flurry of Vietnamese there were usually several English words in the mix. "Pizza" and "Lucia" were being used a lot in this conversation, which was not surprising but Win was supposed to be getting information about what his mother wanted to do for her birthday celebration.

"Con yêu mẹ. tạm biệt, bye Mum, love you!" Win always emphasised his point in English, Kathryn, his sister, did the same thing. Lucia had often wondered if they both did it for her benefit, but she'd heard both of them do it when she wasn't in the room. She couldn't understand the intricacies of being bilingual, or not having English as a first language. Not that she didn't care, or didn't want to understand, it was just cold hard facts that her life experiences were different. The difference between sympathy and empathy, or something like that. Lucia sometimes got the two confused.

"Mum said she wants to go to that French place at Market Square."

"Cafe Les Amoureux."

"Yeah, that one, she wants steak."

"Fair enough," Lucia chuckled, "hey, can you put on some music?"

Win busied himself on his phone, scrolling to find something to play. Win and Lucia had pretty different tastes in music, so she was pleasantly surprised when the first few jaunty chords of "Here Comes Your Man" came on. Win and Lucia could agree on The Pixies, both even passionately argued that Doolittle was their best album. Win sang along, evidently choosing this song so he could dance at Lucia in a comedic faux seductive way for the whole song. Lucia laughed and wrapped her arms around him as the intro to the next song "Dead" played. Lucia looked up at Win's face, her head resting on his shoulder,

"If you could be a vegetable, which vegetable would you be?" Win was very accustomed to this kind of questioning.

"Hmmm, I guess I'd be broccoli. Wait no cauliflower." He gave a decisive nod.

"Why?"

"Look, broccoli is pretty good. Got all those vitamins and minerals. Great in stir fry, but cauliflower is having a real moment. I guess I'm just trendy." Win chuckled at his own verdict.

"Let me guess, even though it's not technically a vegetable, you're a tomato?"

"Of course!" Lucia replied emphatically before heading back to the stove to stir her sauce. She spooned a little out on a teaspoon and tasted it. Only when she was happy with the taste of things did Lucia ever offer up a sample to Win. She scooped another spoonful for him. After seven years, six of which they lived together, they still did an awkward little dance over if Lucia would feed him, or if Win should take the spoon from her. They both preferred that he take the spoon, but it was somehow negotiated every time. Lucia waited for Win's approval before turning off the stove. Sometimes Win would offer a suggestion of what would improve whatever dish he was tasting. The entirety of Win's cooking knowledge came from watching MasterChef, so Lucia seldom took his advice.

As Lucia ladled the sauce onto pizza bases and decorated each pizza with toppings, the pair discussed more hypotheticals. What animal tail they would each like to have, how many cats they'll get when they own their own house, if they would ever own a house, and which aquatic mythical creature would win a fight.

❖

Win stepped off the bus straight into the Adelaide Street thoroughfare. His bus stop was the next closest to the Edward Street crossing; a big four way crossing that serviced the Central Train station, main shopping mall and a bus stop laden street. At 7:30 in the morning this meant it was particularly busy and he had to merge into the footpath traffic without getting trampled. Brisbane CBD is not nearly as bustling as larger cities in Australia or overseas but it gets busy all the same. Win didn't really like crowds, he walked swiftly and with purpose at all times. Getting trapped behind a mob of slow walkers ate at his soul. He also wasn't a morning person; he was pretty capable in the mornings but just really didn't like them. It was crazy to him that he had married an early bird like Lucia. She did all of her best work before 8am, even on weekends. He nipped quickly up Edward Street, avoiding the troublesome crossing altogether. He grabbed coffee from one of the hole-in-the-wall cafes, usually picking the one with the smallest crowd to grab a tall flat white and a muffin. He headed up Edward, coffee in hand. Heat rising from the coffee caused the inner edges of his glasses to fog with each sip. The mornings were already crisp enough to do so, until he reached the next intersection with Ann and the sun appeared from behind the train station warming the glasses up enough to stop the fogging. Win crossed and headed down Ann until he reached his building.

By the time Win reached his floor, he'd finished his coffee. He made his way to the lunchroom to wash his keep cup, eat his muffin and scroll through his phone.

The insurance office was nicer than American offices are on TV, even nicer than a lot of Australian offices. The desks were in groups of four, with partitions dividing them. The partitions only covered two thirds of the desk. It was easy to push back a chair and poke a head into the neighbouring cubicle. This was particularly helpful when getting a second opinion of a case. The cubicles still offered a lot of privacy when hunkering down to get a file closed. The whole East side of the building was lined with full length windows. The natural light countered the fluorescent lighting, making it quite a pleasant environment. Like most offices in the CBD, the windows did not open. The morning sun hitting the windows warmed the office, so the year-round freezing AC only became a problem in the late afternoon.

Win wandered to his desk, still ten minutes until he was officially on the clock. Enough time to turn on his computer, catch up a little and adjust the blinds behind his desk. His quad mates were Sanjay, Mel and Peter. Win's desk was right on the end, in the corner, so he didn't neighbour anyone but those three, which suited him fine. Win and Sanjay caught up on each other's nights while their computers hummed into life.

Win's calendar was full for the day. He had phone interviews for several claimants and witnesses that would take him right up to one o'clock. With any luck he could squeeze in some lunch before doing more investigating into the claims. There are a few jobs that society views as immoral, pitiful, even scummy. Politicians, parking inspectors and insurance claim adjusters. Win liked his job though, he loved being able to find loopholes and offering a big claim. He loved that there was always something interesting and new to learn. He felt a lot like a private detective, but Win dealt with a lot of private detectives, and his job was more interesting.

Win was supposed to finish at five o'clock but didn't get out until closer to six. Mel stayed back too, she had annual leave from the next day and she was busy closing out any loose ends.

"You going?" Win peered over the cubicle wall, his brow furrowed in polite concern.

"Yeah actually. Just sending you guys an email with some info if that's ok?"

"Of course." Win shut down his computer and pulled his satchel up to his lap. He packed odds and ends that he needed to take with him and by the time he finished laying them neatly in his bag, Mel was finished and up ready to start her holiday.

"Shall we?"

They walked together to the Adelaide/Edward crossing. This time Win had to cross to make it to his bus.

"Have a good holiday! See you when you get back."

"Thanks!" Mel was beaming, her holiday had started the second she stepped out of the office and she looked refreshed already. She turned back into 7-11 instead of crossing right away.

The Adelaide crossing was usually the worst part of his afternoon routine and today was no exception. Win was pulled to the ground by a man not looking where he was going. The man seemed to trip down the gutter. As he lost his footing and fell, he reached out and yanked on Win's bag and brought Win down with it. Win was annoyed and a little sore, especially annoyed because he had made note of this man from the other side of the road. While they were waiting to cross Win scanned the people on the opposite side, trying to figure out the freest path across the busy intersection.

This man had been waiting on the other side, but for some reason the man only started moving once Win was close to him.

Cursing only in his mind Win sprung back onto his feet. Another passer-by was helping the other man up. He was older, maybe in his fifties and a bit overweight. The man thanked the passer-by and turned to Win.

"Sorry. One of those days 'eh? You alright?" He reached out his hand to Win for a handshake. Win saw Mel, who was now waiting for the next lights, she was openly laughing at him.

"I'm fine actually mate, gotta run. That's my bus." he gestured to the bus passing them, before chasing after it down the street towards the bus stop. As annoyed as he was, Win felt terrible about declining the man's apology, but if he didn't make this bus he'd be stuck for another twenty minutes. His leg was already acting up, but now it really hurt.

On the bus Win glanced back at the intersection again and saw Mel had collided with the same guy. He must have been incredibly clumsy, probably not used to the city at that time of day. Served Mel right for laughing at him.

❖

Lucia let herself in. The door was always unlocked when Kathryn was expecting company and for lifetime friends it seemed more polite to not make her get up. Kathryn Samaras-Huyhn was curled up on the couch under a blue blanket. Her chin length bangs swept effortlessly over her face from under a grey beanie. Her short hair usually tapered to the nape of her neck but was fanning out under the weight of the band. Despite the beanie and blanket suggesting she was cold, Lucia could see Kathryn was wearing a knee length shift dress, a staple in Kathryn's "at home" wardrobe. Lucia silently mused how good Kathryn looked. She wished her hair could do that but if she got the same cut she would look like Jonathan Taylor

Thomas circa 1993. Kathryn's Old English Sheepdog Butterbean took up most of the couch beside her, his head rested on Kathryn's lap. Upon seeing Lucia he bounced up off the couch and over to her, knocking several things off the coffee table with his wagging tail. Lucia finished kicking off her shoes into the entry hall and greeted him with similar enthusiasm, her hands getting lost in his fur as she patted him.

"I don't know why we even still have a coffee table?" Kathryn sighed, moving reflexively to pick up the spill. This was a very regular occurrence. Lucia helped pick up the items closer to her; a tv remote, three coasters and three bobby pins looped onto a hair tie.

"Maybe you should just get rid of it. Imagine Butterbean and a baby!"

"True!" Kathryn replied, her tone showing that she hadn't thought of her child and dog becoming a tag team of destruction, and the sudden weight of that realisation.

"Is Gianna here? I thought she'd take the day."

"Nah, worked the night shift last night. She's an absolute boss and honestly thank fuck she's the one that actually wants to be pregnant."

Gianna and Lucia became fast friends at university. When Lucia introduced Kathryn and Gianna to each other, she knew at the very least the three of them would become an inseparable trio of close friends. She secretly hoped sparks would fly between the two. They did become an amazing triad of support for each other, just Gianna and Kathryn also happened to be married. And now Kathryn and Gianna were trying to have a baby. Kathryn had not been so instrumental in the set-up of her best friend and brother, that happened almost by accident, but it was a welcome change for Lucia to become Kathryn's sister for real.

"How did it go? Tell me everything!" Lucia smirked and squinted her eyes, "well not everything, you know, tell me!"

"It was weird, good...great, but weird." Kathryn massaged her foot through the blanket, self-soothing. "We made a thing of it, without making a thing of it. A nice breakfast, a bath, good music, good sex." They both laughed. "Then it's just syringing the..."

"Baby formula?"

Kathryn let out a snorting laugh, "Gross! But yeah."

"Oh my God! Imagine she could be getting pregnant right now. I'm so happy for you!" Lucia bent down to wrap her arms around Kathryn's shoulders. She planted a kiss on Kathryn's beanie, getting errant wool fibres stuck to her lip balm and gathering on her tongue.

Lucia slipped into the kitchen and poured herself a cup of coffee from the pot sitting in the percolator. The Samaras-Huyhn household always had a pot brewing in the morning. Then Lucia folded herself up next to Butterbean, who had resumed his place laying across most of the couch.

The pair chatted through several cups of coffee, two loads of laundry and one small wheel of brie. They covered Kathryn's new batch of recruits at work, she was head of Learning and Development at a nationwide sportswear chain and a personal hand in the training of every person that had come through the company in the last four years. As always Lucia discussed her favourite and least favourite patients. Lucia's absolute favourite patient had been admitted to hospital with a kidney infection the week prior. The possibility of her not making it out of the hospital weighed on Lucia's mind and she talked it over with her best friend.

Kathryn and Lucia were just brainstorming present and dinner ideas for their mother/mother in law's upcoming birthday when Gianna arrived home from her shift. After university Gianna went on to midwifery. Gianna and Lucia's careers took such different paths that they bookended life. Gianna would joke "I see them in and Lucia sees them out" whenever they were out together or at family functions.

"Gianna, I'll get out of your hair so you can get some sleep." Lucia apologised. "I'm so happy for you though!" She wrapped Gianna in a big hug, hoping that soon their hugs would be obstructed by a beautiful bump.

Lucia said her goodbyes, but even then the three of them kept talking in the lounge room, then in the entryway and finally in the front yard before Lucia eventually pried herself away. Butterbean poked around the yard looking for the best place to relieve himself and Kathryn wrapped her arms around Gianna's waist, planting an enthusiastic kiss on her cheek just as Lucia offered a final wave before getting in her car.

❖

Lucia lifted her head and listened for the kitchen tap. It had been running for a while now, long enough for her to surmise that Win was actually doing the washing up. Good. There weren't many dishes, but Win knew that he had to hold up his end of the bargain. Lucia cooked and he cleaned. Neither wanted it to be the other way around, or they would be having instant noodles most nights.

The groaning of pipes and gushing of water stopped abruptly and was replaced by the faint, but unmistakable sound of clicking cutlery and sloshing dishwater.

"Lorraine gets back from hospital tomorrow".

"Sorry, what?" Win called back. Lucia was already behind him, knowing he wouldn't have heard. "Lorraine, gets back from hospital tomorrow."

"Remind me who Lorraine is again."

"She gave us those embroidered handkerchiefs for our wedding" Lorraine was eighty-nine. In a past life she was a nurse and loved to bestow Lucia with pearls of wisdom about the trade. The two had grown quite close, sharing bed pan horror stories and gruesome tales about pus filled boils, bursting cysts and weeping sores. The kind of things only nurses can stomach talking about over dinner. Of all her charges Lucia missed Lorraine the most when she moved into the nursing home. Even with Lucia as her carer, it was getting too much.

"I'll go visit her after I finish up with Ruth tomorrow." Lucia said as she wrapped her arms around Win from behind and kissed him lightly on the shoulder.

❖

The streets were still and quiet, the sun just peaking over the edge of the houses as Lucia pulled into Ruth's driveway. The driveway was on a steep slope towards the house and usually the sound of Lucia wrenching the handbrake as far as she could would result in Ruth's two Pomeranians being whipped into a frenzy. Lucia tracked wet footprints in the still dewed lawn on a detour to retrieve the paper. She wiped her feet several times on the mat before letting herself in. The house was quiet.

Hot, stagnant air escaped with the front door opening. As Lucia entered, the room grew hotter and a disorienting smell hung in the air. Immediately inside the front door was the lounge room. Typical "old person" style' two easy chairs and a three-seater, all draped with crocheted squares. The woollen blankets slide over the vinyl upholstery if anyone even thought about sitting. There was a worn, imitation Persian rug devoid of a coffee table, but instead three side tables bordered the room. The closest to the door sported a table lamp and a small painted ceramic cottage, a tiny analog clock face inlayed in it. Lucia glanced around, a half-finished cup of tea sat next to the easy chairs, it would be cold if not for the heat in the room. Lucia saw the space heater still running, one of those older filament styles that they don't even produce anymore. From the feel of the room, it had been running for some time.

"Shit! It's a wonder the house hasn't burned down!" Lucia cursed and shut it off. The constant hum of the heater stopped abruptly and the house became even more quiet, save for the sporadic creaks of the now cooling walls.

Still no dogs. Lucia debated internally to open up the house a bit for some air flow or to find Ruth first.

"Ruth?" there was no reply, "it's Lucia." still nothing.

Lucia crossed the lounge, past the dining room and towards the bedrooms. A quick search of the bathroom and toilet first, usually a trap for people not so steady on their feet. Nothing.

"Ruth?" She opened the main bedroom door. Ruth sat upright on the edge of her bed, staring straight at Lucia but didn't say a word.

"Ruth! You gave me a bit of fright! Let me give you a hand, you going up or down?" Ruth gave no response, just stared blankly through Lucia.

Lucia decided to run some tests. She needed to fetch her bigger bag from the car.

"Ruth can you hear me? I'm just going to the car for a moment. I'll open the place up a bit too. So it's not so muggy in here, ok?"

On the way back through the house Lucia paused to open some windows. A few little, dark brown paw prints spotted the cupboard under the sink, just the right height for an outstretched Pomeranian. They might have been at the groomers if they were that dirty.

Returning with her bag Lucia got to work.

Pupils – Slow
Blood pressure – 65/40
Heart rate – 22

"Ruth, I'm going to call you an ambulance ok? Your heart rate is very slow." It was more than slow, it was barely a beat at all. No sooner had the words left her mouth then Ruth's eyes wavered from her fixed, penetrating gaze and lolled to the back of her head. Now limp and unconscious Ruth rocked back onto the bed.

Lucia hadn't performed CPR in a long while. She was trained. She took refresher courses frequently and kept up to date with every new international standard, but people...real people are very different from dummies.

She rushed forward into action, so fervent and focused that she knocked Ruth's dangling feet with her knee. Hard enough to break her skin with Ruth's overgrown toenails, but too adrenaline filled to notice.

She scooped up the diminutive old woman and placed her quickly on the floor. Feet first, keeping the torso upright, wrestling the pyjama shirt up before laying Ruth down flat, gently. Lucia's eyes analysed Ruth's bare torso. Her skin was papery and thin. She felt along the ribs to the breastbone, knowing that soon the ribs would be breaking under the force of compressions. She had no choice.

In what seemed like one manoeuvre Lucia grabbed her Automated External Defibrillator and mobile phone and placed them in reach and view. Pads on the chest, AED on and reading for a heartbeat, none.

Statistics ringing in Lucia's ears about survival rates.

She dialled 000, put the phone on speaker and started CPR.

❖

Lucia Hughes' head pounded. She had been a home care nurse her whole career. She had lost patients before. It was the nature of the job, but she was never there. Patients usually end up in hospital long before that. Some she had found in the morning after they passed in the night, but she had never felt them slip through her fingers. This was different. Lucia's hands were still trembling, even after the ambulance came, the next of kin notified and the body wrapped up and taken away. Still shaking though no one could tell.

Lucia picked up her phone, now located on the bedroom dresser. A paramedic probably moved it. She dialled Win.

- 17 -

"Hey"

"Hey"

"Ooh, you don't sound good. What's up?"

"Ruth died" It felt stark and wrong to blurt it out so bluntly but her head was pounding. How else could she say it?

"When? Were you there?"

"I tried really hard to save her. I know I did..." Lucia's voice broke as she tried to convince herself more than anyone that she did everything right, "...I know I did."

"I'm sure you did babe. You're a great nurse. Are you ok? Still going to see Lorraine?"

"Yeah, I'm going to head over. She will get it."

She would get it. If there was anyone in the world that Lucia could talk to now and they would understand, it was Lorraine.

❖

It was only as Lucia sat in her car and her knee hit the underside of the steering column, that she noticed a scratch right in the centre of her knee. A few tiny bubbles of blood crystallised like minute rubies lined the cut. It didn't hurt and maybe she would never have noticed if her legs weren't so much longer than her arms, that her knees rammed into the dash every time she drove. Lucia rubbed the dried blood off her knee and started the car.

The drive from Ruth's house to the nursing home was so familiar to Lucia that she could have done it with her eyes closed. She knew every traffic light, every turn, every bump in the road. She even knew exactly when other drivers would make late lane changes or accidentally drift while turning. Other drivers were predictably unpredictable. Lucia reminded herself regularly that not everyone drives this route all the time, not everyone is from the area and most importantly, not everyone was a good driver. She wished she could make this drive with her eyes closed now. Her head pulsed. The pain lashed up from her ribcage, over her shoulders, up her neck and branching out over her temples and behind her eyes. It seared into her skull, retreated and slammed back with every heartbeat. Her jaw felt numb and painful all at once. The swelling agony made her eyes blur and her vision rippled the road like a mirage.

Lucia made the decision not to visit Lorraine and drove straight past the turn to the nursing home.

Lucia made a beeline for the bathroom. A nice hot shower would wash away her short, traumatic day and hopefully take the headache with it. Crumb watched with keen interest from his spot on the end of the bed, lifting his head but not getting up. He could be found here at most times of the day or night. Crumb liked other places; underneath Win's desk in the office, Lucia's lap, any available pillow so long as it already had a head resting on it and underneath the dresser in the spare bedroom if his gut would allow, but mostly he liked the end of the bed. A constant cat sized round of moulted black fur underneath him proved his loyalty to that spot.

Lucia pulled her hair from its bun, but no relief came to her tender scalp. She snapped the hair tie onto her wrist and winced into the shower. Even the tie on her wrist where it had spent countless hours was painful. She knew the effort to take it off would be just as painful too. The water ran over Lucia's aching shoulders, turning them pink. She lathered unenthusiastically but spent most of the shower standing with her hands pressed against the tile in front of her. Head bowed letting the water course over her body.

Sore and wet, with no perceivable improvement except the added obstacle of drying and dressing herself. Lucia pat her body down, pulled on underwear and an oversized t-shirt. Her skin felt like a friction burn all over. She made an unconvincing attempt at drying her hair before grabbing a dry towel from the hall cupboard on the way to the bedroom. She placed the towel over her pillow and curled into bed. The pain biting through her whole body made it hard to relax. She hit play on her podcast. The hosts of *Beg Your Parton* burst into laughter on just that point of the episode. Even if she couldn't find sleep, some country music and Dolly facts would hopefully soothe her. Lucia wasn't a big country fan, on the spectrum of country fans, she sat firmly in the "wouldn't turn it off" position, but she loved Dolly and the hosts were some of her favourite comedians. Somewhere during an in-depth analysis of *Love Is Like A Butterfly* Lucia slipped into sleep.

❖

Lucia was back at Ruth's house, in the bedroom. The dull, peach light from the sun leaking through Ruth's thick bedroom curtains had somehow turned green. The whole room was bathed in muted green. All of Lucia Hughes' bad dreams were a faded green, they had been since childhood. Everything in the bedroom was in its usual place, but everything seemed different. There was a new presence, hanging in the air like a bad smell. It clung to Lucia, forcing her to wade through it and breathe it in. A shroud hanging over the house, changing her, turning her soul bitter. Lucia turned and left the bedroom. Instead of leading into a small hallway off the lounge room, the bedroom door spat her out directly into the kitchen. Food lay out on the bench, a cutting board with carrot and onions and raw steak on the metal plate off to the side. It was all spoiled and Lucia went to clean it all but heard the dogs growl from the other end of the house.

This time she had to walk back through the lounge to get to the bedroom. The dogs were there, two Pomeranians, the green lighting flashing in their eyes with a hellish glow. Once again Ruth sat despondent on her bed. Lucia shone her small pen flashlight in Ruth's eyes. The pupils unmoving but the irises around them flared. Little tendrils squirmed and reached out from the fixed black holes. The dogs began to yip and growl, baring teeth and nipping at Lucia's feet. Again, Ruth became limp. Lucia tried to pick her up to start resus but Ruth's body was heavy and Lucia's hands were numb. Lucia reached forward but Ruth's limbs only slipped through her fingers, she could not close her hands around Ruth's arms. Her grip feeble and weak no matter how hard she tried. Again and again she pushed and pulled with all her might, Ruth flopping forward but remaining in the same place. Her movements like a child's toy that you punch down but always springs back up. No leverage could shift her from the bed and with every heave Lucia grew more tired and weak. The dogs barked louder and louder, clawing at Lucia's legs and ripping her skin.

Lucia woke with a start. Disoriented, she tried to make sense of her surroundings. The morning sun had given way to a cool evening glow, not quite dark, but the amber light of sunset had dissipated. The room was eerily quiet. Confusion wracked her brain as she inspected the bedroom door before her, realising only after several bewildering moments that she was standing. She recognised that she must have been sleep walking, she had been known to do some walking and talking in her sleep. There were lots of things she knew she did in her sleep, occasional snoring, chronic teeth grinding and serial cover stealing, much to the chagrin of her ever-patient husband. Still staring at the door she noted that the headache was gone. She couldn't feel anything and chalked it up to her waking state, waiting for the sensation to return and bring with it a wave of pain. The pain wasn't returning, there was nothing. She willed her body to turn back to bed. Trusting that her brain would send the right signals to her numb limbs, a chain reaction of firing nerves and all she had to do was think about it. She turned, the sensation of carpet absent beneath her feet. There she saw herself, still lying asleep, with Crumb now resting on her pillow.

2

Lucia stared at herself from an entirely new angle. Her hair frizzed against the pillow behind her. She lay on her right side with her right arm tucked underneath the pillow and her left arm curled so that the bend of her wrist rested under her chin. It looked unnatural, uncomfortable but Lucia also felt unnatural and uncomfortable.

"I'm dreaming." Lucia wasn't fully aware if the words were out loud or if they were only in her head. She'd dreamed like this before, out of body. Watching the actions unfold, almost like it was happening to someone else. She was sure psychologists had a word for that.

She'd never known she was dreaming though. Never even had a dream within a dream scenario. Funny how little her life had resembled an 80's horror film until now.

"Sleep paralysis?" Another thing she'd never experienced. She didn't even know exactly what it was, but she assumed she wouldn't be looking down on herself.

Lucia raised her right hand to her left bicep and gave a hard pinch. She wanted it to be hard, but really she couldn't tell. She watched her hand do it and she saw the skin on her arm bulge between her thumb and forefinger but she felt nothing. No paralysis, but when she needed the knowledge the most, she didn't know exactly what pinching herself was supposed to accomplish. Waking her up? She didn't feel the pinch. Did that mean it was a dream?

She shut her eyes and willed herself to be awake when she opened them. As she blinked them closed the world faded away. She couldn't see or feel anything but her thoughts still circled. The knowledge of where she was. Telling herself to stop dreaming.

Lucia opened her eyes. The room was exactly the same. She hadn't moved. Neither of her two selves had.

She went over a few other possibilities in her mind before dismissing them. Astral projection and doppelgangers didn't check out. None of it would check out. Lucia was a sceptic at heart and the idea that she was entertaining anything other than a dream was lunacy, but a dream also didn't make sense.

She reached to check the time on her phone, vainly believing that the time might ground her. Her finger pressing the home button but the phone remained blank. She pressed a few more times with no luck. It struck her that this is exactly the type of frustrating thing that happens in dreams. The lack of control over her body, the repetition, all of it.

Only when she was bent over the bedside table did it strike her odd that there was no movement coming from her counterpart. No rise and fall of breath, no sound at all. Crumb was breathing, his sides gently moved in and out and were accompanied by tiny purrs. She inspected her own face; her usually pale skin was much paler. Her lips and hands showed a slight blue tinge. Lucia knew those signs.

"I'm dead." She heard the words this time, said in her own voice. She knew it was true. She was dead and this, what she was experiencing right now, was her brain dying. She was a figment of her own imagination. A result of a chemical reaction. Soon she would cease to exist because she never really did. She wouldn't be aware of it, she'd just stop.

Lucia tried checking the pulse of her lifeless body, knowing that it would be futile. Sure enough, even though her fingers pressed into the side of her neck, she could feel nothing. Actually nothing, neither a pulse nor the sensation of skin under her fingertips. The muscles and tendons of the neck gave no resistance and though her hand did not fall through the body, she might as well have been not touching anything at all.

Crumb stirred as the sun dropped lower in the sky. He knew very well that he got a morning and an evening meal, but consistently raised the alarm for both hours before his actual mealtimes. As he would in the morning when Lucia and Win lay sleeping, he purred ferociously into the prone Lucia's face. He sniffed at her mouth and nose, clear concern growing in his movement. Crumb tapped at her face, retracting his claws at first but eventually clawing lightly at her lips, nose and inside the nostrils. Light scrapes appeared where he too checked for signs of life.

"It's ok Crumb," Lucia tried to soothe him, not knowing if he could hear or see her. His distress hurt her more than when she herself had realised her death. Crumb looked up at her, staring without acknowledgment before returning his attention to the corpse.

"Crumb, it's ok, Mum's ok." Again, Crumb looked up at her. Lucia shuffled to the side to test his gaze. He followed but showed no real recognition, he didn't show fear or unfamiliarity either. He probably couldn't see her. There was no reason why he would be able to.

Crumb and Lucia both stared at the body for a long time. Every so often Crumb would sniff and claw again. Lucia had tried petting him. She tried touching and moving all kinds of things, but each effort was useless and she gave up. On his final go at inspecting the body Crumb nipped lightly at the flesh on the body's left cheek. Lucia shooed him and he again looked at her briefly before returning to nibble the cheek.

"Can you see me?"

He lifted his eyes to her again and let out a small growl from somewhere in the back of his throat.

"It's ok Crumb."

Lucia was trying to keep her voice calm, but he was ignoring her again. He returned to sniffing around the face. Then he bit in, not so hard to tear the flesh away, but hard enough to cause deep punctures in the skin. Lucia yelled at him to stop and he did briefly before seemingly deciding she had no authority over him. His next bite was cut short by the body rolling over.

The body opened her eyes, lying flat on her back. Her once hazel eyes were glazed and milky white. They had not lost their shine but they sunk almost imperceptibly into the sockets and reflected light in a way that was different from how eyes should look. The pupils were fixed just as Ruth's had been. Lucia and Crumb both watched agog, both afraid to move. The body pushed itself up, it moved slowly and awkwardly, like someone getting up to go to the bathroom in the middle of the night. It swung its legs over the side of the bed and sat, as if working up the motivation to go further.

Lucia could see now the underside of the chin on the right side was flushed red. The redness grew darker down the outside of the right arm, bulging into a large oval on the right shoulder. Further down the thigh and outer edge of the right buttock was bruised a deep purple. The outer edges of the aubergine crescent thinned from a rich maroon to a crimson before fading into pallid skin. The crest of the hip bone was stark white in contrast to the pooling blood. Another couple swells of colour highlighted the calf and ankle on the right leg. Lucia knew it was lividity. A stage of death that showed the position in which someone died. It also showed any unusual movement after death. Still, it was another sign that despite the body moving it was in fact dead.

Deep impressions of the waffle textured blanket the body had been laying on criss-crossed their way across the whole right side of her legs, the purple bruising lighter in the grooves left by the blanket.

Crumb chirped with familiarity and rubbed himself against the body's waist, his tail aloft and he purred loudly. Any concern he had shown earlier gave way to his eagerness to be fed. Lucia was still silent, unable to process what was unfolding before her eyes. The body noticed Crumb and turned her head and shoulders toward him. Lucia winced, unsure what this body would do to her beautiful boy. She had no perceivable way to stop anything. The body didn't do anything though, just looked, accepting Crumb's hopeful affection.

"Can you hear me?" Lucia broke the silence. The body looked right into her eyes.

"You can! You can hear me!" The body, Lucia's body, gave a grunting acknowledgement.

"You're me, you're my body and you recognise me!" A slow creeping thought came over Lucia. Her body was awake, but she was still exactly where she woke up. None of it made sense.

"Can you talk?" Her body just grunted again.

"Can you stand?" Her body didn't really do anything, she didn't grunt again.

"Stand! Can you stand?" Her body rocked to its feet.

"Yes! Ok now walk over here." Lucia stepped backwards to create a larger space between them and watched in amazement as the body lumbered towards her, halting just as she reached her. Lucia reached out, trying to touch her pale skin. It didn't work, she didn't expect it to. She looked at her own hands. They looked like graphics in a first-person shooter game, not literally, but detached somehow. Like they weren't her own. Beyond her hands she could see her feet. Something was off about them too. Not her feet, the carpet. She couldn't feel it, but also there were no indentations from her weight. She might as well not have been standing there.

All at once Lucia knew somewhere in the back of her mind before her critical thinking could prove or disprove it. She was a ghost.

It was automatic, with the news of her own death and weird reality of her ghost self. She sat on the edge of the bed, surprising herself that she was able to even though the bed didn't move under her and she couldn't feel the blanket or mattress springs beneath her. All she could feel, all she had felt this whole time was a weightlessness. It felt like floating in a pool, like tiny current brushing past her skin but nothing permanent. Her body stood, rocking back and forth almost imperceptibly on stiff legs. Then she backed herself back down to sit next to Lucia on the bed. The mattress dipped under the weight and the blankets rippled to follow suit. Crumb jumped back up from the end of the bed and rubbed his cheeks on Lucia's body's elbow. He purred.

Crumb, Lucia and her body all cocked their heads as they heard a rustling of house keys at the front door. Win was home.

3

"Hey babe?" Lucia called out anxiously.

"Yeah, just a second." The carelessness in Win's voice hit Lucia like a steam train. She was about to upheave his whole life. How does she tell him that his wife has died? That's not news the deceased is usually responsible for. He could hear her though, at least that was something.

"Don't come in here yet!"

"In where?"

"I'm in the bedroom, don't come in."

"Is everything ok?" There was a playful mocking in his voice.

"Yeah..." It wasn't ok. She knew her tone wasn't convincing. If anything, that reply would have caused him more concern.

Lucia scanned the room frantically, vainly believing that her surroundings might hold inspiration. Would it be better for him to see her body first or her? Both? Neither?

Crumb bounded off the bed and out the door. A few seconds later his hoarse meow could be heard coming from the kitchen. He was harassing Win for food. Lucia could picture him winding his way around Win's legs, tripping him up and staring upwards hopefully. The image was so normal and comforting that she forgot for just a moment what had happened. Crumb's insistent meow became more erratic, signalling that Win was close to the food source. The breaks in meows were hopeful pauses, followed by admonishing yowls. Crumb didn't stop screaming at Win, even when Win opened the food. He only stopped as the food was poured right into his bowl. Then he gave a satisfied bleat, which both Win and Lucia usually took as condescension.

Lucia heard Win's soft foot falls crossing the lounge.

"Did you see Lorraine?" Win was close to the open bedroom door, but respectfully still out of sight.

"I didn't end up going."

"Oh really?" There was a pause where Win went to ask why, but decided he already knew why. "You haven't been holed up in here all day have you?" In truth he didn't care if she'd spent the whole day in bed. His concern was more that she'd probably spent the day blaming herself for a death she couldn't have prevented.

Lucia positioned herself right inside the bedroom door, blocking Win's view of her body. She didn't know how to break the news, but she couldn't avoid him for much longer. He'd want to change soon and would get cranky if he couldn't get into house clothes. If she had still been able to, Lucia would have taken a big breath before calling out to Win again.

"Ok, can you come in?" Lucia was more nervous now than she had ever been in life. More nervous than their wedding day, than her first overseas trip or every job interview she'd ever been to. Even more nervous than the time she skipped school, only to get immediately caught and the school called her parents.

Win appeared in the doorway.

"What's going on?" His mouth was smiling, but his eyes showed concern. The concern quickly changed to something different. Closer to confusion.

"Are you ok?" He reached for her elbow, intending to pull her closer and in for a hug.

Lucia stepped back. Not wanting him to touch her. Not knowing if he could.

"Huh? You mad at me?" Win's brow crinkled, more confusion and some hurt.

"No! Not angry. Just..." She stepped back again, this time revealing her body who sat silently on the bed watching this all unfold. "I didn't know how to tell you."

Win's eyes darted back and forth over the scene in front of him. In the low light of early evening Win couldn't see clearly exactly what was going on. He could only see that there were definitely two people in his bedroom. Two people that looked exactly like his wife. He reached out blindly to the light switch and flicked it on with the second try. The bulb above the bed buzzed and flickered on, low at first until it warmed up to its full brightness.

"I..." Win tried to make sense of his vision but drew nothing. He held his jaw with a clenched right hand and gestured towards Lucia and the body with the left. Throwing it into the air and slapping back down to his side, the air again and finally crossing his body to encircle himself in a protective hug.

"I think I died." Lucia heard the words coming out of her mouth before registering their weight.

"She's not." He pulled back, running his hand through his hair, something he did when stressed. "She's not dead."

"She is, check her pulse."

She still looked a lot like his wife. Win reached forward and placed two fingers on the side of her neck. He flinched at the coldness of her body. Then pressed harder. He pulled his hand back and shook it, like shaking water off it.

"But she's..."

"A zombie?"

"A zombie. And you?"

"Ghost? I think."

"Why?" Win's voice was pleading but still restrained as he always was. His calmness was sometimes frustrating, but right now Lucia was grateful for his cool head.

"I don't know. Maybe you should sit down."

Suddenly, as if remembering something. Win gasped, "I should call 000."

"What would you tell them?"

"I don't know. My wife is dead. I came home and found her dead."

"How would you explain me? How would you explain her?" She gestured toward the slow but definitely responsive body.

There was a long silence before Win spoke, and then only to say, "I need a minute."

He walked into the living room and held his forehead with one hand, before running his hand up through his soft, black hair and clutching a fistful. He tugged firmly on his hair; the aching pull of his scalp relieved the tension somewhat. He looked down at his other hand to see it was shaking. He was scared and confused.

Lucia stood in the bedroom, listening to Win in the next room pacing and sighing. Her heart broke with every groan. She followed and laid her hand on his back, wanting so badly to sooth him.

"I'm sorry." Her sudden appearance behind him caused Win to flinch. The shock reverberating through his body, leaving pins and needles in its wake. He swung around to face her; Lucia quickly pulled her hand back in shock.

"I couldn't hear you. I couldn't feel you." Win's voice breaking in fear and sadness.

Lucia told Win everything she could remember; about the missing dogs, Ruth dying, the paramedics. She told him about them taking her away and calling Ruth's son. That took them right up to when she had called Win.

"When you called, you said you were going to visit Lorraine. What happened?"

"I got a headache. Well, I already had one, when I called. I thought it was just from the stress, but it wasn't". The pain came screaming back into Lucia's consciousness. She hadn't been able to feel anything up until that point, but she could remember that pain so vividly that it was like it was happening all over again. She forged on and told Win about coming home, going to sleep and waking up dead. She even said the words, "woke up dead," as though her life was written by an eleven year old.

"Crumb nibbled her. I guess that solves the question about how long it would take for him to eat us." She chuckled hoping her joke would alleviate some of the tension in the room. Win did chuckle, but not for long before the reality behind the quip hurt his heart too much.

"What about her though?"

"I don't know, I'm me. She's just...there."

"I think I need to be alone again."

❖

It hadn't even occurred to Lucia; she had been so distracted with her body and Win that she had no idea what she even looked like until now.

She went to the bathroom and stared into the mirror, half expecting to not see anything. She did see herself though, she looked how she did in bed, not dead but weary. Her hair looked damp, kinking up as it dried, suspended in fizz. She looked tired and her skin wasn't the deathly pale like her body but wasn't alive either. After examining herself for some time it finally dawned on her what her reflection reminded her of. She looked like skim milk. Like a glass of full cream milk next to a glass of skim, the skim looked weaker. Still milk, still there, but less than. No wonder she had scared Win. She had been thinking all his fear was about the body. She was scary, corpses are scary and that one could move. Win had only ever seen a corpse all done up for viewing, he hadn't seen them mostly undressed and without makeup or embalming. That must have been what was scary, but now Lucia could see she was just as frightening.

Win stepped into the bathroom behind her. She couldn't see him through herself, confirming that she was opaque.

"You've been in here a while".

- 34 -

"Yeah," Lucia kept staring into her own face. Win's frustration subsided when he saw the bewilderment in Lucia's face. As annoyed as he was, he hadn't stopped to think about what Lucia was going through. He wanted to be angry, how could she do this? He knew it was selfish and irrational. If she was dead, a normal kind of dead, he could feel however he wanted and no one would judge him. If he came home to find her lifeless body, he could be as angry as he needed to be. What kind of emotion was appropriate here?

"I love you." Win broke the silence. "You know that right?"

"Yeah." Lucia still concentrated hard on her reflection.

It was very late when Win finally drifted off to sleep on the couch. Lucia didn't want to wake him; he needed his rest. She didn't know how she would wake him even if she wanted to. She sat quietly on the other end of the couch. Win did not look peaceful or cute while he slept. He lay crooked, his head hanging awkwardly to one side. Sweat, or oil, maybe both dampened his face, not glowing like after a workout, just kind of shiny. His shirt was bunched up around his ears, coming up in the back as he slid downwards on the couch. In this moment Lucia thought he was the most beautiful he'd ever been. His breath was heavy and rhythmic and Lucia took it all in. She could never touch him again. Her gorgeous husband lay so close to her, but she had never felt further away.

Lucia had always diametrically opposed the phrase "love of my life," she, so cynical, believed that the terminology was too definite. How could anyone know for sure who their greatest love would be. She loved Win with everything she had, she had never had a doubt about him, but who's to say. Something bad could happen to either of them, and the other one might find an even better match when they were fifty, sixty, heck even eighty years old. Something bad did happen. Lucia could say definitively that Win was the love of her life. The thought stumbled in her mind and she had to think it over a few times before she had the bravery to truly believe it. He was the love of her life, but there was no telling if she was his.

4

Lucia realised that her body was still in the bedroom. She didn't want Win to wake up during the night, stumble into bed and find her body still sitting there. She set out to try and move her.

"Get up," Lucia shout-whispered. The body noticed her but didn't move.

"Get up" she whispered again, but this time even more firmly. Her body rose slowly.

"Ok, follow me." Lucia walked across the hall into the spare bedroom, her body watched her but didn't follow. Lucia stomped back into the bedroom. Like stomping any way, raising her knees and forcing them back down quickly and strongly with her arms a little too straight. Her feet made no noise against the linoleum though.

"Come this way!" Lucia whispered angrily, emphasising each word and waving her arm forcefully towards herself. The body followed for a few steps before stopping just outside the bedroom door. She stared at the lights in the lounge room. Lucia stopped again and looked back at the body, frustrated, "This way!" Her body reluctantly followed her into the dark spare bedroom.

"Good, thank you." Lucia poked her head out of the room and peered around the corner to see Win still fast asleep on the couch. Returning to face her body, she looked at it in exactly the same way someone might look at a pile of laundry, with annoyed, unavoidable resignation.

❖

Sometime between 1 and 3am, Win took himself to bed. He bypassed brushing his teeth, slipped off his pants and crawled into bed wearing the same undershirt he had been wearing since the morning. Once he was settled, Lucia crept onto the bed. It felt strange to not be under the covers; she felt exposed. Win was tucked up under the blankets, he faced away from her, still awake. He knew she had arrived, a change in Crumb's purring or something unconscious. Lucia didn't make a sound or move the bed; she didn't even cast a shadow.

Win caught some sleep, fleeting moments that didn't add up to much, certainly didn't equate to rest. Lucia didn't sleep at all. She didn't know if that was because she kept replaying the day over and over, or if she couldn't.

Lucia's alarm went off at five. She'd forgotten that her alarm was set automatically and her phone was still on the bedside table. She reached over to swipe the screen to dismiss the alarm. Something she had done absentmindedly hundreds of times. The alarm kept blaring, getting louder and louder, but nothing Lucia could do would turn it off. Win rolled over, he somehow looked both tired and too awake. He scooched over to Lucia's side of the bed, propped himself up on one elbow and stretched out with the other arm. He couldn't quite reach; Lucia was in the way.

"Can you?"

Lucia looked up at him, not sure what she could do to help, thinking he wanted her to pass him the phone.

"Just move."

Lucia sat up fully, making a clear path for Win, and he swiped off the alarm.

"Is that the only one?"

"Yeah."

He rolled back to his side of the bed, under the covers, facing away from her. Lucia slunk away, hurt. Win didn't stir again until his alarm at six fifteen.

❖

"You're going to work?" Lucia asked, cautious not to frighten him.

"Yes, I need to."

Lucia stayed in the spare room until Win had left. Win popped his head in and said goodbye. He hardly made eye contact, but Lucia couldn't blame him.

As the door closed, Lucia got a sinking feeling. She had had this feeling a few times before. A truly overwhelming sense of displacement. Like when travelling. The feeling of when she first arrived at her destination. The journey takes so long, depending on destination hours or even days. Her whole body and mind focused on getting there, checking into the hotel, getting to the room and then, silence. Even if it's just for a brief moment, the goal is achieved and there's nothing left to do.

She had that same feeling now, but the go go go had been her whole life, and death, until this point. She was suddenly alone and unsettled.

❖

Win arrived at work bleary eyed. Thankful in some ways that he got even as much sleep as he did, it was more than he expected. Sometime during the night he had forgotten about the events of the day. It was only when he woke up this morning that it all came rushing back in. He knew that Lucia had wanted him to stay home, he could hear it in her voice. He had to go to work though. It wasn't just that he had a mountain of files to close, he needed some distance.

"Someone looks like they need a coffee." Sanjay joked as he unpacked his laptop bag.

"Ha, yeah...a second cup." Win lifted his empty cup to show he'd downed a large coffee already.

"Rough night? Mrs keeping you up? eh?" Sanjay loved a sexual innuendo.

"Something like that."

"Ahhh, get it Sammy." Win was too distracted to really care about Sanjay's crassness. By then Sanjay's computer had booted up and he was busy checking emails. Win busied himself with work. More phone interviews, a few reports to submit and in the afternoon some in person interviews and site inspections. Win was delighted by his full day. He didn't want time to think.

❖

The quietness of the house did not get easier to deal with. It was nearly winter and the evenings and mornings were crisp, so the windows were all shut. The glass deadened the outside noise, not completely, but enough that it was maddening. The only open window was in the bathroom, opened year-round to stop mould growing. Lucia stood at the bathroom window, listening. Sirens, birds, lawn mowers, wind in the trees, airplanes overhead, passing cars, dogs, insects, she took it all in. The window tethering Lucia to the living world. Until Win got home, the house was full of death.

❖

By the afternoon Win had successfully not thought about the whole rigmarole of his wife dying. Or her then coming back as a ghost and a zombie. It was quite the ordeal to forget, but he had. He had a working lunch so that he didn't have time to think then either. It might have been one of his most productive mornings all year.

Win check out a car for the afternoon. Rather than supplying their employees with company cars, the company had a fleet of cars that had to be checked out if an agent was going out. Most people avoid city driving. Brisbane CBD is not hard to navigate, despite all the one-way streets. It's not clogged like other cities, or even the motorway at peak hour. The fleet were all hybrids; Win clicked the unlock button to locate his.

Win had not factored in his driving time on his day of avoidance. No matter how loud he turned up the radio he could not drown out his thoughts. They stuck in his mind and once there, started to expand like those thick banh canh noodles that take over the whole bowl if you don't eat them fast enough.

Is it a virus? Is she contagious? Am I going to catch it? What if I catch it, it's so close to Ma's birthday. How did Lucia get it? Are there others?

That last thought echoed in his head, so loudly that by the time he reached Indooroopilly he was a mess. He hardly focused on the inspection, writing notes and snapping photos but not taking anything in. Win had broken the seal on his fears and now he couldn't stop them from flooding in, no matter how many distractions he had.

Win returned the keys to the car. He ducked into the office to check his emails before announcing to Sanjay he was leaving early.

"Ok son, go get some!"

Win chuckled dismissively, grabbed his bag and headed out the door.

"Ok bye? See you tomorrow." Sanjay called after him.

❖

Before she knew it, it was the afternoon and Lucia had spent most of the day looking out the window. She had not even checked in on her body, who was still in the spare room. Crumb had gone to lay on the spare bed. Like most cats he tried very hard to be aloof while also constantly spending his time in the same room as his owners. He was fast asleep, the kind of sleep where he might start twitching from his dreams any second.

Win arrived home, surprising Lucia. She didn't exactly know the time, but she knew he was early.

"You can't be the only one!" the words burst out of Win as soon as he laid eyes on Lucia. "There have to be others, right?"

"I guess? Does it matter?"

"It might? What if someone has a cure?"

❖

The sun was just rising but the birds had been awake for a while. Lucia stood at the bathroom window looking out. She had spent the whole night rehashing everything Win had said about there being others. He was right, she couldn't be the only one. She missed the smell of the morning and the feel of the sun hitting her face. When she closed her eyes there was nothing but black, the sun didn't filter red through her eyelids anymore. Her phone died, or Win turned it off. It was still on the bedside table, but her alarm didn't chirp each morning like it should.

Lucia couldn't face another day cooped up in the house. She needed to get out and find out what happened to her. She instructed her body to follow her to the front door.

"Open it." Lucia gestured to the door and offered the action of turning the knob and pulling it towards herself. The body's depth perception faltered as she circled her fist above the knob a few times before grasping it. Twisting and pulling at the same time proved more complicated than Lucia had bargained for. She would twist the knob and release, letting the catch snap back while she refocused her actions into pulling. When she pulled it was hard and Lucia worried she would pull the door right off its hinges. After an eternity of coaching, the door swung open with a force that nearly did just that.

Lucia slipped through the doorway.

"Now close it." She figured it would go a lot faster without her body tagging along. The door automatically locked when it was shut so all her body had to do was push it closed. She heard the door click into place and immediately regretted the decision to close it. Reconciling in her mind that any frustration she anticipated getting back in the house would be far less than if either Crumb or the body went wandering.

The drive to Ruth's house was about six kilometres. Normally Lucia wouldn't attempt to walk a twelve-kilometre round trip without some preparation. She probably hadn't done a walk that big in her adult life to be honest, but she guessed it would be much easier without a body to restrain her. No pesky things like aching muscles or burning lungs. She could probably walk forever.

She almost made it to the fence before she started to feel a resistance, almost like walking into a strong wind. She struggled a couple steps further before hurtling back into the lounge room. As though she was an over stretched rubber band being snapped back.

"What?"

Lucia peered out the lounge room window that faced onto the road. Outside was unchanged. To her right the door was unchanged too. She looked back into the front yard. She had made it exactly to the front gate, only a few metres from the front door. Right to the edge of the property. She had been trying to step on to the footpath when she reappeared in the house.

"Oh fuck." She was one of those ghosts that couldn't leave the place she died. "I'm stuck here." Her whole life Lucia had been a homebody, proud of it even. Now, when she needed it the most, she couldn't leave even if she wanted to.

5

"Hey Win? Can you leave the TV on?"

"Sure, what channel?"

"It doesn't matter" Lucia just needed it to not be so quiet in the house.

She wandered around the house looking for something to try moving. She settled on the tv remote which sat on the coffee table, thinking if she was successful at least the tv remote wouldn't break if it fell. At first she just tried to pick it up. Her fingers clasped around the remote, but it didn't budge. She tried thinking hard about it, but that didn't work. She imagined the remote to be very heavy, but that didn't work. She imagined her hand to be heavy, but that didn't work either. She meditated, she screamed, she asked politely but the remote never moved. Hours passed; Lucia briefly tried to move the tissue box, but that was just as useless. She was concentrating so hard that she had barely noticed her body and Crumb came into the room. Crumb sat on the couch, half watching but mostly snoozing.

"Come on! I'll do anything if you just move!" Lucia pleaded, shutting her eyes and curling herself into a ball.

The body reached for the remote, the sound of it pushing across the coffee table caused Lucia to spring up. For a brief moment she believed that she had telekinetically moved it. The trade-off of telekinesis as a ghostly power would be exceptionally cool for Lucia, who had watched Matilda approximately a million times, give or take. Her joy quickly gave way to a different elation as she realised that the remote was being moved by her body. She pushed it towards Lucia, wearing a quizzical expression behind her atrophying muscles.

"You understood me?" The body didn't give a response other than nudging the remote again. An idea burst into Lucia's mind. Even if she couldn't do it herself, she could still be useful. Lucia had missed taco Tuesday and Win had a frozen meal for dinner. She wanted so desperately to show Win that things would be ok. She had to believe that for herself as well.

"Do you want to cook dinner with me?" Lucia didn't even wait for a response before racing into the kitchen, popping her head back around the corner, "Come on!"

Lucia stood almost face to face with her body. The body was shorter than Lucia had been in life. The disks in her spine compressed as they lost integrity. Lucia's hands rested on her body's shoulders so she could capture her full attention.

"We need to get ingredients."

Non-refrigerated stuff first. Onion, spices, tortillas, all located in Lucia's meticulously organised pantry. Lucia stepped to the pantry door.

"Open this." Seven repetitions and four mimes of opening the door, the pantry was finally open.

"Fuck me, this is going to take a long time." Lucia muttered under her breath. One red onion made its way onto the bench. Paprika, salt, pepper and chilli flakes were also strewn across the bench. Cumin and the tortillas were on the floor, but out of the pantry. Lucia chalked it up as a win.

Next, they grabbed all the utensils they needed, or whatever was close enough. Her body grabbed a slotted spoon instead of the stirring spoon, but that was fine, frustrating, but fine.

Fear bubbled up in Lucia as she instructed her body to get a knife. She didn't fear for herself, obviously she couldn't get hurt, but she worried about how useful she would be if she lost an appendage.

The body's motor skills were what you would expect from a zombie and cutting the onion took many times longer than it would normally take Lucia. Slices of onion were shaved off in uneven discs as the knife kept sliding while cutting. It looked kind of like one of those balloon and sand juggling balls that Lucia had made at Girl Guides. Little bits of onion and flakes of the onion skin were smeared across the cutting board and onto the bench, but no lost fingers.

The tomatoes were already on the bench. Lucia didn't need to get them from anywhere. Cutting them seemed like an impossible task. The less knife work the better. She got her body to put two tomatoes in a bowl, then with another bowl on top press down. Her idea was that she could crush the tomatoes. Where she was lacking fine motor skills, the body made up for it with brute force. As it turned out, too much force; the bowls skidded out from under her body's hands and landed on the floor. Both bowls broke and the top one bounced out and sprayed mashed tomato across the whole kitchen.

Lucia left her body to stand in the kitchen, while she steeled herself to go on. Lucia needed to recuperate before continuing. Normally she could smash this recipe out in under twenty minutes. The mental agility required to instruct such a demanding student was draining, but she was still excited and hopeful to get a meal on the table. Crumb scampered into the kitchen in Lucia's absence. He sniffed cautiously at the mess of tomato on the floor, and at the wet globs where the juice had run into the dusting of cumin. Neither were appealing to him, so he rubbed himself against the body's leg.

4:30pm. Lucia could wait to keep going, but anything could happen between now and Win's arrival home. Better to start now, he could heat dinner up if he needed.

Crumb worked his way under the body's feet and meowed expectantly. He knew that mince was the next step in this recipe. Lucia looked down at her bare feet next to her body's. The skin was mottled purple and a sickly pale but Crumb wasn't bothered as he rubbed against her legs. Lucia's feet were unchanged from only a few days earlier when she was alive. She longed for Crumb to be nuzzling her.

Her body took a saucepan from the cupboard, not the frypan that Lucia had instructed. All good, a saucepan would work. Only half the mince made it in the pan. The rest hung down the side of the pan in frayed, pink tendrils. A whole clump fell all the way to the floor. Crumb scooted quickly but ate it in petite nibbles. It was only tacos for one, half the mince would be fine.

The mince sizzled in the pan, the body nudging it around roughly with the large slotted spoon. The mince stayed in large clumps; the bottom burned before the top cooked through. Lucia tried to get the body to turn the stove down but she turned it off all the way. The residual heat had at least cooked the mince through by the time they got the stove back on. The garlic burned, the spices didn't mix in. The contents of the pan were both burned and soupy.

Lucia surveyed the kitchen. None of it was edible. She'd used all the ingredients but had nothing to show for it. The kitchen floor was a Jackson Pollock of Tuesday night tradition. A tradition that was now just as spent as her attempt at dinner.

Lucia was frantically instructing her body to sweep the floor as Win came home. The broom was just making muddy streaks on the floor and pushing the mess from one place to another, tainting everything in between.

"What are you doing?" Win queried as he turned on the light.

"We're just trying to clean up. We made you dinner. Tried to make you dinner." She wanted to cry.

"She cooked?" He grimaced a little. "I don't think I'd want it anyway, but thank you?" His face and his tone were unconvincing. "You didn't have to do this." He meant that she didn't need to try, he could manage, but he also meant she didn't have to make things harder. "I'll finish cleaning up."

Win scanned the kitchen and let out a sigh that he definitely wasn't aware of. He pushed one hand through his hair, his slender fingers lost in the black, shiny swoop behind his temples. The other hand on his hip, his shoulders dropped noticeably.

"I'm sorry."

Win whirled around, either he didn't realise Lucia was still there, or he hadn't noticed his deflated body language.

"I know." He strode past her and returned after a little while with the vacuum, wrestling the nozzle under one arm.

"I'm sorry." It was reflexive for Lucia to apologise. She wasn't just apologising for the mess, but for the whole thing.

Win offered a weak smile out the corner of his mouth, his brow knitted over his eyes.

"We should name her."

"Whu.what?" Win sputtered out a combination of who and what, making his voice sound a little like a children's tv presenter. The change of topic catching him so off guard that he barely registered what she had said.

"My body. We need a way to refer to her."

"Oh, ummm..." Win huffed the words out while pulling the vacuum cord out enough to plug it in. "What about Lu?"

"Deal."

They both nodded in agreement as the sound of the vacuum filled the kitchen.

❖

It was well past dinner time when Win had finished cleaning. He threw another frozen meal into the microwave and a familiar series of beeps rang out. He was going to say something to Lucia but stopped short when he saw Lu. She was just as much a mess as the kitchen had been. Win sighed again.

"I'm sorry."

"Stop apologising." Each syllable strained on Win's voice. His exhaustion was showing itself, not only in his voice but deep rings were forming under his eyes, that hadn't been as noticeable when he first came home.

"I'm just going to hose off her legs."

"Sounds good."

It was dark now. The back steps were only illuminated by the moon and the light coming from the kitchen. Win guided Lu down the stairs without turning on any outside lights. The hose was not far from the bottom of the steps. Lucia watched from behind the screen door. Crumb stood next to her feet but made no effort to rub against her. He barely even acknowledged her. His attention was with Lu and Win leaving without him. His meows landed somewhere between concern and indignation.

Win positioned Lu on the grass. Pulled her oversized shirt up into a knot around her waist. He then repositioned her, she stumbled back a few steps.

The same resistance tugged at Lucia as the day before. This time it pushed her forward instead of pulling her back. Lu continued to stumble backwards, trying to find her footing and Lucia scooted forward, gliding through the screen and down the first few steps.

"Huh?" It was confusing and disorienting. "Oohhh." It clicked. Lucia wasn't doomed to be trapped in the house at all. She was doomed to be tied to her rotting corpse.

6

She was up against the clock. Summar Ibrahim had woken with a faint stinging behind her eyes and a weird spot in her vision. A migraine was imminent. Her housemates had already gone to work or uni. The cupboards were bare and she desperately needed food. Especially if she was going to make it through the migraine unscathed.

The lights in the supermarket weren't helping. The fluros burned her eyes and their strobing added to her nausea. She was tempted to keep her sunglasses on while she hurried around the aisles, knowing that her body would fall into a useless heap before long, but she didn't. Her hijab attracted enough negative attention. She didn't have the time or energy to handle some boomer getting in her face about it.

She didn't make a list and cursed herself because as the pain started to shift into the eye sockets; it seemed to push out her memory.

She grabbed bread, fruit and veggies, chocolate and Panadol. The medications aisle felt like it was a mile away from the self-serve checkouts. Summar's whole face stung when she tried to focus on the distance. She kept her head down and watched her feet try to shuffle towards the checkouts quickly but without moving too abruptly. She timed it wrongly, the migraine was coming fast.

Summar didn't know exactly what happened. Her apples fell to the floor and went scooting into the aisles. She was standing, so was the man she ran into. Maybe he ran into her. It didn't matter. She held her breath, waiting for him to start berating her. Expecting his face to be flushed with anger, but he wasn't angry. His skin was pale and unfettered by emotion, like their collision hadn't phased him at all.

"Oops." That's all he said. Not sorry, no banter, he didn't offer to help her collect her things. He smiled and continued walking and disappeared into the pet food aisle. A chill ran down Summer's spine when she watched him pass her. She put it down to a cold sweat starting up, or adrenaline.

Everything but the bread was on the floor. She hadn't grabbed a basket. A woman and her son, a gawky looking kid that couldn't have been more than eight, were busy grabbing the groceries off the floor.

"Are you ok?" The mother said, while bundling the pile of food back into Summer's arms.

"Yeah." She wasn't ok. "Just a little fright." Summer smiled sweetly, even though the edges of her mouth were starting to tremble. "Thank you."

"The apples got a bit bruised."

"Oh ok." Summer was lagging. Her reflexes were slowing, including her comprehension. She was ready to just leave the whole pile and race back to bed.

"Tyler, go grab some more apples for the lady."

"Oh no, it's ok. He doesn't need to."

"You sure?" The lady wasn't buying that Summer was ok when she so clearly wasn't. Even in the time they had been speaking Summer's face had started to drop. Her eyes, usually shiny, clear and deep brown, had glazed over.

"Yes, thank you."

She shuffled herself to the nearest checkout and dumped her armful on the conveyor.

Checking out took what felt like an age. Each second that ticked down was one more increment of pain.

By the time Summar reached her own front door, her migraine constricted the whole of her upper body. She felt like she was drowning in cement and it was quickly hardening. She'd had the forethought to toss her heat packs next to the microwave before she left. She threw the entire green bag into the fridge. She'd deal with it later. The handles of the green bag brushed down her forearm as she let it drop from the crook of her elbow to her hand. There was a slight sting on her arm, a tiny snag on her grey hoodie. Something from running into that guy maybe.

She unpinned her hijab with one hand while mashing buttons on the microwave with the other. Walking to her room she pulled the hijab off her head, then her hair cap. There was a slight relief when the fresh air hit where the cap had been pressed tightly to her head.

She could faintly hear the microwave from her room. She pushed off her jeans, leaving them on the floor, and lay on the bed. She'd get up to get the heat packs in a moment.

7

"Well, if we're going to be stuck together, we might as well make you look presentable." Lucia looked over Lu's body, right now, she looked exactly like someone who had died in their sleep. That needed to change if they were going to go out into the public.

Win was still asleep and Lucia didn't want to wake him. Lucia had stopped staying in their bedroom at night. Partly so she could move around, try to entertain herself in those torturous extra hours. Partly because, even though he wouldn't say it, Win wasn't getting any rest with her there.

She instructed Lu to be quiet, not really sure if that instruction would be understood or carried out. They crept into the bedroom. There was an ottoman in the corner of the room which acted as a catch-all for partially dirty clothes. Some of the clothes on there had been there for months. Jumpers and leggings that had been worn once at home on an unseasonably cold day. Waiting for the weather to cool down so they could be worn again. Shirts and jeans that had been worn to do the grocery shopping but nothing else. Lucia thought rifling through the drawers would take too long and probably wake Win. She would take her chances with whatever was on the pile.

She instructed Lu to take the whole pile. There were a lot of Win's clothes in there but this was the easier plan. Lucia and Lu tried sneaking out of the bedroom but Lucia could see Win was awake, just not moving yet. With any luck he'd fall back asleep, if he had been asleep to begin with at all.

Lucia hushed Lu as she shuffled into the spare room. They closed the door behind them to muffle any sounds. There was a trail of clothes behind them and a single sock got caught under the door as Lu shoved it.

Lucia selected a pair of jeans and a loose jumper for Lu to wear. The long pants and sleeves would do most of the grunt work covering up her deathly skin. Getting the clothes on was an ordeal, Lu fell over several times before Lucia had her sit on the bed to pull on the jeans. She didn't even bother buttoning the fly. Knowing that Lu's fine motor skills weren't up to it.

Lu was caught in the jumper, arms over her head and swayed into the spare bedroom wall when Win knocked on the door.

"Everything ok in there?"

"Yeah" Lucia replied unconvincingly.

"Can I come in?" Win stepped through the door to see Lu flailing about, light pink fluff from the inside of the jumper whirling in the air around her.

"Oh!" Win raced forward to pull the jumper down over Lu's head. This was the first time he had touched her since the first day and he felt queasy as his hand brushed her cold skin.

"You don't have to help." Lucia offered an escape for Win who was noticeably uncomfortable. "I'm just trying to make her more presentable."

"It's ok, I can help. What do you need?"

Lucia asked Win to do up Lu's fly and get some shoes. They selected some black slip-on Vans, for the dual benefit of covering most of Lu's foot while being easy to put on and stay on.

As Lucia and Win were discussing if makeup was a good idea or not, Lucia gestured towards Lu and caught a glimpse of her own arm. She too was wearing a jumper. Checking her legs, she found she was also wearing the jeans and Van's. She hadn't thought about what she would wear, figuring that she was destined to be pantsless for her whole existence. Her body didn't reflect Lu's deterioration, until now she hadn't changed at all in days.

Win was thickly applying concealer to the cat bite marks on Lu's left cheek. The concealer was a few shades too dark and was drawing more attention to the area. Win threw his hands up in the air, concealer glazing his fingertips and he urged Lucia to help him with a pained look.

"Maybe we could make them look like freckles?"

"Good idea." For the first time in days there was an enthusiasm in Win's voice that reminded Lucia of how he used to speak to her. For a moment, his apprehension towards her was dropped and she felt their connection again.

Win went to wash his hands and Lucia decided to try something. She grabbed a hair tie. She had died with the elastic on her wrist. It was still there. She couldn't feel it between her fingers but was able to move it in a similar fashion to how she used to. She pulled her hair back off her face and up into a high bun, securing it with the hair tie. Her slightly waved, mostly frizzed hair looking suitably tousled but much neater.

Win returned with a damp washcloth and was dabbing Lu's face to clean it. He held her chin gently with his other hand. Lucia saw how softly and lovingly he was and felt hope. This face was serious, lips barely parted and after watching him for a while, Lucia noticed he was holding his breath. The more she watched, the more crestfallen she felt.

After patting her face dry, Win coloured in the four punctures with a brow pencil. It took a few goes as the pencil kept cracking. Win would mutter under his breath, wipe it off and try again, until the "freckles" looked suitably realistic. He brushed Lu's face with powder to mattify any slickness and combed through her hair to tame the frizz.

Lucia and Win stepped back to admire their work. She looked ok, only ok. If anyone looked closely they would see someone a little worse for wear. She looked like a living person that only *looked* dead. In passing, people probably wouldn't notice her at all, which was exactly what they needed. Lucia looked passable too. Together they looked like identical twins, one having a much rougher life than the other.

❖

The bus would be longer, but also the safest option. Lucia had considered the car but ultimately couldn't reconcile the risk of something happening. The issue with the bus was getting caught out. Lucia had Lu practice swiping her Go Card several times, not entirely sure if that kind of knowledge could be retained.

They trundled up to the bus stop, it was only about 500 metres from their front door but it took a while to get there. Once the coolness of the morning dried up, the day was bright and hot enough to be summer in other parts of the world. It wasn't too implausible for the pair to be wearing jumpers but it was pretty unnecessary and Lucia hoped no one would mention it. Lu handled the walk pretty well, she wasn't distracted by the cars or birds, she seemed to hone into Lucia, only hearing her. Maybe that was fear. She didn't know if Lu could still feel that. For all she knew all nerves that would normally be swarming Lucia had transferred to her counterpart. Lucia retained the emotion of nervousness but only a tiny bit of the symptoms remained. More like a buzzing outside of her than the usual butterflies.

Lucia hailed the bus; she was surprised at how delighted it made her. Being able to actually influence something in the real world. Even something as small as waving her arm at a bus for it to stop, was exciting. She hadn't felt that useful in days.

When Lucia and Lu alighted near Ruth's house, the phantom gnawing in the pit of Lucia's stomach finally dissipated. She had been so nervous someone would realise that they didn't belong there. None of the three other passengers had even bothered to look at them. They were all too busy in their own little worlds.

Ruth's house was quiet. Lucia hadn't really expected anything else. She thought that maybe Ruth's kids would be there, rooting through her belongings for something of value. In reality they'd probably done that while she was alive.

Lu turned the key in the lock, mashing her wrist into the door as it twisted. The door creaked open, which Lucia was almost certain it had never done before. She laughed at the peculiarity of the door being creepy now that house was abandoned after death, like some kind of cosmic joke.

The lounge was exactly as she had left it on Monday. If Ruth's children had been, they hadn't moved anything. Glancing over at the kitchen Lucia could see the small amount of washing up she had done on Monday still on the sink. She didn't know what she was looking for, this was just a hunch to retrace her steps. Ruth's was the last place she had been before she died. Lu swayed in the doorway, taking in the empty house with a glint of familiarity and hesitation. Lucia hadn't seen Lu hesitate, she was slow and took a while to get things done, but that was a processing issue more than anything. Lucia stopped herself from blurting out, "What is it Lassie?" She thought it best not to treat her own body like a dog. Instead, she ushered Lu further into the room and tried to soothe her.

Lucia heard a scuffling coming from around the corner towards the bedrooms. From the uncharacteristic focus on Lu's face, she could hear it too. Lucia crept forward, the instinct to make herself slow, quiet and small still held up even when it changed very little now. She rounded the corner and jumped back at the sight of Ruth standing in the hall just outside her bedroom.

Ruth was completely naked; her olive skin was pale. She did not share the same deep purple bruising that Lu wore, instead her skin was swollen. On her calves and forearms the wrinkles were stretched and the skin papery thin. Ruth's usually perfectly curled hair was wispy and pulled straight in parts.

Ruth heard the gasp escaping from Lucia and whirled around.

"Ruth? How did you?" Ruth grunted in recognition. "You too." This discovery of Ruth, back from the mortuary or wherever they cart bodies, changed everything.

"Lu!" Lucia called back for Lu to come. She didn't move or take her eyes off Ruth. "Did you know about this?"

Lu shuffled into view of Ruth and the pair of them focused on each other intensely. During the zombie standoff Lucia let her eyes search the rest of the bedroom. Ruth's body was there, but she didn't have a ghost anywhere to be found.

❖

Lucia waited anxiously on the couch for Win to arrive home. Lu sat beside her smacking her lips, as though chewing gum, even though she wasn't. Lucia thought gum probably wouldn't be that bad an idea, surely Lu's breath was getting ripe. She was decomposing, slower than a regular body would, but it was still pretty bad. The soft tissue of her organs would be mush, it was a wonder Lu wasn't starting to bloat or ooze. Ruth was bloating, but Lu seemed to be almost drying out. Her skin was loose and sagging but it looked as though it would be hard, like the joint where a limb of a tree had been cut off. Over time the bark ripples over the cut but is firm.

- 62 -

Lucia wondered if she should get an air freshener or something to cover the smell. She knew there had to be a smell. Simultaneously happy to not be able to tell, but really missing having all of her senses. She remembered the spare camphor balls in the bottom of the linen cupboard. That would cover the smell and keep the bugs away. She urged Lu to follow her to the linen cupboard to get the camphor. She had forgotten that they were buried underneath a lot of spare items. Candles, vacuum bags, batteries, sleeping bags and wrapping paper were all strewn across the floor when Win came home.

"Oh my god! I'm so sorry. We'll clean this up." she'd done it again. The second day in a row Win was coming home to a mess.

A pained look fell across Win's face, "What are you doing?"

"We're looking for the camphor, to cover the smell. Does she smell?"

"A bit. You worried she's going to get moths too?" He said it like a joke, but there was a harshness in his voice.

"Flies, more worried about flies." Win nodded, accepting the answer as reasonable. "We had an exciting day. I have to talk to you."

Win spotted the camphor on the ground, three white balls surrounded by a light green cage. He picked it up and shoved it into Lu's front pocket. She obediently lifted her arms out of the way as he did. It looked just like a roll of coins or a lighter in her pocket.

Crumb saw his opportunity and snuck into the mostly empty bottom shelf of the cupboard. He poked his head behind the vacuum cleaner, sniffing heavily.

"Get out of it Crumb!" Win roused and Crumb immediately backed out and ran into the bedroom. "Yeah, ok, just let me get changed first."

Lucia was still telling Lu how to put things back in the cupboard when Win came back out of the bedroom. He stopped for a while watching before just finishing the job himself. He walked away to the lounge without saying a word but glanced at Lucia expectantly from the couch.

"We went to Ruth's today. To retrace my steps or something." Lucia was perched on the edge of the couch, enthusiastically telling Win her news. "Ruth is a zombie too!"

"Did she tell you anything?"

"Noooo?"

"Why not?"

Lucia gestured up and down at Lu. Shoulders raised to her ears.

"Yeah ok, but what about her....you?"

"Oh." Of course he'd assume this. "She didn't have one."

"So she's dead, but just a zombie?"

"Yeah."

Win's face scrunched, then fell. He didn't know what to do with this information.

❖

Win woke several times strangled in blankets. Tossing and turning in his sleep had wound the blankets around his body and was restrained in an uncomfortable hold. Every few turns he would heave the blankets out from under himself and lay them back as flat as he could. The night was cool, a temperature that ordinarily Win would find blissful. After hours of wrestling the covers Win settled into lying facing the window. The light of the streetlamp across the road illuminated the world outside and most of the bedroom. Had it not been for the shifting brightness of the light as the wind blew the tree branches out of the way, Win would not have noticed that his eyes were open. He stared blankly out the window, but his thoughts clouded his vision.

It took several runs through his head for Win to organise his thoughts into something coherent. His mind kept getting stuck on his words, repeating phrases over and over and jumping to the next thought. Once it was all straight in his head, the whole week until now, Win called out for Lucia. He didn't want to forget how to say what he wanted to say.

She was awake. He knew she was awake.

Lucia arrived at the door, announcing herself quietly. It made Win jump, he had been listening for her since he called out, but without footsteps she snuck up on him. He pulled himself upright and sat back against the wall at the head of the bed. He hugged a pillow close and let his gaze fall to the bedspread in front of him.

"I need to talk to you."

"Ok" Lucia moved forward into the bedroom.

Cutting her off, "I just. I just need to say it all. Without you saying anything."

Lucia understood and was unsure if she should acknowledge that or remain silent. She chose silence and edged forward to the corner of the bed furthest away from Win. She coiled herself into a small ball at the end of the bed. Her knees up near her face and arms wrapped around her shins. Once she was settled, Win lifted his head only slightly to check he had Lucia's attention before dropping his gaze again.

"I don't know how I am supposed to be feeling. I love you. I *loved* you so much. Being married to you has been better than I could have imagined, but it's not the same anymore." His eyes darted up to meet hers. Tears nudged the corners of his eyes, but the tiny quiver in his voice gave more away.

"I promised to you that I would try and grow with you, I understood, *understand,* that you wouldn't always be the same person. I wouldn't always be the same. I get that. But this. This is too much. I didn't sign on for this."

Win stopped talking but didn't lift his eyes again, instead he stared at his own hands, winding his fingers around each other.

After a long time Lucia spoke up, "I'm still the same person though."

"Yes, but no. You're not the same person. You're dead Luke!"

Lucia knew she was dead, but Win's tone stung. He so rarely raised his voice; he was always calm. He never called her Luke. He had always teased her when she and Kathryn were kids. His childhood teasing of his younger sister blurred over onto her best friend. Calling her Luke annoyed a ten year old Lucia to no end. It rubbed her the wrong way as a girly girl, and once a twelve year old Win learned that, he didn't stop. He continued into their teens and early twenties.

At Kathryn's twenty first birthday party he called her Lucia. She hadn't seen him since Kathryn's twentieth. She was so taken aback and could hardly believe it. He never called her Luke again.

The way he spoke to her now, this regression. She felt small, and worse, she felt like Win was looking down on her.

All these thoughts swirled in her head. She so desperately wanted to cry and maybe the pain would wash away with the tears. Her face contorted into a deep frown, but no tears came.

"I know it's not your fault." Win knew that face, even without the tears. Lucia had a face for anger towards other people. He saw it when Lucia saw or heard someone being bigoted, when people walked too slowly, or stopped short and definitely when someone else's food came before theirs in the restaurant. She had a whole other face for when her anger was being directed inward. That face he saw a lot more often. Lucia was a very forgiving person, but less so when it came to herself.

8

Win had messaged to tell Kathryn he was coming over. She waited at the door as he pulled up. The glow from the lounge room light behind her, her silhouette only just visible through the screen door. Butterbean's nose pressed between the metal lattice and into the fly screen. He gave out a small growl as Win unlatched the gate but gave up quickly when he recognised him. Kathryn swung the door out towards him and Win caught it before it could clang into the end of its rotation. Butterbean's excited tail wagged forcefully against the wall.

"Have you eaten?"

"Not yet."

Kathryn shot back an incredulous look. It was past eight, and she was only asking out of politeness. Win was usually pretty ravenous by seven. They never booked a table any later than six thirty if they could avoid it, so the food was hitting the table before he got too hungry.

"Woah, what happened?" She was half joking in her tone but pulled up pretty quickly when Win replied with a laboured shrug. "Ok, really? What happened?"

"Can we...just sit for a bit?" He sat on the edge of the couch. His head resting in his hands. Butterbean sniffed enthusiastically up at his face through his forearms, only stopping when he heard Kathryn in the kitchen.

She scooped some pasta from a cooling pan, still on the stove. She hadn't gotten around to putting away the leftovers. She threw it in the microwave and poured a glass of water from the fridge.

"Or did you need something stronger?" Again she joked, but as Win peered up at her from between his hands, she lowered her tone and listed the wine she had on hand. "Got some Glenmorangie as well, if you want?"

The microwave beeped.

"Shiraz. Please."

Kathryn returned with the wine and pasta.

"Thank you. You can finish." He gestured towards the paused TV screen.

Win took in none of the plot in whatever show it was that Kathryn was binging. He just stared at the bottom right corner of the screen. The background noise of the TV hushed his thoughts only a little as he rehearsed in his mind how to tell Kathryn everything. Kathryn didn't pay much attention either. She was waiting for him to say something, her body tensed in readiness to react.

The Netflix next episode countdown popped up on screen just as he was ready to start talking. Kathryn held the remote up towards the screen, ready for the second she was able to pause.

Win spewed out the whole story start to finish under the glow of the Netflix logo. Kathryn stayed silent the entire time. When he finished, she didn't offer any advice. Only telling him that he could spend the night. The amount of wine Win had drunk also indicated he should stay.

❖

Win spent a sleepless night in Kathryn and Gianna's spare room. His body relented eventually but it wasn't a restful sleep.

Kathryn spent a restless night in her own bed, waiting for Gianna to come home from her shift. She was convinced that her brother had lost it, and she needed her wife to help him get some help. She messaged Lucia to let her know he was staying there and asking if Lucia was ok. The lack of reply, to this or any of the week's previous messages worried her too. She loved Win so much, but she couldn't shake the feeling he had done something to Lucia.

❖

Win had said that he was going to see Kathryn. It was a relief if Lucia was being honest. She worried about him keeping it all in. It felt like the more people knew, the more people there were to share the load. She assumed he'd be back. She told herself that nothing had happened, he was ok, safe at Kathryn and Gianna's. There was a little nagging in the back of her mind, a what if. What if he wasn't ok. She couldn't be so sure anymore. Afterall, the thing no one thinks is going to happen, had happened to her.

The only clock in the house was in the dining room they never used. The minutes ticked down slowly, until eventually it was the next day. Past midnight, he wouldn't be coming home until the morning. He was fine. She had to keep telling herself that.

When she was certain she had the house to herself, she curled up in a ball on her own bed. She couldn't feel cool bedspread, strewn with patches of black cat fur. She could not smell the lingering scent of her tea tree moisturiser on her pillow, which always reminded her of a crisp gin and tonic. She couldn't smell that musty, sleeping man scent that every man, no matter their age, size or location seemed to get. She could imagine all of it so clearly. She could hear the memory of Win's heavy breathing in his sleep, but when she rolled over, the bed was made, and his side remained empty.

Win had, justifiably, thrown out the sheets that were on the bed when she died. The sheets on the bed now were a pale blue. Lucia would never have picked this colour, she only liked dark coloured sheets.

She played the words Win had said over and over until they were screaming inside her head. Each replay his tone became harsher until the words hardly meant anything and the ringing in her ears sputtered and spewed only hatred.

❖

Win woke just as the sun was rising. The light through the spare room window was cool and diffused through the swaying trees outside. It took him several moments to recall exactly where he was. But after recovering that memory, he felt almost as though within the four walls of his sister's spare room, he was safe. Here he didn't have to answer to anyone and the thought lulled him back to sleep.

He woke again, much later. The cool, soft light of predawn had been replaced with a harsh brightness. The bedroom window faced west, so the sun didn't beat directly into the room. It bounced off the smooth trunks of the gums outside and glared straight back into his eyes. The operatic song of the magpies was interjected and overpowered by a gang of squawking crows. In between the crows, Win could hear hushed tones in the living room outside. Gianna was home and he could tell, even without hearing the words, that they were talking about him. They weren't arguing, but both sides of the conversation were lowered in the way people do when they're controlling their emotions.

❖

"Do you really think he did something?"

"I haven't heard from her all week. Have you? Zombies and ghosts aren't real babe. I think maybe he's...snapped."

"I haven't heard from her, but that doesn't mean anything necessarily. You know Win."

"That's what everyone says!" Kathryn adjusted herself as she felt her volume creeping up. "It's always the ones you least suspect."

"It's not always the ones you least expect Kat. It's *sometimes* the people you least suspect, just a creepy guy turning out to be a murderer isn't as good a story."

"Gianna, I don't think that's as comforting as you think it is."

Gianna saw the real concern in Kathryn's face. She was worried too but didn't want to let Kathryn's mind run off. Most of all, if Win really had "snapped," she didn't want either of them to inadvertently knock him back to reality. Not if it put her or her wife in danger. She pulled Kathryn in close, wrapping her arms around her and kissing the top of her head.

"What if I stay here and you go to the house?"

"What if she's there? Her...body...I mean?"

"Then call the police. Straight away. You see blood or signs of a struggle, anything. Call the police."

"Ok"

Gianna kissed her again and held a little tighter.

❖

Lucia had never seen so many sunrises in her life. The phrase still holds up, she could count on one hand the number of sunrises she watched in her whole twenty-nine years. She had already surpassed that in death. The night times were definitely the hardest time, but

- 73 -

a tiny glimmer of hope came back with the sun each day. Lucia longed for the days of her insomnia; it was torturous at the time. Lying awake until three in the morning, fragmented sleep from then, but this was much worse. This was insomnia of a different level. The minutes slowed at night and she would give anything for those fragments of release again. Maybe this is what they really mean by waking nightmare.

There was no point getting up, but no real point staying in bed. A car pulling into the driveway urged Lucia to finally make the choice to get up. Cars seemed to pull up outside their house constantly. Apparently it was a good place to turn around or stop to make phone calls. There were even a few cars that pulled over to scoff down fast food guiltily before moving on. The road was wide, so no one ever needed to pull into the drive to turn around. Lucia recognised the car in an instant, Kathryn.

Kathryn's face was drawn and sullen as she made it up from the car to the front steps. She glanced around rapidly at the windows, but Lucia knew very well that from the driveway it was impossible to actually see anything inside the house during the day. Kathryn knocked on the door. Lucia was paralysed and didn't answer. She was not afraid of her friend, maybe the opposite. She loved Kathryn so dearly and that she did not want to reveal herself. Win was so hurt, maybe it would be easier for Kathryn to never see her.

Lucia snapped out of it for the second knock. She stood close to the door.

"Kathryn?"

The closeness of the voice, with no accompanying footsteps shocked Kathryn.

"Lucia? Thank God. Can I come in?"

"You know where the key is right?"

Kathryn was worried again now. Lucia not opening the door. Lucia not welcoming her at the door, was unusual. The door opened and Kathryn slipped through, closing it quickly behind her. For some reason she felt she should keep the outside from getting in. Much in the same way people whisper gossip even when there is no reason to. Lucia stood back in the lounge room, not sure how to hold her hands while she waited for Kathryn's judgement. Kathryn's eyes found Lucia's and she was about to say something when she saw Lu in the hallway, over Lucia's shoulder.

"You look like you've seen a ghost." Lucia joked, knowing it wouldn't land but trying anyway.

"I can't believe it."

Win strained to hear the hushed conversation between his sister and sister-in-law, but he could only hear some clinking of dishes. He decided to brave a trip to the kitchen. Gianna was sitting at the kitchen table, her breakfast dishes already on the side of the sink, her hand rested around what was probably a second cup of decaf. Her other hand held a small paperback out in front of her. The cover an ambiguous shade of purple but Win knew it was probably a mystery novel.

"There's coffee still in the pot," Gianna said without looking up from her book.

She finished the paragraph she was on while Win was pouring himself a cup and she swivelled in her chair to face him.

"How are you feeling?"

"Kathryn told you?" He didn't wait for Gianna to reply, he knew the answer, and she knew he knew. "You don't believe me."

Gianna considered her answer, "I believe you believe it."

❖

Kathryn edged her hand towards Lucia, intent of checking if she was real. No one had tried to touch Lucia yet, so the result was a first for both of them. Kathryn's hand disappeared in Lucia's shoulder.

"Huh" They both said in unison before both laughing at their persistent similarities.

"What does it feel like?"

"Like nothing's there. I thought it would be warmer or colder, something. My eyes are telling me something, you're there," Kathryn corrected herself, "but I can't feel it...you." Kathryn paused to gauge Lucia's feelings. "What about for you?"

"Same. Can't feel anything." Kathryn's eyes darted back to Lu who was looming in the hall. Kathryn nodded towards Lu, eyebrows raised to Lucia. "This is Lu." Lucia introduced them.

Kathryn was more hesitant towards Lu than she had been towards Lucia. A more visceral reaction to the more tangible death and she made excuses to distance herself.

Kathryn nestled herself down on the couch "We need to talk about Win."

"You're handling it better than him." Lucia rested on the couch. Kathryn hesitated, her face unable to hide her surprise at Lucia's ability to sit so normally.

- 76 -

"I had a heads up and I'm not married to you. I don't think I'd be taking it as well if it was Gianna." She paused before abruptly adding, "and I'm really happy my brother's not a murderer."

"What?"

"We thought he might have killed you and then had a breakdown or something."

"I didn't even think of that. Of course you thought that. Oh no, what if everyone thinks that?"

"Fuck, I've got to tell Gianna. Hold that thought?"

❖

Gianna put down the phone, her steely grey eyes lifted to meet Win's. She wanted to hug him and celebrate her relief but even though he wasn't a killer, the reality was just as depressing. Instead, she swallowed hard, the muscles in her jaw stung with tension.

"Kathryn went to my house?" He asked calmly, knowing the answer and not being all that surprised.

"Yeah, she is with Lucia now. And Lu?"

"Lu's the body. Not very talkative, kinda ripe."

"I bet."

Gianna was calm under pressure, at least externally. It was kind of a blessing and a curse, that no one ever knew what she was thinking. She didn't keep her feelings in completely, she wasn't emotionally repressed or anything, in fact she opened up quite willingly to people. In the moment however her feelings didn't show up her face. She was a master at compartmentalising, and now

- 77 -

she had to put her emotions aside. She would later let them bubble to the surface, her long-time friend and sister dying. Right now, she had to be a support.

Win sat down at the table. "I don't really want to go into it right now, if that's ok?"

"Of course."

❖

Kathryn pulled over onto the side of the road somewhere between Win and Lucia's house and her own. Tears welled up in her eyes making it hard to focus on the road. The more she thought about her morning, the more her hands shook. With the car safely pulled over, she sobbed huge heaving cries into the steering wheel.

Several commuters probably saw her bent over in her car, but no one stopped to see how she was doing. Kathryn was grateful for this small mercy. She cried until her tears dried and her hands stopped trembling. She had to get it all out before she got home.

Kathryn knew this theory about grief, it's supposed to be for cancer patients. The patient's circle of friends and family are laid out in concentric rings, the closest in the centre and acquaintances on the outer. Grief should only flow out from the centre, and support flows in. The idea is that the patient only has to worry about themselves. Then the people closest to them are focused on supporting the patient and can only express their grief to the people in the next circle out.

This wasn't cancer, but Kathryn was in that third circle. She held it together while talking to Lucia, and she had to still hold it together when comforting Win. Neither of them should be worrying about how she was handling the news. She wasn't dealing well at all, so the tears had to all come out before she could face her brother.

9

Lucia prepared Lu for another outing. She needed to go back to Ruth, to find something, anything. The bus had worked well before, so she hoped it would again. It was cooler and the jumpers didn't look as out of place as they had on their first trip.

❖

The house was still untouched, Lucia said a quiet thank you that Ruth's children hadn't ransacked the place yet. She was up against the clock to find something in the house before everything got pilfered or sold off. She might have more time than she had expected though. It had been over a week since Ruth had died. Lucia knew that her kids were aware, she had called them herself. But there obviously hadn't been a funeral, there wasn't a body. Lucia knew that because Ruth was standing right in front of her, completely naked.

"What the fuck Ruth? Why'd you take off your clothes?" She would never have said that to Ruth when she was alive. Lucia didn't see the point in keeping things formal or professional. They were beyond that now.

Ruth was not any less strong willed as a zombie, just now she had shed the pretence of civility, along with her clothes. She was bitter and stubborn, and Lucia couldn't hold it against her. Lucia didn't have time to waste by trying to dress Ruth again.

"You know what? Fine, I don't care if you're naked." Lucia decided the best course of action would be for her to do scouting, and only call on Lu to help her when she needed it.

"You stay here." She directed both of them.

After they got over their initial standoff, Ruth seemed to enjoy Lu's company a lot more than she ever had liked Lucia. Perhaps she felt now they had something in common, Lu wasn't a babysitter. Maybe they both resented Lucia. She was kind of babysitting Lu. There was some kind of consciousness there. Animals have different personalities, but Lucia rarely worried about animals conspiring against her. She shook the thought out of her head. The conspiracy and the animal comparison, Lu was part of her, and she knew Ruth. They were people, life impaired people.

Lucia started her search in the bedroom. She looked over every surface, trying to spot anything out of place, anything could be a clue, but she had no idea what was relevant.

The bedroom, bathroom and spare room showed up nothing. She'd spent countless hours in this house. She knew exactly how it was supposed to look and everything looked in its place. Lu and Ruth followed her with their hollow gazes as Lucia scanned every surface.

Lucia stopped at the phone table, just outside the kitchen. There was a diary and an address book laid out on the table. It was one of those things that had always been there, but Lucia never really took notice. She called Lu over to help her go through the diary. The week was marked with a thin red string. Opening it was a challenge on Lu's fine motor skills and by the time the diary was opened on the marked page it had slid most of the way across the small semicircular table.

The week starting Sunday, May 6. Lucia stood in short for a moment as she read her own name on the Monday, the day she died, it seemed so foreboding.

Lucia tried demonstrating to Lu exactly how to turn the page so she could view the week before. Lu's heavy handedness had the diary teetering on the edge of the table after turning the page.

Friday, May 4.

~~Linda~~ Richard + meals

Lucia didn't know a Richard that worked for them. She was friendly with their coordinator, so she knew most of the nurses in her area.

On a hunch Lucia thought she should check the meals that were brought in on the Friday. Lu reefed open the fridge door, it looked perfectly fine. There was an abundance of fruit, yoghurt, Yakult, milk, and small goods. The freezer seemed fine too. The meals Richard would have brought were stacked along one side. On her tiptoes Lucia inspected them, she had her whole head and shoulders in the freezer trying to peer on each side. Looking for evidence of tampering. It was useless though; the meals came on little trays wrapped in cling wrap. If there was any tampering, she wouldn't be able to tell on sight.

There was nothing in the kitchen bin. Not a scrap or anything. There might have been something in the wheelie bin. A door off the kitchen led to the garage, there was a door on the other side of the garage which led directly to the side of the house where the wheelie bins were kept. Lucia weighed up her options. Through the garage or out the back door and round the house. She had to assess everything now, based on what Lu could achieve. If her body couldn't do it, she couldn't do it. There were two doors to get through no matter which way. No keys to mess with through the garage though, so it won.

The garage echoed. Every step Lu took, every word Lucia whispered bounced around the concrete and brick. Ruth's silver corolla was parked crookedly. That could have been normal. They always took Lucia's car, if they took one at all when they were alive.

As Lucia passed the hood of the car, she caught a movement by the front passenger side wheel. A shadow stretching out and then cinching back in under the car. Lucia's eyes followed reflexively, before she had a chance to think about what might be there. A Queensland garage, it could have been anything; a lizard, spiders, an intruder, possum, just basically any form of wildlife. The movement was coming from a wet pile on the painted concrete. Flies.

It took getting a little closer for the realisation of what it was to dawn on Lucia. The flies jerked about, turning on their axis like they were stuck with pins. Every now and then one of them led the charge and flew up into the air. It was followed by all the others, did a little loop into stagnant air and then found another place to land. The hallowed ground for these flies, the thing they were so invested in was a pile of blood, gristle and fur. One of the dogs. On the next fly loop, Lucia saw the hint of a blue collar beneath the clumps of fur. Daisy.

Lucia paced to the end of the car. No Delilah. There were scuffs of blood on the concrete, little claw and paw prints among them. On a hunch Lucia crouched to the ground. She could hardly see beneath the car, so got on all fours and lowered her head to the ground. In the centre of the car she could see another mound. This one was more intact than Daisy. Delilah.

They weren't run over. The injuries seemed wrong for that. They were eviscerated. Ruth couldn't have done this; she was alive when Lucia found her. The dogs weren't there that morning. Were they? How couldn't she tell? How did no one smell it?

"Can you see the dogs?" Lucia cringed as she asked. She didn't want to be there and she certainly didn't want to watch Lu manhandle some dead puppies.

Lu plunged her hand down on top of Daisy's ribs as an affirmation.

"Careful!" Lu pulled her arm into her side and cowered.

- 82 -

"Fuck, no, you're not in trouble. Sorry. Just be careful."

Lu hovered her hand back over the dog.

"Can you pull them out and lay them...here." She indicated an empty laundry basket resting atop the top loader.

She took a closer look at Daisy, now piled up in the basket. Lu was on her hands and knees flailing under the car for Delilah. All the bones seemed to be in the right place. She didn't know for sure. She'd never had a dog, certainly never examined a dog skeleton. The fur surrounding her torso was stripped completely off in places, twisting on itself in flaps. The flesh beneath was torn in long gashes. Claws? Maybe teeth.

Lu dragged Delilah by the hind paw out from under the car. She had considerably less damage. Only a big sore on the side of her neck. The ginger fur on her chest was painted down with dark brown blood and her underside was still wet with it. She bled out.

Lucia's thoughts hurtled back towards the brown paw prints on the kitchen cabinet. Realising that they were probably blood.

Lucia continued to guide Lu round the side of the house. It was mostly sheltered from prying eyes. A tall, slatted gate to the front yard was set back behind the front of the house, so it would take a bit of work to see in from the street. Behind them was a retaining wall, just above knee height, followed by a narrow garden bed. Where the garden bed terminated, there was a small compost bin.

❖

Lucia wasn't even quite sure how Ruth felt about those dogs. She cared for them, coexisted with them, but didn't choose them. In all honesty Ruth didn't seem like a dog person. Whatever a dog person seems like. The widely accepted idea that dog people are friendlier and more outgoing than their feline loving counterparts seemed a little strange to Lucia. Since there are lots of different types of dogs and cats, there is probably a dog or a cat to suit everyone.

Lucia liked the company of dogs, Butterbean especially, but would never own one. Ruth didn't seem like a *pet* person. That was stranger to Lucia, the lack of desire to have a pet around the house. Those kinds of people got her hackles up.

Whether or not Lucia knew Ruth's feelings towards Daisy and Delilah was beside the point, she had to tell her what happened. She needed both Lu and Ruth to do something about it.

The sound that emanated from Ruth was unrestrained pain. She howled, her face twisted into a grotesque scowl. Her sadness was so unfiltered by inhibitions. Ruth pulled the lamp from the lounge side table, dragging the doily and ceramic clock with it. All three fell to the floor. Ruth stamped her feet on them and the cracked lamp broke underfoot. Thick, slices of maroon glazed pottery wedged into Ruth's foot.

"Stop!" Lucia shouted, "You'll hurt yourself!"

She couldn't tell if the tantrum was overriding the pain, or if Ruth couldn't feel at all. Even without feeling if she kept going there wouldn't be much of a foot to hurt.

Ruth fell back onto the couch, her bare, dead skin camouflaged against the seafoam pleather.

"Oh fuck, no."

There was no blood, but shards of the lamp poked through to the skin on the top of her foot, three toes flopped limply, the bones shattered. With no blood and no swelling, the image was far more gruesome than this type of foot injury would be normally. Lucia

- 84 -

thought that if she had her body she would faint at the sight, but somehow couldn't look away.

❖

"You have to wear something. Only to go outside. After that you can take it off." She pleaded with Ruth, as Lu wrestled a dressing gown on to her. She looked at the mess of Ruth's foot and wondered if she should put a shoe on. The toes hung loosely. Lucia had visions of them bending all the way back trying to stuff the foot into a shoe. She winced.

Lu gently rested Delilah on the damp pile, followed by Ruth with what was left of Daisy. They took it in turns piling in leaves, mulch, and wilting, fallen frangipanis before closing the lid over again. Lucia said a few words and all three of them, miserable, returned to the relative safety of the house.

No sooner were they through the side door, than Ruth had removed her dressing gown and disappeared, limping into her bedroom. Lu let out a coo that started small under her uvula and gained power as it rolled to the front of her tongue. She did it a few more times, watching the darkened hall where Ruth had retreated.

10

As far as work was concerned. Ruth had died, Lucia reported it and promptly disappeared. Her phone rang out and eventually went dead.

Lucia was actually kind of shocked that the police hadn't shown up; not shocked, a little annoyed. Lucia could be lying in a ditch somewhere, she could be kidnapped or murdered. Lucia was beginning to think she *was* murdered.

The work offices were located within the reception of a sizable residential aged care facility. There were independent accommodations, assisted living and hospice care all over a sprawling campus. Lucia was not terribly concerned about Lu standing out, she was slightly nervous that a colleague or superior would see her and question where she had been. She would have to risk it if she was going to find out who Richard was.

"Knock knock." Lucia cringed at being one of those people that says knock knock, rather than just knocking, but what else was she supposed to do?

Lorraine was lying in her bed, the head elevated so it was more a reclined seat. The walls were painted a warm, pale-ish pink, skirting and trims a darker shade of the same. It was dated and claustrophobic. In an attempt to make the rooms less clinical, some committee in the late nineties chose this of all colours. It was far from clinical, but equally far from comforting. Lorraine was reading a paperback book; the cover was obscured by her knotted and wrinkled hands. A pencil rested between the pages. Lorraine loved to read, practically any genre. She was worldly and in addition to her vast medical knowledge, she seemed to know something about everything. Not in an obnoxious way, in the way that some people have lived a lot of lives. When Lorraine moved into the home, she started jotting down notes in the margins of her books. Little facts, correcting the author, anecdotes, anything that came to mind. "It's my legacy," she would say, "even if all these books end up at Lifeline."

"Lucia Vivien Hughes! Here I thought you'd forgotten about me." Lorraine jibed as she looked up through the tops of her peach rimmed bifocals.

Lu appeared from behind Lucia as the pair shuffled through the doorway.

"Oh my, you better close the door."

Lucia didn't even need to explain what happened to Lorraine. She did tell her what happened, but the facts of the story, the order of events. Lorraine wasn't shocked, frightened or angry. She asked logical and insightful questions and waited patiently for answers. After having all the facts and order of events straight, Lorraine gave her verdict.

"Lucia, I'm going to be blunt. She doesn't look very good."

"She's dead."

"I know Darling. For a dead woman, she looks terrible. What are you feeding her?"

"She isn't interested in food."

"Oh no, she is." Lucia was now sitting on the guest chair, and looked up at Lu, who remained standing. "She needs to eat."

Despite recovering from a nasty infection, Lorraine decided she was probably the best person to investigate the nursing offices. Her eighty-nine year old hands were still more nimble than Lu's.

"I'm tired of being cooped up here, some espionage will do me good." The way Lorraine said it had Lucia thinking this wasn't Lorraine's first reconnaissance mission.

In any other place, the rag tag team including an ailing octogenarian and adult identical twins in varying degrees of decay, would be cause for intrigue. In this place, with tired and overworked staff, they were hardly noticed by anyone. The only person that even lifted their head was a small boy, around five years old. He was restlessly perched next to his mother and across from his elderly grandfather in one of the many lounge areas spotted around the halls. His eyes widened upon seeing Lorraine scamper past, head tucked, shoulders rolled forward and a steely, determined gaze. His eyes widened further at the sight of Lucia in hot pursuit, gliding across the floor without a sound and the boy gave a little yelp as Lu meandered behind them, her skin wet and green. The boy's mother admonished him without even looking up.

There was a desk, where visitors signed in and residents got signed out. The door to the reception area was to the left of the counter, flanked either side by a wall mounted, acrylic rack filled with pamphlets on aged care issues and local events, the other side was a framed evacuation plan and a fire extinguisher. Sitting in the green, vinyl chairs of the lobby staring anxiously at the door, Lucia thought that she could just as well be in any two-star motel around the world. She had never noticed how oppressive this place was. Even with the high ceilings, and glass panelling along the entrance, it was dark. The brick walls and wooden handrails made it seem dusty, even though everything was perfectly clean. Maybe she was only noticing now, because Lorraine wasn't back yet.

14 minutes, 23 seconds. What could be taking that long?

Watching the clock wasn't helping, but when Lucia wasn't watching the clock, she was watching the door, which was just as bad.

At 14 minutes and 47 seconds the lady behind reception loudly exclaimed, "What are you doing here?" Lucia flinched and could swear phantom heart beats pounded in her chest and sweat rolled down her temples. The lady at reception laughed and greeted someone who was obviously an old friend.

At 15 minutes and 19 seconds, Lorraine appeared in front of Lucia.

"That was fun! Let's go."

❖

Lorraine's room seemed even more stifling now that it harboured fugitives. Lucia was terrified of being caught. She was much more adventurous in death than she ever had been in life.

Lorraine flopped back down onto her bed, taking a moment to breathe before retrieving an A4 piece of paper, folded in thirds from under her shirt. She unfolded it and laid it flat on the bed beside her.

"Here's the skinny on Richard." She gave a wink, and chuckled at the turn of phrase, but the laugh got tangled in a wheeze. She lay her head back on the pillow, allowing her eyes to close for a moment.

Lucia read the paper, a phone number, a home address, next of kin and a work roster.

"Nice work!" Lorraine's eyes shot open as Lucia spoke. She was trying not to show her exhaustion.

"Do you need anything Lorraine?"

"Right as rain Darling. Just a little nap."

"Ok, we'll leave you to it. Thank you."

"No, thank you Lovely, I needed some excitement."

Lucia reached down and squeezed Lorraine's hand just once, Lorraine didn't stir, with her eyes closed she would have had no idea Lucia had done it.

Lucia asked Lu to take the paper, which she scrunched in her hand.

Good enough.

She ushered Lu out the door.

"And Darling," Lorraine called out before Lucia was out the door, "Do see she gets something to eat. She really does look awful."

11

There was a stillness in the air that only comes with an empty home. Win was relieved to have the space to himself after not coming home the night before. He slumped at his computer, idly reading Reddit and Whirlpool. Crumb came into the office after a little while and curled up under Win's feet.

Undead wife

Dead wife

My wife is a ghost.

Google didn't yield any useful results, only synopses of books and movies. No one was searching the same things in earnest. Still, it was cathartic, like screaming into the void.

Zombie care

Haunted house

Ghost wife

Ghost wife support group.

Win shuddered to think of the advertising he would get if he wasn't in incognito mode. Unsurprisingly there were no support groups for his specific scenario. No information on how to care for Lu either, just 135, 000, 000 search results on how to survive a zombie apocalypse. If there were more of them, maybe that information would come in handy. Win read through a couple of articles; he was 100% certain that none of these people doling out advice had actually survived a zombie apocalypse. They probably hadn't even met a zombie, let alone lived with them.

He closed out the tabs, tried to put his anger to the back of his mind and entertained the idea of a nap. It was nearly dinner time, but Win's stomach felt weighty with a churning fullness. He wandered the house aimlessly, willing something to jump out as a tantalizing option. Eventually settling on the TV as a companion. He flicked through Netflix but nothing seemed the right fit. Free to air was garbage at that time of day. He found some 90's reruns, queued up for the next couple hours of viewing. He stared at the screen, not absorbing anything, hardly even keeping his eyes focused, occasionally not even looking at the screen, but looking below it. After only fifteen minutes he transitioned into sleep, the sounds of canned laughter knocking back any nightmares.

❖

Win was awoken by a shuffling at the front door. Barely a knock, more of a nudge.

"Win?"

Lucia hadn't thought about how they would get back in if Win hadn't returned home. She had focused more on the emotional implications if he still wasn't there.

"Just a second." He called out, shaking the sleep from his eyes and stiffness out of his bones as he trudged to the door.

"Woah," Win stepped aside to let Lu and Lucia pass and closed the door behind them. "Is she ok?"

Lu's face no longer resembled Lucia's very closely. She didn't look completely lifeless, she wasn't falling apart, but her face was warped. Win had seen a few people have seizures before and it reminded him of that. Her complexion was sallow, eyes sunken and cheeks hollow. Every facial feature looked simultaneously tensed and atrophied.

"Lorraine thinks she needs to eat."

"You saw Lorraine? How'd - "

"We had to check some stuff out, too early to say what's up yet."

Win was a little annoyed that she seemed so casual, and so secretive. If anyone should be kept up to date it was him. His annoyance gave way to a realisation at the rest of Lucia's original statement.

"Wait. Eat?"

"Mmm hmm" Lucia nodded.

"Lucia...zombies eat people."

"Do we *know* that?"

"I'm pretty sure, right?" All his morning research heavily implied that was the case.

"I don't know Win, there's a pretty steep learning curve here." Lucia immediately apologised for snapping. It felt like every minute was something new and she was tired. Exhausted with no hope for sleep, ever again.

❖

Win appeared in the doorway, his sweaty face pulled into a grimace.

"Beef hearts or pork shoulder?" He pulled the packages of meat out of his green bag and placed them on the kitchen bench.

"Beef hearts I guess?" Lucia suggested, thinking that if Lu liked the beef hearts then at least Win was likely to eat the pork.

Win cut open the plastic vacuum sealed bag containing the hearts.

"Do I feed it to her? Like out of my hand?"

"No! She could bite you. Maybe..." Lucia looked around the kitchen searching for a solution. "...put it in the sink?"

Crumb scurried into the kitchen, his face eager for whatever had been brought home. He could probably smell that it was meat, but he had the same reaction to anything that came out of a green bag. To him, that's where all the food appeared from before being distributed around the kitchen, and sometimes to him. Sometimes was enough of a promise for Crumb to expect a meal every time.

He sniffed at the watery blood drips on the floor between the bench and the sink, before stretching up towards the sink. His body just long enough for his nose to come in line with the top of the bench, nostrils flaring rapidly at the scent of fresh meat.

The image of Crumb's paw on the cupboard for support sent flashes of those poor Pomeranians into the forefront of Lucia's mind.

"Not for you buddy." Win's voice pierced through her memory, shocking Lucia back to the present.

"I...I'll get her." She stammered.

The blood and bits of heart weren't as contained to the kitchen sink as Lucia had envisaged. It wasn't that Lu was a messy eater. It wasn't that she ate the hearts so exuberantly that they got everywhere. Lu had given it a go. She maybe had a nibble, before wailing and releasing the kilo of bloody meat to the floor. It slapped the ground with a wet smack; then Lu, alarmed at the whole ordeal, trod on it.

Lu didn't like the heart, she spat out the small bite she had taken. The thoroughly chewed meat clung to the splashback. The pork did not go over well either. Lucia had the forethought to cut off a bit for her. They managed to avoid the mess issue of the beef heart, but this time the chewed pork ended up back in the sink.

"I'm so sorry."

Win flicked the chewed meat off the splashback into the sink and scooped the sink's contents out in one hand. He held his other hand below, his full, wet fist, aiming to catch any drips between the sink and the bin.

"Stop apologising. You didn't do anything." The foot pedal of the bin released the lid with a tinny clang punctuating Win's response.

"That's it. I can't do anything. I wish I could clean this up."

Win paused pulling paper towels from the roll and turned to face Lucia, just to give her a cynical look.

"I mean it!"

Continuing to amass a pile of paper towels, "You don't." Before Lucia could retort again, "I know what you mean though. Where is...?"

"Under the sink, white handle spray bottle."

"Thanks."

A few sprays, some wipes, more bin clanging and the kitchen looked completely normal again.

"I think it will be easiest if I just wash her off in the shower."

"I've already got her standing in the bath. Didn't get her clothes off though."

Lu was standing in the tub, exactly how Lucia had left her. Most of the blood from her feet had worn off in scraped, pinkish footprints on the linoleum between the kitchen and bathroom. Still her shoes left a grimy paste of blood, water and dirt scuffed on the white porcelain.

Win peeled Lu's jumper up over her head. She resisted him when he came to unbutton her jeans. She liked Win but Lucia guessed that she was just asserting herself. For the most part Lu was pretty compliant but she could get frustrated. Lucia soothed her and assured her it wouldn't take long.

"Haha, I guess it's like we have a kid after all."

Win shuddered at the remark and continued to wrestle the jeans off Lu. Her increasing decomposition made her legs damp and the denim tightened and clung.

"It's not funny Lucia. I haven't changed my mind and everything's not suddenly better because we're trying to feed her." He pulled Lu's right leg up by the back of her knee, pulling her foot through the leg of her jeans. "I don't want anything... I don't want anything more to happen to her. That doesn't make it hurt any less or whatever, it just makes me a decent person." Win pulled Lu's left foot out of the jeans and pushed them to the end of the tub.

"I..."

"I can handle this; can you just wait outside?"

For the second time since she died Lucia felt physical pain, when there was no vessel to feel it in. It felt like the wind had been kicked out of her, but she didn't say anything, only left to sit on the couch.

❖

"I changed her clothes."

Lucia gestured to her own body. "I can tell." Her outfit had changed to a different pair of jeans and a loose-fitting t-shirt and a bulky cardigan as she waited for Lu and Win to reappear from cleaning the blood off.

"Oh, yeah. I put some smelly stuff on the clothes before I put them on." His tone acknowledged his unkind words, without him saying anything out loud. Win sat down on the couch, not relaxing back, but perched on the edge, elbows firmly on his thighs and hands clasped. "I think I have a plan."

Without a word, Lucia moved forward to a more obvious listening posture.

"I could find some people at work. People that are on their way out anyway."

"Win!" Lucia's eyes widened and then her brows quickly furrowed "You can't. We don't even know that it would work. There's got to be another option. Fresh animals, something?"

"I thought through our options. Like medical waste and stuff, I don't think we'll be able to pull it off. Honestly, I don't think we have a choice. She's got to eat, we don't know what will happen if she doesn't."

"It's murder."

"You don't think I know that? Try to think of it as euthanasia".

"Without consent. You know what that is Win?" They actually hadn't had this heated a discussion in a very long time. Not angry at each other but forcefully putting forth their own arguments. They weren't opposed on too many things. "Murder!"

Win looked towards the window closest to their neighbours. It was closed, but the neighbour's window was open. They could probably hear the raised voices clearly enough.

"Shhh." he gestured toward the neighbour.

Lucia lowered her voice. "I don't want to be a murderer."

"Neither do I. We don't know if she'll go rabid or something. What if she does and we don't have any control anymore? What if she kills me?"

"They put rabid animals down."

- 100 -

12

In her race to lay down and free herself from the clutches of a migraine in full swing, Summar had put the wheat filled heat packs on for 22 minutes. Her eyes were squinted closed when she threw them in and haphazardly nominated a cooking time. If her eyes hadn't been closed, they would have been blurred anyway. She had drifted into unconsciousness long before the wheat started to smoulder. Before flames started to burn holes through the pink corduroy. The fire stayed contained within the microwave for a short time. Not long enough. Not that Summar was able to tell. Sparks vented through the back of the microwave and the casing melted until it was no longer capable of functioning. By then the damage was underway and the kitchen wall was smoking.

Flames leapt from room to room, shrouding the three bedroom flat in smoke. Smoke alarms sounded, but Summar didn't stir. While fire destroyed her home, tearing away at it piece by piece, a virus ravaged inside her. It too started small, a tiny puncture, hardly noticeable. It spread through her blood, taking down one organ after another until she was dead. It broke down the chemical bonds in her tissues, until she was not recognisable as a person anymore, not on a molecular level. Then it let her heal. New bonds forming, similar to what they once were, but wrong. Before she had a chance to wake, her new form absent of pulse and breath, she was consumed by the flames.

No one would know that she felt no pain, no one would know it was anything but a tragic accident.

13

In the many sleepless nights since her death, Lucia had carefully examined everything she had ever done. Before and after she died. She tried to replay every significant moment of her life to try and find a reason. What she could have done to deserve this fate. Searching for answers to the two big questions. Why did she die? And why didn't she die "normally?"

One time she and her older sister Ava were gifted lollies from a family friend. Ava was thirteen, maybe fourteen and out with friends. Lucia was under strict instructions to pick the lolly she wanted and give the other to Ava. Which she did, but before Ava came home Lucia snuck into her room and ate Ava's share too. She'd felt guilty about that for almost twenty years, but while it made her feel nauseous with guilt, it wasn't punishable by death or undeath.

Another time as a teenager Lucia saw a crow that had been injured. Its chest pumping in and out too fast as it lay crooked on the ground. Soft, pained caws escaping its beak. It looked up at her, head resting in the dirt, with one pale blue eye and Lucia did nothing. She neither helped it nor put it out of its misery. She just sat there, watching it, knowing it was in pain but not doing anything about it. That guilt knocked its way around her head for close on fifteen years. A doubtful cause for her predicament, even if crows are incredibly smart and every crow in south Brisbane probably has some intergenerational memory of her inaction.

Being rude to an occasional customer in her uni retail jobs, saying harsh things to friends and being too proud to back down or say sorry and the cardinal sin - vaguebooking. None of these seemed like plausible reasons. When Lucia had finished taking inventory of all the horrible times in her life and all the pent-up guilt, she started to analyse the non-important moments. Times when she was oblivious, every time she felt someone was mad at her and she couldn't figure out why. Every time someone was rude to her, searching for a reason that was her at fault.

She was no closer to an answer. Only thoroughly convinced that she was, or had been, a truly deplorable human being. Even now, in death, she had allowed hatred to creep up inside her. She hated Lu. She hated that Lu could touch and feel. That she was tethered to a body that she could not control, neither with force nor willpower. She felt useless, like she was careening down a highway unable to reach the steering or brakes. She was along for the ride but lacked any faculty to do anything about it. Everything she was doing, or not doing was hurting the people around her. At this point, she was nothing more than mould lurking behind the drywall. Slowly poisoning everything around her. She knew that like the mould she should be eradicated, but the will to keep going was strong.

Her life, or her death for that matter was not worth the lives of others. Win was already so eager to be an accomplice to murder for her. That wasn't him, it wasn't her either.

❖

Light stretched across the carpet towards the bed just reaching the tips of Win's toes before being cut off by the shadow of the awning. Win could feel the warmth focused in on his feet and didn't mind. Mornings were cool enough that it was welcomed. In the warmer months the sun would stretch all the way up to his waist, making it hard to sleep in. From around this time of year Win found it difficult to get up, he loved the feeling of the covers up around his ears, his face exposed to the crisp air. He loved pulling Lucia back into himself and wrapping his arms around her waist. Their bodies perfectly aligned and her hair brushing under his nose. She smelled of tea tree shampoo and Moroccan argon oil.

Lucia was an early riser even in the cold. Sometimes she would sneak back into bed, book in one hand, coffee in the other. She wouldn't try to wake him, mostly, sometimes her excitement about her book, or Crumb being particularly cute would cause her to suddenly start talking to him. Win was easy to stir when she did, by then he was mostly going through the motions of sleep, that limbo before waking. When Lucia's eyes opened in the morning, she was awake and as sharp and quick as ever. She had no real concept of how it took Win several hours for his brain to rev up. He didn't mind though, waking to her enthusiasm was always a delight.

Win nestled into his memories of mornings just like this one before he remembered. Suddenly the cool morning didn't seem cosy and loving. It was cold and empty.

Win flipped to his back and stared at the ceiling. They had lived in this house for four years and he had never been so well acquainted with the ceiling above the bed as he was now. The house was old, built sometime in the forties. There were little rough patches where paint had flaked off and been painted over again without sanding back the edges. There were small brown spots, some might have been mildew, or water damage, or even just dirt and grime left there by the breeze. One brown spot was definitely from where Win had tried to capture a spider under a cup. The spider made a break for it just as Win thrust the cup into the ceiling, trapping the spider on the rim. He had never bothered to clean the smudge, until now he rarely ever saw it. Mapping the ceiling, even worrying about if that brown spot was water damage and imagining the whole roof caving in on him in his sleep distracted Win. If he thought about the ceiling, he didn't have to think about the rest of his life. Not about Lucia, or Lu and her decaying body. Not about being an accessory to murder. Murders that were his idea. He loved Lucia, he loved her so much it ached inside him even when they were happy. The ache now was so intense it was consuming the rest of him. His happiness, his reasoning. He wasn't ready to say goodbye to her and apparently that meant murder.

His alarm went off.

- 105 -

Going in early was Win's best bet to look up files unencumbered. He had access to all the files, including ones not in his department. So long as he didn't change anything, no one would know he was looking around. The printer logged who printed, but not what was being printed. If someone went looking, he could say he was printing personal things. Then he would only get a slap on the wrist for using company resources. Win made a mental note to do a test print to make sure the files didn't get backed up in the printer. If that happened he would be found out.

Only the sound of Win's computer whirring and the dim buzz of fluorescent lights disturbed the silence in the empty office. Win had everything up and running but froze looking at the computer screen. He didn't know if he should be looking for people that were already dead, or people that were about to die.

Already dead might have the same issue as the meat. What if it wasn't the species but the lack of freshness? About to die, caused a whole mess of other problems. The increased risk of getting caught and having that person's death weighing on his conscience.

No one was due in the office for at least another half hour but with the office so quiet every sound made Win's heart race. There is a lot of white noise in an office building that goes unnoticed daily, but when someone is on edge already, it's deafening. The elevator clunked up and down, the call button dinged on floors above and below and echoed through the shaft. The pipes groaned, the mechanisms in the printer shifted and the break room fridge ticked.

In general, unless there is something shady going on, people don't claim life insurance for a while after someone is dead. The beneficiaries are usually very close to the deceased, spouses, children, parents. Searching through life insurance claims, Win could see that he would be hard pressed finding someone that hadn't already been buried, or more likely cremated. The idea of grave robbing briefly ran through Win's head before he squashed it down with actual reasoning. Win had a healthy lack of desire to eat human flesh. But he had the wherewithal to know that if he did want to chow down on some people, he definitely wouldn't want them to be embalmed.

Win combed through injury and illness claims, hoping the right candidate would reveal themself.

Hannah Delenko - Coma - Car Accident - in home care

Jeremy Moore - Alzheimer's - assisted living

Michael Kyle - Liver disease - in home care

Nicole McCledd - Breast cancer - Chemotherapy

Gloria Platt - Renal failure - dialysis

What a fucked-up menu.

Win stuffed the files into his backpack and tried to push down his nausea. Fifteen minutes until his co-workers would start rolling in, he turned off his computer and raced out the door, head down, on his way to attain coffee and an alibi.

The sun didn't hit the spare bedroom the same way as it did the main. It was facing north and therefore one of the nicer rooms of the house. It maintained a fairly even temperature year-round. It wasn't so dark that it felt claustrophobic but it didn't receive any harsh sunlight. The only reason they didn't use it as their own bedroom is because their bed didn't fit. They bought a futon, threw it in there and called it a day. At one stage Lucia tried to make it more inviting for guests. She made up a dedicated bookcase with a few spare towels rolled up on the second shelf, old chargers to fit three or four different phones in a basket on the bottom shelf and toiletries laid out neatly on the top shelf. She bundled some knick-knacks; a lamp, a ceramic turtle and two small frames. In them one said, "In this house everyone is accepted," the other had the Wi-Fi password in a curly script.

Those homey touches only served to make Lucia feel like a guest in her own home now.

She heard Win get up and leave. He didn't say anything to her, but she knew he paused in the doorway briefly to inspect Lu. He rushed off as Lucia started to lift her head to say something. She wanted so desperately to reach out to him, with her hands and her heart, they both felt so empty now. There was tension before, but there was more now.

Win seemed to be a lot more accommodating to Lu than he was of her. His eyes didn't flash the same sorrow as they did when he looked at her and a tiny seed of jealousy started to bloom. Jealousy that her husband had more time for that shell of who she was than for her. Jealousy that if Lu wanted, she could touch him, be touched by him. Anger that she was stuck like this. The hateful thoughts circled Lucia's mind, gathering momentum as they turned, until she slammed clenched fists down into the futon either side of her hips. Nothing moved and the anger didn't come streaming out her fists like she wanted. So, she screamed.

Lu turned to the sound, making a quizzical grunt.

"What are you looking at? Turn around!" Lucia's face scrunched as she saw Lu confusedly turn to face the wall. "What is the point of you."

The venom in her words shocked even herself, but the anger was still brimming and she couldn't get herself to calm down. Not yet anyway. She would apologise later.

14

Lucia and Lu greeted Win at the door, his face was drawn and tired.

"Oh wow, she looks…"

"Worse than you?" The joke spilled out like a reflex. Lucia immediately regretted it. She hadn't poked fun since she died and wasn't sure how it would go down.

Win laughed. His genuine laughter washed over Lucia, soothing her like aloe after a burn.

"I have a list of…" he couldn't bring himself to say "people." He was going through the motions of finding someone, an actual person for Lu to eat, but he couldn't make his brain catch up.

Win laid out the files on the coffee table and Lucia scanned them.

"I'm no expert, but I don't think chemo would taste good." What was she doing? These were real people she was analysing, playing God, seeing who should die.

Win reluctantly nodded in agreement.

"I hate to say it but I think Jeremy is our best bet. We need someone that could feasibly go missing."

"Wait we're, you're kidnapping them first?"

"Well yeah, I guess. Think about it. She can't take a bite out of them first and then leave them there. People will find that pretty weird and start looking out for zombies, even if they don't really believe. I would. An Alzheimer's patient wandering off is not out of the question. They'll look, but not *that* hard."

Specks of toothpaste and finger smudges clouded the bathroom mirror. It would take less than a minute to clean. The Windex and cloth were under the sink, a couple sprays and it would be perfectly clean again.

Lucia bent to open the cupboard under the sink, before catching herself. She thought to try and do it anyway, but she couldn't take another emotional hit if she failed. She could nag Win to do it, but it wasn't her place anymore. This was her home, but she had no claim on the running of it anymore.

Instead, Lucia focused beyond the grimy mirror and settled on her face. She had not deteriorated like Lu. Her skin remained intact, hair exactly how it was when she tied it up, untouched by any corporeal forces. She felt disconnected from herself. She recognised the person standing in the mirror, she looked like her. A paler, uncanny version of herself anyway.

Small things that went unnoticed at first, started to become glaringly obvious the more she inspected herself and the more she distanced herself from the mirror imposter. It was only when at rest that she could see how inhuman she was. All the subtle, human movements were absent; no breathing, swallowing, and blinking. Her muscles didn't strain and stretch against themselves to hold her up, her skin lay flat and unmoving. The more she looked the worse it got.

Lucia snapped out of it, prying her eyes away from her reflection. Win was pulling on a work shirt and tucking it roughly into his chinos.

"I can't help you, you know?"

"Huh? What?" Lucia was still deafened by her own thoughts.

"The kidnapping." Win practically mouthed the word, as if suddenly he thought the house was bugged or something.

"Oh, I know. God, I wouldn't expect you...you know?"

"See you tonight."

With that he was out the door. His bus wasn't even due for another 20 minutes.

❖

Crumb sat impatiently in the spare bedroom doorway. His tail swatted behind him, forcefully thudding against the door frame. His eyes were wide but dipped slightly towards his nose, the cat equivalent of a scowl. His meow erupted urgently from his small, black frame as soon as Lucia came into his eyeline.

"What's wrong?"

As Lucia stepped closer he sprang to all fours, tail swishing high in the air. His meows now with a hopeful lilt.

"Didn't Dad feed you?" Lucia hopped to the kitchen to see Crumb's bare bowl.

She reached for his food, coming up empty.

Crumb let out a wail as Lucia went to fetch Lu. When they returned together Crumb had taken up the same scowling, swishing stance in the centre of the lounge room. As if following her all the way back to the spare bedroom was beneath him.

Before Lu could scoop out a cup of kibble from the container, she dropped the whole thing on the floor. One of the plastic snaps holding the lid in place shattered on contact with the linoleum. The

- 111 -

food container was as old as Crumb himself, not too surprising that the brittle plastic hadn't held up. Crumb took offence and cowered from the noise. It wasn't long before he noticed the kibble stretching every way across the kitchen floor and forgave the crash.

Crumb crunched with laser focus, blissfully unaware that Lucia was just as shattered as that frail, blue plastic snap.

❖

Win's phone buzzed quietly on his white veneer desk. An 07 landline flashed up on the screen. He didn't recognise it and even if he wasn't at work, he would have let it ring out. Win thought about declining the call but felt that was a bit of a rude move, even if the person on the other end of the line was trying to scam him. The ringing stopped. Another buzz and the screen lit up with a voicemail notification.

Work wasn't so busy that he couldn't take a short walk to the bathroom and listen to the voicemail on the way.

"Hello Samuel, this is Tanvi Jay. I am seeking Lucia. Please reach me on this number as soon as possible."

An icy dread ran down Win's spine. He knew Tanvi, he'd met her a few times. She was Lucia's boss. She was always lovely and Lucia seemed to like her a lot.

"Shit, shit, shit!" It was a voicemail, of course Tanvi didn't include her fears and suspicions. He needed to just call her back and say Lucia was sick. No, not sick, Tanvi was such a delight that she was likely to bring round meals or flowers. A sick relative maybe? He settled on that excuse.

Win leaned against the wall across from the elevator, left hand in his pocket and the other pressing the phone firmly to his ear. Each ring that went unanswered pushed his heart further into his throat.

"Hi Tanvi, It's Samuel Huyhn. Sorry I missed your call."

"Yes Samuel, thank you for calling." She continued before he had a chance to interject, "I returned from holiday and I am hearing that Lucia has not been to work." She said it like it was a question, but it wasn't and she continued. "One of her patients died and she has not been seen from then. I am not reaching her on the mobile also." Win could feel Tanvi expecting an answer.

"Yeah, sorry Tanvi. Lucia's father isn't very well, she's gone to help out."

"Strange of Lucia to not advise me." She wasn't buying the story.

"I thought she must have...you know what. She's been having phone trouble for a while, hasn't had a chance to get a new one...with her Dad."

Win liked his father-in-law. Ryan Hughes had always been very welcoming, despite there being very little overlap in their interests apart from the welfare of Lucia. A pang of guilt stabbed him in the gut at the thought of somehow jinxing Ryan to become gravely ill. The feeling was washed out by the rising dread of knowing that Tanvi probably didn't buy his story.

15

The facility that Jeremy lived in wasn't terribly secure. There was a large main building, only one story but sprawling. Enclosed, glass-panelled walkways connected the wings, which were colour coded. There was a gate but it didn't require a code, it worked on a sensor. The pedestrian entrance had a pull up latch. It took a few goes and a lot of coaching, but Lu opened it with relative ease even in her declining state.

They followed a hedge lined driveway to a fork; right led to the main building, left down a small hill and into a series of boxy, prefab homes for the more independent residents. Jeremy lived in one of those, which indicated that his family probably cared a great deal about him but didn't have the facilities to care for him. That didn't sit right.

Number 6 was on the end of the first row of houses.

"I guess, we just ring the doorbell?" The bell chimed with a loud melody.

There was movement inside. Shuffling footsteps approaching the door, followed by the sound of glass breaking and retreating footsteps.

"Press it again".

The door opened a little while after the second chime. Jeremy was tall, probably around 6'1" or 6'2" in his prime, less now. He was completely bald, but made up for it with huge wiry, grey eyebrows that loomed over his glasses. He was wearing a navy polo shirt tucked into tan shorts and reminded Lucia of her own grandfather.

Jeremy didn't say anything, only wrung his hands peering at the women on his doorstep. Behind him Lucia could see a vase that used to be on a side table, lying broken on the floor. The side table had framed children's drawings and family photos. He had a family.

She looked at Lu, who was pale, green and slicked with fluids sweeping from her pores. "Sir, you have to come with us."

"Who..."

"We're officers Kelly and Grant, we need you to come to the station." She tried to keep her voice firm but not angry.

Jeremy protested, but he wasn't violent. Lucia kept up the charade of being police to keep him inline. It was far too easy to take him. He shouldn't have been living alone. His family didn't care as much as she thought they might. Or at least they didn't visit enough. He needed more help than he had. That didn't sit right either. It shouldn't have been this easy, someone should have been looking out for him. That person would usually be Lucia.

In all they were at the nursing home for ten minutes before kidnapping someone. Lucia felt evil, she detested herself for lying to this sweet old man.

The only camera was on the front gate. Lucia sent Jeremy through the gate first. She told him to keep walking towards a white car that was parked down the road, telling him it was their undercover police car. She and Lu left a couple minutes after and headed the opposite way. They got far enough on the road to be out of sight from the camera and headed back to collect him.

It all came way too easily and naturally to her. She didn't think she would or should get away with it, kidnapping and impending murder. She knew she would though. It would not be ludicrous for Jeremy to wander off and have some danger befall him. Lucia made a note to hate herself when she knew Lu was ok.

Even in autumn it was hot at midday. The trees in Toohey Forest weren't as densely grouped as Lucia would have liked. She used to enjoy bush walking in the forest. The paths were good and not too demanding, which also meant they saw quite a lot of foot traffic. She hoped that midday would mean there were less people out and about. Even so she led her little troupe off the path pretty quickly. There were a series of ferny gullies so, if someone were to hide a body, it probably wouldn't be found in the undergrowth for quite some time.

Jeremy was getting increasingly agitated. He took a swipe at Lucia a couple times. Coming up empty handed only served to make him more confused and volatile. Lucia kind of hoped he would attack Lu, then she would be acting in self-defence. Jeremy and Lu were both flagging, their bodies stooped closer to the ground with each step, their feet dragging in the dirt. Between the three of them, they left no discernible footprints. At this point she thought Lu might be too weak to eat at all. What would happen to her then? Would she be tethered to wherever Lu's body fell? No way to communicate to any of her loved ones where she was. No search party because she is already dead. Would she become a local legend, her only visitors local kids trying to brave the forest ghost? Or would she simply cease to exist?

The wind blew through the trees, rustling the leaves. Bugs and birds chirped and Lucia thought there were worse places to be. Whether it be forever or only a little while longer. She hoped for the latter.

Jeremy let out a wail as he tripped on a rock sticking up from the earth. The dirt kicked up behind a sharp, rust coloured protrusion. Jeremy landed on his stomach, arms outstretched in front of him. A bad idea. His wrist breaking sounded almost like a twig being snapped only louder. The ground wasn't that hard, there was a layer of leaf litter, but Jeremy's feeble bones were no match.

Jeremy cried, loud terrified sobs. The kind of sound that people can hear over and over again once they witness it. In haste, Lucia decided this was as good a place as any. She just needed to shut him up. She leaned in close to Lu, who was looking alarmed at the thrashing elderly man on the ground.

"Eat him." The words were sour in her mouth. "He's food."

❖

The bush was quiet again, more so than before. Lucia had heard once, she didn't remember where, that when a big predator is nearby the forest goes quiet. It was like that now, every bird, bug and lizard had frozen in its tracks.

Most of the damage was to Jeremy's neck and stomach. His old skin torn in long jagged strips exposing a wet mass of organs. Any similarity to a familiar anatomy diagram was lost amongst the rips and bites. His lower ribs were crushed where Lu had taken an overzealous bite. Lucia had always had sensitive teeth. Hard, sweet, too cold, too hot, they all sent shooting pains through her teeth and into her jaw. Lu obviously didn't have the same problem.

Lu crouched over Jeremy's body. Her feet spread wide and hips resting between her ankles. Her shoulders rounded over her blood glazed arms. The blood on her face smeared outwards from her mouth in translucent, red arcs drying and settling into the skin. Lucia shuddered at the view of something so plainly inhuman, so clearly removed from who she once was.

At last Lu relinquished her hold on the body, she pushed herself back, satiated. What was left of Jeremy's blood, that hadn't been slurped up with his organs had started to congeal. So much so that when he rolled down the hill barely a trace was left in the leaf litter. Some tiny shards of bone jostled loose, still bearing globs of sinew and flesh. Some opportunistic animal would make short work of that, along with any blood.

- 118 -

Jeremy rolled into the ferns. They swayed under his weight, before swinging back up to their rightful position. They swallowed up Jeremy's body like a green shroud. The image seared itself into Lucia. His pale face, wrinkles softened back towards his ears. The blood from his neck wound smeared right up to his jawline like a macabre turtleneck.

Lucia paced past the body from higher up on the ridge, just to make sure that he was obscured. She kept seeing his shredded corpse, each time dread welling inside her. But each time it was only her mind playing tricks.

16

"It's her skin." Kathryn and Win were sitting in Kathryn's kitchen, trying to put a finger on what it was about Lucia that was so disconcerting.

"The silence is what got me."

Gianna interjected from the doorway. "Does she blink?"

"Huh?"

"Does she blink? She doesn't need to."

"Oh man. You're right!" Kathryn said.

"Honestly if you told her how creepy it is, I think she could make herself do it."

The three of them sat uncomfortably in the silence that followed this realisation. Not one of them wanting to change the subject or continue with this one. Grief came in waves. Sometimes as ripples on the calm exterior of someone holding it together. Other times it came crashing down over them, dragging any happiness and progress out to sea with it and leaving behind something that was less than before. This wave of grief washed the joy right out of the room.

"Wine?" It was Gianna who broke the silence. She was stoic and she was strong.

Win and Kathryn jumped on board the wine idea immediately. Opening a bottle, passing around glasses was in this instance, a three-person job. The flurry of movement was just enough to reset and no one felt guilty for leaving their sadness behind, if only for a night.

The movie had finished and Netflix autoplayed the trailer for a new season of a show that Win had never watched. Kathryn didn't stop it from playing, only lowered the volume. When it was over the screen cycled through titles of other shows and movies. The only sound was the alternating light snoring of Gianna and Butterbean, who were curled up with their butts touching in near identical poses.

Kathryn very quietly shifted forward in her seat to snap a photo of them front on.

"Crumb would wake up if I tried that."

"One point for dogs then."

The photo was blurry so Kathryn was now crouching down, hip resting against the coffee table, steadying the phone with both hands.

"Definitely a point for dogs. Cats are, overall, much cuter but notorious photo ruiners."

"Pshht." Kathryn's nose was buried in her phone, cropping and editing the photo before uploading it to Instagram. #catsofinsta #Katofinsta #myheart #love #snooze

"You can stay over if you want." Kathryn didn't look up from her phone. "If you're avoiding going home." She looked up on that last point to emphasise her meaning.

"I'm not avoiding home. I should be going home. They were getting something to eat today."

"Some(thing) to eat?"

- 122 -

"Someone."

"Someone?"

"Don't make me say it." Kathryn kept looking at Win. Her face scrunched and judgmental eyes peering out from behind her raised cheeks. "What am I supposed to do Kat?" Win was more defensive than either of them expected. "She needs to eat. We tried other stuff."

"Duuude, that's so messed up." Her tone was in jest but her face pulled into a frown that portrayed her very real disgust. "You don't even know that this will work either. What if Lucia has murdered someone for nothing?"

"That doesn't help!" His voice cracking under the strain of his tensed muscles. "I can't do anything. I can't turn her into the cops because they won't believe it. Some government agency will probably burst in and kidnap her if I take her to a hospital. If I keep her...if I keep them a secret, anyone that's ever listened to a podcast will think I killed her. And I can't lose her." Tears welled up in Win's eyes but none fell. His body held them back, every muscle pulling in opposite directions, trying to cage his emotions.

Kathryn sat contemplating the best thing to say next. Everything inside of her was telling her to offer advice, but she was way over her head. Nothing she could say would truly help. There are no analogies for a situation like this, no life experiences she or anyone she knew could draw upon to offer any words of comfort.

"Go home. Tell all of this to her." Her brow furrowed so deeply the inner corners of her eyes hurt. Kathryn searched her brother's face for any kind of reaction and smiled weakly. "I love you."

"Love you too."

❖

Win knew that Lucia would be awake. He didn't know if she would scurry back into the spare room when she heard his keys in the lock. He pushed the key in and paused before turning it, he even flicked the keychain with his pinkie to make sure he made as much noise as possible. He hoped that Lucia would get the message and make herself scarce. He didn't want to see her right now, but he wanted to know she was there. If she wasn't, it could mean something terrible happened. He couldn't face her but he also couldn't face her being gone for good.

Win's procrastinating had annoyed Crumb. Crumb waited just clear of the door, looking impatiently at Win and meowing in a way that was more like screaming. His tail swished across the floor behind him, displacing dust with each flick. As soon as Win stepped through the door Crumb was up on his feet, angling his hind quarters towards Win's shins in a way that all cat owners are just as familiar with as they are puzzled by.

It was dark in the house, not a single light on and moon at its meekest. The only light coming from a streetlight across the road, which shone through the open lounge room window. Even with his glasses on, and a fully lit room, Win would struggle to see Crumb's food bowl from his position in the lounge. In the dark he could see unfamiliar shapes on the floor. It set him on edge.

He inched into the kitchen placing his bag on the counter, turned and switched on the light. As he turned, he trod on Crumb, who had grown uncharacteristically quiet just as he decided to settle behind Win's heels. Crumb let out a sharp yelp.

The light revealed the prone plastic container. Crumb had eaten the food sprayed on the floor and a good chunk of what had stayed in the container. The plastic snap had scooted into the corner of the kitchen. Based on the scene, Win was sure Crumb had more than his fill of food already. The guilt of stepping on his foot, meant that Crumb would be getting another meal anyway. Another meal and many many pats.

A trail of wet splodges led from the bathroom to the spare room. They were definitely Lu's footprints as she scraped her feet across the linoleum floor. The bathroom was a mess, water splashes all over the floor and patches of pinkish blood against the white porcelain of the tub.

"Sorry about that." Lucia stood just shy of the bathroom doorway. She was in shadow but her skin was so pale it reflected any trace of light.

"Does this mean that you were successful?"

"If we're calling it that."

"And the body?"

"What's left of it is hidden. Shouldn't be found for a while." Her voice was low and controlled.

"Are you sure?"

"Obviously I'm not sure Win. I've never done this before. I don't know how to properly hide a body! And I don't exactly have all my faculties to be executing a foolproof plan."

"I didn't mean..." Win leaned back, his back softly thudding against the tiled wall of the bathroom. "I just don't want you to get caught."

"I know, sorry. It was a rough day. I can't get him out of my head."

She wanted so badly to hug him. To be comforted by his smell and the feeling of his t-shirt against her face. He wanted to embrace her too, to tell her it would all be ok, but all he did was tense his whole body subconsciously until the moment had passed.

Lucia returned to her room, the sound of the shower following her back as Win got to work cleaning the bathroom.

17

It took nine minutes to walk to the bus stop. Lucia could normally do it in under five. It took Lucia eleven minutes to learn that the undead can still get sun burnt.

"Of course, you can get sunburnt." Lucia muttered while peering into Lu's face. "Add sunscreen to the list, I guess. It's not like you could look any pastier."

Lucia hated getting sunburnt, she would always apply sunscreen if she knew she'd be out in the sun, even just driving or hanging out the washing. If she forgot she could feel the sun sizzling on her skin and she swore she could feel her cells mutating into cancer. She would have a thousand moles cut out in exchange for the warmth of the sun now. Even the scalpel would be better than this nothingness. She understood now why people fall into destructive habits; self-harm, alcohol, drugs, adrenaline, anything to feel something.

"You'll be fine for now, just keep to the shade."

The walk from the bus stop to the address on the employee files that Lorraine had skilfully swiped was thankfully, mostly shaded and devoid of people. Lucia had quickly learned exactly why most home invasions happen in the middle of the day. The streets were deserted from around 10am to 2pm. Before and after that there were people exercising, children walking to school and cars on the road for their commutes. For those few hours, there was nothing. There were sure to be people in their houses; shift workers, retirees, stay at home parents, but even in the cooler months it was unappealing to be out and about when the sun was at its highest.

The house was overtly plain. Lucia didn't know exactly what she expected. Houses in the area were usually built somewhere between the 30's and 50's. They had a quaintness and uniqueness that wasn't present in new builds. Lucia and Win's home was the same. She didn't know the names of the styles. Post-war? Federation? Small homes, slightly elevated, like Queenslanders without the verandah.

This house was a mix of red brick and off-white cladding. There was a small balcony, barely big enough for the wrought iron bistro set that nestled in one corner. Bromeliads in little pots lined both sides of the steps leading to the landing and cobwebs laced between the balusters of the railing. It looked so ordinary and plain. Not that it wasn't a nice house, it just didn't look like anyone responsible for the havoc in her life lived there.

She couldn't just knock. Wait for someone to answer and say, "Hey, are you responsible for my death." In honesty Lucia hadn't thought of what she would do once she got here. So much focus went into the present, the small series of steps that amounted to huge effort. By the time that hurdle was passed, there was hardly any energy to continue.

Down the side of the house where a driveway consisting of two parallel concrete paths lead to a small garage in the back corner of the yard. The lot sloped and Lu was battling the incline of the driveway. It hadn't appeared steep from the footpath, but for someone so uneasy of their feet it was yet another hassle. Lucia tried to race ahead but kept stopping short when her unseen tether to her body couldn't stretch any further. Eventually she made it to the edge of the house and could spy around the corner. A small brick patio under a green shade cloth, more potted plants skirting the edge. There was no one in the yard, only a clothesline turning slightly with the breeze.

When she had the slack, Lucia edged close to the back wall, ducking under the windows. She listened for sounds of someone moving around. Taps running, TV playing, footsteps. There was nothing. She popped her head up to look through what she had suspected and now confirmed was the kitchen window. No movement in the house, she could see straight through the dining room and into the living room. The curtains were drawn. A large ginger cat lay on the dining room table, almost blending in with the wood. It lifted its head, looked at her, then rested it back down, only half closing its eyes.

Certain that no one was home, Lucia decided it was time to break in. She had already added murder to her repertoire, what difference was a little trespassing.

It was at this time that Lucia wished she was one of those, "walk through walls" ghosts. In honesty, everything could be a lot easier if she could do any of the things movie ghosts could do. The afterlife would be so much smoother if she could be invisible, walk through walls, move objects, it would even be great to flicker some lights. The rules that actually came with her death seemed so arbitrary and condemning.

Lu tried the back door. Pushing on the handle till it looked as though it might snap off. The handle turned fine, but the door stuck in place by a dead bolt.

The sliding side of the kitchen window was barred, but the other side was only a pane of glass. The window was over the kitchen sink, a row of potted plants lined the sill.

With Lucia's instruction, Lu hurled a heavy potted plant through the window. It took a couple goes. Lu was strong, but not coordinated, a frustrating and dangerous combination. The pot only made a jagged hole the size of a netball. Lucia was nothing if not resourceful and decided not to go through the pain of more throwing. Instead, she urged Lu to rip a stake from the garden and joust away the remaining glass. Once the end of the stake was through the hole, it was simply a matter of Lu thrashing it about and proved very effective.

Lucia climbed through first, resenting her ghostly compliance to earthly limitations. Hoisting herself up onto the window ledge in the way she was taught to exit a pool in primary school swim classes. With an elegance she had never possessed in life she swung her legs onto the bench and hopped into the stranger's kitchen. A nervousness rose in Lucia. Similar to sneaking into her sister Ava's room as a teenager. Thumbing through magazines she wasn't quite old enough to read, but much worse. She could only reconcile this behaviour with the notion that the occupant of this house was a bad man. A man responsible for her death, Ruth's death and possibly, probably, more.

Lu came crashing through the window, falling to the floor with a thud that echoed around the room. The ginger cat, who had cared very little about Lucia's presence, puffed up and slinked away. It looked back at Lu once partially hidden by the dining room wall, eyes wide in fear, then disappeared.

Inside the house was just as unremarkable as the outside. Knick-knacks, cute sayings painted onto blocks of wood, photos of what was likely grandchildren covered the fridge. Lucia started to feel as though she had made a mistake. This place looked so ordinary, surely the man that lived here hadn't killed her. Then again, isn't that what they say about every murderer.

Any little noise in the house had Lucia racing to the window to check for approaching homeowners. Other times she froze in place, holding herself still waiting for the noise to return. Lu shuffled behind her, disinterested in anything in the house other than the cat. Occasionally the cat poked its head out from the hiding place to check the status of the intruders. Lu flinched each time, until she settled on just turning her body away from the cat whenever it appeared, only relaxing when the little ginger head had retreated again.

Lucia looked over every surface, under tables, behind bookshelves, anywhere she thought secrets might be held. Cupboards were opened, papers strewn on the floor, drawers pulled all the way out, and Lucia inspected it all. She even found some carefully wrapped Christmas presents, gift tags bearing names like Jasper, Cayden and Ayla in swirling cursive. There was nothing weird though, nothing unexpected, not even a secret she wasn't looking for.

"We should try the shed." Lucia announced to the room, not quite ready to accept defeat. Lu looked at her, acknowledging that Lucia had spoken, but not comprehending the words, her face blank like someone trying to hear in a crowded bar.

She'd seen the shed come garage on the way into the property. A standalone structure with the same colour brick as the house. The garage door was old and the corners of the metal sheet were pulled up. Old break in attempts, or an aging door with a sticking catch? It was locked, a small keyhole in the handle, that wouldn't be a problem though. The door was framed in weathered, disintegrating wood Lu could bust it open. Lucia told her to pull the door open, warning it would require some force. Lu wrapped both hands on the handle. Her knuckles grazed the aging white paint of the door and came away coated in the same powdering pigment. She pulled.

The steel latch broke through the wooden frame, it didn't splinter, only pulled out a deep groove of moist wood chips. As the door sprung up Lu flew backwards onto her behind, the door clattered to the roof with a resonating gong.

Nothing. There was absolutely nothing in the garage apart from a rack on the back wall which housed a shovel, a rake, a broom and something that looked as though it could help empty gutters. The floor was solid concrete with a healthy coating of dust and stray leaves. There was no indication there could be anything below the garage either.

The wind whipped at the garage door and after a few big gusts it slapped shut. The sound bounced around the hard walls and Lucia was plunged into darkness. Lu flinched, whirled around and glared at the door, then at Lucia.

"I didn't do it!"

The sudden darkness was abating and tiny shards of light started to show themselves between cracks in the walls. They were too bright to see through. From inside the dark room, it made the outside seem overexposed.

The door wasn't fully closed, the wind kept pushing at it and made thundering noises as it rippled over the steel. Lucia thought she might have heard footsteps outside but dismissed them as rustling leaves.

She scanned the garage again, looking for anything that could serve as a secret hiding spot. There were plenty of loose bricks, but the walls were only one brick thick and removing them would result in a window, not a hiding spot.

The door rippled again, but this time sunlight flooded into the space. Silhouetted in the doorway was a man. He was holding something chunky and heavy, with his hands raised like swinging a bat. It must have been Richard. As her eyes adjusted again she saw thing in his hands was a steering wheel lock. She hadn't seen one of those for decades. Her mother used to have one with orange handles, Richard's was yellow. His car was parked halfway down the house. He'd seen the open door and guessed correctly at intruders. The broken kitchen window probably confirmed that.

"I'm warning you." There was a tremble in his voice. Richard wasn't a young man. He was short, shorter than Lucia and he had a crook in his back, maybe chronic or out of fear, a maroon shirt strained against his protruding belly.

- 132 -

"I'll call the police."

Lu was hanging back, a bit behind Lucia, but when Richard spoke again, she showed herself and growled from the back of her throat. Another growl and she stepped forward. Lucia could tell it was a display only, if she planned on attacking him outright, she would have done it by now. Lu was fed and for the most part she was placid.

Richard didn't know that, his grip on the steering wheel lock loosened until it fell to the ground. He held his arms, then moved his hand to his chest. He stumbled backwards and lowered himself awkwardly onto the ground.

Now Lucia rushed forward. Her nurse instincts kicked in. When she reached him, he cowered.

"I think you're having a heart attack."

She tried to reach out to him and couldn't. Richard wheezed and lost consciousness. He was in cardiac arrest and Lucia couldn't do a thing about it. Without help, she had killed this man, and worse she no longer thought he had anything to do with her own death.

<u>18</u>

After spending the whole morning slumped down behind the steering wheel watching Lucia's house, Tanvi saw Samuel Huyhn emerge. She had been waiting for him to go to work and had been watching the house since 5:30 that morning. A slim gold watch on her equally slender wrist, the one she wore when she was not working now read 8 o'clock. She waited as he walked up the street. Hands in his pockets, wearing a stern face, but one that was from concentration, not anger. He looked tired. She remembered him from Christmas parties, he was attractive. He was very good looking, but the attraction was his manner; calm, gentle, he had a vibrance to him, even when he wasn't talking. He didn't have that now.

She was going to take action, now or never. Her heart beat out of her chest as she raced, careful not to break into a run, across the road towards Lucia's house. Every inch of her nearly five foot frame was trembling as she flitted up the front stepped and readied herself to knock on the door. She felt the shaking coming from deep inside her bones and roused on herself in a similar way to the way she spoke to her kids when they were out of line. She had a very good angry voice, which demanded respect from anyone it was directed at.

She knocked, louder than such a delicate hand should be able to and waited.

It was only the third time in as many weeks that someone had knocked on the front door, but Lucia wished she had had the idea when she was alive to install a peephole. Without knowing who was on the other side of the door she thought it best to just let them give up and leave. At this time of day it was probably a courier, unlikely because she hadn't ordered anything. It also could have been a JW or a political canvasser. Neither were appealing options for conversation and the risk that they would notice something wrong and call the police was too great.

There was another loud knock.

"Lucia?" Tanvi pulled on the last syllable of Lucia's name and it rose to a sing-songy emphasis in her accent. Lucia recognised the voice; she'd heard her name said in that exact way a million times.

"Lucia? Open up."

A stream of expletives ran across Lucia's mind like ticker tape and she wasn't quite sure if she had said them aloud. She must have because the next thing to come from the other side of her front door was this.

"I can hear you, please open the door. I only want to find you are well."

"I'm ok Tanvi." Lucia had moved so close to the other side of the door she barely had to raise her voice to be heard. Tanvi reeled back in surprise, as she hadn't heard any footsteps approaching the door and had imagined Lucia was calling out from the depths of the house.

"Please let me see you. You can trust me."

"It's better if I don't. I'm sick, I don't want you to get it."

Tanvi was very concerned and that bullshit meter of hers was going off. She would bet her life that Lucia was not okay, nor was she sick.

"Lucia, please. You can tell me if something is bothering you." As stern as Tanvi could be she could also be very patient and kind. She was after all only sneaking around and playing at espionage because she had legitimate concerns about the wellbeing of an employee. Now that she had proof of life, the gravest of her fears was put to rest, but that didn't mean Lucia was out of harm's way.

"I know you are not sick also. I don't need to come in, only see you are ok."

If it would get Tanvi off her back, she could open the door and speak to her through the screen. The fly mesh and security screening would obscure her just enough for her to seem pale, but not deathly. There's no need to touch anything if they were just talking either. It would basically be like a proof of life photo, but in person. Instead of holding up a newspaper with the date on it, Tanvi could just see that she was alive and well. And a terrible employee that just stopped coming into work and a terrible friend for not answering any calls. If she was being honest with herself Lucia would rather people know she was dead than to think she was a dead beat.

Another terrible thought jumped into her mind. What if, after Tanvi saw she was alive, she tried to give her something. It was just like Tanvi, a lady who was going out of her way quite literally to see if an employee was ok. An employee that dropped off the face of the earth three weeks ago after six years of dedicated employment, without so much as a text. Tanvi was just the type of person to bring some home cooking to ease whatever hardship she was going through. Lucia knew she was that type of person because when she caught the flu two years ago and couldn't work, Tanvi Jay showed up with a basket full of frozen dinners. She came late at night because she went home after an eleven hour shift and cooked them all. Win had answered the door and Lucia would have thought it a fever dream if she never ate the meals. She remembered it being good but she was starting to forget what food tasted like. She knew in a general sense lemons were sour, pears were sweet, but she had trouble locating the exact taste in the annals of her once encyclopaedic palate.

"Just through the door, right? I'm not up for company."

"Yes, only through the door."

There was a long silence. Tanvi wondered if Lucia was still working up to it. She was just about to say something encouraging when she heard shuffled footsteps from somewhere distant inside the house. It dawned on her that Lucia mustn't have been decent. It was cold, so she probably was wearing pants, but maybe she was without a bra or the shirt she had on was stained. She hoped that was the case, not that Lucia was hurriedly brushing concealer over her bruises or negotiating with an armed mad man to let her open the door.

The shuffling got closer until it was right on the other side of the door.

Lucia leaned in and whispered in Lu's ear for her to open the door, then to remain hidden behind it. She knew that she had to whisper, because if she said it as loudly and forcefully as she usually spoke to Lu, Tanvi would surely hear and the jig would be up.

Tanvi did hear whispers, but she couldn't make them out. There was someone else there though. She had moved back from the door so her ear wasn't pressed to the screen when the door was finally opened. As it was black sooty diamonds from the dust that settled in the security door imprinted on the side of her face and some onto her dipped right shoulder as she leant into the door.

The door opened easily in the cold, so much that chilled air flowed under it in the evenings. Lucia mimed that she was the one opening the door, as Lu scooched herself back into the entry corner.

"Hello."

"Hi"

Tanvi tried to make it not so obvious that she was working Lucia over with her gaze. Inspecting each part of her exposed flesh for signs of trauma. She took in her gait and body language and

- 138 -

listened hard to everything Lucia said and how she said it. Searching for trouble, and only coming up with confusion.

"Are you ok?"

"Yeah, I've just been sick is all." She was looking right into her eyes not avoiding them, but it was still an obvious lie.

"Samuel is telling me something else. Are you sure?"

"You spoke to Win? When?"

"Only a few days ago. This is very out of character for you Lucia."

"I'm really sorry I let you down, but I can't talk. And I can't come back to work."

"I was not thinking of that. I am concerned, very concerned."

"Nothing to be concerned about." It wasn't a total lie. There wasn't anything Tanvi needed to worry about. Win wasn't litigious, he wouldn't sue the company because Lucia died after coming off a shift when she was infected by her zombie patient. She didn't think that would even stand up in court and chuckled to herself at the idea.

Lucia hadn't thought through how she would close the door. She could just walk away around the corner and keep poking her head back until she was sure Tanvi had left and the coast was clear. That seemed even more rude than just closing the door though. It already felt horrible to be talking through the screen to someone she knew. Salespeople, charity collectors and Jehovah's Witnesses were fine. Don't talk to strangers and all that, a thought that didn't really hold up as an adult. A lot of adulthood is exclusively talking to strangers and giving them your personal details. It's a wonder she hadn't been killed much earlier than 29 years old.

"Thank you for coming by, really. I appreciate it a lot." She did appreciate it, Tanvi Jay cared and that felt nice.

"Ok, I will let you be. Promise to call if you are in need."

"I promise."

Tanvi held Lucia's gaze for a beat too long before retreating down the patio steps.

She couldn't put her finger on it exactly, but there was something strange about Lucia's presence. Inconsistencies in the story, who had Lucia been talking to before she opened the door? Win had left, she saw it. She was more certain now than ever that something was amiss and she would ponder that all the way to work.

19

On the third loop of the Market Square car park, Win lost a space he was waiting for to someone coming the opposite direction. They either didn't see that he had been patiently waiting for occupants of the white corolla to say lengthy goodbyes to the rest of their group and back out painfully slowly, or they didn't care. While he was waiting for the corolla to pass him, another car swung in without indicating. Win cut his losses and exited the car park to find a space at Sunnybank Plaza, he didn't even try the streets behind Market Square, at this stage he just needed to find somewhere as painlessly as possible.

The undercover car park was awash with sickly fluorescent lights. Win found a space quickly and before he could reprimand himself for not coming straight to this carpark, hot tears sprung forth from his eyes. They burned rivulets into his already flushed cheeks. Win wiped the tears from his face before they slid under his chin, but they kept coming. He wanted to scream, he wanted to curl into a ball and sob into his knees under his car seat, but instead he stayed where he was. His only movements were mopping his face and turning off the car.

Someone stealing his car park was the last straw and all his emotions came bubbling up the moment he didn't need to focus. It took every part of him to muster up the motivation to get out of his car, and had Kathryn not texted him asking for an ETA, he probably wouldn't have.

"5 minutes, had to park at the Plaza." he punctuated his sentence with an emoji glancing disapprovingly to the side.

Most of the party wasn't seated yet, so he couldn't have been that late. Aunties and uncles were all still greeting each other and exchanging hugs. Kathryn and Gianna raced straight into his face, they noticed the puffy, tear stained cheeks but didn't mention it.

"Are you up for this?"

"Should we have a safe word?"

"I'm sure it will be fine, all the attention will be on Mum anyway." Win wasn't very convincing, he was distracted by his aunties squawking.

"Well if you need us to run interference?" The Aunties didn't like Gianna much. They were polite enough to her face, but if Gianna approached them or tried to make conversation it was a sure-fire way to get them to disperse pretty quickly. Win knew this fact kind of hurt Gianna, she just wanted to be part of the family, so it was a lot for her to be offering up such a thing at the expense of her own ability to get through the dinner unscathed.

"Thanks Gianna." he smiled warmly for what felt like the first time in weeks. Dried tears crackled on his skin with the now foreign movement.

Win's Aunties, Di Hai, Di Ba and Di Ut were circled around his Mother, making stony cracks at each other followed by raucous laughter from the three that weren't receiving an insult at that particular moment.

Win interjected himself to wish his Mother a Happy Birthday and was quickly ensconced by his aunties pawing at his body or with his clothes and finally questioning where Lucia was. Win quickly informed them that Lucia was unwell with food poisoning. His excuse was accepted as real, but not a good one. Di Hai retorted that Lucia should have come anyway. Win's Mother was the only one that seemed a little worried by the news and eyed Win with careful concern.

Win and Kathryn's older brother Henry stepped in and retrieved Win.

"You looked like you needed saving from hurricane aunties. How you doing bro?"

Henry Huyhn wasn't so much of a black sheep as he just had his own thing going on. To Linh and Duc Huyhn he was the golden child. They didn't see him as often because he had kids, lived further afield than a ten minute drive and most importantly, his wife wasn't anybody's childhood best friend. Henry was an accountant, but you wouldn't know from looking at him. On this night he was busting out of a skintight, short sleeved button down with little white palm trees dotted over the navy fabric. Win thought that he must have had the shirt altered, there was no way that any mass-produced clothing would fit so snuggly over every part of his torso and his tree trunks for arms. His chinos were equally tight around his quads and his arms rested a good few centimetres off his body even when relaxed. Had Win not known and loved his brother, he would think he was a total douche.

Win jerked out the crick in his neck from Henry's overzealous hug before greeting his sister-in-law. Mindy gave a knowing smile, as though pain was a common side effect of her husband's hellos.

"Hi Samuel. So good to see you. Kat said that Lucia isn't feeling very well."

"Yeah, something she ate."

"Poor thing." Mindy cooed. She was everything you wouldn't expect from someone who would marry Henry. Mindy was gentle. Lucia and Win used to joke that she was like a wood nymph, or some celestial being from a movie. She seemed unphased by any kind of chaos, which was usually surrounding her as she had three sons who all took after their father.

The party was seated at a long table. Linh Huyhn sat at the head of the table with her sisters still cackling away around her. Then the dutiful husbands and then the children. The actual children, Mindy and Henry's kids did not stay in their seats. They fought, raced and squirmed around the whole restaurant.

Mindy was chatting to Gianna about the insemination process, asking thoughtful questions and avoiding anything too probing for the dinner table. Henry was busy interrupting them both with his take on the whole thing and his misguided belief that he was an expert on the subject. Gianna was getting visibly annoyed to everyone at the table apart from Henry. Kathryn eased her hand into her wife's lap, prying open her clenched fist and slipping her hand in hers.

"Hey babe? I think I'm getting a headache. Would you run to the pharmacy and grab me some painkillers?"

The pharmacy was not far, but Kathryn knew that by the time Gianna returned her temper would have cooled and Henry would be busy extolling his expertise on someone else.

"I need to get some Visine. I'll come with." Win clambered out of the crowded seats to follow Gianna out the door.

"Getting too much?"

"Yeah"

"You guys are pretty quick to name fake ailments. I'm impressed...and worried."

"Oh nah, I fully believe that Kathryn was actually getting a headache from hearing Henry talk."

Gianna laughed, rolling her eyes.

"And my eyes actually are a bit sore."

"From the crying?"

"That too."

"You know it's ok right? You can cry." Gianna checked over each shoulder before adding in a hushed tone "Your wife died."

"That's not it though is it? I mean, it's not that she died. It's that she's still hanging around."

❖

When Win left the house, he didn't turn on the TV or a podcast. Lucia had tried to stay out of the way as he got ready. There wasn't anything in the house that drew much enjoyment, so it wasn't difficult to stay in her room. Physically difficult, it was very emotionally draining to stay concealed from a man who not that long ago, she shared everything with.

She tried not to think about how open they once were. How they never closed doors or shut each other out. How they didn't hide away even the gross, mundane things, flossing, nail clipping, farting realness. They admired one another at least once a day as they frequently strode around the house naked, for comfort or convenience. She tried not to think about that, but her mind wandered back to those thoughts.

If things were different, she would be doing her makeup in the bathroom mirror while he showered. They would stand side by side putting on their "good" clothes for the party. They would effortlessly provide unprovoked compliments to each other, banding together for a united front as they stepped into the outside world.

She knew exactly what he looked like stepping out of the shower, exactly how his hair looked when it was slicked to his forehead before he brushed it back. She could see the water dripping from his limbs and smell the fresh, just-showered scent steamy and humid against her face. She could remember all of that as though it wasn't even a memory, as though it was part of her. She could remember it, but instead she looked out of the window of her room, silently praying to a God she didn't even believe in, that something more interesting than her pain would hop into view.

Lucia didn't venture out of her room but Win poked his head in to ask about their (his) present for his Mum.

"We went in with Kathryn and Gianna. Fruit trees. Kathryn has them."

"Cool thanks!" She believed he was genuinely grateful, for both organising the present and for telling him about it now. His reaction was still somewhat dismissive.

"There is a card."

Win's head popped back around the corner. "What was that?"

"There's a card. In the linen cupboard, in the wrapping paper box. There's a white paper bag with cards in it. One of those, I haven't written in it."

"Ok, thanks."

Can you...can you leave the tv on or something?"

"Sure."

20

The sky was bright and clear slices of brilliant blue between the city buildings. The sun bounced harshly between glass and chrome, but at ground level the streets tunnelled wind off the river and blasted commuters with a chill. Despite having been in Australia for over a week, Laura De Jong and Kevin Mulder were not used to the sun being so bright at this time of the morning. Winters back home dawn would just be breaking.

They arrived in Brisbane that morning, suffering a night in a cramped bus, on a trip three times longer than they thought it would be up from Sydney. They dropped their bags and were looking for something to do, without realising that Brisbane was not flush with exciting attractions like Sydney or Melbourne. It was a pit stop on the way to Queensland's beaches.

The receptionist had given them some unconvincing directions to Mt Coot-tha, since most locals agree the best thing about Brisbane is viewing it from afar. Kevin decided it was best to get a second opinion from someone not ending a night shift. He planted himself on the corner of Edward and Ann, straining to gain the attention of passers-by. Laura slunk back propping herself up with the building, her bare shoulders prickled at the cold where they met the black, tiled wall. She was tired and grumpy; she didn't think a second opinion was needed. Businessmen in cheap suits gawked at her long, tanned legs, following them up the hem of her frayed shorts. She felt exposed and wanted to be out of there as soon as possible.

Swarms of people passed Kevin, occasionally smiling, but most averted their gaze. At last he caught the eye of a man. He was dressed plainly, dark short hair with too much product or not enough washing and a pinched face behind glasses. He was smiling and walking quickly and purposefully to Kevin. Laura had been looking down Edward St, away from Kevin watching the next intersection burst to life every so often. When she looked back she saw Kevin with the man. A chill set down her spine and her gut sloshed uneasily. The man was pointing back where Laura had just been looking, large wet patching visible on his armpit when he lifted his arm. Kevin held out his phone and Laura moved in behind the next wave of foot traffic to get a closer look. Not wanting to be closer to that man, but not wanting her boyfriend to be stuck there alone.

"Aye fuck!" Kevin jumped. Rubbing his arm.

"You get bit?" The man seemed unphased by Kevin's pain.

"I don't know."

"Probably a mosquito mate."

Laura saw a small smear of blood on Kevin's forearm where he had wiped it. The man was giving directions back down the hill. The smell of his underarms stung Laura's nostrils. She followed the line of his finger, only to look away and breathe some fresher air. A pain stabbed her finger. She flinched but didn't say anything. Pulling her hand away and rubbing the small spot of blood peaking from between her fingers. She eyed the man carefully, suspicious of his claims about mosquitos. Not this early, not that big or painful either. The sooner they were away from him the better.

"260 bus will get you there."

"Thank you."

The man didn't even keep walking when Kevin thanked him. He just stood there and watched them as they walked away.

"Wat een griezel" Laura muttered as she rubbed the sting in her finger. Kevin's usual persistent jolliness had made way to a grimace as he rubbed the back of his neck in an attempt to sooth a pain. "Gaat het?"

- 148 -

"Sliep vreemd, het is ok"

Closer to the mall Laura's neck began to ache too. It felt sharp and stinging, like sinus pain in the back of her head instead of a crick from being jammed in a bus for nearly a day.

They tried their best to find the bus the man had told them about, but eventually slumped to the floor in the Myer Centre bus station. The scrolling advertisements across the busway burning neon into their vision as they took their last strained breaths.

21

Tuesday night was not exactly an ideal night for it. Exactly three weeks after Win had come home to find his wife dead, he moved out of the home they had blissfully shared until then. He hadn't packed anything. It wasn't a rush decision though. Perhaps somewhere in the depths of his subconscious Win had thought that things would improve. This whole thing was so far removed from his understanding of the natural order that he had no idea if there was more to come. He couldn't completely dismiss that Lucia could return to life, or Lucia and Lu would merge and life would be somewhat normal again. None of this was completely out of the question.

The shift came when Win realised that even if she were to come back, somehow, he couldn't bear to be around waiting for it. He needed to grieve. For three long weeks he had let his emotions sour inside of him and he needed to cling to the last sliver of sanity he could.

He couldn't avoid breaking the news to Lucia upfront. He owed her that much, but also the suitcases were kept in the spare bedroom. Lucia was laying on the futon watching the ceiling. By the time Win got home the sun had long gone and shadows of the outside trees swaying in the wind danced across the ceiling. Win didn't turn on the light and sat on the floor, his back against the futon at Lucia's hip.

Lucia waited for Win to speak. Her head suddenly filled with optimism. She willed him to say that he loved her and they would make it work. She wanted him to assure her.

Crumb followed Win into the room and rubbed himself furiously against Win's elbow. Win alternated scratching behind both of Crumb's ears and smoothing his hands down his back. Loose fur collected at the base of Crumb's tail with each pat, and heavy purrs informed Win of his approval.

"You know I love you right?"

Hope sprung back into Lucia with his words.

"I just can't."

"Can't?"

"I'm moving out." Win thought ripping the band-aid off was supposed to make it hurt less, but it didn't. It felt like he had taken a shotgun blast to the chest. Maybe even worse because that pain would have been shorter lived.

Lucia didn't know what to say. The words had evaporated out of her and were now just as useless as the rest of her existence. There was nothing to say, his mind was made up. She could beg, but that would be cruel to both of them.

She still hadn't said anything by the time Win had retrieved the suitcases from the spare room closet. He wheeled them out of the room and focused so hard on getting them both through the door that he had an excuse not to look at Lucia as he left.

About half an hour was all it took. Win lifted bundles of clothes out of his drawer and laid them directly into the open suitcases. His clothes were folded neatly in the draw and didn't require any adjustments to fit. He swooped whole arms full of work shirts from the wardrobe, not bothering to remove them from the hanger, instead laying them directly over the rest of his clothes. He lined an empty wine box with a plastic bag and flung his toiletries in there. He didn't have much in the way of toiletries, body wash, razor, shaving cream, toothbrush, toothpaste and some hair pomade that smelled vaguely of pine.

Win piled Crumb's belongings into another wine box. His food, bowls and toys. The toys were easy, they were already in a small crate and he only had to search for a few that were scattered around the house. By this time Crumb had realised that something was going on and had hidden in a small space between the bedside table and the wall on Win's side of the bed. Crumb thought this was an excellent hiding place, but he was literally backing himself into a corner making it much easier for Win to pick him up and deposit him in a cat carrier. Crumb protested loudly until he found the treats that Win had pre-emptively left in the carrier. Win draped his used, but dry bath towel over the carrier in an effort to block out the light, but also cloak Crumb in a (hopefully) comforting smell.

Win pulled one of his pillows from the bed and added it to the pile. He noticed Lucia's pyjamas poking from beneath the pillow on her side of the bed. He pulled them out. A large, faded black men's XXL t shirt. Long ago it bore the face of Alice Cooper on the front, but now he could barely make out the face from the speckles of white peeling paint. A teenage Lucia, still Luke to Win then had worn it as a mini dress, paired with a white studded belt and tights. That was a half a lifetime ago; it was faded and stretched and when she wore it to bed it just grazed her upper thighs. The thinning cotton fibres carried with them the scent of her, of all that time. He tucked it into his pillowcase.

Just like that he was all packed up and shipped out, the only trace left of Win was the tracks the suitcases made across the carpet.

❖

The first night as a new resident of Kathryn and Gianna's house, Win had not done much of anything. He hung his shirts in the spare bedroom closet and lined up his toiletries along the edge of a desk come vanity in the corner of the room. He stacked his suitcases next to it and laid his clothes for the next day across the top of them. After that he lay down. Sometime after that he fed Crumb, who was swatting at his face and sometime after that he fell asleep. The sleep was good. The kind when you cry yourself to sleep usually is, because by then it's especially needed.

Crumb woke him before his alarm went off. For most of the night Crumb lay on the bed next to Win's feet, occasionally getting up to sniff around. He paid close attention to the crack under the bedroom door. Every now and then Crumb's sniffs were met by sniffs from the opposite side of the door. Butterbean didn't care much about who was on the other side of the door. In that way he was a terrible guard dog. He would lose interest quickly. He had much more important and pressing things to do, like eating and laying his head across the lap of whichever mother looked the least likely to move any time soon.

In the early hours of the morning Crumb discovered the windowsill. The view from the windowsill looked out on a big backyard. It had to be big in order to accommodate an Old English Sheepdog. The far end of the yard, and along the northern fence were trees. Some towering gums and a smattering of smaller natives. Possums scampered through the branches. The boldest of them ventured all the way up to the house, decimating the pot plants on the back verandah. Even plants you thought would be safe from the possums were uprooted, tipped over and gnawed on. It was as though the locals put on a welcoming party for Crumb. Two tawny frogmouths caught his attention too when they arrived on the clothesline. Their low throbbing call injected itself into Win's dreams. Crumb squeaked into the window, his whiskers bristled and nose wrinkled. Even Win waking and demanding he get down did not break his gaze.

❖

Wednesday morning was the hardest to wake up. For maybe two whole seconds after Win's eyes opened the confusion about what he was looking at overrode every other thought. Two seconds was just

- 154 -

enough to make it really hurt when he plummeted right back into the pit of despair that he fell asleep in.

He had not thought to make any arrangements for the following day last night. He had no idea of the bus times and only a vague notion of how long or how far away the bus stop even was. Second to that thought was that he didn't know the shower schedule around here. The last thing he wanted was to impose and push back the morning routine of his gracious hosts. All of these thoughts happened as he remained on his left side, facing the window. Crumb noticed Win's awakeness and chirped before pouncing on the bed. Crumb pressed his nose underneath Win's and breathed loudly. More like a grumbling purr. Crumb was ready to leave the room, Win wasn't so sure he was.

"Ok boy." Win heaved himself up, his bones were stiff but they didn't crack. Crumb pushed himself into Win's ribs in an affectionate shove.

"Yeah yeah." Win collected his laid-out clothes and an armful of his shower things. The shampoo slid against the body wash bottle, each pushing the other out of the way. The whole pile balanced precariously in Win's arms as he pried his right arm away just enough to release the door handle. The door stuck on Crumb's side, as he had pushed his way in front of Win.

"Oh for fuck's sake! You right?"

Kathryn had heard the struggle and was standing, toothbrush in hand down the hall outside the bathroom. From her position she had a clear shot right to Win and Crumb's farcical exchange.

"Are you?"

"Yeah." Win noticed the toothbrush and Kathryn still in her pyjamas. "Fuck are you just about to shower?"

"Nah, just brushing my teeth. Just be a second."

Butterbean had also popped his head around the corner to check what was going on at the end of the hall. His tail wagged so forcefully that his hips swung side to side. It was impossible to tell if he was more excited by Win or by Crumb. Probably both in equal measure.

22

Three loud raps on the front door startled Lucia out of her trance. She had found that she could spend a lot of the "down hours" gazing at the ceiling and if she focused just hard enough, the ceiling is the only thing she would think about. It was preferable to ruminating over her current existence.

Win had left the night before. Lucia could tell that it wasn't quite midday, but she wasn't exactly sure when Win had left. It was a Wednesday, again she was pretty sure of it being Wednesday, but the days were bleeding into each other. Like on a holiday, but without any of the good bits.

The three knocks came again.

"Who is it?"

"Lucia Hughes? It's Constable Bentley and Constable Scott can you please open up?"

"Just a minute."

"Mrs Hughes we just want to talk to you."

"Yeah, just a minute. I gotta grab some pants."

Bentley and Scott chuckled to themselves at that line. Not like they hadn't heard it before though. It was astonishing how many people opt out of wearing pants in the comfort of their own home. Bentley was a pants on type of guy, but Scott stripped off as soon as she came through the door herself.

Pantslessness was a good excuse though, giving reason to the movement that surely would be heard from the other side of her front door.

Lu begrudgingly opened the front door and assumed a hiding position behind the front door out of sight. As long as Lucia didn't look in that direction, they would have no reason to suspect anyone was there.

"How can I help you officers?"

"Mrs Hughes…"

"Ms, but Lucia is fine."

"Lucia, we've received a call from someone concerned for your wellbeing." Constable Bentley was doing the talking.

"Huh?" She tried to sound surprised, but in her head Lucia actually thought it was about time. She was beginning to be a bit put out that no one cared she'd gone missing.

"You haven't been to work or been answering the phone?"

Scott interjected, "Can we come in and discuss this? We might all be a bit more comfortable inside."

"Actually I'd rather you didn't"

"Any reason why you don't want us inside Ms Hughes?" Bentley asked.

"Lucia. Well yeah, I've been sick. Horribly and haven't cleaned up. The place is a pigsty and covered in germs."

"I'm sure we'll be fine."

"That's why I haven't been at work or answering calls either. I've practically been asleep for a week."

Scott mentioned quietly to Bentley the inconsistency in Lucia's timeline.

"If there's something wrong we can help Ms Hughes." Scott stepped forward, putting on her best woman to woman voice. Even in her anxiousness to get rid of them Lucia appreciated it. If something was wrong. Or wrong in the way they thought it might be, she would appreciate a woman being there.

"No, no really. I just want to get back to bed."

Constable Scott stepped even closer to the door. This didn't seem like protocol because her partner flinched as though he was going to pull her back. Scott whispered, "Is there someone in there with you?"

"No. I'm alone, and I'm fine." Lucia whispered back, echoing Scott.

"Ok Lucia, you feel better soon."

Lucia stayed at the door waving them off until the police officers were in their car. They talked amongst themselves on the way to the car, but not about that interaction. Lucia swore she heard Scott mention a "McMuffin." Bacon and Egg? Is that too on the nose, for cops to eat bacon on duty. It was guess work though, Lucia didn't gain super hearing or super sight as a ghost. She hadn't gained anything, other than a basically useless sidekick. Not even a sidekick.

After she was sure they couldn't see her, or at least weren't looking. Lucia got Lu to swing the door shut.

Lu did it before grumphing off back to the spare bedroom.

❖

"That's $11.50. Sir?...Sir?" The cashier was more concerned than she was annoyed, but Win was still holding up the line and the stress of a morning rush pile up was imminent.

"I'll get that." Sanjay's smiling face appeared behind Win's left shoulder. He was wearing a pale grey suit, and pink button down. Sanjay never wore suits, but he was very specifically trying to get in good with this barista. He handed over $15, grinning broadly with a cheeky glint in his eye. If Win had been aware of anything happening at that point, he might have noticed that Sanjay had trimmed and brushed his beard and moisturised his hands and face. "Keep the change."

"Thanks. Is he...ok?"

"He'll be fine when he gets some coffee into him." Sanjay nudged Win in the ribs. "You right there Bud?" Win snapped back to reality and for the first time noticed Sanjay was beside him.

"Shit" to the barista, "how much?"

By this time she had moved on to serving the increasingly aggravated line up and shot an awkward look back to Sanjay.

"I took care of it mate; you can grab the next one." Sanjay thought it was better to quiz Win on his absent-mindedness when they were in the office. For now he would just wait with his friend for their coffees.

❖

Win looked at his blueberry muffin as if even one bite would make him ill, in reality he didn't remember getting it. Were they out of every other flavour? That's the only conclusion he could come to, since he would never in his life order blueberry.

His stomach turned over on itself, more like sea sickness than a hangover. Win would occasionally let his blood sugar drop to the point where he felt weak and nauseated. He couldn't actually remember the last meal he ate. Even searching his brain for a memory of last night's dinner was too much for him to undertake right now. No? He didn't have dinner, he was sure of it. He had a vague recollection of Kathryn knocking on his bedroom door and enquiring. He could remember the post dusk blue light filtering over the spare room. How even though he wasn't facing the door he could picture the warm light streaming under the door, disrupting his wallowing. Most of all he could recall that uneasy feeling, the one that comes with hiding away in a dark room while the world carries on without you. Laughter and warmth radiating from the rest of the world while he was in pain.

He hadn't felt like that since a brief angst-ridden phase in grade eleven. The whole thing reminded him of the story of The Little Match Girl, out in the cold while everyone else was enjoying their Christmas. Each match he lit for himself was a painful memory of his wife.

Win's brooding poetic thoughts were abruptly disrupted by what little contents of his stomach he had, surging up past his throat and straight into his bin.

"Nope. Dude! You've got to go home." Sanjay was genuinely concerned but everything out of his mouth always sounded like a bit of a dig.

"It's not contagious."

"Hitting the pub, eh?"

"Haha, yeah." If there was anyone that Win would confide in that wasn't his sister or sister-in-law, it would be Sanjay, but not yet. He couldn't face talking about it just yet. Another wave of nausea hit, but everything had already been expelled.

"Sooo...you gonna eat that?"

"Nah mate, it's yours."

❖

The front right wheel of the shopping trolley spun awkwardly as Gianna tried her best to keep it going straight. She was stronger than her slender frame would suggest, if she was a man people would probably describe her as wiry. It was less of a physical struggle and more of a mental one, the sheer annoyance of a wayward trolley was enough to nearly have her at breaking point. She was chock full of hormones and coming off a long shift, which probably didn't help much.

When Gianna got this way she was prone to making confident, but hasty decisions. As a result the trolley was filled with things they definitely didn't need and lacking things that they really did. Never shop when you're hungry, but also never shop when you're sad or exhausted. Gianna was just about to add two boxes of cereal to her shop, neither she nor Kathryn ate cereal, when a tap on her shoulder stopped her.

"Hello, you are Gianna aren't you?" Tanvi was smiling broadly up at Gianna. She barely reached Gianna's shoulder. Her black hair circled her face in a thick bob that ended at chin length and her eyes waited for Gianna to recognise her from behind thick, red-framed glasses.

Gianna did recognise her, but couldn't place her, just the feeling of dread she needed in the middle of her panicked grocery shop.

"Tanvi. Tanvi Jay. Lucia's boss. You are her sister-in-law?"

"Yeah, oh, yeah yeah!"

"I believe we met at her birthday dinner last year."

"You're right we did. Sorry I just came off a shift."

"Oh yes, you are a midwife. Excellent! How is Lucia? I have not been hearing from her."

Sweat beaded at Gianna's temples and she held her breath hoping that would somehow open her pores to swallow the sweat back up.

"She's doing well. All things considered; it was a nasty accident." Gianna patted herself on the back for coming up with such a believable lie so quickly.

"Very good, I am pleased to hear. Terrible to hear of the accident. I do hope she is feeling better." Tanvi was also a good liar.

"I think it will be a while, but you know Lucia."

"Right. Well, I will let you continue to finish the shopping."

Gianna left the cereal on the shelf and checked out as quickly as she could. She didn't stop sweating the whole way home. It wasn't far but she had the air con on, which just made her cold and damp. The knot in her stomach seemed to be drawing strength from her limbs because they were numb.

The key wouldn't fit in the lock, probably because Gianna still didn't have full use of her fingers and in spite of that she loaded herself up with all the groceries. She let out a strained scream as she mashed the keys against the door.

Win opened the door, not knowing what was on the other side but certainly not expecting a near to tears Gianna. She was usually the most stoic of the whole family.

"Thank you!" She heaved the bags onto the counter and collapsed into a dining room chair.

"Are you ok?"

"It's been a long day." Gianna seized back up, the key ordeal had made her briefly forget her Woolworths encounter. "I ran into Tanvi. Told her Lucia was in an accident. She's recovering."

"Fuck!"

Their eyes met, both widened in horror.

"I told her Ryan was sick."

"Fuck."

"Oooh, family meeting in the kitchen." Kathryn dropped her keys in the dish on the dining table and kissed Gianna on the forehead while she was bent over. She snapped her tongue against her lips as she pulled them off Gianna's skin.

"Blurgh, sweaty babe."

Neither Gianna nor Win were game to say anything yet.

Looking through the shopping bags, Kathryn paused and looked back at Gianna.

"No dog food?"

Gianna vomited straight onto the kitchen floor. Some splashed Win on his bare foot, but he would probably never mention it. The dog food was forgotten for the second time that evening.

Nearly three full decades of being a nurse, meant that Tanvi Jay had a very well-honed bullshit detector. She knew that something was wrong. She knew it when Lucia hadn't shown up for work, when Win gave that feeble excuse and now she knew it for certain. So strong was the stench of something fishy that Tanvi did something very foolish. She followed Gianna.

Tanvi abandoned her cart. She had two high school aged children who wouldn't protest if their mother had the sudden benevolence to grant them midweek pizza dinner. Honestly they would probably think she was incredibly cool for hunting down suspicious characters. Though she would never let them know that's what she was doing.

It was Tanvi's good fortune that the Buranda car park was so small and so busy that she didn't lose Gianna, but also was pretty certain that she wouldn't be spotted. Tanvi started her engine and slumped down in her seat. She barely saw over the steering wheel anyway but it was more instinctual at this point.

Peak hour traffic in that area was always a nightmare. If no one let her into traffic Tanvi would lose Gianna as soon as they left the car park. Both cars wound their way through the streets of the southside for fifteen minutes until Gianna pulled into her driveway. She set the hand brake and left her door ajar while she fussed with the gate. Tanvi drove straight past, knowing that by now Gianna surely would have noticed her. She drove all the way to the end of the street and turned around, stopping a few houses down the street just as Gianna pulled through the gate.

Tanvi slumped down and watched Gianna hoist her reusable shopping bags and fuss with the door. She saw Win open it. She was sure it was him. It wouldn't be out of the question for Win to be visiting his sister. At the very least she knew there wasn't an affair, was there? They did seem happy to see each other, but in-laws can be happy to see each other.

- 165 -

Buzz Buzz

Tanvi's phone vibrated against the plastic cup holder she kept it in while driving and made her jump out of her skin. It was her daughter.

"Muuuuhhm?"

"What do you want Sunny?"

Usually Sunny would expect a sigh or the like, but Tanvi was hushed and harsh. Nearly snapping. A real indication that something was up and whatever Sunny was going to ask would be answered negatively.

"Mummyji?" She was sucking up now. "Could you get some ice cream on your way home?"

"Sunny, I am not having time to go to the shops. We are ordering pizza. If you work on your assignments and finish the washing up also. Maybe, maybe we will order ice cream also."

"Thank you Mummyji!"

"Love you."

"Love you too!"

That was genuine, a real "I love you" from her teenager and there would be chores done when she got home too. Tanvi patted herself on the back and mentally added "super sleuth" and "miracle Mum" to her list of assets.

She pulled out her phone and was just about to message her son to assign him chores to be completed for the ice cream reward when footsteps beside the car quickened her heartbeat. It was just

- 166 -

a pedestrian and Tanvi breathed a sigh of relief, even if her heart hadn't got the memo yet. That pedestrian was Kathryn. That almost definitely ruled out an affair, nothing nefarious could have happened in that time. Something was up though. None of this made sense and Tanvi would get to the bottom of it if she wanted to keep super sleuth in her title.

23

Lucia had watched more episodes of Ghost Whisperer in her time than she cared to admit. She might have only watched it for the scenes with Jennifer Love Hewitt in her nightgown, but nevertheless most of Lucia's ghost knowledge came from that show. Anything she didn't already know from Casper of course. Like a lot of women her age, the standout scene in Casper was when he became a real boy. Casper was no more reliable a source of accurate ghost information than it was about what actually happened when you kiss a boy at a party. The latter was a disappointment to Lucia when she was thirteen, the former was a disappointment now.

Lucia didn't need a medium to help her communicate with her loved ones. She might have needed voice recognition software but when they were in front of her talking wasn't an issue. As far as she was aware, she could not affect the temperature or lighting in the room just by being there. She didn't know for sure though. It was winter and she couldn't feel anything. That was something. She couldn't feel anything. The ghosts on TV were always complaining about feeling pain or cold or something. Lucia felt nothing at all. This was where she was starting to realise the one similarity between her experience and what she had seen. Because Lucia couldn't feel anything, even little things, her emotions were starting to bubble up. Any emotion that would normally have a physical reaction was turning into rage. She could be an angry poltergeist any day now and she would still be tethered to a potentially ravenous zombie.

The feeling crept up most when she thought about Win, or saw Win, or spoke to him. They were also very present when she wanted something from Lu. Sometimes it felt like she was trapped in a box, and her only way to do anything was to pass notes. She had no idea if the notes were being read. They were though, just by a recipient who didn't speak English.

From the outside the house looked exactly the same. Most people have some kind of subconscious way of knowing if a house is unoccupied. Little clues that all together add up to a sixth sense. Closed windows, closed doors, garden in disarray, footpaths unscuffed by regular comings and goings. Neighbours would most likely know that Win had left. Noticed his absence, maybe even saw him leave not long after dark with a suitcase, a cat carrier and tear streaked cheeks. Lucia and Lu were still coming and going. There was movement and noise still inside the house, but when Kathryn pulled up, it felt empty beneath her gaze. There was no life left in the house.

Kathryn considered it a kindness when she stooped to weed between the rocks that lined the walkway to the front steps. Deep inside she knew it was procrastination, she was avoiding knocking on that door.

In the end, she didn't need to. The front door jerked open and Lucia stepped on to the small, paved patio.

"Thank you."

Kathryn had heard the door but the words still startled her.

"I wanted to check in. See how you're coping."

Lucia didn't mean to laugh, but she couldn't help it. "How was she coping?" Like there was any way she could be coping right now. As if what was happening was work stress. If someone dies, or is recovering from a serious illness, people often choose to say, "How are you holding up?" in other words "How much effort is it for you to be acting like a functioning human being right now?" Lucia was neither "holding up" or "coping." There was not a single part of her that was handling her current situation well at all.

Kathryn made herself a tea and folded herself up on the couch. She was wearing stretchy knit black pants, a white t-shirt tucked into the front of them in a way that looked casual but took a concerted effort. Her fluffy maroon cardigan swamped her small frame, in a way that only Kathryn could pull off. Lucia knew that Kathryn chose these particular clothes for the maximum comfort, meaning that she intended to have a long chat. Kathryn placed her tea on the coffee table along with a small dish that they exclusively used for spent tea bags. Her long brassy chain, with a thin but solid pendant struck the edge of the coffee table as she leant forward to dunk her tea bag in and out of the steaming water. Tendrils of sepia circled the cup with each movement.

Lucia took up her spot at the opposite corner of the couch, arranging her limbs to mirror Kathryn. Kathryn was suddenly aware of the quietness within the house, and specifically the lack of Crumb, who if he hadn't taken up residence in the remaining square of the couch, would at least be nuzzling their feet.

"I thought people were being poetic when they said that people can die of a broken heart." There were no tears, she couldn't cry, no matter how much she wanted to. "I can't feel anything, but I can still feel the emotional pain. Does that make sense? Even without a body I can feel it."

Kathryn didn't know what to say, she couldn't answer that. No amount of empathy could stretch across this particular arrangement of emotions.

"I can't even have chocolate to make it feel better!"

They both laughed, and that lifted the mood of the room some.

Kathryn cradled her empty mug in her hands, absorbing any warmth left in the ceramic. Her hands were sweating but not from heat. She was running through her mind, the best way to break it to

Lucia that Win had asked her to collect some things. She wanted to break it gently.

"Hey Lucia?"

"You can take whatever you need to."

Shocked, "Are you telepathic now?"

"Haha, no. I just figured Win would need something. He didn't take much."

"I forgot how good you are at that."

24

The front door was open and there was a pearlescent finish navy Audi parked in the driveway when Lucia and Lu arrived at Ruth's house. They hid in behind some bushes, hoping that whoever was there would be leaving soon. Lucia could hardly make it out because of the glare coming off the Audi's heavily tinted windows, but it looked like it had been piled high with furniture. Resting against the open doorway was the rolled up rug from Ruth's lounge room.

A mixture of annoyance and relief welled up inside of Lucia when she realised that the car and the looting was Ruth's children. Coming to strip the house bare of anything with value. At least it wasn't a professional moving company, or real estate, or some government personnel. Those would be more sinister, more likely to see an undead (most likely naked) old lady and try to capture her, lock her up, maybe kill her. Lucia wondered if she was giving Ruth's children too much credit, they would probably do those things too.

Ruth was probably weak and with any luck she was curled up in a closet somewhere, out of harm's way. She could lay low until the house was empty again. Lucia cursed herself for not bringing anything to Ruth to eat. A backpack full of human organs would probably tip Lu way into the conspicuous end of the scale and she couldn't risk that.

The minutes ticked down and there hadn't been any movement in the house. Lucia readied Lu, and herself to enter the house.

The living room was empty. Free from people and relieved of a lot of its previous contents. The armchairs and couches shifted back haphazardly so that the Persian rug could be taken away. There was an empty space where the TV had once been, several tchotchkes were either missing or moved around. There was a box sitting by the rug that had a lamp, mantle clock and silverware in it.

There was no sound or movement coming from the depths of the house, so Lucia stepped in. The side tables had been picked clean, pots, pans and vintage crockery were piled up on the kitchen benches. The wheelie bin sat in the middle of the kitchen, open and brimming with items of lesser value. The dog's food was just visible over the lip of the bin, apparently the whereabouts of the dogs was of no concern.

Lucia made her way back to the bedrooms. The amount of trauma she had been subjected to by entering Ruth's bedroom, it was a wonder that she could even bring herself to enter. A bloody handprint clutched the door frame about a foot above the carpet.

"Oh for fuck's sake!" Lucia knew that once again, horrors awaited her inside that room.

The body was very familiar. Familiar in the way that Lucia was certain she had met him when he was living and the scene of his death was also ringing bells. The soft parts all torn to shreds while the rest remained fairly intact. An organ soup, half slurped out and spilling on the floor in almost black smears. Lucia couldn't quite remember his name, Liam, maybe Leon, possibly not even an L name at all. His throat had been chewed, but not eviscerated. The angle of his head indicated that Liam/Leon had met his demise by having his neck broken.

It presented a bit of an issue, another dead body. This one would be much harder to clean up. At this rate Lucia was averaging a body a week since she died. Blood and bits of organ flung around the place, onto the bedding and seeping into the carpet. What looked like it might be intestine was stuck to the quilt and dried, Lucia was grateful to be without smell. The intestine had not been empty.

Ruth was calm, satiated and dressed head to toe in the insides of her own son. She needn't have been so exuberant in her killing of him, but it seemed like part of this was payback. Payback for being forgotten, pushed aside, not even a funeral or any proper mourning, just looting. Ruth seemed very pleased with herself.

"Happy Ruth? You know we have to clean this up?" Ruth stood confidently before licking her fingers. "His car is here! He has a family that knows where he is."

Ruth either didn't understand or didn't really care. She was like a cartoon cat, nonchalant and smugly covered in her kill.

"Stay here." Lucia waved her arms in a halting motion before leaving to get Lu. Lu was standing in the lounge room. Lucia whispered thanks to herself that Lu was at least obedient. Maybe just lacking in initiative, unlike Ruth who was a true wild card.

"You hungry?"

Once again pop culture had betrayed Lucia. Movies and TV had led her to believe that zombies are ravenous, insatiable beasts that eat all day every day until the world has fallen apart. Apparently, they're not and even if their last meal was days ago, they were measured and only ate what they needed. In this case it wasn't nearly enough. Lu barely touched what was left of Liam/Leon. She kind of pawed at him and slurped at some of his bountiful belly fat. Doing nothing of use apart from getting Lucia's DNA in a crime scene.

"I guess we'll take him with us?" Lucia shrugged, having no real clue how they got him home.

Lu, Ruth and Lucia all slumped against the side of the bed facing the door. Blood and bits painted the whole room now. Liam/Leon was torn into smaller pieces, literally torn. His bones were practically all broken as Ruth and Lu worked together to break him down like a chook. Lucia herself wouldn't know where to start dismembering a person. That must have been some inherited zombie knowledge.

Lucia did know how to butterfly a chicken, and surely Ruth knows her fair share of butchery. Maybe when it came down to it, she would know how to do it. That was a grim thought.

What was left of Liam/Leon had been stuffed into a rolling suitcase. Not ideal, but the best they had to work with.

The plan was that Ruth would come with them this time. It wasn't a long journey to connect the dots if someone found Ruth, they would definitely be knocking on Lucia's door soon. Better to make it look like some random murder, taking place in an unfamiliar house. Lucia hoped that human meat would keep well, save another body down the line.

❖

Sometime around 3am Gianna crawled into bed. Kathryn would usually wake when Gianna came home. They wouldn't talk, but Gianna could be greeted by a soft hand on her hip. The little press saying, "I love you, glad you're home, sleep well" without the words. This morning Kathryn snored softly without stirring. Gianna glimpsed her wife's face pressed into her pillow. She wanted badly to reach out and kiss her but didn't dare for fear of waking her. Kathryn was beautiful, now especially.

Gianna's eyes closed involuntarily, the only way she could tell she was falling asleep was when a wave of consciousness came over her and she heard Kathryn's snoring, which was now joined by Butterbean's snoring from the foot of the bed. Gianna rolled herself over and facing away from Kathryn she clutched her own pillow into her chest. Eyes still closed rearranging her pillow as it brushed against her chest and walloped her with pain. Three times she tried to nestle into slumber before her eyes shot back open.

Shortly after that Gianna was sitting on the edge of the bathtub, trying to not to watch the pregnancy test on the vanity. Her feet were cold, freezing on the tiled floor. She reconciled with herself that she could leave and get socks and when she came back the test would be ready.

Hope brimmed from Gianna as she walked back to the bathroom. Her mind flipped from positive to negative. Hopes high and lying to herself that she was able to control herself. A second pink line was clear as day.

Gianna slipped back into bed. Kathryn reached her hand over this time. Gianna pulled Kathryn's hand up and scooted forward wrapping her arm around Kathryn's back and pulling her in. Their hips pressed together, Kathryn's warm body against the still coolness of Gianna's.

"Babe?"

Murmuring, "Hmmm."

"I'm pregnant."

Kathryn's eyes blinked open. "Really?"

"Really."

25

"You don't have to visit me so often."

"I want to."

Kathryn had procured Win's keys to make her increasing visits go more smoothly. She showed up unannounced, which felt incredibly rude but she didn't have any other options. Win had left Lucia's phone for her to use but Lu lacked the dexterity and Lucia lacked the corporality for it to be of any real use.

On her way back from fixing herself a tea, Kathryn saw a figure looming in the hall. She assumed it was Lu and she had no real interest in seeing Lu up close. Kathryn didn't have the stomach for it. It was only when she sat across from Lucia and noticed that her clothing was a remarkably different shade than the person in the hall. Without saying a word, she reached her head back to take another look. It definitely wasn't Lu.

"Ummmm."

"Ruth." Lucia knew exactly what Kathryn was looking at.

"She...she's naked."

Lucia sighed deeply "Yeah, she does that."

"Lucia? Why is she here?"

"I've visited a few times since we died. Just trying to get information. She killed her son, so I thought she should hide here."

"Yep, that only gave me more questions." Kathryn angled her body towards Ruth, suddenly quite afraid to turn her back to an undead stranger. "What did you do with her son?"

"He's in the freezer."

She didn't say anything but Kathryn's face was only barely hiding her mortification.

"He was a bad guy!" Lucia jumped in, "If that helps at all."

"It really doesn't."

Outside was bright and as it approached midday, the air warmed to a comfortable temperature. In the sun it was getting hot, not stifling, but enough that even in the beginning of winter you wouldn't want to stay in the heat for too long. It was, or at least it had been, Lucia's favourite weather. Getting around in jeans and tee without being mopped with sweat after only a short while.

It was much colder inside. Lucia could tell it, but she also remembered it well. The cold air of the evening staying trapped in the house until late morning, sometimes early afternoon. A brief window to open everything up and let the stale air out.

Kathryn had exchanged her tea for coffee, drinking it black because the milk had turned. Kathryn made a mental note to throw it out as she was leaving. She let Lucia know her plan because she surely would forget.

"You can take all the food. Better you have it than it goes to waste."

"Thanks, I'll do that."

"Kathryn?" Lucia led off the sentence knowing that the end would be asking for a favour. "Can you turn off a lot of the appliances? There's no point having them running if I'm not using them. I really just need the fridge."

"Of course. Good thinking!"

"One other thing?"

"Sure, what do you need?"

"Can you write down some recipes for me? For Win, from me?"

Kathryn was a little taken aback. It wasn't a big ask, just unexpected.

Lucia continued, "I want him to have the recipes for everything he likes. In case something happens. They're all up here." She pointed to her head.

"Of course!" Already Kathryn was picturing her grief-stricken brother weeping into a handwritten cookbook.

❖

Ingredients

2 x carrot

½ Butternut pumpkin, approx. 400g

1 large brown onion

A couple stalks of celery, equiv 1 cup.

4L salt reduced chicken stock. If you can't get salt reduced, that's ok. Just don't season with too much salt.

½ cup medium grain rice.

500g chicken mince

½ cup fresh breadcrumbs

1 x egg

3 x cloves garlic, minced

Dried thyme

Ground nutmeg

Butter and oil

Salt and Pepper to taste

Method
1. Combine mince, egg, breadcrumbs and 1 x clove minced garlic. Season with salt, pepper, thyme and nutmeg to taste. Mix it with a fork to keep the mixture light and aerated.
2. Roll mixture into small meatballs. Should yield at least 30. About a heaped teaspoon each. Keep a bowl of water nearby so you can rinse your hands. The mince won't stick to wet hands as much. Leave in the fridge to set.
3. Sautee diced carrot, pumpkin, onion and celery in butter. Any amount of butter is fine, oil will do in a pinch. Use the big pot with 2 handles, on the biggest burner. Keep the temperature pretty low and BE PATIENT!
4. When the onions are translucent and pumpkin is soft, add the remaining garlic and deglaze the pan with a bit of stock. Make sure you get all the good flavour up from the pan before adding the rest of the stock.
5. Bring to the boil and add in the meatballs. It's best to kind of ladle them in a few at a time. Stirring gently between adding them.
6. Add water if needed to top up the pot. Season with salt, pepper, thyme and nutmeg. You have to keep tasting it and adjusting. If you season too much in the beginning it will be overpowering, but you don't want it to be flavourless either.

7. Leave to simmer, with the lid on for 20 minutes. Stirring and tasting occasionally.

8. Add ½ cup of rice and leave to simmer for a further 20 minutes. It's done when the rice is cooked and the soup tastes like a roast dinner.

Lucia tried to think of everything she could to add into the recipes so that Win would be able to replicate her cooking. She mostly followed her nose, literally and figuratively, when cooking. It was hard to get it all down, especially with her mind going a mile a minute and poor Kathryn scrambling to catch up.

Page after page of one of the many notebooks Lucia kept around the house was filled with recipes. Dishes that Win loved, recipes that had sprouted from Lucia's imagination. Lucia was sure to be as detailed as she possibly could be.

"Make sure he knows if he's making his own nước chấm to use more fish sauce than he thinks he needs. But it's probably better to buy the one from Woollies and add a little more fish sauce to that."

"I do that!"

"I know you taught me. He's hopeless, and fussy. Remind him."

She moved around the kitchen, re-enacting the cooking so that nothing was missed. She detailed exactly what to look for when picking produce, trying her best to describe the exact amount of give is ideal for stone fruits and how heavy a lemon is if it's laden with juice. She listed appropriate substitutions and what amendments should be made to the recipe if those substitutions are made. The texture, taste and smell of every step.

Kathryn knew her brother couldn't cook and when he ever attempted it, he clung to the recipe for dear life. She knew why Lucia was being so detailed, it was practical, but it also seemed like a farewell. It reminded Kathryn of that story, she couldn't remember what movie it was, maybe it was multiple movies. A mother is diagnosed with cancer and spends her last days preparing letters for the people she'll leave behind. Her writing was getting messier and messier and Kathryn wished she had had the forethought to take Lucia's dictation down on her laptop. She pushed through the pain in her hands and neck and relayed every single detail to the page.

They were done when Lucia couldn't think of anything else that Win enjoyed eating. She had dictated even things he never in a million years would attempt to cook, but it was better safe than sorry.

Lucia's epic farewell letter, in the form of a full-blown recipe book, hit Kathryn hard. She had somehow thought this whole time that Lucia would get better. She knew she wouldn't, that she was dead, but it didn't feel like that would always be the case. She was still stuck in the denial phase of grief. Win moving into her house, felt more like a rocky time in their relationship and everything would work out, but she was now coming to terms with the idea that wasn't the truth. Her best friend was dead, her brother a widower, and nothing would ever be the same.

"I have to tell you something."

"Ok?" Concern drew across Lucia's face.

"Gianna's pregnant."

"Oh my God Kathryn! That's such good news, I'm so happy for you." Lucia reached out to hug her friend but stopped when her hands glided past Kathryn's shoulders. Kathryn's elation dipped into an awkward silence before she shuffled away, only slightly and resumed her happiness.

"Thank you."

"When did you find out?" Lucia tried to put it behind her, an awkwardness she hadn't felt with Kathryn in decades.

"Last night. Gianna took a test when she came off shift." She was beaming.

Lucia did some quick maths in her head. "January due date?"

"Beginning of Feb."

"Oooh , what if we have the same birthday? Matching birthdays with my favourite niece or nephew."

It was awkward again. A weirdness in the air, an unsureness about what would happen to Lucia during the next thirty-eight weeks.

"Haha, should I tell Henry and Ava that?"

"Oh come on, as if they don't know your kids will be the best." She smiled as Kathryn dipped her gaze. "Congratulations, also give Gianna a big hug from me. You're going to be such great Mums."

"Thank you." Kathryn drew in a quick breath and pushed the heels of her palms into her thighs. "So how can I help?"

"You just did. A ton. You've been writing for hours!"

"No, I want to help find out what happened to you. Win said you're investigating it yourself. I want in."

26

Between the cubicles and the break room was a wide, baron hallway. There were three doors, two on the right and one straight ahead. The first door on the right was a server room, it hummed, and both a faint blue light and blast of cold air hit the ankles of passers-by from beneath the door.

The second door was a storage room; it housed stationery, disused computers and accessories, precariously stacked office furniture, a first aid kit and most notably of all, gossip. The breakroom, which was accessed through the third door, held its fair share of gossip too. Usually the more innocuous kind that if it got out wouldn't really matter. The storage room was for the *real* gossip.

One employee would only have to send a discreet email expressing their desire for new pens, post it notes or a fresh notebook, then they and the recipient of the email would rendezvous in the storeroom to discuss. To the best of Win's knowledge, none of the storage room rendezvous were conjugal in nature, but if they were and if anyone knew about it, gossiping about it would also have taken place in the storage room. It housed just as many secrets as it did loose rubber bands.

Win was on his way from his desk to the break room when he heard his own name coming from behind the door. He was the only Samuel to work in that department and definitely the only one that anyone would suspect was having marriage trouble. He had half a mind to pull open the door and tell whoever was on the other side that they were correct. He and his wife had separated and he was living in his little sister's spare room, sharing his bed with the cat. He stopped himself because he didn't think he'd be able to stop at just that. He might word vomit the whole thing or accidently say that actually his wife had died. Either way there would be inevitable follow up questions, and he couldn't handle it. He had paused too long outside the door and the voices from inside hushed before continuing a louder than needed conversation about stationery.

Win was relieved when Sanjay was sitting at a table in the breakroom. He and two other colleagues, Leonie and Hunter, were seated with him. They all had half eaten Guzman Y Gomez and half a dozen beige napkins and empty sauce cups littered the table.

Sanjay called out, even though there was no one else in the room for him to shout over. "Win, over here. We would have got you some but I figured you'd brought your own."

"Ahh yeah, I did, just a minute."

Win retrieved a frozen meal from the overstuffed freezer. Creamy, tuna bake, scraping the bottom of the barrel. He wouldn't normally commit the most heinous of the office space crimes by bringing in anything fish, but he didn't have a choice. He sat while the microwave whirred.

"Mate, we were just talking about the craziest shit. Tell him Lee!" Sanjay had a knack, whether welcome or not, for giving everyone a nickname. Win didn't think he had ever heard him call a single person by their real name. This "crazy shit" story was a welcome distraction though. Leonie launched into her story about a bunch of suspicious life insurance claims that one of her friends had been investigating. The life insurance people were, apparently, all a buzz with some eerie similarities in cases coming across their desks.

"What kind of cases?" For the first time in his life Win hoped for a suicide epidemic, or a serial killer.

"They're all missing their organs. Not like a serial killer; like a wild animal attack or something. Fucking bears in Brisbane!"

"Bears? Really?" Hunter was cynical, anyone would be. Win shifted uneasily. No not bears. He thought he was going to be sick, again, but just in time the microwave beeped and the feeling subsided.

The rest of the lunch Sanjay, Leonie and Hunter postulated different theories about whatever was killing people in Brisbane. Win focused on keeping his lunch down. He wasn't ignoring them. In fact, he was doing the opposite, he was committing everything he could to memory. Win didn't know the exact details of where Lucia and Lu had hidden their body. He did know who it was though. From what he gleaned most of these reported attacks happened randomly. Apart from the manner in which they were found, the victims seemed to have all disappeared off the streets. Homeless or people walking home alone. They were all over the city and there didn't seem to be an effort to hide the bodies.

The conversation turned to something else. Now Win wasn't paying attention. He excused himself and went back to his desk, throwing his half-finished tuna in the bin. Another office crime.

He started to search for reports online. Scrolling through headlines.

3 dead in horrific car crash.

"Friendly" dog attacks toddler in New Farm Park.

12 people that vanished from Brisbane 2018.

Bodies found mauled.

The list was depressing. You would hope that mauled bodies would be easy to find, that it would be a leading news story, but there was just so much death.

Win's eyes darted across the list of people found. None were on the list he had provided to Lucia.

Work allowed its employees to decorate their cubicles with no more than five photos or objects, so long as nothing on the desk was offensive or too distracting. It used to be that only offensive images would be banned, for obvious reasons. They added the "not too distracting" rule when Scott Pastors added a desk ten pin bowling game to his desk and for two days all that could be heard from every corner of the office was him hurtling the large marble across his desk, causing the pins to clang and fly off everywhere.

Win had mostly photos tacked to the partition at the left of his monitor. There was a pop vinyl figurine of Storm from the X-Men centred under his monitor. The photos he had up were a photo of Crumb lazing in a shaft of sunlight, a candid photo of Win and Lucia at Kathryn and Gianna's wedding. Lucia's head rested on Win's shoulder as they embraced, not so much slow dancing as exhaustedly leaning in the most romantic way. Win remembered that he never did get Lucia's makeup off his dress shirt. They were both part of the wedding party and by the time the reception was winding down they were both beat. The last photo was of Lucia on their own wedding day. They had been taking their solo photos and Win was behind the photographer, he said something that tickled Lucia in just the right way because her mouth dropped wide in a hearty laugh and her nose scrunched right up. Lucia hated the photo but Win adored it.

Win's desk painted a picture of a blissfully happy married man. Win decided that the photos now were too distracting and he pulled the tacks holding them up and slipped the photos into his top drawer. He would deal with them later, not throw them out, just move them to somewhere where they could be forgotten. He moved the photo of Crumb along so it didn't look so out of place. Now he was just a dude with a cat and a thing for Halle Berry.

27

Neighbours notice things. It's a trope of the nosy neighbour, peeking through their blinds and being suspicious all the time. Everyone's guilty of it though. Say what you will, Gladys Kravitz had every right to be suspicious of the goings on in Samantha and Darren Stephens house. She was portrayed as meddling and a thorn in their side but if Samantha hadn't been a friendly witch, if she was a murderer, or Darren was beating her, Mrs Kravitz would be a witness to that. It's either a benefit or a curse that in 2018, people still peek out from behind their curtains at anything out of place in their neighbourhood, but very few ever do anything about it.

This is why Ruth's front door lay wide open for four days before any of the neighbours thought to report it. The same navy sedan sat in the driveway and people noticed, but assumed it was none of their business. Surely, they all had seen when Ruth had died, there was quite the kerfuffle in the street. Maybe some had even noticed when she came back. Saw glimpses of a naked old woman through the windows, maybe they even heard her shuffling around in there. Piecing together from what they had learned from the comfort of their own homes, any sighting of Ruth after she died was probably met with the assumption that they had heard wrong and she hadn't died. That was logical after all.

Harriette O'Connor who lived across the road from Ruth was eventually the first person to notify the police that something strange was going on. She worked full time and had noticed the open door and the same unfamiliar car both before and after work each day. On the fourth day she was actively looking to see if the house remained open. She had not seen Lucia or Lu arrive and shortly after that Lucia, Lu and Ruth all leave on foot wheeling a heavy suitcase. That all occurred in the hours she was at work.

On that fourth day something took a hold of her. A bravery she hadn't possessed the preceding days, or an intrigue so great that it overrode any boundaries, be they tangible or not. She parked her car in her driveway where she always parked it, but instead of making her usual route, car-mailbox-front door, she walked over the road.

Harriette felt a nervous heat rise from her stomach into her cheeks. She felt now, more than she ever had that she was being watched. Later she would tell herself that the thing that kept her going was the thought that she was doing the right thing by an elderly neighbour. If she was honest with herself, it was the thrill that drove one foot in front of the other.

She brushed past the Audi in Ruth's driveway. Careful not to touch it but getting so close that her breath steamed on the back-passenger window, negating any effort to not contaminate a potential crime scene. Nothing in the car was anything she couldn't see from the road or her front room. The smell hit her before she even reached the front door. Like the slope down the lawn to Ruth's front door had kept the rotting stench in a little valley. At first Harriette couldn't quite place the smell. She knew it wasn't good though. It smelled like rot, but also something else.

"Hello? Anyone home?" she waited. "It's your neighbour Harriette." Her voice breaking, but she tried to sound firm. "Is everything ok?"

At this point Harriette O'Connor thought for sure she was going to venture into the house and find the decaying corpse of her elderly neighbour. A neighbour who only a short time earlier was brought back from the brink of death. A little zap of excitement sprang to her chest. She let her mind wander into accolades from her colleagues and the police for finding the body. Harriette O'Connor had never even seen a dead body before, let alone one that had been rotting for days. She didn't even think about how damaging that might be. She was just excited to be a part of a story. To have something interesting about herself to tell people.

- 192 -

She walked now with even less hesitation than she had crossing the road. She walked straight ahead, checking the kitchen first. The excitement kept building, looking at the house and someone else's things. She followed the wall cabinet separating the dining and living spaces from each other, into the small oddly shaped hall. The smell was worse now and only when she looked into the old woman's bedroom did Harriette place it. Blood. Lots of old blood.

She hadn't expected that. Trembling she lifted the phone in her hand. Her sweat left little puddles on her Tinkerbelle case. The phone slipped from her hand and bounced top to tail on the carpet, finally landing just inside the bedroom door. Harriette let out a strained squeal. She was not as brave, or interesting or unique as she had thought. She had always entertained the idea that in a crisis she would be cool, calm and collected. She held that opinion of herself even though Harriette O'Connor had never been in a crisis.

She crouched to her knees and reached forward to her phone, keeping her body as far out of the room as possible. Tossing her head back so her shoulders could get closer to the blood, but her head wouldn't, or at least she couldn't see it. She grasped the phone and reeled back doing a backwards crab walk out of the hall that was neither calm nor graceful. Her legs kicked from under her and she phoned 000.

Once out of the house, she regained her composure and her sense of self-importance started to rise again. She was a little put out that there had been no body to bolster her retelling of this story.

28

The train coasted down the Ferny Grove line, commuters lining the carriages bobbed and swayed along with it. Most had their noses buried in phones, some in books, others closed their eyes trying to catch a sliver of sleep before work and a very small number of them chatted. James Clayborne was one of the latter. He stood, while his girlfriend of four years, Andrea Nichols sat on an aisle seat. It was Andrea that he was talking to, or talking at. She seemed to be rapt by his monologue in which he used a lot of words to say nothing at all. The woman next to Andrea was less impressed by James holding court on the 6:30am train.

When other people got on or off at each stop, James leaned forward, thrusting his crotch into his girlfriend's face. His light grey trousers strained against a poorly concealed member, not erect, just stuffed into the skin-tight pants. Andrea blushed each time, making doe eyes at James and let out a little purr through glossy lips. This was likely the desired effect that he had in mind when dressing himself that morning. The lady on the window seat rolled her eyes and shifted uncomfortably, every few stops she even went far enough as to mumble under her breath.

His matching suit jacket was also a couple sizes too small, he thought it showed off his muscles but he just looked stupid. James pulled a phone from his brown, leather satchel, his pants too tight for it to fit in his back pocket. He thrust it to his ear where the screen was sure to come away slick with hair product, no doubt something expensive.

"Hey mate." His voice bounced around the carriage. Commuters who had been successfully ignoring him, now couldn't and several shot him scathing looks. He didn't notice.

"Yeah, yeah, yeah. I can get that proposal to you later today."

No one would have been surprised if there was no one on the other end of the line. Or if it was real, he could have waited until he was in the office, but the pageantry of talking loudly on the phone in a crowded carriage was too appealing. He wanted everyone to know he was better than them, not realising that he was proving himself wrong. Even with Andrea right there he made eyes at other women. Winking over her shoulder. He wasn't sly, she probably knew.

Andrea was a great contrast to him. Always neat and well put together. When she sat, she perched with her knees together, bag in her lap. She was small, brown hair curled around her shoulders in a glossy cascade. Her features were dark and her eyes looked kind. She spoke quietly. She deserved better, but those kind eyes looked at him with nothing but adoration. Every douchy move he made she seemed to love him all the more for it.

He stretched out his lumpy arm to lift her chin to him. Swooping down and planting an overzealous kiss on her compliant lips. The woman next to him shifted, heaving her whole body towards the window and turning herself as far away as the seat would allow. She caught the eye of the man behind them who offered a look of sympathy and judgment all in one.

The train pulled into Central station and all the remaining passengers surged to the doors. James let Andrea ahead of him, wrapping his colossal fists around her waist. The woman beside her let out a sigh and looked bemusedly at a few of her fellow commuters.

James ducked through the train doors, implying a belief in a height that he definitely did not possess. He pulled Andrea in close to him and enacted another inappropriately long and passionate display, this time almost purposefully in the way of others. So they not only had to witness it but were inconvenienced by it. A middle-aged man, also wearing a grey suit but not one as flashy or new as James brushed behind them. As he did he pressed a needle into James' right glute. The pants were stretched so tightly that for a moment the man thought they would burst like a water balloon when the tip of the needle pricked in. A little jab and it was done. James let out a series of expletives and whirled around to catch whoever touched him, but when he turned all he saw was a sea of people crossing which way and the other. He didn't have a clue who was the culprit.

James bid Andrea farewell with another drawn out kiss then headed to a coffee shop on Adelaide St. He flirted with the barista. She was laughing politely, not out of genuine attraction. Collecting his coffee, he brushed her hand, it was intentional. The barista wasn't amused. He took another call. His arrogance wafting on the breeze behind him, every word lined with machismo and insincerity. By the time James reached his office building a strong pain was creeping up his shoulders and into his skull, his phone call was over and very soon so would be his life.

29

The lengths between Lu's feedings were getting shorter. Her decay was quickening and the effect of the meals was getting weaker. The mat that Win had laid down for her was already sodden with seeping bodily fluids. Lu's skin was both wet and dried out. Where skin had peeled up or outer epidermal layers had sloughed off they had become hard and yellowed. Like the jagged and neglected cuticles over her body. There were no bugs, yet. Lucia was grateful for that small mercy. It might have been too cold or the mothballs they'd laced her with were working. Lucia idly thought if they could somehow embalm her.

How many organs do Zombies need? Embalming Lu would be the final nail in the coffin so to speak. It would mean she had no hope that one day Lucia would wake up and suddenly be inside her own body again and alive. That could hardly happen if the organs were removed. Embalming is also difficult to pull off discreetly. By comparison maybe not as difficult as murdering people though. Lucia didn't know how to embalm someone. That's not covered in nursing. She had seen dead bodies. Medical cadavers are all embalmed. They can be kept by the university for years before they've worn out their usefulness. Lucia could still feel the formaldehyde in her nose. It wasn't the worst smell, cloying and astringent, but only as much as any strong chemical odour is. Nothing like some of the other things she'd smelled in her education and career in health. Those cadavers had ruined a lot of perfumes for Lucia though. Chanel IV and that Britney Spears perfume that every teenage girl was wearing in 2008. They smelled like death to Lucia. It's not polite to tell friends, "Sorry, your perfume reminds me of dead bodies." She was sure she wasn't the only one who made the olfactory connection. She had mentioned it in passing at a party once. An older guy, one of those guys that seemed to remain genuinely cool into middle age, equally at home reading story books to kids and rioting in Brixton sometime in the 80s. He seemed to know what she was on about.

The smell wasn't an issue for Lucia now. She was certain Lu in her current state smelled worse than any formaldehyde. If Lu was embalmed, she at least knew how to cover the smell. Better people think, "Woof, go easy on the perfume!" than "That's a fucking zombie."

She knew it was cold though because in the early morning she could see the breath of joggers puffing their way down the street. Some mornings there was a thick fog that nestled into the neighbourhood at around 4am. From her elevated position in the bedroom she could see over most of the fog, less like floating on the cloud and more like Silent Hill. Normally at times like these the bedroom windows would fog up. The heat from Lucia and Win existing together in the house. "Fog at seven, fine by eleven" Lucia chanted compulsively in her head every time without fail. The voice in her head was a mixture of her and her mother's. It was usually fine by ten, even earlier some days. When it did clear up, the sky was blue and the sun beat down on the asphalt the same as any other Brisbane day. While winter days are clearer than summer ones, it still looked hot. Lucia might not notice when it really was heating up. It would soon enough and in a few months' time they would be back in 30-degree days. Lu wouldn't last long then. With any luck, August would bring the westerlies and the dry air would do its part to mummify her body. With any more luck, everything would be back to normal by then.

There was a tiny skerrick of Liam/Leon left in the freezer. Thigh, rump, something that had been large. Lu seemed to prefer eating from the head down. Neck, organs, and then when she had to eat actual fresh she went upper torso, arms, abdomen and finally legs. Was that some kind of instinct thing? Don't snakes do the same thing? Eat from the head down, to make sure their prey doesn't crawl out or fight back or something. Ruth favoured the organs too, but then there didn't seem to be any real order. Ruth ate fingers and toes, practically gulped them down like horse pills. Lu wouldn't touch them. Maybe it was personal preference after all. Lucia knew if she was a zombie she wouldn't want to eat the fingers and toes.

She didn't have to hypothesise really. She actually did know. At that time Lucia would have preferred to have to swallow a toe than to swallow the fact that she was actually relating to her corpse.

Liam/Leon's remains were freezer burnt. This particular piece of him had been pulled in and out of the freezer several times. Kathryn had removed most things from the freezer and taken them home. There were some of Win's favourites in there. All that was left was a few stray peas, an embarrassing amount of dirt, half a pack of fish fingers and a bunch of frozen people meat. It was easier not to try and pack the meat up. Easier access and while very incriminating if someone opened the freezer, less evidence in the rest of the house. A layer of tiny ice crystals covered what had been Liam's thigh. The outer part, there was a large mole, some freckles and a couple of keloid scars.

Lu knew the drill. She could have taken herself to the freezer whenever she was hungry, but she seemed to be bound by some sense of formality about the whole thing. When Lucia told her to go eat, she knew what to do. She knew where it was. She even dutifully gnawed her meal over the sink. Lu didn't quite have the dexterity to turn the tap to wash any meat and blood away. The kitchen sink was visible from the footpath, all anyone had to do was look up and they would see straight through the kitchen window and see a woman hunched over a lump of raw meat. Lucia only remembered this when she looked out the window while Lu was munching a shoulder blade. She swore she made eye contact with a man walking his dog. Now when Lu was eating she stood herself in front of the window to block the view. It felt like teenage girls getting changed at the beach and their friends using their bodies to shield her from prying eyes. Not that Lucia spent any time at the beach as a teenager, but she had the occasion to be both the shieldee and shielder in similar circumstances. This small act made her feel closer to Lu. A small act of sisterhood, despite it being more a move of self-preservation than anything. She did love Lu, somehow. In a way she was not familiar with. Nothing like family, pets or children. Not even like self-love, even though she felt more compassion towards Lu than she ever did towards herself, more hatred and resentment too, but it balanced.

30

Two police cars pulled up on Ruth's street. Harriette went out to greet them. She knew they were there because of her call and she puffed herself up with pride over the situation.

"Finally!" Harriette had been watching the street from her front window. Still wearing her work clothes. The police had shown up quickly, but Harriette wasn't impressed. She rushed down the path from her front door into the street, getting in the way of a second police car that was pulling up.

"Hello officer." She stopped to glare at the other police car as it pulled about her before continuing straight up to the man on the other side of the road.

Constable Andrew Clarke turned to her. He'd seen this before. People that make a big show of reporting a crime, they're the ones to watch out for. He knew straight away that whatever had happened in that house this woman was going to get to him more.

"I take it you called this in?"

"Yes, Harriette O'Connor. I live just here."

"Ok Ms O'Connor, why don't you tell me what you saw while my colleagues take a little look."

Three other police officers made their way across the front lawn of Ruth's house. One, a woman, her red hair pulled into a low bun circled the outside of the car in the driveway. Two other male police officers made for the front door. Harriette was a bit distracted by them, she couldn't peel her eyes away. Waiting to see their reactions. Hoping they would crumble like she did. Waiting for someone to tell her she was right to venture into that house, brave even.

Constable Clarke noticed and shifted her over so her back was partially turned from the house and she had to look at him. Harriette remembered the question.

"We all thought she died. The old lady that lived there. Not now, a while ago."

"How long ago?"

"A few weeks maybe? It was early in the morning, before I'd gone to work. I watched them take her out on a stretcher. But she came back after that."

"So she didn't die?"

"Well no, because she came back." Her tone was downright condescending on this point.

Clarke shifted from one foot to the other. Gathering himself before proceeding.

"So we're looking for an elderly lady? Do you know her name?"

"No. Yes an old lady, no I don't know her. I think she had children but I never saw them. I thought that was her kids. Then the car just stayed."

"How long has the car been there?"

"A few days. Four days? The door has been open too. I didn't want to go over. Didn't want to intrude but then I thought. If I don't, who will? Right?"

"I understand Ms O'Connor, it's a good thing we know." He knew she was seeking his approval. "Why take four days to report?"

"I'd made my mind up that I was going to, as I said, if I didn't, who would? An old lady alone, anything could have happened."

"Right, so you went in the house with concern for your neighbour?"

"Yes."

"And can you tell me what you saw?"

"The house was normal, I guess. Looks like the car was filled with things from inside." Clarke nodded. "It smelled bad, so I thought she might have been in the bedroom. Her body." She whispered those two words for emphasis. "I didn't think it'd be like that though."

"The bedroom?"

"Yes, covered in blood. I've never seen that much. A massacre."

"Did you touch anything in the house?"

"No, I was careful not to."

"Thank you, Ms O'Connor. If you think of anything else, give the station a call."

Andrew Clarke held out his hand for a handshake and Harriette gave it a firm shake, as though she was running through a 'how to' manual in her head, but her palms were beaded in sweat. Constable Clarke waited until her back was turned to rub the transferred sweat onto his right pant leg.

"Clarke. You're gonna wanna see this." The big bulking officer called from the doorway just as Andrew Clarke stepped up onto the footpath.

The house was empty. Missing things, but still neat.

"Witness reckons the car belongs to the owner's kid. Still could be burglary. Think we're looking at a robbery gone wrong? Old lady caught them?"

"Not likely, owner of the house was already deceased. 3 weeks earlier. Cardiac arrest." The ginger cop called from the hallway entrance.

"Hold on Meadows, I've got a witness telling me she wasn't dead."

"No boss, she definitely died. Not her crime scene." She tilted her head back towards the bedroom.

Andrew Clarke brushed past her and into the bedroom where the third police officer was crouched. There was blood everywhere. It seeped into the carpet and splashed up onto the old lady ruffled valance.

"Oh shit Tran, get outta there, Seal it off. Fucking hell."

- 206 -

31

It took less than a day for Sanjay to notice the missing photos from Win's desk. He was brash but observant, which made him good at his job. If Sanjay wasn't actually a good guy at the heart of it, Win would not be his friend, his real friend, not just a work friend. Sanjay swung his chair around the divider of their desks and assumed the manly pep-talk position. If they didn't have broad office chairs with armrests, he would definitely have sat cross armed and backwards on the chair. Instead, he spread his knees wide, leaned forward to rest his forearms on them and clasped his hands together.

"Ok mate."

Win slumped his shoulders forward and head back, like his upper body was sighing without bothering to get his mouth involved.

"What is it Sanjay?" He had an idea what it was, but it could honestly have been anything. A sincere pitch for a paintballing weekend, a story about his last date (Win probably would have heard that one already) or, unlikely, but it could have been work related.

"What's going down?"

"With what Sanjay?" Win scraping every skerrick of impatience out with his words.

"You're acting weird. You took down your photos. Dude, you can tell me." He was sincere and trying to convey it as best he could.

Win sucked in a big breath, before turning his chair to almost face Sanjay. He looked him in the eye for the first bit, he knew he wouldn't be able to muster the courage to look him in the face for any follow up questions.

"I moved out."

"Nah" Sanjay knew something was up but he thought it was a joke. Win and Lucia were "goals" and he couldn't think of a couple more suited to each other. They weren't showy about their love. Not the kind of couple to finish each other's sentences or make big sweeping romantic gestures for the benefit of other people. Nor were they private about their love. He'd hung at their house plenty of times. He noticed things, as Sanjay was prone to. How they always touched each other as they walked past one another, not in a gross way, just like a little silent, "I love you." He had, on more than one occasion, caught each of them quietly telling the other that they love them. They said thank you, constantly. Like no gesture, no matter how small was taken for granted. They bantered, little jibes, but they were never mean and knew their limits.

Win almost never complained about Lucia, if they had an argument it was always resolved by the time Sanjay heard about it. They talked about everything and held nothing back. So it was ludicrous to Sanjay that they would separate.

"I thought you guys were a 'til death kinda deal man. What happened?"

Win fought back tears, he didn't want to cry at work. Though maybe if he cried, he wouldn't have to answer any more questions.

"Irreconcilable differences."

"Dude no, you gotta give me more than that. How long have you been fighting?"

"We weren't fighting, it just got weird ok?"

Sanjay could see Win barely holding it together now and even though the photos had been taken down, Win was still wearing his wedding ring.

"Where are you living?"

"I moved in with Kathryn."

"Ok, cool man. Is there anything I can do?"

He placed his hand on Win's back, kind of patting and kind of rubbing. This kind of gesture is usually for the benefit of the comforter and doesn't do much for the comfortee, Sanjay knew that.

"No, I'll be fine."

"Come on man. Let's go to paintball on the weekend!" Win spit out a sudden cackle. "What?"

"I knew you were gonna bring paintball up somehow."

"Bro, bonding? and you get to shoot things. Eh?"

"I'll think about it." Sanjay was already rolling himself back around to his side of the desk.

"I heard a yes." All Win could see of him now was a wagging finger over the partition between them. "I'm booking it!"

❖

Kathryn had dressed herself head to toe in black, in an unconscious effort to look more stealth. It didn't work. She looked like someone wearing all black, not someone incognito. Lucia watched a YouTube video by someone in the CIA that said spies pretty much wear business attire, charcoal suits, white button downs; men wear plain, non-flashy ties, she guessed that women wore the same just no tie. It's the same as ninjas, real ninjas didn't really wear black. They dressed like the working class.

In suburban Brisbane an Asian woman wearing an all-black ensemble wouldn't attract much attention at all. She could have worn jeans and a blue t-shirt without garnering attention. Heck if they were only heading to the Woolworths she could wear a tracksuit and no shoes and still no one would bat an eyelid. Lucia noticed though, because Kathryn must have thrown together all the black items she had, or more likely raided Gianna's wardrobe. Gianna was taller than Kathryn by a long shot, 6 inches maybe, they were similar sizes though. Kathryn cornered the petite market and Gianna had lanky covered. Gianna wore more form fitting clothes, as opposed to Kathryn's trademark tent-like, voluminous style. Lucia could actually see Kathryn's shape, something she only usually witnessed in a swimming pool.

"I'm ready!"

"I can see that." Lucia chuckled.

Not embarrassed, more indignant, "I don't own any black."

"Yeah, but why did you need to wear black?"

"To *feel* more like a spy."

"Sure ok, you look good."

"Thank you." Kathryn stepped in and shut the door behind her. The glaring morning light had been bouncing off the house next door and straight through the front door. The absence of the sun after the door closed was more startling than the glare had been. Kathryn and Lucia had to wait for their eyes to adjust before proceeding.

"Ok, what do we need to do today?"

Kathryn had the same energy as that one friend in every group that pumped to do something that everyone else had to be bribed to do. Moving houses, yard work, stuff like that. Kathryn never showed that exuberance for actually moving house. Lucia was learning that the everyday person was excited to play spy if the situation called for it.

"Before we go anywhere, can you help me with something?"

"Of course."

"I need my phone."

One hassle of being dead is that Lucia didn't have her phone. She was cut off from everything without it. This whole time her phone had been sitting on the bedside table, where she put it when she came home from Ruth's that day. She hadn't plugged it in because she still had 60% battery, that and she was, quite literally dying. It ran out of battery, or Win turned it off. She wasn't sure.

She didn't have any voice recognition set up on her phone. Lucia always thought anyone who wasn't impaired in any way that spoke to their phone was a bit of a douche. Now she saw the benefit, but now she was impaired, in a big way.

A green pulsating battery showed on the screen when Kathryn plugged it in. It would take a little while to charge enough for them to be able successfully do anything of use with the phone.

"Coffee?" Lucia asked as if she was making herself one and wanted to know if Kathryn would partake, rather than the plain suggestion that it actually was.

"Yeah. Do you miss coffee?"

"Yes." she didn't have to think about it. "I miss all of it. If I could smell it I think I would miss it more though."

"You can't smell?" Of all the reveals that had happened, this is the one Kathryn seemed the most shocked by. More so that when she learned Lucia was dead, or when she found out about the body in the freezer.

"I guess in some ways that's a good thing." Kathryn gestured towards Lu, who had decided to join them. Lu seemed to have warm feelings for Kathryn, maybe some kind of remnant memory. Lucia didn't know how much of her memories were knocking around in Lu's brain, if at all. In all honesty, she had never stopped to think about it. If she allowed herself to think that Lu could remember her life, that would be allowing herself to think that Lu was the real her, and she was just a shell. Maybe an echo.

"Oh no! Is it that bad?"

"Oh nah, it's not too bad. I've smelled worse on the bus." she laughed at her own joke. "It's not great though."

"Can you stuff more moth balls in her pockets. Or we could give her a shower?"

"I don't think I'm ready for that to be honest."

That was the last of the moth balls. They would need more soon, or some other way of disguising the smell of decay. Lucia might have to revisit the embalming idea. She was pretty sure that formaldehyde was on some kind of register though.

Kathryn rested against the kitchen bench, holding her empty coffee cup. The same bouncing sunlight that had streamed through the front door, was coming through the open kitchen window. It warmed Kathryn's back and her front was still cold, causing goosebumps to prickle up her arms.

"What is it?" Lucia questioned, noticing Kathryn subconsciously rubbing her arms.

"Oh, just the difference in temperature."

"Oh." Another thing Lucia missed, temperature. She didn't say any more, but her face told Kathryn all she needed to know.

Trying to change the topic, "Your phone is probably charged now."

Within seconds of Lucia's phone being turned on, it practically buzzed off the table with all the notifications. 27 missed calls, 48 text or WhatsApp messages and literally countless app pop ups.

"I guess we should go through these."

"Right"

"Half of these are from me. So that's easy."

Kathryn thumbed through the messages. Most of the WhatsApp messages were from group chats and no one had noticed Lucia's lack of response.

There were messages between Lucia's sister Ava and her mother, a conversation she would usually be a part of. The conversation was dominated by Ava asking Evelyn for advice on this and that. None of it was cooking related, so it wasn't out of the question that Lucia hadn't replied.

There was also a thread of Evelyn telling them that she and Ryan were off to their anniversary dinner and some subsequent poorly lit and poorly framed photos of what looked to be a seafood pasta, a pork loin and a slice of something chocolatey. Ryan Hughes was in the background of most of these shots and when Kathryn showed the photos to Lucia, she could see that by dessert both of her parents had switched to scotch over the white wine they had been drinking. When she saw them she also got a pang of guilt. Guilt that she had not wished them a happy anniversary and that so far her parents had no clue that their daughter had been dead for weeks.

Guilt was pushed back by the feelings of sorrow that she would never hug either of her parents again, nor would she eat with them at the family table.

"There's a Facebook message from someone called Rachael Connors?"

"Nah, fuck her, it's 100% going to be some MLM bullshit. Don't even open it."

"Ok sure." Kathryn kept scrolling through the phone. "There's a bunch of messages from me, and Gianna. Calls too. Calls from Tanvi"

"My boss. She came and saw me though."

"Wait what? That's pretty big."

"Only saw me, she doesn't know."

"She knows something though. Chasing up Win and Gianna? Did you know about that?"

"Fuck, I knew about Win. She called him. Not about Gianna. What?"

- 214 -

"Talked to her in the supermarket. They both lied...different stories though. AND she came to you? Fuck Lucia. I think she's on to something."

"She did send the police."

"What the fuck Lucia!"

"It's fine. Trust me. They believed I was fine."

Kathryn furrowed her brow at Lucia, then a moment later even deeper while looking at the phone.

"What is it?"

"There's a message from Win."

"Yeah?"

Kathryn paused and looked at Lucia. She didn't want to read it. It was an innocuous text, one that Lucia wouldn't normally think much of. Kathryn held her breath, without realising it until she had to read it. She read over the words a few times before starting.

"Hey babe, just getting the bus now. Hope your day improved. Big hugs when I get home. Love you."

The text hit Lucia hard and it felt like every single thing that had happened to her was happening all over again and all at once. She got up and walked away without saying anything. Kathryn didn't follow, not yet. She would, soon, but for now she knew her friend needed to be alone.

Lucia curled herself into a little ball. There was no comfort in it because she couldn't feel her own arms wrapping around her. It was pure intuition at that point. It did help to bury her head in her knees, because then she couldn't see. She was blocked off from the world. She waited and wished for the feeling of hot tears streaming down her face. Wanted so badly for there to be some kind of release, any release, and for the feelings to not get caught up inside of her, so she screamed. Less of the scream more of a wail. Lucia didn't know she could make that noise. She certainly never had before. She had only seen it on TV when people learned of someone's death. She wailed until there was nothing left and the initial sting had subsided.

❖

With each swish of his spoon through the soup, little layers of soup attached themselves to the base of the handle and hardened there, just enough to stay put. Even the smell as it wafted up and encircled Win's face in plumes of beefy mist, made his stomach turn. Stomach acid gurgled up his throat and coated his tongue, making the food taste awful, similar to drinking orange juice after brushing your teeth. When his stomach wasn't flipping on itself, it felt hollow. A nauseous emptiness wound its way from the pit of his stomach up into his jaw and rested there, behind his tongue like a sentinel guarding his gullet.

Crumb sat below Win's feet, watching eagerly and awaiting food to be passed down to him under the table. He eyed Win shifting his weight forward with every movement ready to jump up and accept any donation. Crumb did this routinely despite never being fed food from either Lucia or Win's plates and surely Crumb also possessed the knowledge that human food did not sit well with him. Any time he has managed to finagle some people food, it resulted in lethargy, if lethargy was something noticeably different in cats and painful, frequent trips to the kitty litter. Each time Crumb lurched forward, Butterbean lifted his head and propped himself up, ready to also partake but not willing to do any of the begging, after all he did not fit as comfortably under the dinner table.

In all of her twenty-nine years, Kathryn had never seen her brother avoid food like he had since he moved into her home. Win usually exuberantly scoffed down plates of food, any food. With the exceptions of some very badly cooked or spoiled food, he'd never met a dish he didn't love. He ate from fine dining restaurants with the same joy and enthusiasm as he ate from frozen meat pies.

At first she took offense, she knew she wasn't a great cook, but she was a darn sight better at it than he was. She even tried cooking one of his favourites, hers too. Com Tam with grilled pork, partly to prove to him that she could in a pinch whip up something delicious. After she had wiped her plate clean, Win was still ruminating over his. He ate maybe a couple mouthsful of rice and a bite of the pork, he didn't touch the egg or any accompaniments. Win was sure to express how good the food was though, but he lacked sincerity. Not in a "oh this is good!" way while depositing half his food into a napkin, or a "I can't stay for dinner" way of a child that has choked down too many of their friend's parents' meals out of politeness. In a way where he really wanted it to be good, but it wasn't working, the "It's not you it's me," of dining.

It only took a few days for Kathryn to realise it wasn't her cooking at all. She still insisted he eat. That he sit down and spend the duration of dinner in her company, most often silently, or she did a lot of the talking. She refused to let him hide in his room and avoid any interaction.

In the very least he had started sleeping with the door ajar so that Crumb and Butterbean could come and go as they pleased. Butterbean would divide his time of an evening between sleeping at the foot of Win's bed and the foot of Kathryn and Gianna's. Kathryn would like to believe and Win probably did too, that he did this because he sensed Win's heartbreak. It was more likely Butterbean just wanted to be close to Crumb though. He was enamoured with that cat. Crumb kept up the pretence that the galumphing canine cloud was a barely tolerable imposition. But when no one was home and if it was cold enough, Crumb was happy enough to curl up in the warmth of Butterbean's belly.

"Do you want me to put that in a container for lunch tomorrow?"

Breaking Win from his hypnotic stirring, "Yes please."

They both knew he wouldn't eat it for lunch either, but half a bowl of soup, spread over a couple meals was still better than nothing at all. Certainly, better than him buying a meal that he wasn't going to eat either.

Kathryn poured the soup into a container and placed it in the fridge next to another full soup container that was waiting for Gianna when she came home.

"It's the one on the right."

"Got it."

"Wanna talk about it?"

"No"

"Wanna watch TV?"

"Sure."

Thursday night was SVU night, so there was about an hour to kill before it started. Kathryn set a reminder on the TV to notify her when it was 8:30 and flicked to Netflix in the meantime. She put on a comedy series that she'd watched a million times before without consulting Win. He wasn't watching anyway.

Wallowing on the couch was better than wallowing in bed, she told herself. Kathryn did not know how to comfort someone in his situation just as much as Win didn't know how to deal with it. She would be there for him though, she had to be, even if she was hurting

- 218 -

too. He didn't need to see her cry into her pillow at night, because as much as Kathryn was aching from the death of her best friend, she was worried she might lose her brother too.

32

Win typed out his message, then backspaced, only to type it again. He did this four times before abandoning the text all together. He was trying to find the best excuse to stay at home. No part of him wanted to leave the house or be social. He especially didn't want to lug himself over to Petrie. He knew he had left it too late. He couldn't cancel on Sanjay now, not that Sanjay would accept a cancellation. It would normally only take a few minutes for Win to get ready. Change out of house clothes into whatever he wanted to wear; shoes, socks, deodorant and maybe he would need to run some product through his hair.

In between all the moping his usually quick routine stretched into an hour-long ordeal. Every one of Win's joints was weighed down with dread. Each movement was an effort and he lacked the conviction to push himself. After every task he was completely wiped out and collapsed into a pile. He felt like a man trudging through the desert; sinking closer to the ground with each step until he expired, arms outstretched in the sand. But he didn't die, he mustered just enough strength from his prone position to start again. The cycle continued until he was dressed and for all intents and purposes set to face the world, but he was in no way ready. With a final heave he pushed himself out of the door. The outside air lifted him into the car without too much effort but his hand paused on the hand brake. He was not sure he had it in him to release it.

Win stared blankly into the middle distance of the car port. He tossed his car into reverse and the rear camera reminded him that he hadn't opened the front gate. His forearms ached as he pushed the car back into park. He lugged his concrete bound feet to the gate, his fingers stinging and clicking as he worked the stiff bolt out. Back in the car Win planted his head on the steering wheel. All he had to do was back out, park, close the gate and get going again. On any other day, that would be nothing, it wouldn't warrant a second thought. He would be grateful if someone would shut the gate for him, but that would be a luxury. It took everything he had to get the car out of the driveway. He felt an emotional pain that was sadness and anger and apathy all combined. He knew it was only emotion, but it sunk into his bones. He could feel it, actually feel it, tingling in the back of his neck as he strained to keep his chin from falling back to his chest.

The gate was shut and as soon as the car was moving, Win felt as close to normal as he had in weeks. He was out of the house now and it would be smooth sailing until he had to get out of the car.

❖

Sanjay rested on the rear of his hatchback. It was a small blue car that his hulking frame barely squeezed into. He had clad himself in camo from head to toe. The only bare skin was his arms where he had ripped the sleeves off his shirt and smeared green and black grease across his biceps. He had a kerchief around his neck which Win could see had previously been covering the lower half of Sanjay's face, but was now pushed down. The top half of Sanjay's open and grinning face was smothered in the same grease.

Win pulled his car in a few spaces down. Sanjay had seen him, so he did not have time to close his eyes and rest his head working up the courage to exit the car. He only had time to take in one large breath before Sanjay appeared at his window making a series of hand gestures that Win took to be Sanjay's interpretation of military tactical signals.

"In spirit I see."

"Today is going to be baller mate. Just what you need." he nudged Win in the ribs, "You didn't wear your gear?"

"I don't have "gear," It's just gonna get covered up anyway right?"

- 222 -

"It's to give you an extra edge," Sanjay tapped his temple and mouthed, "in here."

Only once their paintball guns were handed out, coveralls were donned and protective gear all set did the big reveal happen that Sanjay had booked a special paintball "sesh." He had selected the Zombie Apocalypse setting, today they would be killing zombies. Win thought he was going to vomit.

❖

With the phone plugged in and voice recognition in operation, Lucia found the long stretches of time where she was doing nothing were marginally more tolerable. She had music and she had a backlog of podcasts to catch up on. It felt a bit less lonely with familiar voices wafting through the house.

A third of the way through her second episode of Beg Your Parton, Lucia began to drift into a downward spiral about never being able to see Dolly live or ever visit Dollywood. Which in turn became never being able to visit Tennessee, then a laundry list of places and things she would miss out on. In reality, even alive Lucia had neither the time nor the money to get around to all the places she wanted to go and things she wanted to see, but that was beside the point. What jerked her out of the pit of despair she was nestling herself into was an ad for another podcast. She had heard it before, but never paid that much attention.

"...presents *Bite* an in-depth investigation into the mysterious deaths of seven Brisbane locals. Listen to the case as it unfolds when Simon Higgson presents the breaking news on this unusual case. Is there a wild animal loose in the inner suburbs of Brisbane?..."

Lucia swore that she felt tingles zapping through her arms and into her fingers. Fuck! Had they found Jeremy? Her DNA was all over at least two crime scenes. She had to listen. She had to know what he knew. She also had to go check the forest, she needed to know if Jeremy had been found.

Rain pelted down, really hindering her plans. Rain did happen in the winter. The early months of the year were usually reserved for the torrential downpours and flash flooding, but winter rain was a regular occurrence too. A couple days of misery and then back to sunny days. Lucia remembered a time when she was a child and they hosted a foreign exchange student from Germany. She had been looking forward to the sunshine, a Brisbane winter is positively sweltering compared to a German one, but it rained the whole time. They tried to still hit up all the usual tourist traps, but it was bitterly cold and wet. Lucia also remembered getting quite sick. Probably less from being damp and more that they were out and about in peak flu season.

Cold, wet and listening to the symphony of retching coming from a sick ten year old. It's a wonder the exchange student wasn't traumatised.

Lucia wondered what the rain would do as it passed through her. Would it fall to the ground as if she was never there at all. Would people notice the absence of sopping footprints and droplets on her face, or would their heads be turned to the ground and they wouldn't notice at all. Could Lu work an umbrella, without getting her fingers caught in the clasp.

The rain wouldn't bother Lu. At least Lucia didn't think it would, she showed very little physical discomfort towards anything. It was probably best to keep her as dry as possible though.

Kathryn was at work. Otherwise, Lucia could ask her for a ride. She readied Lu to set out. Ankle high boots and a somewhat water-resistant jacket pulled over the jumper.

Standing on the front steps under the awning and still shielded from the rain Lucia instructed Lu on the way to open an umbrella to no avail. Lu lacked the dexterity required to pop it open and slide the stopper past the catch. The prongs of the umbrella were rusted at the hinges and along the rod. It was one of those compact deals, which required a bit more effort to push and pull simultaneously. Miming the actions were not helping the situation. The umbrella crashed to the patio tiles as Lu pushed with her right hand and forgot to pull with the left. On the third, loud fall, not that anything could be heard over the pounding rain, Lucia frustratedly grabbed the umbrella herself. It popped open and it was only as Lucia was handing it back to Lu that she realised exactly what had just happened.

She had touched something.

"Oh my fucking god!" the words escaped Lucia involuntarily and so loud and high pitched that they were barely recognisable as words. Had any neighbours heard over the rain and this they probably did hear; they would not have been able to discern the shriek from that of an animal or a small child. If it did rattle around the neighbour's brains until the sounds formed a sentence in hindsight, Lucia and Lu would be long gone from the patio before anyone had a chance to peer through their curtains.

Lucia pushed Lu back inside. Their mission could wait, Lucia could touch things again. She tried to remember if she felt the umbrella, between her fingers. If the metal was cold or had been warmed by the attempts before it. Did she feel the click, or fear the snap of her fingers getting jammed? She couldn't remember, she didn't know at all how it happened, only that it had.

The closest thing to them, was a small vase on a table just inside the door. Green, viney pothos sprouted from the vase and onto the lacquered wood. The glass was thick, an old soft drink bottle with a Japanese daruma face illustrated on the front. Lu stood uncomfortably in the corner opposite the table, she had not been instructed on where to go from there and the sudden flurry of movement had confused her. Lucia didn't care, she was excited to try her new-found ability on whatever was closest and right now it was that vase.

Lucia pushed out her diaphragm to replicate a deep breath. She reached her hand forward, clasped her fingers around the neck of the bottle and pulled up. Her hands came up empty. She had watched her fingers lock onto that vase, she knew she had a hold of it, but still nothing.

Lucia tried, over and over, each time she thought she had it and each disappointment stabbed at her will. Lu saw her and tried to help, she didn't understand the reason for Lucia's attempts, only that she could help. Lu was a bit like a cat in that way, cat's thinking their owners are big dumb, bald babies. Always trying to show them how to clean, hunt and talk.

"Leave it!" She shouted, raising her hand, not to hit but to shoo Lu out of the way. At the same time, Lucia's right forearm pushed hard against Lu's shoulder and her left knuckles pushed the neck of the vase down. She felt it, she felt them both. She didn't need to try to remember because it was happening right now. The vase was cold and hard and smooth. Lu's shoulder was padded by the layers of clothes.

The vase tipped backwards and water spilled out and ran over the back edge of the table falling in a puddle on the floor.

"Oh, shit!" the elation of regaining one sense was quickly overpowered by the inconvenience of a mess. "Grab a towel!"

She pulled the table away from the wall, it was one of those small tiered things, probably inherited from some great aunt on Win's side of the family. Well built, but very light. She didn't want to risk the water getting into the wood and warping it.

Lu stood dumbfounded, she knew what a towel was, but didn't know where to get one. Especially at such short and frantic notice.

"Forget it."

Lucia whipped the hand towel from its place over the oven handle and dabbed dry, first the top of the table, then each shelf, and then the floor. By the time she reached the floor the hand towel was very wet, she could feel the cloth barely holding onto the water. Any pressure and drops would start to release from it. She sat, practically laughing at the rush of it all. She could swear that while she was doing that she could even smell the rain that was still hammering down outside. Most people love the smell of rain and Lucia was no exception. If she had a heart to race, it would. Tears of joy might just have sprung from the corners of her eyes. She felt for the first time in quite a while, safe. Like she wasn't vulnerable to everything in the whole world. Like she could make it through, she could maybe even lead a life that resembled something close to normalcy. A completely comfortable life with her undead body and undead former patient in tow.

She pulled herself up and swiped at the sodden towel on the floor. Her hands were empty though.

33

Win came to check on Lucia. He noticed immediately the crooked stand by the door and the wet towel on the floor. The towel was still damp, and Win didn't think that the moisture might be anything other than water until the towel was already grasped between his slender fingers. He instinctively smelled it even though his reason for smelling it was because he feared it might contain something gross. There wasn't a pleasant smell. It was musty and smelled like laundry that had been left to fester before hanging out. There was a faint herbaceousness and the empty vase with a limp, thirsty looking plant told Win that's where the water had come from. He threw the whole thing in the bin rather than bother with washing. Lucia didn't explain the mess and Win didn't ask.

It felt like an age since Lucia had seen Win. In the whole time since they moved in together, they had only spent a handful of nights apart. So few that Lucia could count them up in her head if she wanted. Even before they officially lived together, they spent most nights of the week together.

Win would come over on Monday night and stay until Thursday morning. Thursday night they would have to themselves, then Friday and Saturday nights depending on their plans. At that time Lucia lived alone in a small downstairs unit of someone's house. Win had lived with Kathryn until she and Gianna moved in together. They wanted a place to themselves and didn't want an older brother cramping their style. Win found a room on Gumtree with two housemates. They were fine people and they weren't friends and he kept to himself. At the end of that lease he and Lucia found a place together.

Shortly after that they obtained Crumb. Crumb and a skip worth of trash were left by some neighbours when they moved out. Lucia and Win were glad to see the back of them. Lucia had been feeding Crumb for a few months when she noticed his declining weight. So Crumb moved into the house approximately 12 hours after his owners left him and there he stayed. It was the three of them from then on.

Win was standing in the living room and he felt like a stranger to her. A stranger she happened to know everything about. Because she knew everything about him, she noticed immediately that he was smaller. What little body fat he had had dropped off and if he took off his shirt she knew that his ribs would ripple against the muscle on his back. He was stooped like his spine folded over to protect his heart, or maybe she was reading too much into that.

Win's face thinned under his chin and at his temples. His hair, which usually slicked back in a thick, glossy black wave, was now limp and greasy more than it was glossed. He had been running his hands through it, pulling at his hair, just enough to feel his scalp stretch, but not enough to rip the hair from the scalp. His face was tired, but more than that, there was fear in his eyes. He swallowed hard before saying anything.

"How's it going?" Win asked. He knew how it was going. What he really meant was. Is this nearly over?

"Fine." That was a lie. Nothing was fine. He knew that too.

"Should I see her?"

"They need more to eat."

Win gorked. "They?"

"Didn't Kathryn tell you? Ruth is here."

"What the fuck? Why is she here?"

"She killed her son. Last time I went to see her, she killed him. They would find her, it wasn't safe."

"It's not safe here either Lucia, geez! What if they trace you back here? What then?" He was angry.

"I don't know Win. I just, I thought it was better if she came back home with me."

Win lowered his voice, acutely aware that the neighbours could probably hear them. Even with the windows closed, sound seemed to travel between the houses on their block no matter what. He swore that he heard the neighbours clipping their nails once.

"Lucia, I just don't want you getting in trouble."

"What are they gonna do Win? Kill me?" The joke landed and Win was ready to discuss feeding the pair of undead residing in his old house.

"Lucia, how am I supposed to get the bond back if you're taking in stray corpses?" There was a bite to his words and Lucia would analyse his words many times over when she lay looking at the ceiling.

"She's not a stray, neither is Lu. And *your* bond will be fine!" She wasn't as angry deep down as her response implied. She was just being reactionary.

"Ok let me see."

Lucia told him where to find each zombie subletter. Win grumbled as he moved past Lucia to look in the spare room. He stepped around her. There wasn't a chill as he walked past her, only an absence of heat. He didn't know that he was so used to the feeling of someone nearby until now. Heat radiating off other people is not something he ever took note of unless it was very hot or very cold. The air pressure didn't shift around her, everything was exactly as though he was walking through an empty room.

Suddenly his house was like a sad zoo with exhibits of lonely and unstimulated animals. He half expected Lu to be rocking in place, that's how bad she looked. She stood, not completely still, but hardly moving. No rise and fall of her breath. Swaying slightly from side to side, as if the muscles she would have used to stabilise herself when she was alive were slacking off. Not enough for her to collapse to the floor, just enough for her to look weak. Her skin was waxy and wet looking. Win had an uncle that died after a long time on medications that made him retain fluid in his limbs. Win was too young at the time to remember what exactly it was that he had. Maybe he was so young that no one ever told him. He could remember seeing his uncle after he died. He had the same waxy wet look. Like once chilled ham that had been left on the bench for too long.

The hole in Lu's cheek looked punched in and as though pus or blood had been seeping from it but had dried now. He made a note to dab at it later but for now he didn't have the energy.

Ruth looked a little worse for wear than Lu did. Her skin was also waxy and bore the same green tinge, but her lips peeled back from her teeth as her jaw hung open. Her foot, where the shards of lamp had poked through were putrefying. Her hands looked purple and her cuticles were pushed back way too far. Win didn't want to step too close to check that. Most jarring of all, this woman he didn't know was naked.

"Their last feed didn't last that long then." He didn't need to announce himself; Lucia was waiting where he left her in the lounge.

"If it's the food that helps them."

"Did it last time? Ruth's son?"

"Yeah, they both seemed good after that."

"Does it reverse the.." he gestured to his body with a flourish of out turned hands at the end.

"Grossness?" She offered the end to his thought.

"Yeah, or just stop it."

"I think it repairs it for a while, but not much."

Win pulled out the list of options he had presented before. It was a toss-up between Gloria Platt, a sixty five year old on Dialysis and Hannah Delenko, a twenty four year old in a coma. Gloria lived on the other side of town and despite her failing kidneys, was doing well according to what they could glean from Facebook. Hannah was in home care at her parents' house not far away and that was the clincher.

The less Win knew about the logistics the better. While he was cleaning up Lu a bit, Lucia mulled it over. When Lucia was alive she consumed concerning amounts of true crime. She wasn't obsessed with murder; it was more that she was endlessly intrigued by human nature. In a way that she could never wrap her head around it and she had to learn everything she could about something so foreign to her. She could not imagine killing anyone. Even if it were legal she couldn't see herself ever wanting to. She could barely imagine killing in self-defence. Planning a murder now, no matter how she dressed it up as a mercy killing, or hunting, sat uneasily on her.

Through the open bathroom door, she could see Win struggling to get Lu clean. He had undressed Lu and had her standing in the bath. His sleeves were rolled up to his elbows, but sudsy water was dripping down his slender forearms and moistening patches on his shirt. Lu's body was splotched with various hues, none of which rightly belonged on a person.

The water was barely warm. He kept it that temperature for fear of gently cooking the body of his wife. No steam rose into the cold bathroom. Unlike the last time Win had bathed Lu, he did not have her stand under the shower. Instead, he situated her just beyond the spray and splashed water from his cupped hands on her body. He didn't use a loofah or washer either but lathered his hands and rubbed the suds over her skin. He didn't want to risk compromising her skin further with abrasions.

The body beneath his fingers did not feel like his wife. He had run his hands over Lucia's body countless times. Sometimes in a manner just like this, in the shower with soapy hands. It was not just the cold of her, and Lu was cold. Getting colder by the day as winter crept in. Her skin hung differently over her muscles and fat, both of which were sagging and softening now. Her shape was changing, at first in a way only discernible to someone who had known her body very well. Now the changes were big enough that he thought even someone that had never seen Lucia naked, would notice a difference in Lu.

Win untied her hair and scooped water onto the ends. He ran shampoo lather through it careful to only caress her scalp and not scratch with his fingernails. Still clumps of hair turned up in his palms. It was not noticeable yet where the hair was thinning.

His forearms were slick with water and the pale blue of his work shirt was dark with water. Win turned the taps off and water gurgled down the drain, taking hair, soap and scum with it. He unbuttoned his shirt and hung it over the towel rack, cursing himself for not doing that in the first place.

Lucia had been watching but not focusing. She saw Win's bare back reaching across to the towel rack to retrieve Lucia's towel. His tanned, even skin was taut against his ribs. She was right, he was thinner. Thin but strong, muscles flexed on his back and disappeared beneath the waistband of his work pants. He held the towel, a corner in each hand and wrapped it around Lu. For only a moment his arms enveloped her and in that moment a pang of jealousy waved over Lucia.

Win was no longer hugging Lu, but dabbing slightly at the outside of the towel, before removing it and gently pressing at any water still on Lu's skin. He wrapped her hair up in a towel turban hoping most of the moisture would take care of itself before he had to sort it out. He did not want to towel dry it or blow dry it, for fear of damaging her scalp, but the idea of waiting around for it to air dry, especially in the cold, was just as bad.

From the lounge room Lucia watched his torso flit back and forth. Her eyes grazed up and down the length of it and took in every detail. She knew his body and his face well; it was like she was learning them all over again. Like an old song that you haven't heard in a long time, familiar but like new.

He left Lu to air dry, hoping her now clean skin would harden somewhat, like a Mummy. Or at least he thought it might have a chance to dry out and make dressing her easier, and less smelly. Lu's wet skin smelled like the gecko that got caught in the door hinge a few months ago, mixed with the bright blue cast Win had on a broken wrist when he was 9.

"I'm not going to wash Ruth."

"Fair enough. I think she wouldn't hold up to it anyway."

It was awkward, Lucia hadn't felt awkward around Win since she was a kid. She felt like a child all over again, she had forgotten what it was like. She was transported to youthful sleepovers and the occasions she would end up alone in the room with Win. Not knowing they would grow up and fall in love. Not knowing then, that

- 235 -

he would know her better than even Kathryn did one day. In that moment he was the cute older brother of her best friend, she never knew what to say to him and he wouldn't be interested if she did.

There was a weight in the air, like all the thoughts they had but weren't saying hung above them like a shroud.

"How's Crumb?"

"He's doing well. He and Butterbean are getting on better than I thought."

Win turned to go check on Lu again. He had decided to dress her and save himself from his discomfort. Lucia watched him leave. He preferred the company of Lu than he did her.

34

It would usually be around this time of night, if Lucia couldn't sleep, that she would drink half a bottle of water or head to the toilet for a middle of the night pee. Needing to pee and being thirsty were two things that kept her awake that were easy fixes. Usually both were required simultaneously, or the water and half an hour later, the toilet. Lucia didn't need either of those things though. She never thought that she would miss urinating, but here she was missing it. Lucia heard footsteps coming from the lounge room. She thought maybe she was imagining it, that she was so bored that her mind was playing tricks on her. There were two other people in the house, it could have been one of them. The footsteps were quiet, not the heavy shuffling steps of both Lu and Ruth. It sounded like someone creeping around. If she had been asleep, she certainly wouldn't have heard anything and maybe they were counting on that.

Lucia had imagined an intruder in her house nearly every night since she was thirteen. She would fear it and planning out what she would do if someone did break in would settle her mind somewhat. As a teenager, still living with her parents she planned to sneak to the linen cupboard. She knew from many games of hide and seek with her sister that she could deposit herself in one of the lower shelves very quickly and quietly. The door of the linen cupboard was such that she could pull it completely closed from the inside.

In this house there weren't as many secure options but she had decided within a couple months of their first lease in the place that she could hide behind the office door. Most of the doors in the house leaned right up against the wall when they were open, but the office door had a small recess behind it, between the wall and the built-in wardrobe in that room. It gave a snug, but doable clearance for a terrified woman without it looking as though there was any room behind it at all. Lucia kept a small Lebendwell hunting knife behind that door, just in case. She didn't have a knife in the bedroom, but she had a very hefty torch in the bottom drawer of her bedside table, which would pack a good wallop. She couldn't use it anymore, but an intruder also couldn't hurt her. Not physically.

Her whole life she never needed any of these plans or weapons but felt safer knowing they were there. In the same way she felt safer having two mini fire extinguishers in the house. Ryan Hughes, Lucia's father and SES volunteer for longer than Lucia had been alive, wouldn't have it any other way.

More footsteps. There was definitely someone in the house, someone living.

In spite of being unable to make any noise, Lucia slid off the bed and crawled across the floor to the edge of the bedroom door. She could poke her head around the corner and see whoever was there, they could see her too, but maybe they wouldn't be looking on the floor for someone. She poked her head around but couldn't see anyone. Pale moonlight streamed in from the front window and since Lucia hadn't closed her eyes all night, they were well adjusted to the low light. She could see the whole room with relative ease and it was empty. Devoid of human life at least.

A breeze blew in and shuffled the curtains, shifting the tissues in the box that lay on the coffee table. It wasn't noticeable during the day, when things were happening but the wall clock ticked loudly. Lucia had forgotten she even had an analog wall clock to tick. She so rarely looked at it. She could faintly make out now that the small hand was resting on the 3 and the minute hand showed 5 past. She was sure that was not actually the time. It was more likely to be closer to 3:30, not that she had anything to go by other than intuition.

Through the ticking, under the sound of distant birds and the drone of the streetlights, she could hear breathing. It was quiet and muffled, but fast. Like someone was holding their hand over their mouth so as not to give away their position. Exactly what she could imagine herself doing if she was still alive, afraid of death, and hiding behind the office door. In this way being a ghost had its merits, the only one that she had encountered so far. She was unafraid of the consequences of a home invader. It would be a major inconvenience if this intruder decided to loot the place, or trash it, but that was more on behalf of Win. It would be hard to rent a new place if this was burned to the ground, but not impossible. Win would have to be moving for good soon anyway, he wouldn't be able to keep up with the rent by himself.

The devastating thought of Win leaving for good and of her having to find a new haunt, literally, was so consuming that Lucia almost forgot why she was laying on the floor peering into the empty, but maybe not empty lounge room.

The breathing, faint as it was, was close. Very close. She shifted her gaze closer to her and that's when she saw it. A pair of feet mostly hidden by shadow against the wall closest to her. She hadn't seen him because he was so close, but there was definitely a man standing with his back against the wall between the lounge room and her bedroom. A gloved hand covered over his face and she could see a glint of two eyes, from under a pulled down baseball cap. He was looking right at her.

Lucia pulled her face back and sprang to her feet. How did he know she was there? Lucia ran through an inventory of what she saw or thought she had seen.

Baseball cap, clean shaven (possibly) his gloves were in the way, jeans and a black t shirt, his shoes were lace up canvas sneakers, not chucks, but a cheaper version where the toe was also black. He was holding something, in the hand that wasn't covering his face he was holding something. Not a weapon, surely that would have caught the light, a bag?

"I saw you." A low voice came from the opposite side of the wall. "Are you alone?"

Visions of the man pinning her down and raping her while she struggled against him, screaming for help that wasn't coming flashed behind her eyes. An amalgam of every story she had heard, movie she had seen and every other time a man held her down against her will, clouded her vision until she remembered. He couldn't, the joke was on him. He couldn't rape her if she didn't have a body. He couldn't kill her if she wasn't alive. But she did have a body. He could rape Lu, he could hurt Lu. Who was this necrophiliac fuck in her house?

"No" she called back, elaborating "I'm not alone. My husband is here, he's already called the cops." Try as she might the lie didn't come out as confidently as she had hoped. She kicked herself for even coming up with that lie when the truth was scarier.

"I better be quick then." This time the voice came harsh and crumbs of hatred were spilling everywhere no matter how he tried to contain them. He swivelled round the corner; Lucia could see now that he was not tall. She couldn't tell that from her ground level perspective earlier. He was clean shaven as she thought and older, in his 50s at least but 60s wouldn't be out of the question. The man scanned the room. He entered pushing past her, Lucia instinctively moving out of the way, he was searching the room.

"No husband here." He grinned back at her, the light through the window glistened on a string of saliva stretching from lip to tooth. "Sneaky fucking bitch." He was even more angry now. Lucia barely had time to say anything before he lunged at her. She jumped out of the way and he collided with the bedside table, sending a framed photo flying off the side. Obviously winded he unzipped his bag. A knife.

"This won't hurt a bit." Now it was getting a bit much of a cliché and Lucia certainly would have laughed if she wasn't busy dodging his attacks. This guy really did fancy himself a super villain. He gripped the knife firmly and readied himself to lunge at her again.

She thought about letting him. He might crash through her and hurt himself on the other side.

Instead, he pushed forward and she was trapped on the bed. He pushed the knife against her neck, there was no resistance though and the knife hit the mattress behind her.

"How'd you do that cunt?" He raised his knee and attempted to pin her right thigh down. He was trying to get the upper hand. He was trying to make sure she was scared, pinned down, helpless. Without any actual power over her, she did feel helpless and scared. Lucia was paralysed. She could scream, wake the neighbours, lock this man up, but in doing so expose herself. The fear of that gripped her so tightly she thought she might die all over again.

He thought he had won, she could tell that from the smug look he wore on his face.

"Get off!" That's all she could say.

"Don't worry you little bitch, I will."

Lu was the first to appear in the doorway of the bedroom. Drawn in by the noise. Or some other zombie sense. Ruth wasn't far behind, lingering back in the hallway.

The man followed Lucia's relieved gaze. He lifted himself off her holding his knife up again.

"Goodie, I've always wanted twins."

"Who even says that?" Without him on top of her, remembering she had not one, but two killing machines under her roof, Lucia relaxed enough to notice how much of a total douche this guy was. On top of obviously being a serial rapist, he was so gross.

"Shut up cunt!" He snapped back at her. "Ohh look, this old bat has done half the work for me." Ruth's nakedness was a plus for this creep, never mind the fact that she was old and dead. He turned to face Lu, turning his back completely on Lucia. A real rookie error for someone who thought he was going to overpower three women at once. He saw Lu's drooping features.

"Bit too much time in the sun this one?" He laughed at his own joke. "You right there luv?" He wrapped his knuckles on Lu's head. Lucia hadn't seen this look before. Rage. Lu didn't like this guy.

He turned back to Lucia. "She a retar..." his slur cut short by Lu taking a bite out of his neck. "Oi what the fuck?" His hand found the gushing wound on his neck. His eyes found the piece of him Lu removed between her lips. She snapped her neck back and threw his flesh into her mouth like a pelican with blood lust.

His eyes widened, "Fucking bitch," and he thrust the knife into Lu's hip, leaving it there and pushing past her. Ruth reached out, almost casually and swiped three long fingernail cuts through his hoodie and into his forearm. Then he was gone.

The house returned to being quiet. The man's footfalls slapped the footpath leading away from the house, to the main road. Lu and Ruth stood nonchalantly, as though what just happened was already gone from their consciousness.

"What the fuck was that? Thank you. What the fuck?"

Lu noticed the knife protruding from her gut and clawed at it until she was able to wrap her fingers around the handle and pull it out. She looked at the knife with a puzzled expression. Lucia could see her synapsis sparking to try and figure out where the knife had even come from.

35

The phone buzzed a message. Lu had learned how to swipe across the screen to open the phone and another swipe the opposite way to pull down the message preview. Lucia could duck in and read it before the screen faded black again.

This text was from Tanvi.

"Hi Lucia, I don't want to put any pressure on you to come back but I thought you should k..."

"Press it."

Lu pressed a finger strongly into the screen. Her forefinger bending her tendons unnaturally the wrong way under her force of strength.

"...thought you should know that Lorraine passed away last night."

"That's enough." She pulled away. "Thanks Lu."

It wasn't shocking news, Lorraine was very old. She had not been well over the last few months. Lucia had seen it before. A simple UTI progresses into a bladder infection, that becomes a kidney infection (which was what Lorraine had been hospitalised for) then the weakened immune system makes way for all sorts of other infections and viruses. Even though she was out of the hospital and seeming quite vital when Lucia had seen her last, she most likely died of some secondary illness. Lorraine was also the type to remain steadfast through illness, not revealing the symptoms to anyone and not likely to complain before it was too late. She was a nurse, she knew better, but she was a nurse so was prone to ignoring her own health.

By now Lorraine's children and grandchildren would have been informed. They'd be planning her funeral. Lorraine probably had all the arrangements sorted anyway. She was exactly the type of person to plant a few surprises in the funeral, her way of getting the last laugh. A wave of emotion hit Lucia. Sadness, yes, of course she was sad. Sad for the loss of a dear friend, and that she wouldn't be at the memorial, that surely would be a turn out for the books. There was also something else, unmistakable and baffling. She was jealous.

Lorraine was dead, dead-dead. If she was only kinda dead that would be news. If it happened last night, if she was going to become undead she would have done that by now. She was gone. Forever. Not this hanging around bullshit that Lucia was dealing with. Lorraine was dead, she died for normal reasons in a normal way. It was boring how normal it was and Lucia had never wanted to be so boring in her whole life. More than her whole life, her death. That's how stupid it was, there wasn't even a colloquialism to express her feelings accurately. Her friend was gone, she was sad and she was angry that her own selfishness was getting in the way of that. How could she be thinking of herself now? She should be thinking of life without her confidant, but it wasn't even life. She was not living, she was existing and there was a big difference.

She could never speak to Lorraine again. Lorraine who so readily accepted her. Who somehow knew that Lu needed to eat and talked to her like she was still a real person. Lorraine who was the only patient she ever visited after they no longer needed her. She was gone, leaving behind four kids and who knows how many grandchildren, probably nieces and nephews too. Lorraine whose life had meant so much to so many people, especially Lucia and all she could think about was herself.

❖

Goosebumps rippled their way down Win's arms and he reflexively rubbed his forearms. The morning sunlight hit the window behind his desk, warming his back like a radial heater. The glass was tinted so the heat didn't spread further than a foot into his cubicle. A vent over his desk blasted cold air on his front and his body reacted appropriately. Win looked to the ceiling, crinkling his brow at the vent and rubbed his arms again, this time for warmth.

Sanjay lay his bag down on the floor and nudged it under the desk with the side of his left foot. He peeled the headphones out of his ears.

"Cold?"

"Yeah" Win crooked his eyebrows in a comical wave, which he did not mean to be funny, but knew it was anyway.

"Need to beef up a bit man." Sanjay flexed his large biceps like a strongman. He was built solidly, basically a wall of muscle, without the definition of someone that had to work towards that physique. His arms strained against his short sleeved, button down. Even in the early June chill, Sanjay would wear shorts if he could. "Nothing compared to Melbourne weather!" Like all people living in Brisbane after having lived in Melbourne, Sanjay loved to tell people about it.

Win had lost weight from his already small frame in just the short time he had been off food. That wasn't the reason for his sensitivity to cold though. He had always run cold. One of his friends had a theory that in each couple there is one person that is always cold and one that is always hot. This theory was in no way scientific or tested in any official capacity, but it was true of Win and Lucia. She was always hot and him cold. Win shuddered at the thought that now Lucia was also cold and it sent the goosebumps back up his arms. This time he could feel them prickling across his ribs too.

By midday, the temperature in the office had evened out to a light chill. A few hours of bustling insurance claim agents brought up the ambient temperature. Win was set to work through lunch. There was a claim about a spate of slip-and-falls, caused by a burst water pipe. Everybody was passing the blame up or down the line depending on where they fell. An ordinary slip-and-fall is usually pretty open and shut. If there were no measures taken to protect the public, or if the incident was reoccurring. Then the business was at fault. If all appropriate measures were taken, then they weren't. Ones like this case were interesting because he had to determine whether it was the plumber, the council or the business owner who were at fault. A lot of interviews and trawling through records and it felt a lot like being a detective. Win's favourite cases were like this, that or they were just interesting. Collapsed balcony, boring, collapsed balcony at a scandalous party, interesting. Accident in the workplace, pretty boring, an accident where a deadly virus was spilled on the floor, interesting.

He didn't mind working through lunch either because that way he would not be subject to the break room crowd that by now almost certainly knew that he and Lucia were separated. He could be vague and broody but that didn't come naturally to him and he did not want to alienate his friends. They were just trying to be kind.

"You coming?"

"Nah, I want to finish this."

Sanjay gave him a cynical look, as cynical as Sanjay's broad, jolly face could muster anyway. He didn't probe any further though.

A third through reading the scrawled notes of a plumber that had quoted for the burst pipe to be completely replaced, Win's immediate boss appeared over his shoulder.

"Hey Samuel. Have you heard from Mel at all?"

It took a second for Win to register what he was being asked. His quad mate Mel was absent.

"Nope, she's on leave."

His boss narrowed his eyes and looked at the empty desk over the top of the cubicle dividers, as if staring at the empty chair would give some other answer.

"She was supposed to be back today. Haven't heard from her is all."

Mel had been on annual leave for 4 weeks. She was headed overseas, Europe with some lengthy stopovers in Singapore, or Malaysia, maybe Hong Kong? Win wasn't sure, it had been 4 weeks since he'd heard anything about the trip and a lot had happened in that time. He was friendly with Mel, but they didn't talk heaps, not unless they were consulting on each other's cases.

The awkward lingering of his boss's gaze made Win feel as though he had to provide some kind of answer for why Mel was still absent.

"Maybe her flight got delayed?"

He didn't say anything and walked away, that was obviously not the kind of speculation that his boss was after. Glancing back at the photocopy of handwritten notes, Win decided that while his sudden headache was work induced, a coffee would fix it. He grabbed his coffee cup from his drawer and headed to the kitchen.

36

On the second day after Mel was due back from her European holiday, Win's boss asked HR to ring her next of kin. He wasn't worried, men aren't as quick to assume something bad has befallen a missing person as women are. Faith King from HR was immediately concerned and furious that she had not been told of this earlier. Faith had to hold her breath to stop from panting into the phone as her heart raced. Her concern could not be detected in her phone voice though. She, like many that have worked in office environments for any amount of time, had a phone voice. Her phone voice was so alarming to those around her that they commented on it nearly every time she answered a call.

Mel's next of kin was her brother. When she had started at the company she and her brother lived together, but he had since moved out and lived in a share house across town. He vaguely knew that Mel was going on a trip, and somewhere in the periphery of his mind he knew that it was Europe. He could not say at all when she was due back, in the same way he could not recall her exact job description, who she might have been dating, or her birthday.

He told Faith that he had not heard from Mel but assured her he would ring around to find out where she was. He didn't do that because no sooner had he hung up the phone, he got a message from a friend asking if he was available for a game. He accepted and didn't give a second thought to his potentially missing sister.

Mel lived in an apartment building with long corridors and heavy doors. Where everything echoed but people lived there for security and prestige. Mel had lived there, when she lived. She didn't live there anymore, but that's where they found her. Mel didn't have any housemates or pets. She was enjoying spending time living alone. She wasn't scared because of the multiple layers of security that apartment living offered her. She was 26 and had the ideal that she would meet the love of her life soon enough and she would never have the chance to live alone again.

She padded around her one bedroom in the nude, she ate what she wanted and watched what she wanted. When she decided to go on a European holiday, she didn't need to leave lights on, or have someone check in on her house. It was safe. None of her neighbours knew she was going away. She liked that too. She lived very close to a lot of people, but she couldn't say that she had had a conversation with any of them. They offered polite nods in the hallway, but nothing more. None of her neighbours raised the alarm when they heard a loud thud about a week ago. None of them that heard it could be exactly sure of which apartment the noise came from. A few bangs and big thud, then nothing. If anyone had thought it was suspicious, the thought left their mind quickly and before they could take action.

The caretaker opened the door at the request of the police. A stench not quite like anything the caretaker had ever smelled before poured out of the apartment into the hallway. The officers had smelled it before, there was a dead body in that apartment. A body that had been dead for a long time.

For one week, Mel had been a member of a very elite club. People who had managed to die twice. She died for the first time four weeks earlier; when on her walk home from work, she bumped into a stranger. An incident she later chalked up to her brewing migraine. By the time she got home, the migraine gripped her whole body. She took painkillers and went straight to bed. Her bags were packed and her alarm was set. The last thing she needed was a migraine to ruin the start of her holiday, so she hopped into bed and willed it to vanish as quickly as it came. By the time her alarm went off to get her to the airport in time, Mel was dead.

The Mel that woke up was not urgent to get on a plane to Europe. She likely had no recollection of booking the trip at all. The suitcase on the floor of her bedroom was now nothing but a tripping hazard. The Mel that existed inside that apparent for three weeks, had very little in common with the Mel that was looking forward to a European trip of a lifetime, apart from looks. As she spent the days without food, even that likeness diminished rapidly. Skin sloughed off onto the floor, and putrid liquid oozed from the splits in her skin. Cockroaches swarmed the apartment to the feast on the festering puddles. Mel, the new Mel, ate the cockroaches in desperation. When they caught wise and outran her with ease, she too slurped up the remnants of her decaying body from the tiles. At some point the need for food took over and Mel thrust herself against the front door, trying to break it down. She was weak, but still stronger than the average person. She slammed her body against the door and on her last push she headbutt the door too. Her temple landed on the coat hook on the back of the door and Mel died for the second and final time.

The police that arrived on the scene didn't know any of that happened and it certainly wasn't clear while inspecting the scene. Mel was slumped on the floor behind the door. The officers had to squeeze through the partially open door, at first not clear what was blocking the way. Being impaled would ordinarily be ruled the cause of death and that's certainly what the first responders thought it was.

The bloodless gaping hole in the side of her head told otherwise.

❖

The last time the whole branch was called into a meeting was when their last boss retired. That was 3 years ago. They have announcements and meetings, but never everyone at once. At the last-minute Win was pulled, stopped from heading to the meeting and directed to one of the smaller board rooms. Sanjay was already in there, along with other colleagues from his team.

Win mouthed to Sanjay. "What's this?"

Sanjay mouthed back, "Don't know," along with a raised eyebrow and shrug.

Faith King from HR was in charge of the smaller meeting. She didn't waste any time.

"Hi everyone. We've called you in for some bad news."

Faces around the room dropped, not that they were expecting good news. Win could see the thoughts of redundancy ticking behind the eyes of his co-workers. Sanjay seemed to be the only one without a sour expression. He was always the optimist. A chill ran down Win's spine, he thought he might know what was coming next, and redundancy would have been more welcome.

"Your colleague Mel was found dead in her apartment yesterday." Faith rushed to hush any immediate questions. "We don't know much more at this point. We are offering the rest of the day off for anyone that feels they need it, but you are welcome to stay at work. We have phone counselling at the ready."

The room sat in stunned silence. Shortly after their announcement a collective gasp came from the meeting outside their boardroom. The sound of fifty other people hearing bad news all at once.

Mel was well liked by everyone in the office. She was generally a pleasant person to be around. She kept mostly to herself, in that she didn't get caught up in office drama. She never gossiped, which in an office the size of theirs, went a long way towards making her an office favourite. She never came out for drinks, mainly because she had her own thing going on, but she was never rude about it and somehow avoided being included or excluded from any cliques.

Fifty people all at once felt an immense sadness, but the reality of it was that Mel's absence wouldn't make any real difference in any of their lives. She was friendly, but no one there could call her a friend. That's how no one noticed that she didn't go to Europe and no one noticed when she wasn't back. If Sanjay had scheduled a holiday and then didn't post anything to social media about it, people would notice. They might even have noticed if it was Win that went missing. People had definitely noticed that something was up with Win. Throwing up in the bin was a pretty good tell though.

Win looked at Sanjay who was visibly shaken. He always seemed so unshakable, but colour had drained from his face and he seemed for the first time since Win had met him, lost. He snapped out of it pretty quickly when Win's hand landed on his shoulder.

"Pub?"

"Pub."

Win could pretend that he was trying to cheer up Sanjay, when he was only trying to distract himself. It was too much of coincidence for Mel to die so unexpectedly. People die every day and ordinarily it wouldn't be out of the question for two young people to die within a month of each other. At this point he didn't know exactly when Mel had passed away. It was suspicious though.

❖

In one movement Sanjay placed two full pints on the wobbling, pub table and straddled the backless bar chair. His hulking frame perched precariously on top of the chair, knees out wide in a kind of sumo squat for extra stability.

He pushed one beer towards Win, slowly and deliberately to not spill the beer. Win watched the frothy head ripple, with very little worry about it splashing over the edge. He let his eyes relax and the foam became a wobbling, indefinable blob. The world around it faded away into a blur. He pulled his eyes back into focus and rubbed his eyes beneath his glasses before hugging the glass with his hand.

Sanjay let out a big sigh between grimaced lips.

"Oh man." He stacked his hand on one of his outstretched knees, tilting his right shoulder forward to raise his glass in Win's direction. "To Mel."

"To Mel." Win waited a beat before asking, "How do you think it happened?"

"I dunno mate, don't know if we'll ever know."

"Should we go to her funeral?"

"Do you want to?" Sanjay replied.

"I don't know. I didn't really know her very well." Win was trying to piece together everything he knew about Mel and it was next to nothing.

"How long you sit next to her?"

"Since my first day. She trained me. Six years?" He counted in his head on an imaginary calendar. "Yeah, six years next month."

"I didn't really know her either." Sanjay thought for a moment. "She had a brother. I know that. I caught her humming Nirvana once, so guess she liked them?"

"That doesn't mean anything. Songs get in your head even if you don't like them."

"Right. How old was she?" Worry was returning to Sanjay's face.

"I don't even know that. Are we bad?"

"No." Sanjay took a sip. "No, I don't think so. She was quiet."

"Nice though."

"Oh yeah, really nice. Good at her job."

"For sure."

Win sat on his beer until the sudsy remains at the bottom of the glass were warm. He sloshed the whole lot into his mouth to get rid of it. Sanjay was already finishing his second beer. "Another?"

"Nah, not today. I'll stay though."

Win had not really understood the term "navel gazing" until right now. Mel was dead, who knows how and he was thinking about what it meant for him. While Sanjay was at the bar, he was quite literally staring at his own lap and thinking about his feelings. And Lucia. He wondered when he would stop thinking about Lucia. It was reflex still, to think of her when he thought of himself. Anything that affected him would affect her too. He got used to that. He got used to wanting to tell her the good things and the bad things. She was the first person he thought of when he saw something weird, funny or sad. He wondered when that would run out. When she was dead? More dead? All the way dead?

Sanjay arrived back with his beer and a water for Win. Water in a bar is never as refreshing as water anywhere else. They only ever served in pots and chock full of ice. There was hardly ever more than a couple mouths full of bitterly cold and strangely stale water in the glass.

He thanked Sanjay all the same. Sanjay pulled his phone out of his pocket and Win could hear the last notes of its vibration as it was liberated from Sanjay's pants.

"Hunter and Leonie are heading down."

Win wasn't in the mood for more people, he hoped it would be a good distraction though. As much as he didn't want to be surrounded by people, being by himself would be worse at the moment. The body count around Win was racking up. If he was by himself, he would let himself think about that fact too much and start to think he was somehow at fault.

Hunter slung his satchel under the table as he arrived.

"Anything? Anything?" he asked Sanjay and Win in turn. They both shook their heads no.

Leonie nodded up to him, half in her seat, "A pint of Pure Blonde if you're buying." They chuckled before Hunter headed for the bar.

"What a day, hey?" Leonie smiled the kind of smile that doesn't denote happiness, more awkwardness and incredulity at a situation. "I didn't really know her, but you guys sat with her right?"

"We did," Sanjay answered, "but it seems like we didn't really know her either."

"I heard she was found wedged behind her front door. Like she was sick and trying to get out."

"Sick how?" Win didn't want to give away too much eagerness. He also thought Leonie was often full of shit, but she had been known to get some things right in the past.

"Apparently, she was bloated and puffy, and there was all kinds of shit all over her apartment. Like vomit and puss and crap. Not crap ya know, just like, other stuff. Maybe shit too. I don't know."

"You really think she spent a month shitting all over her apartment Leonie? Fuck off!" It was the disrespect that got Win offside.

"I didn't say she shit everywhere. I said they found stuff everywhere. Like she was really sick and got confused or couldn't clean up or something."

"Blood?"

"I dunno, I don't think so. People usually mention blood, don't they? A bloody crime scene, not a puss-y crime scene"

"Crime scene?" Win tried to make his voice more inquisitive than nervous.

"Not a regular fucking death that's for sure, so I guess when it's not regular it's a crime scene." Hunter added as he plonked two glasses on the table.

Not a regular fucking crime scene that's for sure. The words repeated over and over, throbbing in Win's head. They would continue to swim around up there for days. Part of Win knew that as soon as Mel died. Part of him knew that Lucia and Mel were linked. He didn't think they had ever actually met each other, but they were linked.

Not a regular fucking crime scene that's for sure.

A crime scene with cops, detectives. Detectives that, if they found out Lucia was also dead, would put two and two together. Two plus two equals Win looked guilty. He was guilty. By now he had the files of two murdered or missing people in his house. He printed them from his work computer. Accessory to murder? Fuck, that was it. He was guilty of that, maybe other stuff too. He didn't know anymore. Sweat beaded across his forehead and under his eyes. The sweat under his eyes dripped down his face and looked like tears. He could pass them off as tears. One of the only times when it was an appropriate cover. No one noticed though, or if they did, no one said anything.

37

For some reason, most likely arrogance with a little obliviousness thrown in, plenty of people let their dogs off leash in Toohey Forest. These same dog owners would be the first to complain about a cat being left to roam free in the neighbourhood. Mostly the issue with the dogs was that they scared human and canine pedestrians alike. The next issue was that Brisbane City Council left baited traps for wild and feral dogs. After that the obvious threat to wildlife. Not so much a problem, but a side effect of careless pet owners was that the body of Jeremy was found sooner than anyone involved would have liked.

Like something out of an urban legend, a three year old, tan mastiff x bull arab named Lexi trotted back to her owner with a big strip of human skin hanging out her mouth. Her owner would not have noticed anything if Lexi hadn't spat the skin on the walking track making a terrible retching sound. He hardly even knew what he was looking at, a wet, jaundice lump. It looked like a rotten jellyfish 13km from the ocean. The smell hit long before the realisation did and small jelly like globs of dark brown blood on Lexi's nose confirmed something was wrong.

Sometimes when Lucia walked in Toohey Forest early in the morning before it was too hot, too crowded and motivation hadn't had the chance to dwindle; she would let her mind wander to the idea that trekking through a forest when the sun was barely up, she might be unfortunate enough to find a body. She would check for phone reception and be careful where she trod and she definitely wouldn't touch the body. Lexi's owner was not prepared for finding a body in the bush. He had never thought about it. He was a man with a large dog, the idea that dangers existed in Brisbane was just as foreign to him as responsible pet ownership.

About an hour after Lexi had another chomp out of Jeremy and both she and her owner had trampled the whole crime scene, the police arrived. A crime scene was cordoned off and Lexi's owner made a statement. A little while after that media vans pulled up. Vans with aerials poking out of their roofs lined the shaded sides of Toohey Road. A uniformed police officer was relegated to moving the news vans on as they were prone to block access for more crime scene vehicles.

Traffic slowed through the otherwise fast-moving section of road. The speed limit was 60, not many adhered to that as they whipped around the broad road that bisected the urban bushland. Now the traffic was a crawl as rubberneckers got their fill. Uniforms did their best to wave the traffic through, but a jam was inevitable.

Police and techs trekked up the dusty path to the gully where Lexi had found her unexpected snack. The initial path was wide enough for cars but quickly narrowed into a path around about a foot across. It was a desire path that cut through the thicker bushland and eventually became more official. Planks of wood were stepped into the path to stabilise the footing, but the steep incline and loose soil eroded the stairs and now the planks were tripping hazards the whole length of the path. The gully was accessible by many directions and from none of them was Jeremy's body visible. The ferns were thick all year round and shrouded him well. Most of the focus was centred around Jeremy. There were already several numbered markers where evidence had been collected. Crime scene tape strung between trees in a rough square shape. Grids were set up through the rest of the gully for techs to forage through the underbrush for evidence. Brisbane's cold weather was not enough to slow the bodies decay too significantly. It wasn't clear what weapon was used in this slaying, so care was taken to check the surroundings. The ferns had concealed a body for so long, they were probably hiding other things too.

They didn't find a weapon, but the ferns gave up four more bodies before the sun dipped behind the horizon. It was estimated that the longest dead of the bodies had laid beneath the chlorophyll shroud for over two months.

Lorraine's funeral was at the crematorium in Holland Park. Tanvi had arranged for there to be a coach from the nursing home to the service. Lorraine was well loved by everyone and many of her fellow residents would not have been able to attend otherwise. She had never been religious, not in any real way. Got married in a church and had her children baptised, but that was just what was done. She came from a time when Christianity was the default religion applied to all white people. It never suited her.

A poster board stood at the entrance to the chapel.

Lorraine Margaret Danvers 14 August 1929 - 7 June 2018.

Lucia recognised the photo they used. It was from Lorraine's eighty-fifth birthday. The photo was cropped in tight to make a nice portrait, but Lucia knew that in it Lorraine was wearing a fuzzy knitted jumper that bore a hen on the front. Once upon a time she had four older brothers, they passed long before her, as men often do. Her brothers called her Henny. The poster was as far as Lucia made it into the service. She hung back in the gardens, trying to posit Lu behind hedging so she wouldn't be seen. When the service started was when she crept up the steps to the chapel.

Lorraine's children chose a charismatic funeral director to do the service. His voice encircled the mourners in a sense of calm and he spoke with a familiarity that seemed as though he knew Lorraine firsthand. She couldn't hear everything, but there was an appropriate amount of sadness in the air, peppered with laughter. A perfect funeral for a wonderful woman.

When the service ended Lucia ducked quickly down the steps again, hiding Lu and herself in the gardens once again. She watched droves of mourners file out of the church, damp tissues clutched in their hands.

Only one mourner saw her.

"Lucia?" Without turning Lucia knew who was calling for her. She wondered how she could so miss her name being called out in the familiar South Indian accent and dread it at the same time. Miss it because she missed work, missed Tanvi, missing living. Dread because her new existence was so unstable. The smallest act could change everything. In some ways the risks of living were removed, physical pain, fear of death. She had none of that, but with so little left, she had everything to lose.

"Lucia is that you?"

There was no avoiding it now. Lucia turned to faced Tanvi front on. "Hi Tanvi."

"You did not want to come into the service?"

"Uh, no I just wanted to pay my respects alone." It wasn't a lie. "Thank you for telling me Tanvi. I appreciate it." It was now that Tanvi saw Lu. She was poorly hidden behind a pillar. Her ever present swaying did not help in her concealment.

"Who is she?" Tanvi pointed at Lu. Dropping any civility, partly out of suspicion, partly out of fear.

"Ummm." Lucia had no excuses.

Tanvi pushed past Lucia on her way to confront Lu. Just as she passed, she stopped in her tracks. Something was wrong, but she couldn't place it. That feeling had plagued Tanvi all too often recently.

"Come out here."

"Tanvi don't" Lu cowered a little. Favourable to Lu's other reaction when confronted. Lu had only just attacked someone with no intention of eating him.

Tanvi gasped and jumped back. She held her slender hand to her throat, guarding it without thinking. "Who is this, Lucia?" Lucia nodded at Lu, trying to tell her it was alright. The jig was up. They'd been caught. Before Lucia could answer, "Is she dead?" The smell had reached Tanvi's nostrils and she retched. The hand she had clutched to her neck moved swiftly to cover her nose and mouth.

"Ummm, yes." Lucia raced to stand between them. "She's me. I mean. I died. That day, with Ruth. I died too. She's my body."

For someone just now learning a lot of confronting information, Tanvi was calm. She looked Lucia dead in the eyes, "And you?"

Lucia gestured down her body. "A ghost."

"Oh no Lucia. I am so sorry." She held out her hand to Lucia, wanting to take her hand and hold it tightly, but her fingers slipped through Lucia's skin, coming to rest in the still air where Lucia's hand should have been. "I wish you had told me earlier."

"I'm sorry."

"No dear, I am the one that is sorry for it." She looked Lu up and down once more. "Do you need a lift?"

❖

The streets, people, buildings that sailed by the passenger side window of Tanvi's car were all so familiar. Lucia could recreate much of Brisbane so clearly in her mind that she very well could be dreaming right now. She felt safe, not like being on the bus, worried

- 263 -

about who would see them. Safer than walking, hoping no one would notice the abnormalities in both hers and Lu's steps.

Lucia could remember the smell in Tanvi's car. She'd only been in it a handful of times. Top notes of Tanvi's perfume, white tea and pear, or something like that. The perfume smelled like a mojito, or an especially sweet-smelling gin and tonic. Mid notes of general car smell and very faintly the smell of coffee and school bags. Lucia had never noticed the smell before, not consciously at least. She could recall it vividly now. Without inertia, skimming through the streets of Brisbane's inner south, she felt like she was flying. In her dreams, Lucia could never fly high or fast. It felt just like that now, full of potential, but ultimately frustrating.

Lu slumped in the back seat. She was buckled in but had slid her butt forward and curled over her own lap. Hovering limply where her hips halted their flexibility and she couldn't fold any further.

Tanvi had questions, all of them fighting to be first out of her mouth. She swallowed them down and wrapped her thumb and forefinger around the steering wheel, picking at her thumb nail without even knowing she was doing it. Lucia noticed Tanvi's slender fingers ending in neatly filed oval nails. A small groove starting on the thumb nail where Tanvi was picking.

"You must have questions."

"I do." She took in a deep breath before stopping mid inhale when the smell of Lu hit her palette. "Samuel?"

"Oh!" The question wasn't what Lucia had expected. "He's fine. Well not fine." She shrugged, "You know. He moved out, he's staying with his sister."

"Kathryn?" Tanvi confirmed.

"Yeah, so there's that." Lucia had difficulty not sounding casual about it. She was anything but casual. She was devastated.

"How are you feeling about that?"

"Ummm uh, not great. I get it, but that doesn't make it hurt any less."

"What are you wanting?"

Lucia kept her eyes focused on the road, but she could see Tanvi glancing her way. Examining her face on the straight stretch of road. She considered her answer, no one had asked her that. "I want for it to not be happening."

"Are you thinking that is possible at this point of time?"

Now Lucia looked at Tanvi. There was a hollowness where tears should have been welling up in her eyes.

"I..." Lucia stopped. Not because she didn't know or not only because she didn't know. Because anything she said now wouldn't be founded in anything but regret, because it was too painful. She turned to look out the windscreen again, feeling Tanvi's eyes on her for a brief moment. Lu broke the silence with a gurgle coming from deep within her chest, it culminated in a blown spit bubble on her lip, far smaller than the rumbling would have suggested.

The car pulled up to the curb outside the house. Tanvi idled the car and looked at Lucia.

"There will be a way, definitely." Tanvi went to place her hand over Lucia's but stopped herself.

"Thank you."

Silence hung in the car again. Tanvi looking into Lucia's eyes, wearing her best comforting nurse face. Her eyes twinkled in a way Lucia missed from her own reflection.

"I can't open the door. You have to let me out."

"Oh right, certainly." Tanvi's tiny frame scampered out of the driver's side and raced around the car to open Lucia's door.

38

It was a few hours into the day before Win became fully aware of the dream he had the night before. Dreams are weird and Win had never really had dreams about anything in his real life. People, places, sure...but he never had dreams that echoed situations he had lived through. He didn't know anyone that did, that was more of a movie thing. The dream that he was remembering felt like something he had lived through. Maybe that was why it took some time for him to realise that's what it was. Even now he could only remember senses, if he tried to describe it to anyone else, it would be disparate and weird.

Lucia was there, that was what tipped him off. He caught himself feeling comforted by the feeling of closeness with her. Out of place enough in his current life for it to spark recognition of what really happened.

They were in bed or maybe they had just gotten out of bed. There was a bed. Or comfort. The feeling of crisp white sheets. Like a Chris Isaak film clip. There were probably crashing waves too, not that he thought the dream was explicit by any measure. That was another thing that reminded Win it was only a dream, the sheets. He had never had plain white sheets in his life.

Win's hands hovered above his keyboard. His eyes glazed and unfocused on the screen ahead of him. He was trying to remember the rest of the dream. He was a sucker for punishment and wanted to feel that feeling again, even if it wasn't real.

In his dream, Lucia was whole, she slept while he lay. He couldn't see her directly. He was looking at the ceiling, but knew she was there. He knew what she looked like; her face crinkled against the pillow, strands of her wavy hair crossing her nose. The hair fluttered with each deep, restful breath. He reached his hand out to wrap her in a hug. She didn't wake, only rolled towards him and rested her head on his chest instead of her pillow. Her free hand rested against him and he could see it rise and fall on his chest with each of his breaths.

Maybe at this time he fell asleep in his dream or he moved to the next dream. However many people are supposed to have in a night. Win hadn't remembered many dreams lately. He figured his sleep had been so poor that he just wasn't getting the chance. He didn't usually hold much stock in them. He wasn't a person who usually tried to remember them and certainly never regaled other people with his subconscious nonsense.

Now they were up, in the kitchen. Lucia was cooking. Scrambled eggs, toast, chorizo. It played out like he was watching a movie from a distance back. He was in the kitchen with her, but didn't move, only watched. Lucia sliced the chorizo on a slant, making long ellipsis of sausage. The eggs cracked into a bowl and she whisked vigorously. She said something to him, but he couldn't hear over the whisking, or maybe he couldn't remember. She smiled though; it wasn't a question. Win thought she might have said she loved him, but he wasn't sure. He knew the look though. The look when she decided she ought to say it out loud.

Lucia kissed him on her way to the pan. He felt her breath brushing his lip and the softness of her face. He could barely remember the real last time they kissed. She might have kissed him as she left for work. She left before he got up, so if she had kissed him it wouldn't have been on his lips. Cheek, forehead, shoulder. Sometimes she kissed him on the crest of his hip if he lay on his side, back to her. Tingles hit each of those parts of him as he recalled how it felt, comforting and warm. They kissed goodnight in the evenings, was that the last time? Did he make the best of it? Would he have kissed her longer if he knew it would be the last time?

He wrapped his arms around her as she folded the egg on itself. Glossy waves of silky eggs trailed behind her spoon until it was a beautiful parcel of scramble.

By the time it made it to the plate, the eggs were pancakes. That's how dreams work and pancakes are the most romantic breakfast food. She said something again and smiled, this time he knew it was "I love you."

Win's hand shuddered painfully, cold and stiff from not moving, and the nerves firing up in response to his mixture of love and pain. His jaw started to sting and he knew his cheeks were flushed. Tears would come if he didn't do anything to stop them. He turned to Sanjay.

"Coffee?"

"From downstairs?"

"Nah, just heading to the kitchen."

"Sure, thanks."

Sanjay passed up his coffee mug to Win as he walked past. Dregs of the last coffee were drying in milky rings at the bottom of the cup. The cup was emblazoned with the words "Straight Outta Fucks To Give" on the side. It was a gift, Sanjay actually had many fucks to give, it was more in his nature to give a fuck than not.

Now Win had a task, it was easier to not cry when his hands were busy. The hot water tap that jetted piping hot water from a small attachment to the sink wasn't working. It streamed chilled water just fine but the hot hadn't worked since last winter. Win filled the kettle and turned it on. He cleaned down the sink while he waited, busy hands after all. The regular hot tap was working enough to run some washing up water. He winced as his finger landed in some icy water being used to soak yesterday's lunch containers. It wasn't his job to clean. Each person was responsible for their own dishes. Still with sixty people using one kitchen, it got pretty disgusting very quickly. He washed the dishes and lined them up to dry. He washed his and Sanjay's mugs. There were no clean tea towels to dry them though. So he turned them upside down in the sink and poured a thin stream of boiled water over them. The boiled water evaporated very quickly and after a few seconds he had dry mugs.

He spooned instant coffee into each mug. Sanjay about half milk, Win only a touch. Boiling water to finish and any tears that had been brewing were swept away with the dish water.

❖

It wasn't on purpose. It was a long day and it was only when Win reached into his satchel for his keys that he realised where he was. He was at his own front door. He was there now, so might as well go in.

The door peeled open and Lucia was right behind it.

"Fuck!"

"Sorry, I didn't know it was you."

"Who were you expecting?" He would have made a tasteless adultery joke then, if he was in the mood for joking at all.

"Uhh no one."

"Ok Lucia, I know that was a lie. Who did you think it was?"

"You have to promise not to overreact."

"Ummmm?" Win put his satchel down at the end of the couch and sat. Lucia wasn't used to this sight. Normally he would strip down to house clothes as soon as he was through the door. He seemed like a guest now, being polite, perched on the couch.

- 270 -

"We had a break in."

Win blinked with emphasis. "What?"

Lucia swooped down to sit side-saddle on the couch. "We're fine!"

"Yeah Lucia, I knew you would be fine. What happened?"

"A dude broke in, he…" she had to put this the most delicately. "He attacked me, tried to attack Lu and Ruth." Win's neck craned forward and his eyebrows waved her on to keep going. "Lu bit him and he left."

"Fuck Lucia, so you're telling me a zombie bit a rapist and you just let him loose?"

"What was I supposed to do?"

"I don't know! Stop him? Kill him? Something!"

Lucia's eyes widened and she bit her tongue. She didn't want to get into the argument right now. Didn't want it to take up what little time she had with him. He was still staring at her. Waiting for a response, a retort, an admission, anything.

"You're right." She did think he was right, it would have been better to not have an extra zombie running around, but he wasn't there. He didn't know.

"Maybe Kathryn can help you find this guy."

"I don't know if she should be helping me anymore. Too dangerous."

"Too dangerous?"

"Yeah, she shouldn't be putting herself in danger, for the baby."

"Baby?!" Win thought for a second that Kathryn was pregnant. It crossed his mind that she had gotten pregnant accidentally which would involve more than one drastic life change. Then he remembered. So much had happened since then, he had completely forgotten that Kathryn and Gianna were trying.

"Oh fuck. She didn't tell you?"

Win flopped himself back like a tired cocoon. His body hung awkwardly. Legs bent, butt slipping from the seat and torso completely straight and armless. His hair fell onto his face and he stared straight at the ceiling. A wave of love crept over Lucia, seeing him in such a silly position. It felt like the mornings, when she would wake before him and see him asleep, wrapped up and carefree. Not that he was carefree now. Behind his hair, Win's brow furrowed.

"She didn't tell me." he said to no one in particular.

Lucia sat beside him on the couch, but he didn't feel it. Nor did he feel her hand touching his thigh.

"Maybe she didn't want to upset you. Introducing a new life, when you just lost someone."

"She told you!" He shook his hair back. "You're the one who's dead!"

"I'm her best friend."

"I'm her bro-ther!" His voice cracked in incredulity, but neither of them acknowledged it.

Lucia shrugged before falling back into silence. Win was sad, but she listened to his breath. She could hear a tiny whistle in his left

- 272 -

nostril and if she listened even harder, she could hear his heart thumping quietly. With his gaze trained to the ceiling, Win lost track of Lucia. She made no sounds and the air around her stayed unaltered.

Lucia broke the silence, "So why are you here?" She quickly added "Not that I'm complaining...but why are you?"

Her voice didn't shock Win, but his eyes flashed open at the sound.

"I forgot."

"Forgot?" Not knowing what exactly he forgot.

"Autopilot I guess."

Lucia grinned to herself. She stayed silent. Not even looking at him, just revelling in his presence. Win's body softened and conformed to the couch. He let it support him and after his long day, he slipped into unconsciousness.

The glow of the lounge room lamp radiated to the edges of the room before fading into darkness. The rest of the house seemed darker now. Moonlight which normally shone through the windows anointing the surfaces with a cold sheen gave way to the warm light coming from the lounge. The moon was approaching full, Lucia didn't know if that was waxing or waning. Linguistically it felt appropriate that waxing would be leading into the full moon and waning out of it. It could well be the opposite though. She was never a "moon girl." She wasn't really a "sun girl" either. Never described herself as a water baby or anything like that. She liked nature plenty, but that's where it ended. No real affinity for any element, colour or animal. Lucia didn't know if that made her boring or more interesting. Probably neither. Sometime in his sleep Win pushed the sleeves of his hoodie up his forearms. They were smooth, smoother than Lucia's had been and little muscles flexed as he hugged his ribs. He looked almost like he was made of marble, the plains of his skin so angular and perfect. He might as well have been stone. Lucia could not feel the life in him. She could not lay her head on his lap and feel his stomach gurgling against her ear. Nor could she feel or smell the hoodie that she sometimes stole and wrapped herself in just for security.

Lu had been swaying in and out of view for most of the night. Eager for attention, missing her undead companion, jealous of Win, hungry? Lucia couldn't tell. She didn't want to be worried about Lu now. She wanted to focus on her husband. She wanted to forget. Wake up from this terrible dream. A ghost, a zombie, a murderer and a victim all in one.

Lucia balled herself into a crescent, feet tucked beneath her and fell into Win. She nestled her head on his ribs, nose trapped behind his elbow. She did not feel him and he did not feel her. She closed her eyes and shut everything out.

When Lucia was a child, she had a fear of being seen in transit. Her family home had a long hall that zigzagged through the house. She hated to be caught in the hall. If she was moving from one room to another, and someone was also moving from one room to the next, she hated crossing paths. She even hated if someone else caught a glimpse of her as she turned a corner. There was no deep-seated reason for this. She wasn't afraid of her Mum, Dad or sister. It caused no fear if she was in a room and someone passed by the door. Only in the hall. Lucia was a jumpy child, maybe she got a fright one too many times bumping into someone and developed a strange phobia. She grew out of it too. As an adult she never had the same reaction. Even in her parents' home, which they still lived in.

Right now though, the same fear bubbled up inside. She was not in a hallway and she could not hear footsteps at the other end of the hall. She was on the couch with her sleeping husband, and he was stirring. The same feeling that had her racing through the hallway as a child, had her spring up from the couch and seek refuge in the spare bedroom.

Maybe somewhere deep-down Lucia thought no one would want her face to be the first thing they saw. She was saving Win a fright. Very few people would want to wake up to a ghost, even if it was their wife. Especially if it was their wife?

Win didn't notice Lucia racing away from him. He had not noticed her curled into his side as he dozed. There was a mild confusion in general when his eyes began to flutter open. A place so familiar, his own living room with his belongings all around him. He didn't remember falling asleep.

The house was quiet, eerily so. He could hear possums outside, rustling through the trees with a characteristic thumping and squeaking. Nothing else though and even the possums sounded further away than they usually were. When he started to move, Lucia reappeared in the doorway. She had been listening from around the corner. Worried he would sneak out without saying goodbye.

"Good sleep?"

"Yeah actually." Win picked up his phone from the coffee table and pressed the button on the side to light up the screen. He had only been asleep for just over an hour. There was a message from Kathryn, only a couple minutes old. Might have been what woke him up.

"Are you far away?" Kathryn was worried that something had happened to him but hedging her bets that everything was fine and asking what she thought, was the least annoying question.

"Not far. Tell you about it when I get there." He thought, "I ended up at my house by accident. Fell asleep. Why didn't you tell me Gianna is pregnant?" was too weird a message to be sent by text.

"I've got to get going. Kathryn is worried about me."

Lucia hesitated; she didn't want to push it.

"Just say it Lucia." One eyebrow raised behind his black hair, which had flopped over his face again. "I know you." He reminded her.

"Will you come back?"

"Yes. But I don't know when ok?"

"Ok."

He scooped up his satchel from the rug and swung it over his body. The strap rested against his chest and outlined his physique. Lucia's eyes brushed over him. She wanted to hug him. Press her hands into his back and feel his lean, but strong muscles twitch as he hugged her back. Win leaned towards the lamp beside the couch, his shirt stretched against his obliques. Lucia did not objectify him this much when she was alive. She did a bit, she always found him very attractive. It was weird because he basically looked like a male version of her best friend. She had never had feelings for Kathryn, but Win was a different story. She regretted every time she could have touched him and didn't.

"Do you want this off?" Win's finger was poised on the lamp switch. Lucia had been so focused on his body she hadn't really seen what he was doing.

"Ahh...yeah."

The lamp switched off, it's lightbulb still glowing the slightest amount and rapidly fading. The room was pitch black for a moment and then the moon light started streaming in. Win moved to the door, moonlight glowing on his back and over his shoulders. He looked like an angel.

"Good night."

The door closed behind him, his footsteps trailed to the footpath without hesitation. His footfalls faded down the street and the silence in the house was screaming.

"I love you." Lucia announced into an empty room.

Butterbean had draped himself over Kathryn's lap. His nose buried under a fold of the blanket she also had laid over her lap. He looked like a big furry throw. Kathryn's legs curled up under him and only one toe poked out from under his tail. She steadied an empty mug on the back of the couch. The contents of the mug were long gone, but Kathryn was kept in place by a dog that weighed not much less than her. The TV light flickered across Kathryn's face.

Walking down the street to Kathryn's home, Win could see this scene through the lounge window. He made a note to tell Kathryn that there was a clear view of inside her home from a few houses down. Butterbean heard Win a few seconds before Kathryn did. His ears pricked up and then his big plush beachball of a head lifted to the sound. His tail wagged ferociously before he made an effort to get up. By the time Win was in the house, Butterbean was up and enthusiastically helping Win take off his shoes. The intent was there at least. Win lost his balance a few times under the force of the huge dog nudging him.

"Good! I've needed to pee for ages!" Kathryn threw the blanket off, brushed herself down before sidling her way out from behind the coffee table.

"You know you can tell him to get off if you need to pee?" Win joked.

"Have you tried pushing him off when he's asleep?"

Kathryn disappeared into the hallway; Win heard the door click closed a few seconds later. A few seconds after that, Crumb sauntered into the doorway leading from the hall. He blinked his eyes slowly and licked his lips repeatedly before preening his paw and rubbing it over his ears. Then the whole process a couple more times before walking right up to Win to give a hearty nudge somewhere just below Win's knee.

"Hello boy!" Win scritched the very top of Crumb's head.

After Kathryn's return to the couch, Butterbean maintained the pretence that he might not jump right up onto her immediately. Instead, he just laid his head on the couch beside her, biding his time before making his move.

"So, what happened?"

"Gimme a minute." Win gestured with his head and his right hand holding his work satchel towards his bedroom.

"I spaced. Ended up at home."

Kathryn didn't know what response was the most appropriate so she stayed silent. She nodded her head up as a catch all kind of gesture, leaving her chin in the air to urge more conversation out of him.

Win changed the topic swiftly.

"So, I'm going to be an uncle?" His tone was pointed, just shy of accusatory.

"You're already an uncle."

"You know what I mean."

Kathryn heaved a big sigh, emotion caught behind her eyes and in the back of her throat. Her exhale coasted over words unsaid or at least words organising themselves into the perfect arrangement.

"We didn't want to upset you."

"How would Gianna being pregnant upset me?" Win had been avoiding Kathryn's gaze, but now whipped his head towards her. Not to relay his emotions, but to check Kathryn's eyes for hers.

"Because Win, you're grieving. We didn't think you would be ready to hear."

"I'm happy for you." Kathryn's brow sunk deeper into a frown. "I am! I can be happy for you. I'm not..." He didn't finish the sentence. He was going to say he wasn't broken, but he wasn't sure enough that was the case.

39

She hadn't been there for a month but now Mel's desk looked emptier than ever. Before, when she was only on holidays it was like her desk was just paused. She had cleaned it up, how people do before they leave. Clearing off papers and notes from her desk. A clean slate after time off. Her coffee cup was washed and turned upside down beside her monitor.

Now they knew she would never be back; her desk radiated an uncomfortable emptiness. Win tried to ignore it, but it buzzed in his left ear like a grief caused tinnitus. He launched himself into work, focusing his attention fully toward Sanjay when he braked.

Faith King stood back from Mel's desk. She held a file box against her pudgy middle. She let out a feeble sigh. She was usually so cheery but now she looked lost. Another sigh and she got to work dismantling Mel's desk. She carefully laid personal possessions one by one in the box. The mug, a little placard that read "keep calm and file a claim" and a few photos. Then she went through the desk. Sorting it into piles; personal things went to the box, work resources on one side of the desk, customer files on another and a lot of it went straight into the bin.

When she was done Faith let out another deep sigh and carried the box away to her office. The disruption to the desk had increased its melancholy reach. Everyone that walked past flashed a sorrowful look when they saw it.

The lunchroom had a big TV, which played almost constantly throughout the day. Very few people were ever invested enough in any particular show to change the channel. The channel did seem to get changed, but not often. Some days it stayed on channel 7 for the whole day, then the next week it'd be stuck on 10, before dropping back to 9 for a few more days. Win wasn't even sure why it was there. It was surely distracting to the people whose desks were close to the lunchroom. Eating lunch together was supposed to be good for morale or something like that, so having midday, free to air programming blasting into the room seemed counterintuitive.

On this day the TV was on the tail end of a panel show. A ticker tape of news scrolled along the bottom of the screen.

ADL 7*C / BNE 14*C / CAN 10*C / DAR 20*C....

PLANT FIRE IN NTH SYD - MORE AT 5 - 7TH BODY FOUND IN TOOHEY FOREST - FACTORY CLOSURES HUNDREDS OF JOBS AXED -

7th body found in Toohey Forest.

Win wasn't the only person to notice it. Two of his colleagues discussed it loudly from different tables.

"So many bodies lately!"

"Right? Remember in 2012 when there were all those murders in North Brisbane? DV stuff?"

"I think that's regular, just they got reported on a lot then."

"Hmmm true."

"Reckon it's a serial killer?"

"I heard it was feral dogs."

All of a sudden it was too much for Win. The bright windows, the food smells, the murder talk. He started to see stars and made a hasty exit. He dumped his barely touched lunch in the bin as he left. The smell that puffed out of the bin stung his nostrils and caused his stomach to churn. He heard the women continue talking behind him.

"Ooops, maybe he's the murderer...haha"

"Boys just don't like true crime."

Win felt the floor getting away from him as he walked back to his desk. It felt like he wasn't seeing with his own eyes anymore. The world was moving too fast, or he was, he couldn't tell and everything seemed too big but far away. He pulled up next to Sanjay's desk.

"Dude, lunch didn't agree with me." He lied.

"Ok" Sanjay looked up at him. Apart from a pained expression, Win looked normal. Sanjay assumed Win was politely letting him know that he was going home to do some explosive shits. Best for everyone if Win could do that in the comfort of his own home. Or his sister's home as it were.

"I'm gonna head home." Win made a move to shut down his computer but his knees buckled and suddenly he couldn't feel his hands. He sat staring into the middle distance, paralysed even though his mind wanted to propel him right out the door.

"You good?" Sanjay was leaning over to Win's desk. "Shit yourself?" He was only half joking.

"It all feels...weird."

Sanjay, always way more compassionate and observant than his outward persona would imply, noticed Win's chest pumping shallow breaths and Win wringing his hands.

"Dude, are you having a panic attack?"

"I don't know!" Win snapped back, not angrily but in a shrieking confusion.

"Oh yeah, I think you're having a panic attack."

"Is it supposed to feel like I'm dying?" The same confusion painting the question but it sounded more like someone trying to talk through bad indigestion.

"Yeah mate."

Sanjay guided Win into his chair. Win shifted uncomfortably trying to squirm above the pain.

"Lean back."

Win complied.

"Close your eyes and put your hands on your thighs."

Win offered a weak smirk before following Sanjay's order. Sanjay's voice was lower and calmer than Win had ever heard. Even smoother than Sanjay's "giving bad news" phone voice.

"So what's your cat's name again?"

"What?" Win opened his eyes and sat up. Sanjay rested a hand on Win's shoulder. His hand was big, soft and warm, but the pressure was firm.

"Just answer the question. Trust me."

"Uhhhh... Crumb."

"Crumb a boy or a girl?"

"Boy." it still sounded like Win was fighting to talk through heart burn.

"How'd Crumb get his name?"

"His previous owners called him Cookie. We thought that sounded too cute, so we renamed him Crumb."

"You get him as a kitten?"

"Yeah, not real little but young."

"A shelter?"

"No. Old neighbours abandoned him."

"Oh yeah? He's lucky you took him in."

"Yeah, he's a good boy."

"How old is he?"

"5 in September, we think" Win's forehead was crinkled and strained but his voice was evening out. His breathing was looking more normal from where Sanjay was sitting.

"Is that middle aged? For a cat?"

"Nah, like teenager, I guess."

"How you feeling?" Win kept his eyes closed but rubbed his palms down his pants.

"I feel better?"

"Good!"

"Ummm thank you." Win blinked his eyes open.

"No problem my dude. My little brother gets mad panic attacks." Sanjay's voice was back to its usual tone and pitch. "You should still go home though. Work'll just make it worse."

"Thank you."

Win scrolled through his computer. Closing things and checking on emails. He pulled his satchel into his lap and closed down the computer.

❖

Though Win had been to the city during non-peak hour countless times, the city felt strange to him. In an eerie way, like going to work on a public holiday or working weekends when you normally don't. He felt that he was the one out of place, rather than the streets not being what he was used to. The panic attack from before had subsided but it was still lurking in the background. There was a fresh fear of having another panic attack. Which cycled into Win reprimanding himself for panicking about being panicked. Somehow Win's body was informed that it should avoid any more panicking and the result was him moving in a way that seemed like he was wading through a pool of wool. Elevating his heart rate would be too similar a sensation to the ones he had felt moments earlier.

The day was bright, he knew that from when he started going wonky in the lunchroom. A frigid breeze floated down Adelaide Street, whipping the leaves gently in the gutter. Coffee, sushi and bus exhaust fumes perfumed the air. Win avoided eye contact with everyone as he waited to cross Adelaide St. He felt exposed, like everyone knew that not long ago he was being talked off a ledge by a large Indian man.

The ground felt somehow softer than usual, but it was just the sun radiating off the bitumen. He could feel warmth, not softness. Everything was normal. Not for Win, in spite of Win. His world was falling apart. His brain flip flopped between scolding him and telling him that everyone knew his life was in tatters and then screaming that no one knew and he was completely alone.

Win peered down Adelaide street to see if his bus was on its way. He couldn't see very far very clearly, even with his glasses on. The glare made him not even want to see that well and he had to keep fighting the urge to pull his glasses off to see better. A silly impulse, but one he experienced pretty regularly. He could have switched the sunglasses, but the thought of trying to balance his glasses and sunglasses while making the switch seemed like a huge bother. He could shift the glasses to rest on the top of his head while he wore the sunglasses for however long he needed to, but then he would be the douche wearing two pairs of glasses. Nearly as bad as the guy who wears sunglasses at night. So many sunglasses wearing faux pas, that's really fucking stupid Win thought to himself. He was a smidge grateful that his thoughts had turned to weird societal idiosyncrasies rather than his own failing mental state. In any case, if he moved his glasses to the top of his head it would be just as much bother to have to clean them of any hair grease later.

Pretty certain that the bus wasn't coming, he felt safe enough to look up the times on his phone.

Still another fifteen minutes.

In that case he would take a seat. There was only one elderly woman with a wheelie cart sitting on one bench. He took the other, crossing his right foot over to his left knee and resting his satchel in his lap.

Win was about to start scrolling through his phone when he took one last glance across the street towards the 711.

He'd seen it nearly every day, but from this angle he remembered wishing bon voyage to Mel before her holiday, before she died. At first just a little glimmer of remembering the last time he saw her alive, then he focused in on the exact circumstances. The man he had run into and knocked to the ground, that man running into her too...and shortly after that encounter she died.

40

Twenty-four is young, every year in your twenties seems to feel forever apart. A twenty-four year old thinks of a twenty-one year old like a baby, when a fifty-four year old would feel kinship with a fifty-one year old. Lucia was twenty-nine and twenty-four seemed like a lifetime ago. Hannah Delenko had been in a coma for close to three years, she had been home for most of that time. Insurance no longer covered a carer to nurse for her and Hannah's mother gave up her job to do all the work herself.

The Delenko house looked like any other house bought off the plan. The front yard sloped gradually to the road, a charcoal driveway led up to a double garage with matching coloured roller doors. The Delenko's house has an off white, rough finished brick. It appeared to be one of four different brick colours on the whole block. There were no cars in the driveway, but that meant nothing.

Fortunately for Lucia and unfortunately for anyone with this type of home, Lucia could tell the basic layout of the house immediately. Entry way, leading past a master bedroom at the front of the house, into a "formal lounge", followed by an open plan kitchen, dining and second lounge room. On the right side of the house, behind the garage would be the main bathroom, laundry and any remaining bedrooms. Lucia made a guess that one of those bedrooms would house Hannah. If she snuck around that side of the house she would likely not be seen and could scout out the best route for Lu to follow.

Lucia got Lu to follow her in beside the house and told her to stand at the gate, beside the wheelie bins. Lu followed Lucia dutifully with each step. She'd left Ruth behind for this exact reason. Lu had some kind of biological bond with Lucia and it was far easier to control her because of it. Ruth was a wild card.

"No, stay." Lucia whispered. She really wanted to stop commanding Lu like a dog. Having a dog to lug around might be easier. A fly that had been resting on the lip of the wheelie bin flew up and onto the side of Lu's nose. It darted around her face, proboscis throbbing against Lu's waxy pores. Lucia watched in horror, silently begging that the fly not find a crevice of Lu's face to nestle in. She turned away before witnessing something she couldn't handle.

Lucia walked close to the brick, closer than that kind of rough brick would allow any living person to walk. She pictured the layout of the house, its neutral coloured walls and white tiled floors. A clothes dryer thrummed at the first door along the wall. If there was someone in the laundry, Lucia couldn't see them. The heat of the dryer had fogged up the glass door. Through the fog, and the security screen, she doubted that anyone would see her either, unless they were seated in the laundry intently watching the door. The next windows were frosted glass, the kind that was smooth on one side and kind of the texture of a worn bitumen road on the other. If she was right, and by this time she knew she was, the next two windows would lead into two bedrooms. The first window was a sewing room. There was a table with a sewing machine and stacked plastic tubs in the corner filled with fabric. There was a quilted wall hanging strung on the wall above the sewing machine that said, "Home is where the Husqvarna is."

In retrospect Lucia scolded herself for just poking her head up in the window to have a good look. She had expected the room to be a bedroom and not likely to be occupied at this time of day. She knew someone was home though, because the dryer was on and there was every chance that they could have seen her. She collected herself before looking into the next window. She crouched so her eye was just above the windowsill, and slid herself slowly to her right, so just her right eye could see over the sill and into the room. She hoped that this way the least amount of her could be seen if there was someone in the room. The room was a mirror image of the sewing

- 290 -

room, but where the table had been, there was an elevated hospital bed. Hannah Delenko lay in the centre.

Lucia glanced back at Lu, who was dutifully standing where she had been told to stay. Now Lu was swatting the flies away from her face. They had multiplied and Lu only seemed annoyed when they came near her eyes or ears. She brushed at them, the frustration apparent from her expression and the forceful downward swings of her arms. Lucia realised that in order to get Lu up near her, she would have to yell louder than was appropriate for the time and place. Instead, Lucia crouched under the windowsills and right to the edge of the laundry. She had to wave her hands to get Lu's attention. Lu was still very focused on keeping the flies from her face, they were relentless and Lu was too slow moving to really disrupt them.

"Come here." Lucia let out a hoarse whisper.

Lu shuffled to Lucia, still flailing her arm at the gathering flies. Lucia had the fleeting thought of wondering what might be in the bin to warrant the presence of so many flies. The thought slotted into her mind behind her foremost concentration on commanding Lu's actions.

The pair crawled on their hands and knees back under the window to Hannah's bedroom. Crawling was more accessible to Lu than the crouching that Lucia has been doing. Her limp feet dragged behind her and she gathered debris with her knees.

As Lucia looked in through the window, watching the monitors beep and respirator hiss, she realised her mistake in leaving Ruth at home. She had no clue how they were going to bring food back to her. On this occasion, two undead bodies were better than one, a situation that had not been true until right this second. Once again, a stray thought wedged its way into the back of her mind. She could set Ruth loose. Just let her out of the house, but she would be damning some poor pedestrian to an untimely death. She could let her waste away, but the thought was too gruesome, less gruesome than another errant thought that Lu could regurgitate part of her meal for Ruth. Zombies probably weren't fussy about their meal being partially chewed. Lu proved that when she joined in finishing off Liam, or was it Leon?.

The openable portion of the sliding window was barred with a security screen. The other side was just glass. Lu would have to break the glass. There was no quiet way to do that.

Lu plunged her hand through the glass. It was quieter than Lucia imagined it would be, but not quiet enough to go under the radar. They had limited time now. Lu withdrew her arm from the window. Long grey grooves had appeared where the shattered glass tore into her forearm, the muscle beneath pale with a disconcerting lack of blood. A couple of more punches and the window was clear enough to climb through. Lu basically backflipped through the window, levering her stiff body over the windowsill. It was an impressive tactic that Lucia would not have thought of if Lu didn't just tumble through of her own volition.

Lu didn't waste any time biting into the young, atrophied neck of Hannah Delenko. It took her longer to get to her feet after her fall than it took for her to make her way to the bedside and start dining. There was, of course, no struggle like the other meals Lucia had witnessed. The monitor showed that Hannah was yet to die, but there was no change in her apart from the blood pressure dropping rapidly as blood pooled onto the side of the bed. It was less of a spectacle, but somehow, much more chilling than the others.

The crashing, the beeping and now the flatlining had attracted attention and the closed door of Hannah's room swung open. Fleur Delenko burst through the door, she was wearing a slight smile. She held her breath with hope that her prayers might be answered. Fleur had stopped praying for her daughter's safe return to the land of the living quite some time ago. Three years is a long time to care for her comatose child. Three years knowing nothing would change and her daughter would likely never improve. Three years for any sense of self Fleur once possessed to fade into nothing. She was nothing beyond her identity as Hannah's mother. Her marriage had dissolved into bitterness and silence. Her friendships were torture under the pitiful gaze of her girlfriends.

Fleur had made her mind up, this was all going to end. For all of them. She only needed the courage. The shrill beep coming from Hannah's room was one she had imagined countless times. The sound of one life ending and maybe hers beginning again. At first Fleur wasn't sure if she was dreaming. When she was sure she wasn't, her heart out paced her feet as she ran to her daughter. She hoped there was freedom on the other side of that door.

Fleur Delenko didn't know what she was seeing, or more so she knew exactly what she was seeing but the comprehension got lost somewhere between her eyes and her brain.

It looked like there was a woman eating her only child. She could see quite clearly strips of her daughter's flesh hanging loosely from this stranger's mouth. Her daughter Hannah, who had once been so vibrant and full of life, was nothing but a bag of bones. People told Fleur, her husband included, that Hannah was still in there. Prayers and patience would bring her back but Fleur lost all hope. She was keeping her daughter alive and clean for no purpose other than that was what she was supposed to do, until she could release them both. Guilt had crept in increasingly since the bright spark of Hannah's personality had been extinguished. If she got her daughter back now, she was certain she wouldn't be the same. Of course, she loved Hannah unconditionally. If she woke up, Fleur would care for her, no matter what physical, emotional or mental obstacles presented themselves, but Hannah was never going to wake up. The doctors knew so and Fleur knew too.

When Fleur heard the heart monitor ring out while she was watching her midday movie. She was ashamed to admit that a wave of relief washed over her. Her daughter would be at peace. Whether she believed that it would be God or something else that lay in wait at the end of life, or even if there was nothing. It would all be more peaceful than the life Hannah had been trapped in the last three years.

Hannah Delenko had been the spitting image of her mother. She still was, as Hannah wasted away, so did Fleur. They both once had plump cheeks, not fat, they were always quite slender. They had round faces, which if all you could see of them was their heads, you would think both Hannah and Fleur were much larger women than they were. Illness and stress had ravaged them both and now their cheeks drooped and skin stretched loosely over their joints. Hannah had a small balding patch on the back of her head, even though Fleur religiously turned her and moved her daughter to avoid exactly that. Fleur was losing her hair too, but in more of an all over sense. If you saw her in the street, you would think her body was riddled with cancer.

Fleur had heard of the animal attacks happening around Brisbane. A friend heard from a friend whose daughter listened to the podcast "Bite". At the time, Fleur didn't think anything of it. Even though she lived close to a bushy area, animal attacks were just not at the forefront of her mind. Australia, with its reputation for deadly animals, was not a place for big game attacks. The deadly animals to worry about hid in the crevices, they just weren't out there mauling people. She stored the knowledge in the back of her mind and it only sprung to her consciousness when she was standing, frozen, watching an animal eat her daughter.

"What's going on here?"

Lu didn't stop. She pushed her fingers into Hannah's neck and liberated muscle from the tendons of her throat with a dexterity that Lu never showed on any other occasion. The tendons didn't snap back to their usual position. Instead, they sagged out of the tear in Hannah's throat.

Lucia froze. She knew that there was no way for them to make a speedy get away. The jig was up.

"I won't call the police." The words even surprised Fleur as she spoke them. She was calm, or calmer than she thought she would ever be when face to face with someone murdering her daughter.

All Lucia could splutter out was, "I'm sorry."

She couldn't tell if Fleur was only saying she wouldn't call the police because she was scared and that's what people say when they're trying to get intruders to leave. There was a genuineness in her face. It seemed like Fleur really wouldn't rat them out. Lu had half of her daughter's neck in her gullet and still this lady didn't seem urgent for them to go.

"I'll unlock the back door and tell everyone it was one of those animals."

"She should bite me, make it look like I tried to stop her."

"No." The word rose out of Lucia's throat much more sternly than she expected. "She's infectious. We won't infect you."

"Will Hannah?"

"No." this time Lucia's voice was softer and the comforting tone she used with her patients. "She won't be infected. You might not want to see why though."

Lu was preparing for what Lucia could only think of as a zombie's version of a digestive. She ground her incisors on Hannah's nose. Already Hannah's face was not recognisable but now the cartilage of her nose snapped under Lu's teeth. Hannah's thin, youthful nose was a mangled tear in the centre of her face.

"Really." Lucia addressed Fleur again. "You need to look away."

Lu hooked her thumbs into the hole that used to be a nose and prised her thumbs apart. The result was a series of squelching crunches which were Hannah's orbital bones collapsing in on themselves.

Without knowing exactly what had happened or what was going to happen next Fleur realised that Lucia's warning truly was a kindness. She spun her back to the bed and covered her ears. Hunching she left the room and sank to the floor in the hall. Out of the room, hands over ears, Fleur couldn't help but focus on the sounds. She didn't know if they were still happening, or if they were replaying in her head.

Lu was sucking Hannah's brains through the opening she made, like some crazed monkey extracting juice from a coconut. Similar to cracking a coconut, the prize inside was peppered with flecks of shell, or occasional crunches of skull.

Lucia knew that as horrifying this was, for her and for Fleur, as bad as it would be for Hannah's father and anyone unlucky enough to investigate this death, it was nothing compared to the horror of watching someone you love turn into a zombie. She had seen such terror and anguish on her husband's face. She had felt it herself.

Fleur Delenko lugged herself down the hall. She felt as though her legs would not support her if she tried to stand. The tiles pushed into her knees and the grout scraped small layers of skin from them. Pain seared up through her joints and into her hips which felt weak and bound all at the same time. She reached the laundry and was hit with a wave of detergent and fabric softener misted in the heavy, humid air. She clicked the latch of the door and pulled herself up to standing before sliding the door open. After this she summoned the strength to race towards the hall wall opposite the laundry door, she jumped and tilted her shoulder into the plaster. Her thin frame left a small depression. She fell to the ground. Crumpled on the floor,

Fleur felt a ringing in her ears and when her head cleared from its knock, she realised it wasn't ringing, it was screaming, her own. She was howling in pain, only some of which was physical. Her eyes were clouded with tears, the laundry and hall becoming only a shimmer. She heard Lu dragging her feet past her, but her eyes couldn't make her out and her head was swimming. Lucia saw the woman in anguish and it hurt, but not as much as when she saw Win. Lu pulled a dirty towel from a load still in the hamper and on Lucia's instructions wiped the blood and viscera from her face and arms. Then they left before Fleur could change her mind about the police.

Fleur slid down the wall and her head lay awkwardly on the cold tile. Her body heaved with each inhale and her bony shoulder ground into the floor painfully. The pain felt far away and did not bother Fleur as much as the heaviness in her limbs. She could not tell if she was still crying, but her saliva got caught in her throat.

A clear image flickered into her mind and calm overcame her. Fleur pulled herself up. Her midday movie played in the lounge, unironic synth playing over strained dialogue. Hannah's respirator was still pumping, the tubes sputtering puffs of air into quickly congealing blood. She could see clearly that she was never going to have a life after Hannah and she needed to do something about it while she still had the nerve.

Fleur pulled the box the Delenko's kept their medication in from the pantry. She set aside her husband's blood pressure medication. The rest of the box she emptied into her palm. 1 and a half packets of Panadol, three cards of anti-anxiety medication, 7 sleeping pills, 10 codeine tablets, an out-of-date chesty cough syrup. She washed them all down with what was left of a bottle of cab sav. As the weight of her limbs got heavier and her stomach bubbled, Fleur stumbled into Hannah's room and curled herself in a ball around her daughter. Blood trickled from Hannah's throat down Fleur's neck and just the slow-moving drip reached the mattress, Fleur was dead.

41

It was hard to know for sure how many people saw a naked, elderly woman shuffling her way through the streets of Brisbane, without raising any alarm. Pedestrians, passing drivers and looky-loos peering out their windows. It was a long walk, just under an hour for a healthy person. Ruth was not young, not healthy and easily confused. The sun was low in the sky by the time she reached her own house. Even in death Ruth was fiercely independent and not one to be told what to do.

Liam/Leon's car was gone from the driveway. In evidence some place. There was a thin strip of police tape across the front door, the only vestige of anything awry. The tape had slipped down and curled, so even it wasn't a blaring advertisement for what had gone on inside.

The door was locked and after several banging attempts to break it down, Ruth flew headfirst through the window above the couch. It was a spectacular sight. From her vantage point from across the road, Harriette saw it in slow motion, like an action movie. The glass shattered in larger sections that it's onscreen sugar-based counterpart, but just as thrillingly.

Shards slid through Ruth's body like soft butter. Large flaps of skin cleaved from her wasting muscles and hung in loose, wet folds. Some pieces cut through the layers of her limbs and jutted from their final sticking place.

Harriette was kneeling on her couch looking out the window. She partially hid herself behind the curtains, trying not to move them, instead moving herself up and down, back and forth trying to get the right angle. She didn't want the curtains to give her away. She was up on her couch because she heard someone walking outside her window on their phone. It was only a man who decided to share his conversation on speaker with the whole neighbourhood while he walked his dog. Harriette forgave him the intrusion only because he had a dog. It was fluffy and seemingly enamoured with its obliviously rude owner. After the man was down the street someway, Harriette saw, below the dip of the sloping yard of Ruth's house, a slow moving naked old woman. She thought she was naked anyway, she could have just been wearing an unfortunate colour. Skin hung differently from clothes though and wobbled rather than swayed as the figure took long dragging steps. The banging made Harriette duck lower in the window but soon she creeped up to her knees again when she got frustrated with the view. By the time she could see across the road clearly again, Ruth was hurtling herself through the window.

"Oh fuck, fuck, oh shit." Harriette's mouth snapped open between words. She grasped her own throat reflexively, the way many women do when they see someone in peril. She bounced herself over to the other end of the couch where she had been about to start last night's episode of The Good Doctor. Her phone was wedged down beside the cushion and her hands trembled terribly as she tried to reach it.

The 000 operator was all business and Harriette started to feel foolish as she answered every question.

"My neighbour's house. Someone just. She went through the window."

"Someone went through a window at your neighbour's house?"

"Yeah."

Do you think a robbery is in progress?"

"No, she went through the window, the glass."

"Can you see her, is she bleeding?"

- 300 -

"I can't see her. I'm here. I'm in my house. Someone was murdered."

"Sorry, who was murdered?"

"A man was murdered in that house. Now she went through the window."

The story didn't make sense to the 000 operator, because it didn't make sense even with most of the facts."

❖

Glass crunched under Ruth's body as she rolled herself off the couch and onto the floor where her Persian rug once was. The rug had been collected in evidence and was locked in a cage somewhere, never to be appreciated. Ruth did not pay much attention to the missing items. Neither did she care much about the fingerprint dust that stained a number of surfaces. She struggled to her feet; small flecks of window embedded themselves in her palms as she pulled herself up. Ruth was home.

The bedroom was cast in shadow in the afternoon. With the curtains closed it was quite dark. The bed was pushed at an angle towards the lightless window to reveal a large portion of exposed foundation. The carpet and underlaying rubber were cut from the floor where there had been a pool of blood only days earlier.

The sheets had been stripped from the bed and there was only a bare mattress. Ruth seated herself on the side of the bed. Her new angle had her facing out the bedroom door and towards the bathroom. Of all the irregularities in her home, this was the one that disconcerted Ruth the most. She grew agitated. After a short while she abandoned the bedroom in favour of the dining room.

The sideboard was decorated with photos in thin, wooden frames set on doilies. Photos of her children, Ruth's wedding to her late husband Vic and Vic in his RAAF dress uniform. Scattered among them were metal folding frames for small loves. In one there was a photo of herself and Vic, another had Daisy and Delilah.

The grief Ruth, while living, had felt for Vic's passing was such a part of her. So deeply ingrained into the person she had become in the twenty years before her death that it was barely a blip in the radar as she scanned the room. She still mourned Vic, even now in death, but it was a constant, she didn't need a photo to remind her. He was one of the only things etched so vividly in her memory that she hadn't forgotten him when her body became a shell and her soul was long gone. The memory of her dogs had not made such an impression, but it was enough that on seeing them, it awakened something.

Rage swelled inside Ruth. She pounded against the panes of the sliding glass door which took up most of the rear wall of the dining room. The thick brown curtain was pulled across, exposing a person's width of glass. The late afternoon sun streamed in a rectangular, orange block across the dining room floor and illuminated the skirting board beside the fridge. The setting sun shone through the lace covered kitchen window too, lighting up the cupboards on the other side of the galley style kitchen. The fridge had been turned off and cleared of what little remained at Ruth's time of death. The fridge had not been cleaned and if Ruth's soul still inhabited her body she would be mortified by the smell. Blood and decay still clung to the air, it converged with the rancid fridge smell somewhere between the lounge and dining room.

The harsh sun practically shone through Ruth's body. The flailing flaps of skin on her upper half let the light through and between them like gossamer ruffles. The glass dotted among them dispersed the light in glimmering fractals. Her face and muscles were strained as she pushed with her full force on the door. The door hopped the runner and swung, first bending the lock, then breaking it off the door frame. The door crashed to the ground loudly and spectacularly in a waterfall of shimmering sunsets.

The first breaking glass wasn't enough to attract the attention of the neighbours. Most of which were a lot less invested in the street's goings on than Harriette O'Connor. Harriette O'Connor would notice anything that happened in a three-block radius of her living room. A second, much louder crash, emanating from the same place and not too long after did garner attention.

Virgil Lotu had been Ruth's neighbour for thirty something years. He moved his family in next door when they only had one child and another on the way. Ruth was a good neighbour. She never complained about Virgil's kids, in the end he had four boys running around and many neighbours would be annoyed. They knew each other by name and waved when they saw each other. Ruth, like many people in her age bracket, was a little racist, and their thirty-year relationship never progressed beyond courtesies because of that. Since the last of his brood moved out a few years ago, Virgil started converting his backyard into a veritable orchard. He could be found pottering in the garden every weekend.

He knew the house next door was empty. His wife, who had a later start in the morning than he did, told him all about the early morning kerfuffle of Ruth dying. They were both home when the narrow street was suddenly filled with police one afternoon. Harriette had joyously told anyone that would listen what happened and how the police "looped her in." Harriette had also told everyone that Ruth wasn't dead, it was a false alarm. When the police came door knocking, canvasing for witnesses to whatever it was that most recently plagued the house next door, they confirmed that Ruth had died the month earlier. Such a tall tale from Harriette was not unprecedented.

Virgil heard the first crash coming from next door. He thought it was next door. The sloping street bounced sound around the houses, making it hard to discern an exact orientation. Virgil's wife, Miriam had even popped her head out the kitchen window to ask what the sound was. They decided it wasn't worth investigating. The second crash, which had been preceded by a whole lot of banging, warranted a little look.

The sliding window crashing to Ruth's back patio was a much easier sound to track. Her yard was lined with ornamental hedging and the sound probably wasn't heard much beyond the boundary of her property. Virgil heard it though and pretty soon his whole 190kg was tiptoed on a step ladder by the fence. Virgil's ankles buckled and rolled when he saw a figure that was definitely his ex-neighbour stepping over a carpet of broken glass into the back yard.

The compost bin was Ruth's object of desire, what she so badly wanted to get to that she smashed through a plate glass door. She did not mind the smell of decay, her own nasal cavities were quite literally rotting. Unlucky for Virgil Lotu, the compost bin was situated by his shared fence and very close to where he was teetering.

"Hey Ruth?" he called out at the woman scuffing her bare feet through the slightly overgrown grass. "You alright? The police think you're dead, ey?" It wasn't until she was much closer to him that Virgil could see her properly. He didn't wear his glasses to garden. "Aww shit Ruth, you don't look so good." Now she was very close, only a hedge and wooden fence between them. Ruth glared up at Virgil and snarled, like a dog guarding a bone. Virgil saw her glazed over eyes and rotting, weeping, torn flesh and he knew, against all reason, the police were right. Ruth was dead.

He stepped backwards off the ladder and reached for the closest thing that resembled a weapon. Lawn edger in one hand, trowel in the other, Virgil was going to fight this thing. He'd seen enough movies with his boys to know this was exactly how zombie apocalypses start.

By the time Virgil had made his way into Ruth's backyard, Ruth was standing over the compost bin. She had removed the sun-bleached domed lid and it scraped down the ridged side of the bin, landing against a pile of bricks beside the bin. Grass clippings loosely covering the rapidly decomposing bodies of her beloved Pomeranians let off steam in the cooling twilight. The smell was eye watering, something Virgil Lotu noticed as soon as he was through the gate down the side of Ruth's house. The bins were in his immediate vicinity and they smelled bad enough. Then the breeze carried the smell from the compost over to him. His eyes ran, his nose stung and he had to find his feet as it hit him. At least he thought that was the only putrefying stench, Virgil's heart leapt out of his chest and his underarms moistened with their own foul odour.

Ruth paid very little attention to Virgil. She had a one-track mind and it was set on reuniting with her pets. She scooped Delilah out first, she was the least concealed by clippings. Mats of red fur were scattered across blackened flesh. The organs had been cleaned away by insects and some beetles still clung to the skeleton. Ruth pulled Delilah to her breast, holding her there firmly with one elbow as she scavenged for Daisy. Daisy looked even worse off, she was deeper into the compost and her already black fur looked like scabs of mould on fetid flesh. Ruth pushed her forehead against Daisy's skull. Her eyes were closed and she swayed, little grunts escaping her that may have once upon a time, formed a melody.

Ruth's eyes snapped open barely a second before the business end of a lawn edger cracked into the side of her skull. The dirty and rusted spikes left reddish powder on the rims of the three identical holes left behind.

"Get the fuck out of here!" Virgil was pulling back the edger over his head, ready to bring it back down again with just as much force. Any thought of Daisy and Delilah had evaporated from Ruth's feeble consciousness. She was angry now. She threw her dogs to the ground; they were so light from decomp that they hardly made a sound as they landed at her feet. As the edger came down again, she was nowhere near its swing and had launched herself at Virgil's throat. As fast as a zombie in full berserker mode can be, her movements were still predictable and she moved in short bursts.

"Ahh shit!"

The first lunge missed him, but the edger slammed into the ground where Ruth had been, which was now where two long dead dogs lay. Streetlights started to flicker on, distracting Ruth for a moment. Enough time for Virgil to ram his trowel into her shoulder. It crunched between bones. A twist snapped the collarbone, not forcefully enough to break the skin, but causing the disconcerting bulb to appear. The trowel was stuck and as much as Virgil yanked at it he couldn't budge it. Broken collar bones or protruding garden tools didn't stop Ruth. She lashed her arm around and caught Virgil by the neck, she ripped a handful of skin and fat from it. Not enough to cause any real damage but exposing the crucial bits. It hurt like hell and Virgil screamed.

Miriam heard the scream from the kitchen. She hadn't heard Virgil scream that way before, but she knew for sure that it was him. She raced into the garden fearing the worst, thinking she would find her husband maimed by a gardening tool. He wasn't there and she called out for him, but Virgil didn't hear her over the blood pulsing in his ears. Shock was starting to claim him and he felt like he was falling through the grass. It felt like punching in a dream, Virgil's limbs were cold and numb. Pins and needles racked his fingers as he tried to strengthen his grip on the lawn edger.

He swung wildly. The head of the edger whacked into the side of Ruth's neck with a squelching thud. Her loose tendons offered little resistance and the edger continued on its arc, dragging rags of skin with it. Virgil pushed his whole-body weight against the direction of the edger and brought it swinging back the other way. The flat side of the wheel connected with the same point on Ruth's skull as it had earlier. Skin split open from her skull in a grotesque tear. Fine fractures on her skull exposed, when on a living person they would be obscured by blood.

There wouldn't be another whack. Ruth reefed the edger from Virgil's grip. She threw it behind her and out of reach. Ruth never had particularly long fingernails, she kept them trimmed and filed down with an emery board. Where the skin on most of her body had puffed, swollen and become a fragile mess, the skin on her fingers and toes had started to dry. The palms of her hands were shrunken and dry, pulling her fingers forward into a claw. Dried skin exposed her nails into ten deadly, sharp implements for gouging and slicing.

Miriam pinpointed the sound coming from their neighbours' yard. She stepped onto the step ladder, but she was much shorter than her husband. Instead of looking over the fence, she peered through the slats of the fence. She could only see flashes of blood and flesh squabbling on the other side of the fence.

"Virg! Virg! Are you ok?"

"Honey, go back..."

The end of his sentence was strangled by Ruth's fist punching into the pulsing hole in the side of his neck. Her fingernails clenched into the muscle on the side of his neck and tore it out with a snap. Ruth pushed the end of the meat into her mouth and tore through it with her teeth, swallowing in one gulp.

Virgil fell back onto the grass. It was damp with the night air, his blood gushed in warm spurts, but he could only feel the cold. Ruth knelt above him, one knee pressed into his stomach, the other by his hip. She buried her face in the side of his neck, tearing and slurping. Virgil reached around him on the grass, it was slick with blood, so were his hands. His hand connected with decaying puppies before he found at last one of the bricks stacked beside the compost. Virgil's large hands enveloped the brick. It normally would be nothing for him to lift a brick and fling it around. His shoulder was decimated and his whole arm trembled. With a final grunt he pulled him right arm across and slammed the brick into the weak side of

Ruth's head. Her skull caved into the grey goop, enough to short circuit whatever it was keeping her moving.

Ruth slumped over. Virgil's eyes dimmed and soon he wafted into unconsciousness, hearing his wife screaming his name.

42

"We should have taken the body." Lucia thought to herself. Thinking about the near empty freezer at home and the two zombie mouths she had to feed. She had left Ruth at home to limit the attention she drew getting around. Ruth would be fine alone. She had been alone for a long time, both before and after she died. For the most part Lucia's undead wards kept to themselves. They didn't really do anything unless they were told to.

She thought they might have thoughts. Or at least feelings, but Lucia imagined they were so few and far between that they didn't change any behaviour. They seemed content to just exist. Ruth did kill that man, her son, but Lucia knew that Ruth thought very little of her children even when alive. She probably would have taken her daughter out too if the opportunity arose. As long as no one broke into the house, Ruth would have no one to kill and she wasn't likely to do any property destruction. The most Ruth would do is maybe leak on something. Her elderly skin had a little less integrity than Lu's did. Ruth had also eaten less meals, as far and Lucia was aware. There was the unaccounted for time between Ruth being carted off post cardiac arrest and when she reappeared in her home again. Ruth could very well have killed someone then. That might be why there hadn't been a big fuss about a body going missing from the morgue. Or would there have been a bigger fuss if she killed someone? Lucia had no idea how many people worked at the morgue. She couldn't have taken them all out, surely. Even if she just got up and walked out, someone would have seen her on the way. How soon do they remove the clothes? Ruth was wearing pyjamas when she died. An old woman walking down the street in her pyjamas would attract attention, so would a naked woman. Then again, Lucia had ventured out of the house with Lu, wearing identical outfits and no one had so much as raised an eyebrow. People are in general pretty oblivious, or self-absorbed or both.

As soon as Lucia left the house she was counting down the seconds until she could go back again. But it didn't feel comforting in the same way as it used to. No longer an island in the stream where she could rejuvenate. No longer a home with her husband. It was just a house, but a safe one nonetheless. Anxiety started to rise up in Lucia. Her eyes darted side to side and every few steps she looked behind her. A wind whipped against Lu. She could see it bending back the stray waves of baby hairs off her forehead. The hood of her jumper billowed as it caught the breeze and the blood smears down the front of it dried into a deep brown rapidly. Only a few more steps.

When she was younger Lucia used to get a sick nervous feeling when she was close to her goal. Usually finishing a test. The last few questions felt like torture because she just wanted to be done. She felt the same now. Only a few hundred metres to her front door. The danger wasn't over, only nearly. If someone saw Lu's bloody clothes and called the cops they could see exactly where they went.

Lu pushed herself over the crest of the small hill on their street. Fighting against her own limbs, gravity and the wind. Lucia wished she could just race ahead, let herself in. Through the frangipani trees that lined the fence a few houses down, Lucia caught glimpses of her house.

The door was open.

She raced forward but her ghostly tether pulled her back. Lu was in no rush.

"Hurry up!" Lucia whispered hoarsely, getting in close to Lu's ear.

Lu didn't react. She was trudging at a steady pace now, but it wasn't fast. A million things ran through Lucia's mind. A break in. A real estate inspection. The police raiding the place. Images of police finding the dead man in her freezer clogged her brain. Ruth attacking whoever broke in, or some poor twenty something property manager. The police finding Ruth and taking her into custody where she would slowly decay and go rabid.

Win could be home. That thought was a shining little beacon in the swampy gore filled nightmares that were flooding in.

"Hurry!"

They were so close, still the tether held Lucia firmly in place like a child on a leash. Just as frustrated at her squandered liberties and close to tantrum. If it was Win, she didn't want him to see Lu looking this way. That would be favourable to any of the other options that were screaming at Lucia.

At last Lu reached close enough to the house for Lucia to rush forward. She was up the steps but she couldn't quite make it to the door.

The house was dark, unmoving other than a few leaves that had blown into the entry. They rocked back and forth with light crinkles. Lucia got some slack and pushed the door further open stepping over the threshold into a quiet house.

There wasn't anyone there. Nothing was moved. She couldn't sense anyone. Fuck. No one at all. She knew it even before she had to look. Ruth wasn't there anymore.

Lu ambled up the stairs and into the house. Lucia raced room to room. Double checking everything. The house was eerily untouched. Ruth was gone. Taken? Had Lu left the door open. Lucia searched her memory for the sound of the latch clicking. She couldn't find it.

❖

Dinner smells floated on the frigid night air, garlic from one house meeting with another house's steak and the next neighbour's curry. Then they disappeared into the night. It was early, not even six, but the sun had set a while ago. Win had been called. There wasn't much else Lucia could think to do. Lucia moved from room to room trying to find any evidence of why Ruth left.

Ruth's room was the way it had been left. Clothes were scrunched in the corner by the door. Ruth's that she'd been wearing on her way over. Pale pink capris, a white button up blouse and a darker pink jumper. The top few buttons of the blouse were unbuttoned but the jumper had covered that. The pair had been pulled off together the first chance Ruth had gotten, sleeves wringed inside one another. Ruth had not so much as touched them again since the night she came here. Curled, thin, grey hairs collected in the dust of the office desks. The house was old, not quite a Queenslander, but the same feel. Win and Lucia managed without air conditioning or ceiling fans. They made do with a cross breeze and a few pedestal fans to cool the house. The open windows and that most of the casement windows were original to the home, meant dust accumulated everywhere. Computer desks seemed to bear the brunt of it though. There were a few odd shapes on Win's desk where his computer had been. The dust was starting to cover any trace of it though. The top layer of dust was where the hair was.

Win's thin strands of black hair blended in with Crumb's fur. Both shed like crazy but formed a kind of black furry homogenised dust bunny in the corners of the rooms. Lucia's paler and longer hair was easily distinguished. It was odd to see another person's hair catching the light. A lot of that dust was probably Ruth's skin too. Lucia tried not to think about it.

The other rooms had even less evidence Ruth had ever been there. If it weren't for the office, Lucia would start to think she imagined the whole thing.

Coming back into the lounge, the breeze pushed hard against the front door. It shifted on its hinges, rocking the latch. Not enough to open. The latch was strong and installed well, even a gale force wind wouldn't change that. If the door hadn't been closed properly though.

Lucia moved in closer to the door, as though looking at it hard enough would tell her if that's what happened. Edged herself closer and closer as though it might suddenly burst open. Nothing could hurt her, but the impulse was still strong. She was sure Lu closed the door. Pushed shut with force and then pressed the heel of her hand on the door to make sure it didn't budge. Had Lucia been paying enough attention? Was that how it happened or was that memory from a different day?

Lucia had been focused hard on the task ahead. Getting there was one thing, what they had in store when they arrived was another story.

Lucia played the events of arriving home back in her head. The fear, what she saw, coming inside and Ruth not being there. She went over everything again and again. She came home, pushed open the door. It was already open, but not that far. She had to push it to get in.

She had to push it to get in! She didn't remember that. Doing it was instinct. Thinking back now she couldn't feel the door on her hand, but she must have touched it. She moved it for sure. She touched something.

Lucia stretched out her hand. Still scared of the door, but this time of what it represented, not the actual door. She reached for the handle. It was bronzed with dark shiny smudges where her hands had been countless times before. She wrapped her hand around the knob, it looked unnatural, but she couldn't remember how it was supposed to look, or if she had just not paid that much attention

- 313 -

before. She twisted her wrist anti-clockwise but the handle stayed put. Still rattling in the latch against the wind.

"Fuck!"

"Oooh" came a voice from the other side of the door. It was Win who arrived with Kathryn in tow. They were standing on the other side of the door when they heard the exclamation come through the wood.

"Shit sorry, didn't notice you pulling up." Lucia stepped backward away from the door.

A key slid into the lock and Win's face appeared through the crack.

"You right?"

"Well no, but yeah."

She wanted to tell him that she touched the door. That it was the second time she had been able to do that. She wanted to let him know that everything would be ok and if she kept getting better at it. It'll be like nothing ever happened. They could return to normal. Instead, she held her tongue and smiled a meek, relieved smile.

Win darted from room to room in the exact same way Lucia had when she arrived home. He reappeared sweaty faced and slightly out of breath. Kathryn had turned the lounge room light on and was standing back against the wall with her hands behind her back.

"How did she get out?" Win questioned, his breath returning to normal.

"I...I don't know. I think maybe Lu didn't close the door properly."

"You didn't check?" He was snappy more than he was angry, but it hurt all the same. "How could you not check?"

"I'm sorry. I didn't think. I'm so stupid."

"Hey" Kathryn interjected. "You're not stupid. I wouldn't have thought to double check either." Win didn't agree with Lucia's assertion that she was stupid, but he didn't agree with Kathryn placating her either. He crooked his head and narrowed his eyes at Kathryn. She ignored his judgement. "What were you doing that you left the house?"

Lucia paused. Win already knew what she had been doing. Kathryn knew that Lu ate people, but the reality of it wasn't something she had been able to stomach yet.

"I...we.."

"They were getting food." Win snapped again.

Kathryn nodded, then the image of what that actually entailed hit her and she shifted uncomfortably against the wall.

Lucia quickly changed the subject, "She made it home before." Lucia shifted her gaze from Kathryn to Win. He was standing a little straighter. Less defeated. "Ruth, she found her way home the first time. Maybe she did it again?"

"That actually makes a lot of sense." Kathryn added. "We could go to her place. See if she went there." She pointed at Win, eyebrows raised waiting for his approval of the plan.

"Should I come?" Lucia asked?

"No." Win snapped again before pulling back. "It'd be easier with just us."

He meant just the humans. They all knew it.

❖

"The next left." Kathryn was directing. They hadn't put the address into Google maps. A step that seemed too little given all the evidence tying them to the deaths.

Turning the corner into Ruth's street the yellow glow of streetlights gave way to flashing red and blue. Police and ambulances lined the small street.

"Is that it?" Win asked.

"Yeeaap."

They had to drive down the middle of the road as cars had lined both sides of the street. New crime scene tape covered the old, this time stretching to the neighbour's yard as well. Harsh green tinged light spilled out from forensics vans into the street. Bodies cloaked in PPE moved about the scene, ducking in and out of the side gate. A forensics tech crouched beneath a tree in the front yard. She'd taken off her gloves and held her head in her hands. Her face glowed with frustration and confusion. Barefoot nosy neighbours collected round the edges of the perimeter and a middle-aged islander woman was wrapped in a blanket wailing into the night.

They didn't say anything, just rolled carefully down the street. Flashing lights lit up their faces through the car window. Win kept easing the car down the street until they were around the next corner. Kathryn looked past him and tried to see through the gate that people kept disappearing behind. It was no use though.

Win started the trip back to his house in silence. Halfway home Win clicked on his indicator and pulled to the side of the road. He leaned his head on the steering wheel and started to sob.

His breath came out in ragged, heaving cries. He clutched his hands around the wheel until his knuckles made bright white crests and his fingernails scratched into the plastic. His chest jerked in painful motions when he tried to breath in.

"Hey, hey!" Kathryn turned and rubbed tentatively between his shoulder blades.

"It's so fucked Kat."

"I know."

Win pulled himself up, hands still on the wheel. His eyes were puffy, cheeks wet with tears, his black hair had flopped over his brow and there was a small streak of snot dribbling down to his upper lip. Kathryn had not seen Win cry this hard since they were children and it hurt her to see his pain. She made note of the snot for later though.

"I don't want to deal with it anymore." He was still having trouble speaking through the hiccoughing sobs.

"I know."

"I'm so tired."

Kathryn pulled her brother in for a one-armed hug. Their bodies awkwardly stretched across the centre console. Neither of them was comfortable, but they hugged in silence for a long time. Win's breathing smoothed out and Kathryn was surprised to find she didn't cry. She needed to be strong for now. Strong for her brother and her best friend. She was terrified. Something bad had gone down and the unknown was going to gnaw at her. Not a chance of sleep tonight.

Kathryn broke the silence "Are you getting snot on my jumper?"

"Yes." A reply came tearful but through a smile.

She pulled away, sure enough a wet patch was noticeable on the shoulder of her green jumper. There was a dot of white mucus in the middle.

"Gross!" She pulled at Win's sleeve to wipe it off.

"My bad." Despite having his snot transferred to his sleeve, Win's mood had been significantly lifted.

"Do you want me to drive?" Kathryn asked.

"Yeah".

43

"We could get a hotel."

"I don't want a hotel, I want to stay here. I want to snuggle in my bed with my wife."

"Yeah snuggle." Kathryn delivered a chiding chuckle.

"And other things." Gianna slipped her arms around Kathryn's waist from behind and lay tender kisses on her neck. During disagreements like this one, Gianna was prone to being demonstrative. They both loved Win, but Gianna wanted him out of the house on the night of their upcoming anniversary. Kathryn's body softened and she tilted her head to give Gianna more access. Then remembering the conversation she stiffened, twisting in Gianna arms to turn and face her. Kathryn dangled her wrists over Gianna's shoulders. Gianna pulled tightly on Kathryn's hips bringing them even closer to her own.

"I can't ask him to leave. He's supposed to feel safe here. He doesn't have anywhere else to go. I think pushing our anniversary and our baby in his face is a little...insensitive."

"It's one night. I won't be on shift. I can take you out, we'll have great food and then come back here." She punctuated her point with another kiss on Kathryn's neck. "It might be my last chance to get you alone before the baby." Another kiss, this time on the lips. She rested her forehead on Kathryn's, stooping so she could still look into her wife's eyes. "Come on."

Gianna's hot breath caressed Kathryn's lips, her big grey eyes filled with pleading and lust. She could tell Gianna was trying to distract her or seduce her into kicking Win out of the house. While she most definitely wasn't immune to Gianna's womanly wiles, she was wise to them being used against her.

"That's my point too. Once the baby comes, we might not get a holiday for a while. A night in the city, we'll be in walking distance of the restaurant. Check in early. We'd only have to get out of bed to go eat." Kathryn's dark brown eyes looked up into Gianna's. She pushed wisps of curled, dark hair that had fallen from Gianna's low braid back behind her ear. Kissed her on the cheek and lingered long enough to whisper in Gianna's ear, "I'd insist on it."

Gianna sucked air through her teeth, threw her head back, sighed, then pulled Kathryn's in for a tight squeeze. After releasing Kathryn from her embrace, Gianna flung herself backwards onto the bed. Knees bent and her toes tucking in close to her butt, one forearm draped over her eyes.

"Augh!" Propping herself back up on her elbows to look at Kathryn while she made her last-ditch effort to persuade her. "What if? We stay here *and* I take you on a babymoon closer to my due date?"

Kathryn hooked one leg under herself and rested on the edge of the bed. Her heart and hands reaching out to Gianna. "Babe, I can't ask him to leave."

"I know," Gianna conceded. Kathryn nestled into Gianna's ribs, hugging her with one leg curled around her waist and her head on Gianna's shoulder. She traced her fingers across the bare, olive skin of Gianna's other shoulder.

"He's my brother and he doesn't have anywhere to go."

"You're right, hotel it is then."

"Thanks babe."

❖

Since Tanvi had seen Lucia, she couldn't shake her from her head. How could she? It was a revelation that was earth shattering. Not only her social circle, that it happened to someone she knew, but her whole idea of this life and the next.

The food on her plate, half eaten egg idli, sautéed mushrooms and tomato, had gone cold while Tanvi stared blankly into space. Her hand rested around the still warm mug filled with black coffee. Tiny specks of dust whirled in the shaft of light that traversed the cold kitchen tiles. Tanvi's mind was trapped in a whirl with them.

News came last night, from an article on Facebook, not any official channel. Tanvi's daughter Sunny mentioned it, almost in passing.

❖

"A guy was murdered in Rocklea."

Sadly, that news, on its own, was not substantial. On any other day, Tanvi would barely have taken any notice. She would have offered some kind of absent-minded platitude, "That's a shame," "What is the world coming to?" "Terrible!"

Instead, her ears pricked up, "Another?"

"Huh?" There was silence while Sunny scanned through the article, "Second in as many weeks" she quoted the article. She kept reading, skimming for any more pertinent information to share from the murder two suburbs over.

"Oh shit!"

"Language chellam!"

"Sorry Mumi. It says he was killed at the same address." Reading straight from her screen.

"Lotu (54) is the third person to meet an untimely end at the Rocklea address in recent weeks. The property has been empty since the owner, Mathews 79, died of heart failure in early May. Police are still investigating the suspected death of a missing man at the property discovered 10 days earlier. The man has been identified as the late property owner's son, Liam Mathews 57."

"Shit."

"Mumi! Language!"

There was no doubt about it. Ruth Mathews was the patient who died. Lucia's last patient before she died. Tanvi had signed so many forms with that name on them, she knew it. She knew the address too, but no one was reporting that. Late last night, while her children and husband were sleeping, Tanvi searched for news of Liam Mathews death. There was not much. His name mostly yielded business announcements and a wanky looking LinkedIn profile. There was a smattering of reports about the suspected death. Suspected because a body hadn't been found yet. All the articles used the same information, barely even bothering to rearrange the words from one news outlet to the next. There was one photo, taken from outside the police barrier, not out of focus, but not focused on anything. Tanvi checked the address she knew on street view. The garden was a little different, but it was the same house.

The dust that Tanvi was watching nearly settled to the floor at the other end of the dining table. Just moments before it disappeared on the tiles, it was whipped up again by the movement of Tanvi's children walking into the kitchen.

"Morning Mumi!" Sunny chimed as she bypassed the idli and poured cereal into a bowl.

Arun pushed her out of the way to take the whole plate of idli. He didn't need to push, he wanted to. The plate was meant to be enough for the whole family to have some breakfast, but he popped the whole thing in the microwave for himself. The microwave was above the fridge and Arun didn't move from in front of it while he waited.

"Arun move." He didn't budge. "Arun, let me get milk!" This time he did move, only to kick straight backwards towards his little sister. "Arun!"

"Leave your brother alone Sunny!" Tanvi was not paying attention. She was weighing up if she needed to go to work, or if it was more important for her to visit Ruth's neighbours.

In the pro work column she had; it's her job, keeping her job is important and she had already had three half days since her return from annual leave.

In the pro ditching column she had; she wouldn't be any good at her job if she was distracted, she very well could be stopping a serial killer. That should probably also go in the cons column. A small nurse in her late 40s probably shouldn't be messing with serial killers. She didn't have any pressing work to do in the office...serial killer or not, taking a look wouldn't hurt, she was sure of that.

"Mumi, I didn't do anything! Arun won't let me open the fridge."

"Arun, be kind to your sister."

The microwave beeped, "Just a second, I've got to get my breakfast." He took his time, carefully pulling the plate down to chest height.

"I could have been done by now!" Sunny whined.

❖

Pulling away from her kids' school, Tanvi felt a lump in her throat and a trail of butterflies down into her gut. Her hands zinged with fear and excitement and she pressed them harder into the steering wheel to settle them.

She rehearsed in her head what she would ask of anyone who was home. She wondered if she could tell which house was Virgil Lotu's. She should avoid it.

It turned out easy to tell which house was the Lotu home. The street was lined with cars, even this early in the morning. Several large men wearing beautifully patterned lavalava and crisp white button-down shirts strolled across the street from their car into the neighbouring house to the South. From the looks of the cars there were many more inside.

From inside her car Tanvi could see the edge of some plywood in the front window. Little metal prongs stuck out of the footpath and down the sides of the property line. Plastic police tape perched atop each spike at shin height. There was fingerprint dust covering the door frame. It could have been old. She knew from a break in a few years back that the fingerprint dust was difficult to remove.

Tanvi felt very conspicuous. Sitting in her car, barely peering over her steering wheel. She felt eyes on her. No one she could see was actually looking at her. The only people in the street were disappearing down the slope into the Lotu house. Everything was quiet, no mowing or school children that she would expect for 8:45 in suburbia. The car deadened everything and Tanvi could hear the blood pulsing in her ears. She touched her slender fingers to her lobes to cool them. She pulled on her ears slightly, stretching her ear canal in a comforting way, her heavy gold earrings knocked on her jawbone as she let go.

Cold, damp air rushed against her face as Tanvi left the relative safety of her car. She paused a moment to orient herself before angling herself towards the neighbours to the other side of Ruth and setting off with determination.

Even from her elevated position on her living room couch, it took only a few steps for Tanvi to disappear from Harriette O'Connor's view. She had been watching out the window since the first car pulled up in the morning.

Either no one was home or they weren't answering when Tanvi knocked on the door. Two murders next door, she hardly blamed them for avoiding unexpected guests. She knocked again. Her hands barely bigger than a child's, thin, small and encrusted with bands of gold, sapphire and rubies. Small as they were, they delivered a loud, strong rap on the timber door. She listened for movement, there was none.

Walking to the next set of neighbours, their roller door opened and released a silver sedan to the workday. Tanvi stopped short of their driveway, eyes watching her from the driver and passenger seats. Any awkwardness Tanvi felt was not shown on her face or in her body language. She didn't have resting bitch face, she had resting badass bitch face.

Tanvi turned around, back to the door, her eyes followed the concrete path down to the road, skipped over onto the lawn opposite Harriette's house and down to Ruth's house. Bunches of flowers lined the property edge between Ruth and Virgil's houses. Piles of colour, written messages, soft toys, and candles. A small shrine was forming. There were no flowers that bore Ruth's name, or her son's. Liam's death was just as tragic, but from the outside it was as though it never happened. Tanvi had expected there to still be some scant police in the area. Crime scene techs combing through the lawn or something like that, but there wasn't.

The door opened behind her, startling Tanvi. Tanvi spun around, her upper half making it around just before her feet caught up. The door was open, but the screen was closed. Tanvi couldn't see into the house. The screen was dirty and the house was dark. There was an immediate sense of colour, brown carpet, but behind the couple inches of light, everything faded into a hazy darkness.

"Can I help you?" Harriette spat out the words, hoping they would arrive at the stranger with the force she intended. Instead, they tripped on a boulder of uncertainty and lost all steam before making it.

"I hope you can." Tanvi stepped right to the door, nose practically against the screen. She shielded her brow with her hand and squinted up to the voice in the darkness.

Sometimes when people are too similar, they clash. That is no truer than for a noisy middle-aged woman. Harriette was caught off guard by the intruder so confidently presenting themselves. She was even more put off that someone else would be so nosy as to come knocking on her door. At least Harriette gathered her intel from the safety of her own home.

- 326 -

44

It wasn't exactly something he could just slip into conversation. Especially when the conversation was so awkward already. It was astonishing how little time it took for all of the comfort and familiarity between Lucia and Win to melt away. Washed down the drain with the blood of all the people that had died at their hands.

Win still loved her. He loved her just as much as the first day he realised he loved her in that way. The size of his love had never changed, only its intensity.

It wasn't anything special or momentous that made him stop seeing her as his kid sister's friend and as "girlfriend material." Lucia and Win had been talking more and more. Ever since Kathryn and Lucia could legally drink, the friendship groups kind of merged. Some of their friends were in the same classes at uni, others were school friends, cousins, just a bunch of people that already were familiar with each other. With the merging of their friendship groups and the fact that Lucia had basically grown up at the Huyhn family home, it wasn't crazy that they spoke without Kathryn acting as a liaison. It was shocking to Win when he realised that she was the person he wanted to talk to most. Soon her name was at the top of his contacts across every platform. It wasn't a one-sided exchange either, Lucia wanted to talk to him just as much. She clued on much earlier that she might have feelings for her best friend's brother though and kept them under wraps.

The day Win realised for sure though, was a barbeque at their friend's house. A housewarming, birthday, something like that. Kathryn was going too, but she was coming from Gianna's house. Gianna at the time lived on the north side and the party was at Paddington, so it made no sense for her to meet up with anyone beforehand.

Lucia sometimes had anxiety about social situations. Primarily arriving at a party solo. Maybe she had been burned too many times before arriving on time and there was no one she knew to talk to. She also hated arriving and the idea that people would see her walk in. This was especially bad at public places where the people inside the party can often see the new arrivals long before they can be spotted in the crowd. Even though this was a house party, Lucia had never been there before. She mentioned it in passing, but with Lucia quickly becoming Win's closest friend, he knew she was downplaying her anxiety. He arranged to drive to her place, park his car and they would catch the bus to the party together.

Lucia answered the door wearing denim shorts and a pale pink linen top. She was barefoot and her hair was down. She hardly ever wore it down. Her natural waves rolled over her shoulders and nestled on her collar bones. She was the most beautiful woman he had ever seen. Truth be told, seeing her that day was not the moment of love. It didn't matter what she was wearing or how she looked, she still would have been the most beautiful to him. He realised he loved her seconds before the door even opened and he was aching to see her.

He still had the same ache. Being away from Lucia was a slow torture to him. He still wanted to share everything with her. She had died and his heart was grieving just the same as it would no matter how she passed. His mind wasn't following suit. Now he had guilt too, because even though she had died, Lucia wasn't dead. He could talk to her, he could still tell her anything, but it wasn't the same.

A second wash of anxiety clawed its way up through Win's gut and came to rest uncomfortably in his throat. It wasn't the anxiety about broaching a difficult topic, or the pangs of guilt, shame and fear that had plagued him recently. It wasn't the creeping mournfulness that quietly grew until it was a screaming panic attack. This was regret. It felt similar to the yearly existential crisis when Win lamented all of his career choices since high school and wished he had somehow picked a career with great earning potential and some meaningfulness. Like he somehow could have known that radiology would be a good idea at the age of sixteen. This bout of regretful panic was not stemming from his career though. Instead, it was caused by his belief that every choice he had made since his wife died was exactly the wrong one.

No matter what he did now, it seemed like he would spend the rest of his life in jail for the death of his wife. Or some other facility because no one would believe him that she was both a zombie and a ghost. Honestly, he might need to be removed from society because he wasn't quite sure that this wasn't all in his head. What if he had been imagining the whole thing?

The house didn't smell as much as he thought it might. Still Win visited every window and cracked them. He swung strategically placed windows open fully to best utilise the cross breeze, even though the air was very cold. He went to tidy the place but nothing was really out of place.

Lucia and Lu weren't home. He considered doing a load of washing. Lucia might need another change of clothes once she got home. On second thoughts he decided that while he hadn't needed it the last few weeks, there would come a time when he would stop living in his sister's guest room and he would need his washing machine again. He would hate to turn up to work with some stray bit of rotting flesh on his shirt. He firmed up his decision against it because he wouldn't be back anytime soon and they didn't have a dryer. He once had neighbours that left their washing on the line for 2 weeks, until it was torn from wind and rain, all that hadn't already fallen onto the ground. He had noticed at about a week and a half that the clothes hadn't been brought in. Lucia, who was far more observant than him, had noticed almost immediately. It later turned out that the tenants next door had moved out very quickly. It was an old house and there was mould covering everything. They only found out when tenants came back to salvage anything they could, but Lucia had watched that house like a hawk. She knew something had gone wrong and she was very close to calling the cops just to check. Lucia had been dialling the phone one time ready to ask the police to do a welfare check on another neighbour when he showed up. They usually said hello to him every day and when he wasn't seen for a whole week, mail was piling up and the smell of his nightly cigarettes hadn't wafted in on the breeze. Lucia assumed he was dead. He had been interstate, but Lucia's concern made sure he gave them a heads up if ever he left again. Win knew neighbours were always nosey, they lived in the suburbs and people couldn't help but notice anything out of the ordinary. A few minutes on any local Facebook group would make sure of that. Best he didn't do the washing and forget to bring it back in. On the other hand, the fact they hadn't done washing in weeks might be just as much cause for concern. For the neighbours that hadn't already noticed a dead woman walking around.

The spare room had little drops of something oily in the corner. He didn't need to sniff that, he knew exactly what it was. Or if he didn't know exactly his imagination could paint a gruesome picture. On closer inspection the drops were resting on the surface but there was a deeper stain covering the whole area. A misshapen oval about 75cm long. It wasn't bad and he didn't know how to clean it. The crime scene cleaner shows on TV have some kind of enzyme spray to break down bodily fluids and fats. He pulled the carpet spray that was usually reserved for Crumb's spiteful nocturnal vomits. He sprayed the area, and just as the instructions said, he left it.

Win pulled a bathmat from the linen cupboard and lay that in another area of the room. Lu would have to stand on that. The bottom of the mat was already rubber lined and Win didn't mind sacrificing it to the cause.

While he waited for Lucia to get home from wherever she was he walked aimlessly around for a bit. Trying to come up with things he could be doing to occupy his mind. All he could think to do was take the spare cat food and lay it by the door so he would remember to take it home. Crumb seemed to be doing ok, but Win was sure he missed Lucia. Cats hold their physical pain in, maybe they hold their grief too.

Though he didn't know what it was at first, Win heard Lu scuffing her way down the footpath towards home. It sounded a bit like someone sweeping their driveway very forcefully. For a brief moment he thought it might be a children's bicycle with a flat tyre. From the kitchen window he could look through the tree in the neighbour's front yard and see both Lucia and Lu. It might have been that he knew to look for them, but they were mighty conspicuous.

Lucia glided over the footpath smoothly. She was a little way ahead of Lu. In death Lucia was just as fast a walker as she always had been. Win's stride was a good half a foot longer than Lucia's, yet he always ended up trailing behind her. He wasn't even a slow walker; just Lucia was just faster. She said it was because she grew up with a tall Mum. Lucia's mother was taller than Win. Her little legs worked double time to keep up and when she grew, she just kept the pace. Win didn't believe it because Ava, Lucia's older sister wasn't vying for a racewalking medal every time she had to get somewhere.

Frustration radiated from Lucia's face, she was annoyed at Lu straggling behind her. Annoyed but not willing to leave her out there alone. Not that Lucia could protect Lu in any quantifiable way. From this distance his wife looked almost normal. He couldn't really see the translucent quality of her skin. He was too far to see if she was blinking, or miss the rise and fall of her breathing, or the gentle warmth her body gave to the air around it. She looked like herself. She looked like when he was waiting for her at the end of a long day and he could see her coming home, anticipation building because he just wanted to be with her again. Things were better together. Cliched, but true. TV, food, jokes, sleep, all were better with his wife. He hadn't realised until now how much that was true. He hadn't realised until now, he couldn't have any of those things anymore and life would just stay worse.

He could hear Lucia instructing Lu to turn into the yard. She was using her work voice. The voice she uses...used on the old people to make them feel encouraged and safe. The voice that covered any frustration, it was happy and lyrical, but firm. Now it seemed like a coping mechanism. It did make Win think about how tremendous she was at her job though. So patient with the oldies, knowing that walking that slow would be torture.

Lu's shoe slapped the riser of the stairs, one by one, until they were at the door. He pushed the door open. Lucia looked a tiny bit startled but thanked him sincerely. She held his gaze in hers, her eyes deep and brown. In this light Win hardly noticed how the light didn't reflect in her eyes the way it should, or that her pupils were exactly the wrong size for the dimness of the room. His swelling of love and longing was fading the closer she got. By the time Lu was close enough to smell, those feelings felt like a distant memory.

"I saw the car."

"I thought you might. Thought it would be easier for me to open the door."

"Definitely! Thank you."

Lucia smiled sweetly. It felt like old times. She didn't want to ask why he was there. She didn't want to ruin it. She could hope he was there because he missed her, because he was moving back in, or had some excellent news and everything would return to normal. She knew there weren't any good reasons for him to be there though. Nothing she would want to hear anyway.

It was approaching dinner time and Win's stomach was giving off tell-tale growls. Even though his stomach was obviously aching for something to digest, his mouth and brain were too preoccupied. He wouldn't have noticed the hunger if the roar from his gut hadn't echoed through the quiet lounge room. Seeing Lu was enough to stave off the hunger. He couldn't believe he had once contemplated eating dinner she had cooked for him. At that time she was fresh dead and even though she was completely absent from life and looked it back then, he couldn't have imagined how much worse she would get. All the more reason to say what he had to say.

Win swirled words around in his mind, he arranged them all kinds of ways trying to work out the most suitable order. The words stuck in peculiar sentences, repeating over in his head. Not sure if they were the right ones, or if they even made sense. Try as he might he couldn't shake the jumble they had settled in.

"I think we should kill her." Fuck. That was exactly wrong.

He meant it but didn't want to say it like that.

"Huh, who?" Lucia asked in genuine confusion. She had been privy to a lot of murders recently and really had no clue which "her" Win was talking about. It was strange to both of them that Lucia's first reaction now was a simple query of who they should kill rather than dismay at the thought at all.

"Lu." Lucia's brow dipped over her eyes, she was still confused at this notion. "I think we should kill Lu," Win said again.

"I...huh?..what?" There would have been a why in there but Win interrupted what he could tell was going to be a downward spiral.

"It might already be too late. She's dead already and I'm worried."

"About?"

"Jail. Being stuck." He pulled back. Once again, he said what he meant, but in a tactless way. Of course, that was the part Lucia clung to.

"Stuck? With me?"

"Not with you. With her." He paused. "But with you too. I've never been married to a ghost before. I don't know. I think it might be… I want to move on." Once again, his tactlessness lingered after the sentence jutted its way out of his mouth.

Lucia was silent now. Working over his words and her rebuttal in her mind. His words and all the meaning she added behind it clinging around in her mind and knocking all other thoughts clean out.

"But," Lucia composed herself again, shimmying her shoulders back as if to shake the start of that sentence away. "What if, her dying, means I die too?"

"I thought about that." Lucia waited for him to keep going. It was obvious what her question would be. "If that's the case. Maybe it's for the best."

"For you!"

"Lucia." He set his voice in a reassuring tone.

"I'll be dead!"

"Lucia, you're already dead!" Try and avoid it all they could, everything came back to that.

It can get so quiet when two people's minds are racing too hard for any words to come out. This conversation definitely wouldn't have benefitted from Netflix playing softly in the background but this silence would have. The only noise now was the possums crawling out for their first nightly jaunt and the sound of Lu shifting her weight between feet. Even the dead girl could feel the awkwardness. Night had fallen quickly over the conversation.

- 334 -

It came as a relief to all three of them in the room when a protracted fart eked its way out of Lu. Lu wasn't intentionally trying to break the tension, she didn't intentionally do anything.

"What the fuck?" Win laughed.

"She's been doing that."

"Wild."

Win had no intention of starting the conversation up again. He knew Lucia well enough to know she would have to sit on it a little while, before her knee jerk defensiveness calmed down. He didn't want to get her hackles up for fear that she would double down on the whole thing. Even more out of fear that the resulting fight would be his foremost memory of his wife.

Win wanted to leave. To let the dust settle on his proposal and he certainly didn't want to sit around to smell whatever just came out of Lu.

45

Saturday mornings Carindale shopping centre was at its busiest. Pre-teen girls raced around the shopping centre colliding with each other in giggling fits at the smallest things. There was the usual fare; young families out for brunch, elderly couples doddering around window shopping and visiting the bank before its early Saturday close time.

Ruby Klein was spending the weekend with her grandparents, Barbara and Greg McMillan. It was three days before Ruby's eleventh birthday. When her parents asked her what she wanted for her birthday, Ruby asked to visit her Grandparents in Brisbane. Already at such a young age she was gaming the system. Yes she loved her grandparents very dearly, but that wasn't the only benefit to her plan. Spending a week with Oma and Grampy on her birthday, this was a caveat of the request, meant a week out of school. She'd be back just in time to be on June holidays. It also meant a week away from her siblings, and her grandparents were sure to spoil her. Which they did, of course, especially after time with them was her special birthday wish.

"Oma can we go into Lush next?" Ruby slurped on the dregs of her iced chocolate. Grampy had finished his cappuccino already, but Oma was still only halfway through what was now a lukewarm flat white.

"Ummm, what do you want to go to Lush for?"

"I dunno, looking at stuff. It looks pretty."

"It looks crowded." Grampy added, craning his neck over his shoulder and trying to see between gaps at the next table.

"Please!" Ruby knew not to whine, that behaviour would get her nowhere.

"Look Oma doesn't really like the smell in there. It gives me a headache. How 'bout Grampy takes you while I finish?" She eyed Greg hopefully, flexing a telepathy that only people that have known each other for most of their lives have.

"Yes!"

"Alright." Greg winced a little as he rose from the table, his knees ached. "Lead on Macduff."

Barbara held her coffee mug up to her lips. She watched as Greg, led by Ruby, walked the short distance to the shop. His stiff gait getting freer with each step. Then they disappeared into a throng of busy shoppers.

It wasn't that she didn't love Ruby. She did, more than she thought was even possible. She also loved having Ruby stay with them, it was a treat and she wasn't so blind or naive that she didn't know Ruby was aiming to be spoiled on the trip. It's just, she hadn't had an eleven year old in the house for thirty years. She was tired.

Barbara pulled her reading glasses from her handbag. She took one last look in the direction of Lush, trying to spy her family, before placing them on her nose and pulling up her phone.

One notification - WhatsApp - Mum and kids chat - 4 missed messages.

Does anyone remember the episode of Round the Twist with the fox?

I forget, why did he have to eat the lemons to get his eyes back? Was the cupboard magic? Jess, her middle daughter.

Because they replaced his eyes with glass ones. The lemons were someone else's eyes. Nell's Grandfather? Simon, the youngest.

I thought Nell's Granddad was the ghost in the dunny? Mum how's Ruby going? Behaving I hope. Megan, the eldest, Ruby's mother.

Barbara clacked away at the phone. Forgetting her coffee for a moment.

Yes she's behaving. We're having a lovely time. We're all out and about at the moment. I'm finishing a coffee. Ruby and Grampy are doing some window shopping.

I don't remember that episode I'm sorry Jess.

Another sip of her flat white. Way too cold now. The WhatsApp message kept flashing "Jessica McMillan is typing" when Greg appeared. He stood behind a slightly dejected looking Ruby.

"Ready?"

Barbara checked the phone once more, the message hadn't come through yet. So she closed the phone and piled the phone and her glasses back into her handbag. "Yes."

"Anywhere else you want to go?" Barbara checked with Ruby.

"No." Ruby knitted her brows together and wiped tiny beads of sweat off her forehead.

"What's the matter?" Barbara asked, very much expecting to hear of Ruby's disappointment in not coming away from the store with anything.

"I don't feel very good. I have a headache."

"Hmmm must take after your grandmother." she said roughly massaging Ruby's tiny shoulders. Not noticing that Ruby flinched when she did so and not noticing the tiny dot of blood pricking up on her neck, a spot where Ruby kept rubbing. Then swooped down to kiss her on the head. "You are a bit warm actually. I've just gotta grab some things in Woollies, then we better get you home Muffin. Hope you get better. I just told your mother we're having a wonderful time. Can't send you home sick."

Ruby complied, suddenly quiet. Her feet dragged across the shopping centre floor, making tiny squeaks that were lost in the rest of the noise.

In the car Ruby fell asleep. Barbara and Greg exchanging slightly concerned looks, but still suspecting overstimulation was the culprit. Before long and before they reached their house, they were rerouted and heading as quickly as possible to the hospital. Ruby had stopped breathing.

46

It wasn't clear where she was headed. Not at first. She could keep going as long as Lu could keep walking, that's exactly what Lucia intended to do. The streets were quiet. The sun set hours ago and now the sky was at its darkest. The cold air had people's windows closed to the streets, deadening any sound blaring from TVs. Lu's lumbering footfalls could go unnoticed at this time more than ever before.

Lu knew her part in this was to keep treading, following her liege into the night.

He had actually asked her. He said it out loud to her face, he had said it might be for the best if she died. He was supposed to love her. Lucia played the scene over in her head. Each run through his words became more malicious, his tone more debasing, his eyes more cold.

By her estimate she'd walked about one kilometre already. She didn't know how long it took. Longer than it normally would, if she had use of her own body. The stars had shifted. She was sure of that. They were on higher ground now though and the stars that had just come into view when she left the house could be skewed by her different perspective.

Lucia hadn't done this in a long time. When she was younger she pent up all the feelings until the only way to get them out was to walk for as long as she could. Things hadn't been pent up in a long time though. Her life, when she had it, had been good. She actually had everything she wanted. People aren't supposed to say that. There's some fine line where you're supposed to be happy with what you have, but still striving for something a little more. Unhappy is depressing, your fault, undesirable. Too happy is complacency, settling, basic. On the list of things Lucia wanted out of life she had them all.

Happy relationship - tick

Wonderful friends - tick

A job she loved - tick

Surrounded by family - tick

A cat - tick

More money would be nice, a lush house would be good, but in the grand scheme they wouldn't make her happier. Easier is different from happier. So, Lucia hadn't needed this kind of catharsis in a good long time.

This walk wasn't working the same as it used to. Her lungs didn't burn, her calves weren't aching, she couldn't feel the night air whipping her face. All she had was a quietness where her thoughts could fester. She wasn't angry, that wasn't the word, not sad either. She wasn't sure this emotion even had a name.

Lu hung back as much as the tie between them would allow. She had the energy but lacked the coordination to keep any kind of pace. That wasn't the reason though, she sensed something. The way dogs sense fear; a foulness that scented the air around Lucia and Lu decided to keep back.

They reached the trailhead of one of the Toohey Forest walking paths some time before 11pm. Lucia stopped to check Lu was doing ok briefly before forging ahead into the forest. She'd never been there at night. The bush was alive with animals, rustling, chirping and squawking out of sight.

The trail climbed up and up then ended with caution tape stretched between trees. There was a small sign that read "closed for track work." If the sign had said it was closed for any environmental reasons Lu wouldn't have kept going, but if the track was faulty it didn't matter to her. She hadn't spoken to Lu since she left the house. She only spoke now to show her how to get around the tape, not wanting to break it so it still served its purpose to other, less immortal folk. A bittersweetness came with talking to Lu now. Hearing her own voice out loud was stark and strange in the night. For a brief moment preceding her voice piercing the quiet she could almost forget that Lu was there at all.

The track was rougher after crossing the tape. Rain or animals had worn large potholes into the dirt path. Short, wooden poles stuck out from the earth on each side of the track, the foundations for a boardwalk. In the retreating moonlight Lucia couldn't make out if they were new or remnants from something that previously stood there. The path spat them out onto a rocky outcrop. Beyond the rocks the forest floor gave way to a steep drop and a view over the suburbs. The soft glisten of the rock, its tiny smooth facets told Lucia it was granite. She wished she could run her fingertips along the cold stone. She could remember being a kid camping with her family and nestling her back into the ancient grooves of the rock. Looking at the sky, only a few hours from Brisbane but already much clearer. She was alone then, wandering off from her family as they played board games under gaslamp light. She liked being alone then. It felt calm and free when she was ten and had everything ahead of her.

The stars she had been tracking earlier had disappeared, clouds hung low in the sky. A few small cracks in the clouds let the moonlight through, then vanished again. It wasn't calm and free now that everything was behind her. She had never felt further from that child than she did now.

Lu had pushed her way to the front of their little two-person caravan. She rocked her signature sway at the edge of the last and biggest rock. Lucia came up beside her, not shocking Lu the way she would anyone else by coming up from behind them. Lu didn't frighten easily or the tie between them informed her somehow. All this time living outside of herself, Lucia didn't think she had stood side by side with her body before. There was a unity in it and she let out a scream. Her anguish cracked against the rocks and came back to her as an unfamiliar voice. No breath to run out, no vocal cords to tire. Lucia could go on forever like this if she wanted. Was she screaming at Win, or for him? At losing him now, or at losing him weeks ago? Her pain carried on the wind and drowned out the world that had gone on so easily without her.

Now taking Lu's hand or resting hers inside Lu's fist, Lucia let Lu know she could scream too. Right now she didn't need to conceal herself. Lu's scream came lower, more guttural. It cracked and gurgled over her dying vocal cords, but Lucia's voice rose into it. They screamed into the night together until the low clouds started to release their cargo onto the city and the rain tempered the rawness of it all.

When they stopped, the rain carried on. Fat drops slapped the granite beneath them. It filled the facets until they were slick and smooth. Lu shifted her feet and she hurtled to the bottom of the rock, taking Lucia with her off the cliff and crashing to the ground below.

The rain was less cleansing from the bottom of the cliff. Lu's leg wedged in a crevice of the rocks below. The bone snapped with a gut-wrenching crack. Her ankle stayed firmly in place, the water lubricating it enough to slot in there, but now it was stuck tight. Even as the stone tore away at the already delicate skin, pulling it from the muscle, the foot stayed in place. Lucia could see the broken bones peeking through the fabric of Lu's pants. From the movement she guessed that somewhere mid shin only a few tendons were keeping the foot attached at all.

Lucia could picture her phone, plugged into the charger and sitting on her bedside table. Utterly useless to her now.

She rose to her feet. Her leg was still intact. The fall didn't look that big from where they were now. The angle, the night, it was deceiving because it was a big drop. Lu lay crooked and at all wrong angles. Her bottom was planted firmly in a wet pile of leaves, they were colouring her jeans with slender tea stains. One leg was pulled up and away from her, the one caught between the rocks. Lu's back lay into the leaf litter behind her, but there was not enough clearance for her to lie completely flat, so her body arched to the side awkwardly and her head cocked to the side so her chin hit her right shoulder. Lucia could see now that she was doing a survey of the damage that Lu's other leg was twisted. The knee hyperextended too much to be natural. Possibly a dislocation, but it could have been broken. The bones weren't protruding in the same way they did with the other leg.

Now was the time for Lucia to be able to touch something. Not at completely useless times like mopping up a spill or using an umbrella. Her pushing and pulling, heaving and hoeing were all in vain. Lu was trapped and so was she.

❖

The kids were in their rooms. Tanvi didn't even entertain the idea that they were asleep. They were in their rooms and weren't likely to emerge until morning. She had initially set up shop in her living room, but she had since decided that she needed a more permanent set up. She spread a stack of papers over her bedroom floor. The absence of her ex-husband's wardrobe opened up a large space. Some light foot work would be required if she needed something from that side of the room. For the most part she wouldn't. That side of the room was never her domain. She could crawl in her side of the bed easily enough and left a small path to her closet. Tanvi had very dainty feet and good balance. She didn't need to leave much space.

She tucked one foot under herself, her slender brown toes poking out from under flannelette pyjamas. Her other leg bent out in front of her, the soul of her foot planted firmly into the plush carpet as she leaned her weight forward to arrange her notes. Even in pyjamas her neck, wrists and fingers were all weighted with gold jewellery. Her bracelets clinked together, keeping pace with her movements and only punctuating the sound of papers sliding across each other. She looked less like a frenzied detective arranging their murder board and more like someone engrossed in a jigsaw puzzle.

What Tanvi had was lists of suspicious deaths from all over Brisbane. There were more than she thought there would be, and her perception of the city would never be the same. Several times a minute a little voice in her head told her she was being stupid, but her gut was a more powerful voice. She didn't know what she was looking for, but she had faith she'd know when she saw it. What Tanvi Jay had in more abundance than the pile of names decorating her floor was tenacity.

For the first time in her life, Tanvi made a Facebook profile. She took the first name on the list and opened several profiles until she found the right one. She made notes of education, employer before scanning the friend lists for other familiar names. Anything from the list. She kept doing this for every name until she fell asleep, exhausted and under a blanket of papers.

❖

At two days Lucia learned three things.

In general people obeyed the signs telling them to keep out.

No track work was actually being carried out.

And in a pinch Lu could lure, trap and eat mosquitos.

The mosquitos came possibly for the same reason that the other bugs stayed away. She was dying. Lu's body, formally Lucia's body was decaying. It was slow but it was definitely happening. There was something though that fooled, a glamour or something that hid the death. She had no blood to drain but the mosquitos still arrived, they drove their proboscises into her rotting flesh and ended up being eaten themselves.

One morning. Lucia couldn't remember if it was that morning or the day before; she heard some people on the track. They weren't above them, somewhere in the distance. The sound of their footsteps was far off and hard to place. Lucia screamed for them. In the breaks of her scream, she waited for a response, but none came. What would they do with her when they found her anyway? Her rescuers could be anyone, and she would be exposing herself and Lu. She could very well be rescued only to end up trapped somewhere else, somewhere sure to be less scenic.

Still at night when she heard a dirt bike ripping through the bush, Lucia called out again. She knew it was useless. No way they would hear her over the engine.

❖

"Arun!" Tanvi shouted up the stairs to her son. She stood at the bottom of the stairs, one hand on the railing, head tilted up listening for his response. She was certain he was awake. Sunny had already left for band practice, so Arun was her only shot.

"Arun!" Her thick black hair was pulled into a ponytail on the top of her head. Her hair was so thick and short that the hair curled back on itself and looked more like a bun. The hair on the nape of her neck hung down in large portions. With her hair up like this, her greys were more visible and her ponytail bobbled back and forth each time she called out.

"Yes Mumi." Arun appeared at the top of the stairs, "I was answering." He looked tired, grumpy. Too many late nights, probably gaming, not studying, Tanvi surmised. Better he be gaming with friends than not have friends at all she thought.

"The printer is doing the wrong things again."

"Ugh." He harrumphed down the stairs.

Arun had at least a foot over Tanvi. He was big and solid like his father. Though small, Tanvi crossed her arms and gave her son a look only a mother could. She didn't need to say anything.

"Sorry Mumi." It was a mumble, but she heard it just fine.

A few clicks and the printer made an agreeable noise. Paper started to edge its way out onto the tray.

"Mumi, when it does this you just cl…"

Tanvi cut him off, brushing past him to sit at the desk waving her hand and nodding her head to tell him his explanation wasn't needed. Arun sighed.

"Anything else?"

"No chellam. Thank you. Please do eat before school."

Arun agreed, glancing over his shoulder at his mother. She pulled in her seat and exchanged her red rimmed glasses for her petite blue reading ones. She thrust forward her chin and held it firmly with one hand, her eyes darted back and forth in the iridescent blue light.

Tanvi piled a stack of pages into a bag. Highlighter stained her fingers and left a tiny green streak where she held the paper. On top she laid a notebook with a list of things she thought Lucia might be able to fill in the blanks about.

❖

Win saw Sanjay ducking out of the cafe near their work. More accurately a wall of pink polka dotted navy and strong cologne

- 348 -

overwhelmed him and he knew who it was. Sanjay's smile was bigger than normal and upon seeing Win he held up his coffee cup. Ten digits written neatly in Nico on the cardboard sleeve and a note that read *Coffee somewhere else?*

"Nice!" Win was genuinely excited for Sanjay that his crush on the barista was returned.

"Gotta run dude, got a message to write." Sanjay smiled so big his eyes were nearly completely hidden behind his broad cheeks.

"She's at work."

"So am I my dude." Sanjay shrugged and patted Win on the arm before practically jogging towards the office.

Win's pocket buzzed. He pulled his phone out and peered at it, trying to read the numbers through the glare on the screen. A mobile number he didn't recognise. He went to hit the little red x, to cancel the incoming call and go about his day. Something in the back of his might told him it was important though.

"Hello, Samuel speaking."

"Samuel, it is Tanvi speaking."

"O-kay?" He was trapped in a weird limbo, caught between his natural instinct to switch into his phone voice and greet her enthusiastically and his other instinct that there was no way her call was good news.

"I am visiting at your house. Former house, Lucia did tell me that you moved out. Lucia is not here."

"She told you? What? Sorry?"

- 349 -

"I know Samuel."

"Know?" still trying to suss Tanvi out.

"That Lucia is dead." Win flinched and looked around for people that might have overheard the other end of the phone call. "I am looking into her death. And the death of others. I am needing to speak to her."

"But she's not home?" He sidled his way out of the line for the cafe and strode to the furthest corner of the building, trying to find some seclusion.

"No. Is it usual for her to go out? Do you know a way to reach her?"

"Ummm." He hadn't noticed until now that his left fist was clenched tightly in his pocket. "I don't actually know. I know she can leave. But I don't know where she would have gone now."

"Ok. Please phone if you hear anything. I will leave a note also."

"Uhh, sure, yeah ok." His face was clammy "Umm, thank you for letting me know Tanvi." He wiped his brow; the back of his hand came back with a milky smear of sweat. "I do care, about her. About Lucia. Even now." He kicked himself at seeming so defensive. What must she think? Not only was his wife dead, but he'd also moved out and he had no idea where she was. He didn't dare tell Tanvi that the last time he spoke to Lucia he hurt her with his selfishness. That he asked her to die. What if that is what happened? What if she did it already? That now, she truly was dead, for good.

"I know Samuel." There was a small pause on the other end of the line. A little scrabble, Tanvi's bracelets clinking and her fingernails tapping the phone screen as she found the end call button. Then nothing.

The morning came back into focus, sounds grew louder and clearer, even the sun seemed to shine a little harder. It was so incongruous, him and everything else. How all these people were so close to him, but none of them knew.

Before he even had time to finish his thought Win's hand fell away, numb and tingly all at the same time. His heart leapt against the front of his chest, like it was trying to shoulder barge its way through his ribs. Not the hard and fast thwack of exercise or even nerves. It felt hollow and like his ribs were insulated with jelly at the same time. If he didn't do something soon his heart would beat so hard that it would crush his lungs. He was going to die here and no one would know. He tried to press his hand into his chest to brace it but his fingers didn't feel like his own. He couldn't call for help because his tongue had become a shrivelled stone in his mouth. Even if he could, he wasn't even sure his throat could open to speak the words anymore.

He should get inside. At the very least die in the lobby of his work building where people would see. If he made it there, he might make it to the lifts, then it wasn't far to his desk. He walked, his gait no different from usual but Win kept having to check that his feet were actually touching the floor. A dissonance between his eyes and his legs making him unsure of the depth of the room, how far he'd walked and how far left to go. He thought it could be a panic attack, he was almost sure it was. He'd had a panic attack before and it wasn't like this, not this bad. This time he was surely dying.

❖

Lucia had noted Lu's deterioration had increased. That it took less time between feedings for her skin to start sweating like raw meat left out on the bench. What little colour Lu retained from a fresh feed was draining away rapidly. Perhaps the trauma to her lower body was using up any food reserves, because three days is too quick for her to be declining like this.

The rocks behind them looked higher than Lucia could venture from Lu. She tried a couple times to wander straight ahead as far as she could and tried to imagine a big arc from where she was. Tried to picture if she could make it to the top of the rocks. It wouldn't hurt any to try, even if she couldn't make it to the top, maybe she could get a view of a path or something from as far as she could get.

"I'm going to climb up here. Ok?"

Lu didn't reply, she never had. Instead, she looked up at Lucia with her mouth hanging open stupidly, eyes tracking movement, but not taking in much of anything.

Lucia eased herself behind Lu. The first ledge, more a narrow crevice in the rock, was behind Lu. Lucia wouldn't have tried to stick her foot in there while she was alive. Memories of a broken foot stopped that. It was a tree that broke her foot, not a rock, but it was a similar situation. Trying to climb up using a fork instead of a horizontal surface, her foot slipped between and crushed one of the bones. It hurt a lot and the cast was horribly itchy. Without a foot to be broken, she proceeded.

Lucia clung to the rock near the top of the cliff. She felt like one of those goats you always see photos of standing on dam walls. Unlike a goat though she was face into the rock, clutching to it more like a koala. She could turn her head and look out over most of the view she'd seen from the top days earlier. From this angle it was dense bush until the edge of the forest, where it was an industrial area. She couldn't see any footpaths or people clearly. If she craned her neck she could just see over the top edge. The stone sloped there and obscured the view further. If there were people at the top she would be able to see them though. Even if they couldn't see her. If she shuffled herself up any further, she would shrink back down the rock, the elastic band that secured her to Lu reaching the end of its reach and snapping her back.

She was going to have to get Lu free.

❖

If she was gone, it might be a blessing. Win kept returning to the thought that if Lucia wasn't at home then it might be a good thing. Each time that thought crept in, another came with it. That if she was gone, if Lu was dead, dead-dead, then there would likely be some sort of investigation. While he would be free to mourn, he very well could be doing that from prison. Then another thought always came next; he wasn't ready for her to be gone for good.

It's not like she could leave a note. Not like he would know if she was missing or if she had just left. No way to tell if she was in trouble. Calling the police was out of the question. So, Win sat and waited.

He sat until his legs got jittery and he had to roam the house. Doing a sweep for any clues he might have missed. Looking over the objects that filled the house. Things that were his, now more than they ever were before, things that he always had thought of as Lucia's influence. Now he unequivocally owned them, but they seemed more unfamiliar to him than ever. He looked at every single knick-knack that decorated shelves, books that lined the shelves and pieces of art. Some of these things he swore he had never really looked at before. He had seen them every day without taking them in as individual pieces.

When he got too tired or too overwhelmed he sat and waited again. Then ran through the whole cycle all over again.

His things were there, his life had been built there, but this house was no longer his home. He didn't have one anymore, not really. Maybe she had been his home, and when Lucia died that was taken from him too.

❖

"Lu?" She didn't answer to her name but Lu recognised that Lucia was talking to her. Lucia could have said anything at that point and it would have achieved the same result. Kind of how you can call a pet by any name so long as you say it in the right voice.

"Lu. We've got to get out of here." Lu's face drooped, not out of a reaction to the words, but her form was fading. "Are you ready?"

Lucia wished she could get her fingers around Lu's leg. Feel for breaks and what was actually happening under the jeans. The denim was stained, but not with blood. Nothing like a big accident scene from a TV show, where the blood would wet the fabric and it would get dark red and slick looking. It looked more like an oil spot left to soak in. It was dry now, any wetness from the initial trauma had dried up days ago. There was dark staining, it could have been old blood, less of a steady pressure flowing from a wound, more like smears of jelly. From there the stain radiated out in concentric patterns. It reminded Lucia of the chromatography experiments from school. How the colours all separated out.

There was a small tear in the pant leg and there was bone poked out only a tiny bit. The bone that Lucia could see, just pipping the surface like an egg tooth, was dry. The exposure to air had wicked away anything left living in it.

"Lu? Can you take your shoe off?" Lucia gestured to Lu's shoe. The toe pointed at a strange angle. Then Lucia pulled at her own shoe. Showing what she meant.

Lu looked back at Lucia with a look Lucia had only heard about, but never seen for herself. Her own death stare. Lu looked so far removed from herself now. Her face was sagging and yellowish jowls hung below her once round cheeks. The eyes themselves were sunken and clouded, their shape changing so much that Lucia wondered how much Lu could actually see. The stare though, that was hers. The eyes steeped in judgement and peering from behind low crooked eyebrows.

- 354 -

"Shit Lu. Can you just do it?"

Lucia ran through the whole mime again.

"If we get out of here, we'll be able to get you some food."

At that Lu hurled herself forward. It took a few tries. Each time she folded the top of her body with enough force that her bottom inched backwards. The gap between the shin and the rest of her leg grew bit by bit.

It made a horrible sound. Squelching, ripping and a popping noise that made Lucia want to fold up her ears in on themselves, but the leg was mostly free. Only the pant leg held Lu in place. Where the holes from the bone were Lucia showed Lu how she might tear the fabric further apart.

Lu pushed her fingers into the hole and heaved apart. The denim tore with relative ease, until the rip stopped at the thick seams. Lu's already long legs looked peculiarly stilt like. At this point Lucia was ready to get Lu to take off the pants completely. She looked at the two busted and broken legs and thought the jeans might be the only way she would stay in one, or two pieces until they could get to safety.

❖

At 6am Win made three phone calls. The first to Kathryn and the second to Tanvi. He told them both to meet him at his place. They needed to talk about Lucia. The third phone call he made to work, telling them he would not be in.

Tanvi was the first to arrive. She had already been up. Both because she was one of those people that seems to go to bed late and still get up early in the morning and because she was trying to figure out where Lucia could have gotten to. For the moment she had set

- 355 -

aside her investigation into the how and why of Lucia's death. Now she was just worried for where she was.

"I do not know how fast a zombie is walking. I have estimated and made a map." Tanvi walked straight into the lounge and laid a map on the coffee cable. It was pages from a Refidex taped together to make one big map. Even if it was a map from 2012.

"Hi Tanvi."

"Oh yes. Hello Samuel. Are you ok?"

"Not really."

She sighed, not in an exasperated way, in a way that said every word of comfort all at once.

Win returned his attention to the map. A big black circle ran around it, at the centre was his house. Win felt a little drop in his stomach and his palms slicked with sweat.

"Is there any place in the circle that she would go to?"

A thin line of sweat ran from Win's eyebrow into the corner of his eye. He blinked it away but it spread across his lashes, obscuring his vision in that eye. He had to blink several more times for the map to come into focus.

"Ummm." The more he looked at it the more nothing stood out. He looked over the streets and landmarks of a town he had spent his whole life in. A place he knew like the back of his hand, but it was totally unfamiliar to him now.

"She has caught the bus before. What if she caught the bus?"

"Don't worry about that now." Tanvi placed a hand on Win's shoulder. Her grip was firm but didn't hurt or feel threatening. Like she was steadying him. She knew he needed it.

"Ummm. There are some stores she likes. "He pointed, "Here-ish." Win pushed his head between his hands "Uhh, the turtles are here." He pointed to another part of the map. Each time he did Tanvi put a little cross on the area. Neither of them heard her pull up but Kathryn appeared at the door. Her hair taking an odd sculptural form. She hadn't showered after Win woke her with his call.

"Thank you for coming Kat. Do you know anywhere in here that Lucia might go to?" Win pointed to the map.

"Ummm" Kathryn dropped her bag to the floor and moved her body aside to look at the map better. She kept her eyes trained on Tanvi.

"Oh, um, have you met Tanvi before?"

"Yes? I think so, at a party?"

"Lucia's birthday last year." Tanvi confirmed. The mention of Lucia's birthday reminded Kathryn that her baby was due then too and how painful it would be to celebrate that without her best friend.

"Tanvi knows." Win added, as if he knew what Kathryn was thinking.

Kathryn pointed to her house, which was within the circle. Then to the large green shape on the map that represented Toohey Forest. "Somewhere in there?"

Tanvi side eyed up at Win, looking to gauge his reaction to that statement. She hoped his face would portray doubt that it was

- 357 -

where Lucia would head, but instead he looked as though he was about to faint. It was possible she was there.

A truck rattled up the street, they all jumped.

With her body free of the rock, Lu had a lot more purchase to be able to wrench her foot free. Her fragile skin tore from the muscle as she pulled at it. With a little twisting and a lot of brute force the foot, ankle and all snapped out of the crevice, sending Lu backwards into Lucia. In her hand Lu held the lower half of her right leg triumphantly. A thin strip of crusty, denim encircled the ankle, frayed from where Lu had ripped it. Her sock was still on, but without the shoe a faint impression of Lu's foot seeped through the cotton. It might not have been fall related, but general corpse seepage. At the shin, muscle, skin and tendons were all in soggy tatters, the bone broken almost lengthways and tiny shards embedded themselves through the end of the stump. Gruesome, but she was finally free and, in a pinch, maybe Lu would eat her own foot.

Looking at Lu's left leg now. It might be easier if she took that one off too. The knee swayed in the wrong direction, not load bearing at all in its current state. No chance of hopping on that leg.

"Can you walk?" Lucia asked in a tentative tone. She knew that Lu couldn't feel pain, or wasn't affected by it, but she couldn't wrap her head around the idea either. Lu rocked herself to standing, she hoovered upright for a millisecond before her knee arced to the side and she fell again.

Lu was unphased. Now she lurched forward onto the knees, the right bent normally, but pulled her fraying lower leg through the dirt. The left hung behind her and tossed from side to side with each "step."

She was slow before. Now she was glacial. Getting back home or at least to a phone with Lu like this might take just as many days as they had been trapped.

❖

"She wouldn't go anywhere with a lot of people, would she?" Kathryn said to no one in particular.

"I doubt she would."

"Then we are looking for secluded places at this point of time?" Tanvi added.

"Yeah, I think so. What does that leave?" Win mopped his brow again. The breeze coming in through the still open door was cool and didn't evaporate the sweat as quickly as he would like.

"Toohey. And the drive back to my place?" Kathryn arched her back, and twisted side to side making the bones in her spine pop at the end of her movement. "I mean, I didn't see her on the drive here. But it wouldn't hurt to check again?"

"The cemetery also." Tanvi looked up at them over the red rims of her glasses. "She could be visiting Lorraine."

"For," Win counted in his head, "three days?" His tone was harsh. Without Tanvi he might not have known she was missing at all. His own wife. Anger felt better than guilt though.

❖

They each took their own cars. Kathryn searched the roads leading between their houses. She took several different routes, in both directions. Stopped at storm drains, parks and underpasses along the way. Her car grew hot with the stopping and starting. Even though it was a cool day, Kathryn started to drip with sweat. Her hair, which started the day out as crazed and unruly matted down against her brow, only adding to her discomfort and desperation.

On her third round trip Kathryn pulled into the shade on the side of the road. The car bonnet crackled as it cooled. She rang Gianna. She got the message bank, she knew she would, Gianna was in the middle of a shift.

"Hey babe? You don't have to call me back. I just wanted to talk to you. I've been driving around looking for Lucia. Babe, I can't find her anywhere." Tears weren't flowing, but they were close and Kathryn sniffed them back pre-emptively. "Win is out looking too and Tanvi. Apparently, she ambushed Lucia the other day and found everything out. I'm hot and tired and I just want to find her." Kathryn sniffed again and watched the dappled light dance over her dashboard. It looked cooler and calmer than she felt. She tried to summon up the words to explain how she felt. "Babe, I think we might have lost her for real this time. I don't know what to do." The end of her sentence dissolved into tears. She sobbed quietly trying to gain enough composure to finish her message. "Talk to you tonight. I love you."

The phone was hot against her face and little smears of oil and sweat covered the top right corner of the screen when she pulled it down. She cracked the window, let the cool breeze caress her face and closed her eyes for a little while. She'd get going again in a moment.

❖

Tanvi searched the crematorium and the roads to it. There was some overlap between the route she took and the way to Kathryn's house. There was a small group of mourners milling outside the chapel. Off in the distance she could see a woman in a wheelchair seated next to a middle-aged woman. They looked too similar to be anything but mother and daughter.

Lorraine was already set into a wall, a little bronze plaque summing up her whole life. Someone had placed a white silk rose in the little holder next to the plaque. It hadn't been Lucia, Tanvi knew that. Tanvi ran her finger over the lettering on the bronze. She was mourning Lorraine too, all the nurses did. It was sad, it always is to lose a friend. When someone is old it doesn't hurt in the same way. It's expected and in her whole career Tanvi had lost more people than she could count. She'd attended more funerals than most people ever would. Lucia was different. Losing her was an injustice that she couldn't reconcile. Lucia was still so young, she worked hard. Tanvi was social with her employees but Lucia was one of only a handful she ever called a friend. She was taken, unnaturally, unwillingly and all she was doing was her job. It wasn't fair and Tanvi felt a bitterness creeping into her.

"Oh sorry!" An older man appeared around the wall. He held a few sprigs of lavender in his hand, they looked vibrant against his green jumper. The scent of aftershave and powder followed him into the alcove. He bent to remove some wilting lavender from one of the lower plaques and replaced it with the lavender he was holding.

"My wife." He said, standing back up. "You?"

"A patient." She turned the name badge clipped to her blouse towards him. "I work in aged care."

"That's commitment."

"Some are special. I'm sure your wife also." She offered a consoling smile and excused herself to let him mourn alone. She had to keep looking anyway.

❖

Win parked at the dead end of Timothy St. Not long ago he would have loved to afford a house on this street. The elevated and immaculate homes struck him with envy any time he accompanied

Lucia on her walks. Now it wasn't the homes that he felt envy for. He would do anything to return to his perfectly adequate rental, if he knew Lucia was alive and well there. The envy that blossomed inside him was for what he imagined were perfectly happy families inside these homes, blissfully unaware of his heartache. Part of him hoped that some upper middle-class couple would emerge from their mini house and accost him for sullying their street with his squealy-braked, third-hand car. He was itching for someone to focus it all on, all the emotions; grief, fear and most of all the anger. The anger made him feel like the bolts on his rollercoaster carriage were loose. He was so tenuously connected to something wild and already out of his control, but everything could get a million times worse and he didn't know when.

Timothy St was the entrance to the forest that he knew Lucia liked the most. Win didn't quite understand why. It was quite a hike from their house to even the edge of the forest and it was a fight uphill to even get there, without the benefit of nature. The entry track also spat you out right in the middle of the main track, and it felt stupid to always be doubling back. Right now, Win cursed it because he couldn't tell which way she would have gone on that path, if she even had and he hadn't brought any water.

The track was damp. Win didn't think he had walked it when the path was anything but dusty. Muddy water in the depressions of the track held fidgeting bugs. They caught the corner of his eye and set him on edge.

Win reached Pegg's lookout, he stopped to regroup. He looked out to the south and couldn't tell if it was dust, rain or haze in the distance over the mountains. It may have just been his short-sightedness. At this distance the mountains reminded him of the scenery in The Wizard of Oz. Lucia had made him watch it not so long ago. He knew the story, had even read the book, but had never seen the movie. For all the human rights atrocities that everyone knew happened during the filming, it still held up. Lucia's voice singing every part of every song in character played in his head. Her face in his memories backlit by the lamp on her side of the couch making it hard to see. That was what she looked like every night on the couch, but it felt like the memory of her then was fading.

Win's thoughts were interrupted by a middle-aged lady stopping a couple metres short of the bench he'd sat on. She drank from a straw that wound around her shoulder and disappeared into a thin pack on her back. She was soaked in sweat, when she finished her drink, she started to stretch. Win sprang up and offered her the bench. She waved him off.

"Can't sit now. Only halfway." She wasn't as out of breath as it looked like she should be.

"Oh wow!" Win's admiration was genuine.

"6km down." The woman looked at her watch and beeped some buttons. "If you're going to the other side, there's a lot of paths eroded from the rain. The ones that weren't already closed."

"Thanks for the tip." Less genuine this time, he just was embarrassed to imply he would be heading straight back to his car.

The lady pushed another button, jogged in place for a little bit and started off again. "Have a good one!"

"You too." Win called but she probably didn't hear him.

❖

The bad thing was that Lu had fallen a long way and without her legs she had to hobble back uphill. The good thing was that the fall was off boulders, not a sheer cliff. If they followed the base of the rocks along, they would reach the end and there was surely a less steep way to the path. The ground was covered in thick leaf litter. It was wet and as Lu dragged her stumps through it, she made peculiar dash like furrows. The leaves clung to her clothes as far up as her thighs. Lu was giving it all she had, she hadn't stopped moving this whole time but when she looked back Lucia could see they had only gone a very short distance.

They reached a gentler slope. Lucia didn't remember where the sun was when they started to be able to tell how long it took them to get there. Hours, that was certain.

The slope was still more steep than she would have liked. In her own body she would have got to the top with ease. Concerned only for any slippery patches instead of the actual hill. She wasn't in her own body though and she had to come up with a plan to get to the top and prevent more damage. Lu would have to crawl on her belly.

❖

Win didn't call Kathryn until he could see the street again. He knew he had service, the whole of Toohey Forest did, one of the perks to suburban bushland, but it felt like he was disturbing the peace.

"Anything?"

"No." Kathryn's voice was ragged on the other end. He could tell she'd been crying. He wanted to comfort her but part of him resented it. If she was crying, she wasn't looking.

"I couldn't see any trace of her here, but it's rained. I think we should look in more of the forest."

"That makes sense to me." Her voice was clearing now. "Where should I meet you?"

"Do you know the carpark on Toohey Rd?"

"I think so, see you soon."

Win's phone beeped in his ear, when he pulled it down from his face a missed call message flashed on screen. Tanvi had called.

❖

Lu's hands were caked in mud. She plunged her fists deep into the ground, making four holes for her fingers and then heaved herself up. The soil between her fingers pulled away and made little divots that every now and then she could push a knee into and gain more purchase. She'd thrown her right foot up the hill a few times to avoid leaving it behind. Lu's left foot dragged behind her. Every so often the pants inched up and Lucia caught a glimpse of the battered skin.

Lucia watched Lu persist. From above she looked a bit like an insect. She seemed to be erratic but she completed tasks with an unfamiliar perpetuity. The only time she slowed or faltered was a result of a physical inadequacy and she kept pushing until that was overcome. It was strange and fascinating and Lucia felt separated from her body now more than ever. It was completely broken and everything about it was unfamiliar to her.

Lucia didn't hear it at first, Lu did. Like a dog who knows the sound of their owner from very far away. The sound of a couple of hikers speaking in low voices to each other. Not even raising their voices. Lucia wouldn't have even known which direction they were if Lu hadn't raised her head and sniffed in their direction. Lu's face contorted into a grimace that Lucia had been fearing. Lu's body was literally falling apart and she was hungry. The first person they came across might be on the menu.

Excitement, hunger, or both; Lu made an extra effort to heave herself to the ridge of the incline. At the top she stopped, to get her bearings. She picked up her foot with her muddy hands. Her skin peeled away from her nails, making room for more dirt to be trapped beneath them. She looked like she had dark brown claws.

"Wait!" Lucia didn't have a reason for Lu to not keep going. She was desperate to get back home; she just didn't want to cross paths with the hikers. It sounded as though they were getting further and further away. With any luck they were on a different track and wouldn't come within biting distance.

She did have to find Lu food though. The climb had worn down her body more and if she didn't get something to eat, she might fall apart altogether. Lucia would be bound to a pile of something that used to be a person.

❖

Win was first to arrive at the car park, then Tanvi. They saw the reason for Kathryn's delay when she got out of the car. She cradled three cold bottles of water and three white parcels in her arms. The condensation on the water left wet streaks over her oversized shirt.

"We should eat first. No use anyone getting sick." Kathryn passed out the supplies.

It was nearly noon. He hadn't stopped to think about it until now, but Win's stomach was aching for food.

"I wasn't sure if you were vegetarian." Kathryn said to Tanvi as she passed one of the white paper bags over. "So, I got us all just salad sandwiches."

Tanvi thanked her. Kathryn walked to the empty picnic tables and sat facing away from the table on one of the bolted down benches. She unwrapped her sandwich. Beetroot spread bright pink onto the white bread. Tanvi came and sat on the other bench, facing the same way as Kathryn. Win leaned against one of the poles cornering the area. The warmth seared through his shirt and into his shoulder blades.

They ate in silence.

Win finished his sandwich and gulped down some water. He swished the last mouthful in his mouth before swallowing. It was the most he'd eaten in one go in a long time. He crumpled the paper bag into a ball, walked over to Kathryn and held his hand out. She pressed her crumpled bag into his palm. Then he held his hand out to Tanvi, she did the same. Win threw the three white balls into the rubbish bin. He wiped his palms on his thighs as he returned to the shade.

"I saw a lady, she said some of the tracks on this side of the forest are closed, others are washed out but not closed yet. Normally I wouldn't be worried about Lucia in here. But Lu."

"Not as steady." Kathryn saw where his thoughts were headed.

"Right. If she fell and hurt herself, they might be stuck."

"If they're here." She didn't remind him to be cruel, only to temper his enthusiasm.

Win shot Kathryn a glare, which faded into disappointment. He had made up his mind they were trapped somewhere in the forest. He had no idea that was the case though. She was right, they could be starting a fruitless search.

"Yeah, if they're here." He conceded. He looked at the path leading away from them. It looked mild. In truth there were no difficult tracks in this area. Some of this section of the park was even paved, wheelchair accessible. His hope that Lucia was around this area was fading fast. "We should split up. Take different paths."

"I feel like that's one of the first things they say you shouldn't do."

"Yeah, in dangerous terrain. If one of us finds her, or has an accident, we can just call each other. Toohey Forest has reception."

"I guess."

"I'm happy with this plan." Tanvi had taken a back seat in the presence of Win. She didn't want to step on his toes.

Looking at a crude map at the start of the path, they each chose one to take. Kathryn and Tanvi shared the path for a bit together before branching off, Win took a different start point.

It was cooler again once they got a little way into the bush. The wet leaves smelled like an earthy tea.

"Lucia!"

"Lucia!"

"Lucia!"

They all called from their respective places, paused to listen, walked further and called again. The further they travelled from each other the more one another's calls sounded like a response.

Tanvi came to a fork. The right led down a paved path and the left was dirt. In the distance she could see a flutter of red. She chose left. Not much chance of Lucia being stranded on such a pristine path.

Win heard something in the distance. He called out for Lucia again.

A reply came, it was far away, but it sounded like "help." His heart jumped into his throat, he called again. This time he was sure she was calling for help.

He raced, his feet slapping the ground in time with his heart beats. His knee sent shooting pains down his shins and into his groin. He hadn't run this hard in years and his leg had already been acting up. His run morphed, still fast but lopsided as he tried to protect his knee as much as possible. He yelled for her again. The response seemed closer but he could only kind of hear it over his gasping breath and feet slamming into the ground.

The path came to an end. He didn't know which way to go, so called out again. She was close now. The left was a steep dirt path, he was sure she was this way. Another call to make sure.

He wasn't running now. The incline was covered in loose gravel and long patches of dirt. The rocks all clattered down the hill with each step. He didn't want to lose his footing and be the one in need of saving. His knee ached with each step. It was throbbing just as much with the weight off it now. The next step and it buckled. Win landed on it and shrieked. He rolled to his side and skid down the hill a little way, enough for his shirt to climb up and to get gravel rash on his flank.

"Lucia?" He called again.

"Yes? Help!"

"I'm coming." He rolled back onto all fours and pushed himself up to standing and hovered his right foot behind him. Rocks made little indents in his palms and he brushed off the dirt.

"Come on." He whispered to himself.

One more step, he winced hard as the weight transferred to his right. Win clenched his fists so hard that the nails started to pierce his already tender palms. Bit by bit he climbed his way to the top of the hill, it kept going, but less steep now. Still, he had to be careful with footing. The bush to his left was dense and the side of the path led away near vertically, the right dropped away nearly as steeply, but ahead and to the right was another picnic area. He called out again.

No reply right away, but a chorus of giggles came from the picnic area. Then a girl's voice called out for help. Now he was closer he could hear the mocking in the tone. More giggling. Now he could see them, a group of teenage girls lounging in the playground. Cigarette smoke wafted his way.

Win's shoulders fell. He didn't want them to see him up close; he was embarrassed and sore and he thought he might cry.

"Oi mister!" A girl called to him.

"Where you going?" Another girl this time.

"Help! Help!" one girl yelled out, standing to project her voice to Win.

The first girl screamed "Lucia!"

Win's phone buzzed in his pocket.

❖

First Tanvi saw the closed track tape fluttering in the breeze. It was strung loosely between fence posts, but there was neither a fence nor a gate to be supported by them. She could see why the track was closed, potholes had been filled with rainwater and from this angle she couldn't tell how deep they were. She ran her eyes down the track, there she saw two bodies, one kneeling and the other standing.

"Lucia?"

"Tanvi?"

- 370 -

"Lucia! We found you." Tanvi's pace quickened as she navigated herself around the obstacles between them.

"Stop! Tanvi stay back."

Tanvi stopped short. "What's happening?"

Lucia walked forward as far as she could. She stood between Tanvi and Lu, blocking both of their eyelines as much as possible.

"Lu's hungry. I don't want her to attack you. She's hurt and looking for food."

Tanvi froze, not sure what to do. "She's hurting?"

"Yeah. It's bad."

"Ok. I will call Kathryn and Samuel also. Tell them I found you."

"Win's here?" Relief washed over her. Win was looking for her.

Tanvi made the calls then returned her attention to Lu. "Can I have a look at her Lucia?"

Lucia allowed Tanvi to creep up to them, all the while explaining emphatically to Lu that Tanvi was not food. They were both cautious but so long as Tanvi stayed out of Lu's immediate reach she wasn't in any danger. She could outrun Lu easily, especially in her current state.

From afar Tanvi assessed the damage to Lu's legs. It was grim. She could probably set them with the right tools, make it so Lu could walk again, but the damage was so severe that it probably wouldn't hold out as a long-term solution. She didn't know the repairing capabilities of Lu either, she was much more exposed to bugs and decay. If they couldn't do anything, she would rapidly decline into

- 371 -

putrefaction. Tanvi didn't need to tell Lucia that. Lucia had the same training Tanvi did, she already knew.

In the distance, Lucia saw two black-haired heads bobbing in the distance. Kathryn and Win walking very closely and not too quickly. As the rest of them came into view, it was clear that Win was heavily relying on Kathryn for support. His limp was the worst she had seen it in a long time.

Selfishly she wanted the sight of her to numb his pain. Her mind slipped into a daydream where he raced to her, the agony in his knee inconsequential when he was so close to be reunited with the love of his life. In the daydream he would collide with her and wrap her in his arms. He smelled of sweat, lust and safety and she would rest her head on his chest and breathe it in. His hair would fall over his forehead and she would brush it back again and kiss him. It was only a daydream though. None of those things would happen, and when he came close enough he would probably be mortified at the sight of her mangled body.

Kathryn and Win's faces were puffy with tears. Lucia warned them the same as she did Tanvi.

"I thought of that." Kathryn swung her backpack from around on one arm and pulled another white paper bag out.

"Kat, Lu doesn't eat human food." Win told her.

"I know." She opened the bag and held it in front of her. "I got this from the freezer." She tipped the bag upside down, still out of reach from Lu. A freezer burned lump of Liam Mathews fell to the ground, rolling once and picking up dirt on its edges.

Lu lurched for it and took two steps forward. Her left leg swung awkwardly in leaves. She put the whole thing into her mouth and

- 372 -

ate it with big open mouth chews. Flecks of frozen blood dotted her lips and she gurgled appreciatively in the back of her throat.

Win started for Lucia, but she saw his wincing and closed the gap herself.

"I was worried." He said and stretched his arm between them. He caught hold of her and Lucia crumpled into his arms. She felt his sweat, damp on her face. Everything that was so familiar and comforting about his embrace. Win hugged her in tighter.

Kathryn and Tanvi watched. Completely confused by what they were seeing. Tanvi went to say something and Kathryn pulled her back by the elbow. She tossed another lump of flesh to Lu who stuffed it appreciatively into her mouth.

Win pulled himself away from the hug to look at his wife's face, to tell her he loved her. But as they separated, she slipped through his grasp and he couldn't feel her anymore.

"You weren't trying to." He asked and clicked his nails together nervously.

"No. It was an accident." She pointed blindly to the precipice she had fallen off, but he didn't know what that meant exactly.

"How did you get here?"

"Does that matter? It was stupid."

He smiled at her, looking her right in the eyes. There was love there, and relief. She hadn't seen either when he looked at her in months.

Tanvi lay out towels in the back seat of Win's car and they bundled Lu into the back. As a whole they decided it was a good idea to strap her down with as many seat beats as they had available to them, to restrict her until she had more to eat.

When they got back home. Tanvi made crude braces for the left leg and bandaged the stump of the right. She promised she would return in a few days with a better dressing and more long-term solution. She didn't press on any of the questions she still had, or explain her research, or how she came to know Lucia was missing. She would bring it up, but not yet.

Kathryn rang Gianna again. This time she was able to pick up. Kathryn cried again, happier tears for now. A rush of relief but their lives were still just as shaken as they were six hours ago. Nothing had changed, not really.

After Tanvi and Kathryn left, Win stayed behind. He wasn't ready to say goodbye just yet.

47

The movers were scheduled to arrive the following morning. Win managed to pay rent through to the end of the lease in just over a month. Lucia and Lu could stay there until then and then would have to find somewhere else to go. She imagined she would end up squatting in an abandoned building somewhere. She wasn't in need of any amenities, just shelter. It was hard to believe she could be any more isolated, but that was surely what she had to look forward to.

Win asked her to make herself scarce while the movers came. That was fair. Lucia walked from room to room. Looking at all her beautiful things. By this time tomorrow there would be nothing in the house.

She lay on the bed. The covers had not even creased since the last time it was made. She understood. The memories of this house were too much. He couldn't live here, not now, not after everything, especially not with Lu. She also understood better now than she had before, about Win needing to move on. He still had a life to move on with. The happiness of their reunion had been brief and it became more apparent than it had been, that the cycle would continue forever if they let it. She was dooming him to lose her over and over again and it wasn't fair. "If you love someone let them go," a platitude of unrequited love and incompatible choices. It wasn't meant for the dead to let their loved ones continue without them but it fit.

There was noise outside. Not one Lucia was unfamiliar with, just she didn't expect anyone. She kept still. It was probably a door knocker, someone collecting money or trying to sell her electricity.

The door opened. Win? He said he wouldn't come over. Specifically, he said that and now it was the middle of the day. He was never sick. Surely not him. Had Lu locked the door?

Lucia crept up and poked just to her eyes around the corner. It was Win. He dropped his satchel to the floor, leaving it practically in the doorway. He kicked off his shoes. His face was crinkled and his hair fell over his face. It puffed out at the back where it was getting a bit long, like he'd been asleep. He was rubbing the nape of his neck. A tiny sheen of sweat glistened on his forearm as his muscles flexed with his caressing fingers.

"I wasn't expecting you?" She felt somehow embarrassed, after they'd said goodbye earlier.

Win looked up to her, but his eyes weren't focusing. "I don't feel so great. Got the worst headache."

Win pulled his hand away from behind his head and even from across the lounge, Lucia could see a tiny red jewel of dried blood between the webbing of his thumb and forefinger.

CPSIA information can be obtained
at www.ICGtesting.com
Printed in the USA
LVHW040839150321
681579LV00020B/231